BookTok is raving about *The A*

"Pure genius! Penner takes magical realism to a whole new depth, leagues under the sea. Sarah's words are a breathtaking treasure that will captivate the imagination of readers and pull their heartstrings."
—Alanna Grace @alannagraceauthor

"[*The Amalfi Curse* is] written beautifully and will have you turning pages until the end. The author's words are magnificent and will have you captivated."
—Red @redbookreview

"It's authors like Sarah who are able to mix history, adventure and a sprinkle of love that make historical fiction and the stories come to life."
—Becky @beckybingbooks

"Sarah Penner uses love, sunken treasure, heartbreak, and magic to seamlessly weave together past and present in two compelling and emotional stories. This was a beautiful story, and perfect for anyone who likes to read stories of powerful women."
—Amanda @amandamegreads

"Sarah Penner has done it again. Mystery, history, and magic. Classically beautiful writing, devastatingly compelling characters, and seamlessly intertwined timelines. This book is a treasure!"
—Erin K. Larson-Burnett @e.k.b.books

"100% this is my new favorite book of Sarah Penner's. Whether you're a fan of mystery, romance, and historical fiction, I think this is a book that stretches across multiple genres and so many readers will fall in love with it."
—Martina Barrow @martinas_library

"Magical realism, sunken treasure, dual time lines, in an epic setting on the Italian coast mixed with mystery, love and adventure… Sarah Penner has outdone herself in *The Amalfi Curse*!"
—Mindi D'Elia @readtraveleatandrepeat

"A mysteriously magical story about the power of love, told through writing that's as enchanting as the Positano landscape in which it is set. This is Sarah Penner at her absolute best."

—Shannon Demaio @bookish_boy.mom

"Penner immerses you in an addictive and enthralling voyage along the Amalfi Coast. A story full of enchantment, betrayal, sacrifice, and finding the greatest treasure."

—Alexis @_alexisinwonderland

"This book was a perfect combination of magical realism and historical fiction! Sarah has a masterful way of writing dual timelines, delving into the historical aspects and relating to the current-day struggles as well."

—Christine Patronick @christineanne4

"This absolute page turner weaves intrigue, romance, magic and adventure in a story that will force you to keep reading to see where the twists will take you next!"

—Pamela Siegel Zinnel @bookwormpbz

THE AMALFI CURSE

SARAH PENNER

PARK ROW BOOKS

PARK ROW BOOKS™

Recycling programs for this product may not exist in your area.

ISBN-13: 978-0-7783-0800-3
ISBN-13: 978-0-7783-6031-5 (International Trade Paperback Edition)

The Amalfi Curse

Copyright © 2025 by S.L.PENNER, LLC

All rights reserved. No part of this book may be used or reproduced in any manner whatsoever without written permission.

Without limiting the author's and publisher's exclusive rights, any unauthorized use of this publication to train generative artificial intelligence (AI) technologies is expressly prohibited.

This is a work of fiction. Names, characters, places and incidents are either the product of the author's imagination or are used fictitiously. Any resemblance to actual persons, living or dead, businesses, companies, events or locales is entirely coincidental.

TM is a trademark of Harlequin Enterprises ULC.

Park Row Books
22 Adelaide St. West, 41st Floor
Toronto, Ontario M5H 4E3, Canada
ParkRowBooks.com

Printed in U.S.A.

For my husband, Marc

Upon the whirl, where sank the ship
The boat spun round and round;
And all was still, save that the hill
Was telling of the sound.

—"The Rime of the Ancient Mariner," 1798

REGISTRO DEGLI INCANTESIMI MARINI

REGISTER OF INCANTATIONS
PRACTICED BY
THE STREGHE, OR SEA WITCHES,
OF AMALFI

incantesimo di riflusso	An incantation to urge water away (ebb). *Attrezzo*: a belemnite fossil.
incantesimo di flusso	An incantation to draw water forth (flow). *Attrezzo*: a mother-of-pearl shell.
incantesimo divinatorio	An incantation to discern the location of items in the water. *Attrezzo*: a strand of six sea-derived hagstones.
incantesimo raffreddare	An incantation to lower the temperature of the water via a cold-water column. *Attrezzo*: a dried Chondrichthyes egg-sack, or "mermaid's purse."
incantesimo dell'elemento	An incantation to alter the composition of the water. *Attrezzo*: a fossilized sawfish snout, or "mermaid's comb."
incantesimo vortice	An incantation to conjure a maelstrom or whirlpool. No *attrezzo* required.
vortice centuriaria	An incantation to conjure a powerful maelstrom or whirlpool enduring for one hundred years. No *attrezzo* required, but the *strega* must remove her protective *cimaruta* necklace to perform this incantation.

PROLOGUE

Letter to Matteo Mazza in Naples, Italy

Monday, April 9, 1821

Signor Mazza:

We have not formerly made each other's acquaintance, yet I pray you will take very seriously what I have to say.

You are the owner of Naples's most preeminent shipping company, and your business is at the mercy of the sea. Yet as of late, I've become convinced the sea is at the mercy of something else: a small group of women living in Positano.

Many have marveled, in years past, over the tiny fishing village's good fortune and its consistently favorable seaside conditions. The tides, for one, are suspiciously calm. Mariners often remark on the village's lack of erosion, yet it is hardly protected by a natural reef, and it is not nestled inside a cove. Why do the battered cliffs of Amalfi and Minori suffer collapses and dangerous cascades of rock, yet Positano does not?

The glut of redfish and *pezzogne*, too. How is it that on days when the fishermen from other places return with by-catch or empty nets, the men of Positano have—yet again—a superb haul? Even at a quarter moon. It is as though the lunar rhythms have no effect on this village.

Ah, but tides and fish are one thing. Pirates, well, they are quite another. Now, I don't mean to make assumptions about those with whom you associate, Signor Mazza, but surely you are aware of this incongruity: there is no record of pirates having ever landed in Positano.

These buccaneers sack ships in Sicily. They ransack from Salerno to Capri. If I were to prick a pin in a map marking everywhere pirates have landed along our coast, it would appear a perfect band, skirting the whole edge of the Amalfi coastline—every village but one. One!

Dare I say, Positano seems insulated. Protected. Favored.

Elsewhere on the peninsula, men lament their filthy seawater, the looters, bad catch. *Yes, Positano has been prosperous*, they tell me, *but we will never move our families there, for their luck will run out. Any day now. Mark my words.*

Even some of Positano's own are bewildered by their good fortune. The men keep well-armed, sure they are due for a pirate attack. Others salt and dry and bottle their fish, certain their waters will soon dry up. Still others refuse to build too close to the shore: the cliffs will crumble eventually, they say, sending those hilltop residents to their rocky deaths.

There is something going on in Positano—a secret, very closely guarded.

And I believe I know precisely what this secret is.

Might we strike a deal, Signor Mazza? For a price, I am willing to reveal what I know—to tell you what I have learned, what I have seen. *Who* I have seen.

I can only imagine the fortune such information would bring you.

Please respond at your soonest convenience.

Signed,
Your devoted friend, associate &c.

1

MARI

Wednesday, April 11, 1821

Along a dark seashore beneath the cliffside village of Positano, twelve women, aged six to forty-four, were seated in a circle. It was two o'clock in the morning, the waxing moon directly overhead.

One of the women stood, breaking the circle. Her hair was the color of vermilion, as it had been since birth. Fully clothed, she walked waist-high into the water. A belemnite fossil clutched between her fingers, she plunged her hands beneath the waves and began to move her lips, reciting the first part of the *incantesimo di riflusso* she'd learned as a child. Within moments, the undercurrent she'd conjured began to swirl at her ankles, tugging southward, away from her.

She shuffled her way out of the water and back onto the shore.

A second woman with lighter hair, the color of persimmon, stood from the circle. She, too, approached the ocean and plunged her hands beneath the surface. She recited her silent spell on the sea, satisfied as the undercurrent grew even stronger. She gazed out at the horizon, a steady black line where the sky met the sea, and smiled.

Like the other villagers along the coast tonight, these women knew what was coming: a fleet of pirate ships making their way northeast from Tunis. Winds were favorable, their sources said, and the flotilla was expected within the next day.

Their destination? Perhaps Capri, Sorrento, Majori. Some thought maybe even Positano—maybe, finally, Positano.

Given this, fishermen all along the Amalfi coastline had decided to remain at home with their families tomorrow and into the night. It wouldn't be safe on the water. The destination of these pirates was unknown, and what they sought was a mystery, as well. Greedy pirates went for all kinds of loot. Hungry pirates went for nets full of fish. Lustful pirates went for the women.

On the seashore, a third and final woman stood from the circle. Her hair was the rich, deep hue of blood. Quickly, she undressed. She didn't like the feeling of wet fabric against her skin, and these women had seen her naked a thousand times before.

Belemnite fossil in one hand, she held the end of a rope in her other, which was tied to a heavy anchor in the sand a short distance away. She would be the one to recite the final piece of this current-curse. Her recitation was the most important, the most potent, and after it was done, the ebbing undercurrent would be even more severe—hence the rope, which she would wrap tightly around herself before finishing the spell.

It was perilous, sinister work. Still, of the twelve women by the water tonight, twenty-year-old Mari DeLuca was the most befitting for this final task.

They were *streghe del mare*—sea witches—with unparalleled power over the ocean. They boasted a magic found nowhere else in the world, a result of their lineage, having descended from the sirens who once inhabited the tiny Li Galli islets nearby.

The women knew that tomorrow, wherever the pirates landed, it would not be Positano. The men would not seize their goods, their food, their daughters. No matter how the pirate ships rigged their sails, they would not find easy passageway against the undercurrent the women now drew upward from the bottom of the sea. They would turn east, or west. They would go elsewhere.

They always did.

While the lineage of the other eleven women was twisted and tangled, filled with sons or muddled by marriage, Mari De-Luca's line of descent was perfectly intact: her mother had been a *strega*, and her mother's mother, and so on and so on, tracing back thousands of years to the sirens themselves. Of the women on the seashore tonight, Mari was the only *strega finisima*.

This placed upon her shoulders many great responsibilities. She could instinctively read the water better than any of them. Her spells were the most effective, too; she alone could do what required two or three other *streghe* working in unison. As such, she was the sanctioned leader of the eleven other women. The forewoman, the teacher, the decision-maker.

Oh, but what a shame she hated the sea as much as she did.

Stepping toward the water, Mari unraveled her long plait of hair. It was her most striking feature—such blood-colored hair was almost unheard of in Italy, much less in the tiny fishing village of Positano—but then, much of what Mari had inherited was unusual. She tensed as the cold waves rushed over her feet. *My mother should be the one doing this*, she thought bitterly. It was a resentment she'd never released, not in twelve years, since the night when eight-year-old Mari had watched the sea claim her mother, Imelda, as its own.

On that terrible night, newly motherless and reeling, Mari knew the sea was no longer her friend. But worse than this, she worried for her younger sister, Sofia. How would Mari break this news to her? How could she possibly look after spirited Sofia with as much patience and warmth as their *mamma* had once done?

She'd hardly had time to grieve. The next day, the other *streghe* had swiftly appointed young Mari as the new *strega finisima*. Her mother had taught her well, after all, and she was, by birthright, capable of more than any of them. No one seemed to care that young Mari was so tender and heartbroken or that she now despised the very thing she had such control over.

But most children lose their mothers at some point, don't they? And sprightly Sofia had been reason enough to forge on—a salve to Mari's aching heart. Sofia had kept her steady, disciplined. Even cheerful, much of the time. So long as Sofia was beside her, Mari would shoulder the responsibilities that had been placed upon her, willingly or not.

Now, toes in the water, a pang of anguish struck Mari, as it often did at times like this.

Neither *Mamma* nor Sofia was beside her tonight.

Mari let out a slow exhale. This moment was an important one, worth remembering. It was the end of two years' worth of agonizing indecision. No one else on the seashore knew it, but this spell, this incantation she was about to recite, would be her very last. She was leaving in only a few weeks' time, breaking free. And the place she was going was mercifully far from the sea.

Eyes down, Mari slipped her naked body beneath the water, cursing the sting of it as it seeped into a small rash on her ankle. At once, the water around her turned from dark blue to a thick inky black, like vinegar. Mari had dealt with this all her life: the sea mirrored her mood, her temperament.

As a child, she'd found it marvelous, the way the ocean read her hidden thoughts so well. Countless times, her friends had expressed envy of the phenomenon. But now, the black water shuddering around her legs only betrayed the secrets Mari meant to keep, and she was glad for the darkness, so better to hide her feelings from those on the shore.

Halfway into the water, already she could feel the changes in the sea: the two women before her had done very well with their spells. This was encouraging, at least. A few sharp rocks, churned by the undercurrent, scraped across the top of her feet like thorns, and it took great focus to remain in place against the undertow pulling her out. She used her arms to keep herself balanced, as a tired bird might flap its wings on an unsteady branch.

She wrapped the rope twice around her forearm. Once it was secure, she began to recite the spell. With each word, *tira* and *obbedisci*—pull and obey—the rope tightened against her skin. The undercurrent was intensifying quickly, and with even more potency than she expected. She winced when the rope broke her skin, the fresh wound exposed instantly to the bite of the salt water. She began to stumble, losing her balance, and she finished the incantation as quickly as possible, lest the rope leave her arm mangled.

She wouldn't miss nights like this, not at all.

When she was done, Mari waved, signaling to the other women that it was time to pull her in. Instantly she felt a tug on the other end of the rope. A few seconds later, she was in shallow, gentle water. On her hands and knees, she crawled the rest of the way. Safely on shore, she lay down to rest, sand and grit sticking uncomfortably to her wet skin. She would need to wash well later.

Terribly time-consuming, all of this.

A sudden shout caught her attention, and Mari sat up, peering around in the darkness. Her closest friend, Ami, was now knee-deep in the water, struggling to keep her balance.

"Lia!" Ami shouted hysterically. "Lia, where are you?"

Lia was Ami's six-year-old daughter, a *strega*-in-training, her hair a delicate, rosy red. Not moments ago, she'd been situated among the circle of women, her spindly legs tucked up against her chest, watching the spells unfold.

Mari threw herself upward, tripping as she lunged toward the ocean.

"No, please, no," she cried out. If Lia was indeed in the water, it would be impossible for the young girl to make her way back to shore. She was smaller than other girls her age, her bones fragile as seashells, and though she could swim, she'd have nothing against the power of these tides. The very purpose of the incantation had been to drive the currents toward the deep, dark sea, with enough strength to stave off a pirate ship.

Lia wasn't wearing a *cimaruta*, either, which gave the women great strength and vigor in moments of distress. She was too young: *streghe* didn't get their talisman necklaces until they were fifteen, when their witchcraft had matured and they were deemed proficient in the art.

At once, every woman on the shore was at the ocean's edge, peering at the water's choppy surface. The women might have been powerful, yes, but they were not immortal: as Mari knew all too well, they could succumb to drowning just like anyone else.

Mari spun in a circle, scanning the shore. Suddenly her belly tightened, and she bent forward, her vision going dark and bile rising in the back of her throat.

This was too familiar—her spinning in circles, scanning the horizon in search of someone.

Seeing nothing.

Then seeing the worst.

Like her younger sister's copper-colored hair, splayed out around the shoulders of her limp body as she lay facedown in the rolling swells of the sea.

Mari had been helpless, unable to protect fourteen-year-old Sofia from whatever she'd encountered beneath the waves that day, only two years ago. Mari had spent years trying to protect her sister as their mother could not, yet in the end, she had failed. She'd failed Sofia.

That day, the sea had once again proved itself not only greedy but villainous—something to be loathed.

Something, Mari eventually decided, from which to escape.

Now, Mari fell to her knees, too dizzy to stand. It was as though her body had been hauled back in time to that ill-fated morning. She bent forward, body heaving, about to be sick—

Suddenly, she heard a giggle, high-pitched and playful. It sounded just like Sofia, and for a moment, Mari thought she'd slipped into a dream.

"I am here, *Mamma*," came Lia's voice from a short distance away. "I am digging in the sand for baby *gran*—" She cut off. "I forget the word."

Ami let out a cry, relief and irritation both. She ran toward her child, clutched her to her breast. "*Granchio*," she said. "And don't you ever scare me like that again."

Mari sat up, overwhelmed by relief. She didn't have children, was not even married, but Lia sometimes felt like her own.

She steadied her breath. *Lia is fine*, she said silently to herself. *She is perfectly well, on land, right here in front of all of us.* Yet even as her breath slowed, she could not resist glancing once more behind her, scanning the wave tops.

The women who'd performed the spell changed into dry clothes.

Lia pulled away from Ami's embrace, sneaking toward Mari, who welcomed her with a warm, strong hug. Mari bent over to kiss the girl's head, breathing in her fragrance of oranges, sugar, and sweat.

Lia turned her narrow face to Mari, her lips in a frown. "The spell will protect us from the pirates forever?"

Mari smiled. If only it worked that way. She thought of the pirate ship approaching the peninsula tonight. If it did indeed make for Positano, she imagined the captain cursing under his breath. *Damn these currents*, he might say. *I've had my eye on Positano. What is it with that village?* He would turn to his first mate and order him to alter the rigging, set an eastward course. *Anywhere but this slice of troublesome water*, he'd hiss at his crew.

"No," Mari said now. "Our *magia* does not work that way."

She paused, considering what more to tell the girl. Nearly every spell the women recited dissipated in a matter of days, but there was a single spell, the *vortice centuriaria*, which endured for one hundred years. It could only be recited if a *strega* removed her protective *cimaruta* necklace. And the cost of performing such magic was substantial: she had to sacrifice her own life in order for the spell to be effective. As far as Mari knew, no one had performed the spell in hundreds, maybe even thousands, of years.

Such a grim topic wasn't appropriate now, not with young Lia, so she kept her explanation simple. "Our spells last several days, at the most. No different than what a storm does to the ocean: churns it up, tosses it about. Eventually, though, the sea returns to normal. The sea always prevails."

How much she hated to admit this. Even the *vortice centuriaria*, long-lasting as it was, faded eventually. The women could do powerful things with the sea, yes, but they were not masters of it.

"This is why we keep very close to our informants," Mari went on. "There are people who tell us when pirates, or strange ships, have been spotted offshore. Knowing our spells will only last a few days, we must be diligent. We cannot curse the water too soon nor too late. Our fishermen need good, smooth water for their hauls, so we must only curse the water when we are sure there is a threat." She smiled, feeling a tad smug. "We are very good at it, Lia."

Lia traced her finger in the sand, making a big oval. "*Mamma* tells me I can do anything with the sea when I am older. Anything at all."

It was an enticing sentiment, this idea that they had complete control over the ocean, but it was false. Their spells were really quite simple and few—there were only seven of them—and they abided by the laws of nature.

"I would like to see one of those big white bears," Lia went on, "so I will bring an iceberg here, all the way from the Arctic."

"Sadly," Mari said, "I fear that is too far. We can push the pirates away because they are not all that far from us. But the Arctic? Well, there are many land masses separating us from your beloved polar bears…"

"I will go to live with other sea witches when I'm older, then," Lia said. "Witches who live closer to the Arctic."

"It is only us, dear. There are no other sea witches." At Lia's perturbed look, she explained, "We descended from the sirens, who lived on those islands—" she pointed to the horizon, where the Li Galli islets rose out of the water "—and we are the only women in the world who inherited power over the ocean."

Lia slumped forward, let out a sigh.

"You will still be able to do many things," Mari encouraged. "Just not everything."

Like saving the people you love, she mused. Even to this day, the loss of little Sofia felt so senseless, so unneeded. The sisters had been in only a few feet of water, doing somersaults and handstands, diving for sea glass. They had passed the afternoon this way a thousand times before. Later, Mari would wonder if Sofia had knocked her head against the ground, or maybe she'd accidentally inhaled a mouthful of water. Whatever happened, Sofia had noiselessly slipped beneath the rippling tide.

She's playing a trick, Mari thought as the minutes passed. *She's holding her breath and will come up any moment.* The girls did this often, making games of guessing where the other might emerge. But Sofia didn't emerge, not this time. And just a few months shy of fifteen, she hadn't been wearing a *cimaruta*.

Lia began to add small lines to the edge of her circle. She was drawing an eye with lashes. "*Mamma* says you can do more than she can," she chirped. "That it takes two or three of the *streghe* to do what you can do by yourself."

"Yes," Mari said. "Yes, that's right."

"Because of your *mamma* who died?"

Mari flinched at this, then quickly moved on. "Yes. And

my *nonna*, and her *mamma*, and so on. All the way back many thousands of years. There is something different in our blood."

"But not mine."

"You are special in plenty of ways. Think of the baby needlefish, for instance. You're always spotting them, even though they're nearly invisible and they move terribly fast."

"They're easy to spot," Lia disputed, brows furrowed.

"Not for me. You understand? We are each skilled in our own way."

Suddenly, Lia turned her face up to Mari. "Still, I hope you do not die, since you have the different, special blood and no one else does."

Mari recoiled, taken aback by Lia's comment. It was almost as though the young girl sensed Mari's covert plans. "Go find your *mamma*," she told Lia, who stood at once, ruining her sand art.

After she'd gone, Mari gazed at the hillside rising up behind them. This beach was not their normal place for practicing magic: Mari typically led the women to one of countless nearby caves or grottoes, protected from view, via a pair of small *gozzi*, seating six to a boat. But tonight had been different—one of the *gozzi* had come loose from its mooring, and it had drifted out into the open ocean. This had left the women with only one boat, and it wasn't big enough to hold them all.

"Let's gather on the beach instead," she'd urged. "We'll be out but a few minutes." Besides, it was the middle of the night, and the moon had been mostly hidden behind clouds, so it was very dark.

While a few of the women looked at her warily, everyone had agreed in the end.

Mari stood and squeezed the water from her hair. It was nearly three o'clock, and all of the women were yawning.

She shoved the wet rope into her bag and dressed quickly, pulling her shift over her protective *cimaruta* necklace. Hers bore tiny amulets from the sea and coastline: a moon shell, an ammonite fossil, a kernel of gray volcanic pumice. Recently, Mari had found a tiny coral fragment in the perfect shape of a mountain, which she especially liked. Mountains made her think of inland places, which made her think of freedom.

As the women began to make their way up the hillside, Mari felt fingertips brush her arm. "Psst," Ami whispered. In her hand was a small envelope, folded tightly in half.

Mari's heart surged. "A letter."

Ami winked. "It arrived yesterday."

It had been two weeks since the last one, and as tempted as Mari was to tear open the envelope and read it in the moonlight, she tucked it against her bosom. "Thank you," she whispered.

Suddenly, Mari caught movement in the corner of her eye, something on the dock a short distance away. At first, she thought she'd imagined it—clouds skirted across the sky, and the night was full of shadows—but then she gasped as a dark form quickly made its way off the dock, around a small building, and out of sight.

Something—someone—had most definitely been over there. A man. A late-night rendezvous, perhaps? Or had he been alone and spying on the women?

Mari turned to tell Ami, but her friend had already gone ahead, a hand protectively on Lia's back.

As they stepped onto the dirt pathway scattered with carts and closed-up vendor stands, Mari turned around once more to glance at the dock. But there was nothing, no one. The dock lay in darkness.

Just a trick of the moonlight, she told herself.

Besides, she had a very important letter nestled against her chest—one she intended to tear open the moment she got home.

2

HAVEN

Monday

On my first morning in Positano, I woke to the sound of sirens.

I turned over in bed, fumbling for my phone, which read 8:22 a.m. I could steal another hour, maybe two. Typically, I'd be up and going by now, but my internal clock was stuck at home—the Florida Keys, where I'd lived all my life.

The echo of distant emergency sirens went on, a series of high-pitched, nerve-grating wails. I threw back the covers with a sigh of annoyance and spun my dark hair into a messy bun.

Having arrived at this rented villa only yesterday, it took me a moment to mentally retrace the layout of what would be my home for the next year. Shuffling along the cool terra-cotta floors, I walked toward the small terrace, facing southeast. It had a panoramic view of the village of Positano and its many buildings, splashes of pink and orange and white stacked vertically up the hillside like the layers of a cake. At the bottom lay the main beach, Spiaggia Grande, with its hundreds of umbrellas lined up in perfect rows. And beyond this, the Tyrrhenian Sea, showing off her luster in every shade of blue.

This view was why I'd chosen the villa, and my team—four other women, all of us nautical archaeologists—had readily agreed. It had been well within our project's budget, which surprised me until I realized that in exchange for the view, we were giving up space. There were only two bedrooms, which meant we'd be double-bunking, with one of us on the pullout couch.

Still, the view. There was a reason Positano was the gem of the Amalfi Coast. Even after a lifetime of diving wrecks throughout the Keys and the Atlantic, I'd never seen ocean like this. I'd never seen *blue* like this.

The distant wail of the sirens continued, and once outside, I turned my gaze to the ocean. A quarter mile off the beach, a pair of boats sped westward, red lights flashing and sirens squalling.

"Morning," came a voice behind me.

I turned to find Mal stepping onto the terrace, her hands wrapped around a mug of black coffee. She and I had arrived together yesterday, earlier than our other three team members, who would join us next week. Mal and I, both thirty-five, had met in our PhD program years ago at Texas A&M. As the only two women in one of our conservation lab courses, we'd become instant friends.

"Morning," I said back. "Sirens wake you up, too?"

She nodded. "I saw some paramedics up there, going west." She pointed toward Amalfi Drive, the road we'd taken into town yesterday. The drive from Naples to Positano had lasted ninety minutes, but I could hardly complain. We'd stopped a few times to snag photos and then again at a sun-drenched roadside stand to buy a bag of apricots and prickly pears. It was easy to understand why Amalfi Drive, especially now in early summer, was one of the most famous roadways in the world. With the limestone cliffside plunging into the ocean just inches away from the road and a dazzling sea beyond, the views were incomparable.

"Harbor police, too," I said, motioning toward the ocean. I bent over the railing, the stone already warmed by the morning sun. "Can't see where they're headed, though."

Mal ran her hand through her short spiky blond hair. "Wonder what's up."

I eyed her coffee. "No idea, but I need a cup of that."

"I found a Nespresso machine inside," she said, smiling. "All stocked with pods."

As I made my way toward the kitchen, I tripped on the handle of a suitcase and cursed under my breath. Only two of us had arrived, but already the inside of this rented villa was, in a word, *chaotic*: unpacked luggage pushed up against walls, scuba dive kits tossed onto furniture, underwater camera equipment crowding the countertops. Mal and I hadn't worried about settling in yesterday. Instead, we'd made straight for the nearest *ristorante* in search of fresh seafood and cheap, local wine. We only had a few days of downtime before our project kicked off, and we planned to make the most of it. Today, we would take the villa's two-person Vespa to a nearby beach.

Returning to the terrace with my coffee, I found Mal leaning over the railing, her eyebrows knit together. "You see that white boat out there?" She pointed to the watery horizon, and I spotted a different, faster vessel, this one also heading west.

"Shit," I said, spotting the red band on the boat's hull. The Italian coast guard. While harbor police handled all sorts of matters, even relatively trivial ones, the coast guard in any jurisdiction meant something serious. Search. Rescue. Recovery. That sort of thing.

"And they're in a hurry, toward something thataway." Mal pointed west, but our line of sight was blocked by the rocky cliff separating Positano from the villages farther along the coast. "If only that hillside wasn't in our way…"

We glanced at each other then, eyes glimmering mischievously. I might have been the lead on this project, but Mal was dive marshal, the one ensuring my team's safety underwater. If there was a local incident worthy of calling the coast guard, Mal's curiosity would get the best of her.

And mine, too, if I were being honest.

I threw back my coffee, enlivened. "Let's go," I said.

Water had always been my playground. But as the daughter of an internationally esteemed nautical archaeologist, I suppose I didn't have much choice. It was inevitable that my father would teach his only child to love the ocean as much as he did. He had me snorkeling at age three, scuba diving at age eight. I dove my first shipwreck soon after.

Not incidentally, we lived in the right place for it. The Florida Keys are riddled with more than a thousand wrecks, many of them in water so shallow that a wet suit isn't necessary, and a single tank of air can last two hours. My father surveyed and published site plans for many of these wrecks, which was how he'd made his name in the world of nautical archaeology.

With the Gulf of Mexico as my backyard, I had an adventurous, unorthodox childhood. Without fail, Saturday mornings meant wreck-diving. The two of us would anchor offshore, raise our red-and-white dive flag, and explore our backyard underwater paradise. Early on, my father taught me basic dive skills—underwater navigation, buoyancy control—and in time, I began to master technical skills, too, like safely diving the cavelike environment of sunken wrecks.

Skills and technique were one thing, but my father also never let me forget the joy. Shipwrecks were full of mystery, and he taught me to explore them as a nautical archaeologist might. What brought the vessel down? What cargo did she hold? Where was she going, and why?

Don't overlook the archives, either, he liked to say. Sailors' logs, vessel blueprints, incident reports—they often revealed far more about a wreck than the rubble itself. *Sometimes the answers aren't in the water, but out of it.*

Even so, there was more to my father's interest in shipwrecks than just research and academia—he'd also been a self-declared treasure hunter. Framed in his study were several articles about the approximate value of the world's sunken treasure: more than four billion dollars, experts estimated. And only a select number of people, those skilled and brave enough to slip into the depths of the ocean, had any chance of finding it.

Even then, it took luck. Luck my father never seemed to stumble on, though it wasn't for lack of trying. Year after year, dive after dive, that Big Discovery always seemed to elude him.

His friend and old schoolmate, Conrad Cass, liked to give him a hard time about it. "Have you found anything but sea junk lately?" Conrad asked anytime the two got together. Easy for him to say: Conrad, a fellow diver, had supposedly stumbled on a few lucky wrecks over the years, though he never revealed where these wrecks were or what sort of loot he'd found.

It felt unfair to my father: he believed in following the rules, and he knew well the importance of reporting any finds to the proper jurisdictions, even if it meant he wouldn't see a dime in the end. But guys like Conrad? My father wasn't convinced he adhered to the same values.

Always a peacemaker, he just shook his head at Conrad's teasing. "Not yet," he always said with a laugh.

Still, I knew frustration lay beneath this facade. My father had come close so many times. Once, off the coast of South Africa, he recovered what he thought was a gold coin from a ship sunk in the early 1600s. It would have been worth more than a hundred thousand dollars.

Alas, it was pyrite. Fool's gold.

Another time, he'd been slated to join a group of fellow archaeologists on a promising dive near the Azores. But the morning of, he woke with a severe head cold. Every diver knows it's dangerous to dive with sinus congestion—it can rupture an eardrum—so my father stayed on the boat instead.

That wreck ended up yielding a quarter-million dollars in sunken Spanish doubloons.

It was his evergreen dream, making a big underwater discovery, yet time and time again, it slipped through his fingers.

Then finally, six months ago, he found something. *Something big*, he said, bigger than anything he'd ever seen. But without a means to excavate it, he'd been forced to return to the surface. Back on shore, breathless, he'd immediately begun planning his return dive to the wreck.

Only, bad luck wasn't done with him yet, and he never got the chance to return. A few weeks after first laying eyes on that *something big*, my father was dead.

Mal drove the Vespa, leaving me to marvel at the smaller details comprising Positano's charm: hot pink bougainvillea climbing up walls, swallows darting in and out of roof soffits, seagulls circling high above. It was a perfect June day with a few cottony clouds and a light breeze. If there had indeed been an incident on the water, no one could blame the weather.

At an intersection, I felt my phone buzz in my pocket. I took a quick peek. It was a message from Conrad Cass.

Thinking of you today, kid, it read. **If I could, I'd send him a whole case of plum wine.**

A knot formed in my throat. Today, my father would have turned sixty years old. And plum wine was his favorite.

I tucked my phone back into my pocket, appreciative of Conrad's kind gesture. He was a big deal these days, retired and living in a nine-bedroom estate in Naples, Florida, with a glut of financiers and politicians to call friends. I was touched he'd thought of me. Not even Mal had acknowledged my late father's birthday yet.

On Amalfi Drive, we took a left, heading west. A few minutes later, we rounded the cliff. From this new perspective, we were able to make out miles and miles of glimmering Italian coastline, and even the Isle of Capri in the distance.

We could see Li Galli, too—the archipelago of three tiny islands where we would, over the next year, be doing our underwater fieldwork. As I looked out at the islands, a chill stole over me: dozens of shipwrecks riddled the seabed around Li Galli. A veritable graveyard, thirty meters beneath the ocean's surface.

Who knew what secrets hid among those wrecks? An untold amount of information might be gleaned from surveying and inventorying them: historic trade routes, piracy incidents, crusades. And this wasn't even accounting for what might be *in* the wrecks. Loot, gems, treasure.

We made a few hairpin turns, and I felt my palms growing sweaty—in part because Mal was taking the turns harder than I'd have liked, but also because we were approaching the first big project site of my career. After so many months of preparation, here we were at last.

Given its many wrecks, our chosen project site was an unexplored mess: archaeologists were at a loss for how to investigate it. Existing technology like echo sounders and side sonar were meant to find anomalies on the seafloor—a stretch of seabed interrupted by a single ship's hull—but Li Galli was a quarter-mile-wide pileup of dense, sunken rubble. No technology existed to survey, much less excavate, such a chaotic site.

Which was precisely what my team of nautical archaeologists aimed to change.

Mal and I drove a few more minutes, the Li Galli islets coming clearly into view. Yet as the details of the islands grew sharper—now I could even make out the ancient stone watchtower on the easternmost islet—I felt my pulse quicken.

The islets were surrounded by rescue boats. Toward the middle of the archipelago, I spotted a yacht, but something was not right—

Suddenly, I drew in a sharp breath.

Mal must have spotted it at the exact same time, because she pulled the Vespa to the side of the road and turned the engine off. I rushed toward the metal guardrail, crocus and chicory weeds blooming at my feet. Below me, the craggy cliffside dropped sharply toward the ocean. I looked out at the sea and blinked, unable to believe what I was seeing: amid the islets of Li Galli, an enormous yacht—worth many millions, surely—listed severely to one side, its port side heaving toward the water.

"Mal," I said, hardly able to form words. According to my research, the last wreck in Li Galli was almost a decade ago, and it had been blamed on a bad storm. And though we'd selected this project site due to its abundance of shipwrecks, those wrecks were...*old*. So old they felt detached from reality, even mythical. But this? This was a modern-day yacht, sinking right in front of our eyes.

My dive training kicked into gear as I considered the hazards, any possible explanation for what we were seeing.

Depth. I frowned, recalling the nautical charts I'd been studying for months. I knew the water around the sinking yacht measured twenty-five meters deep. They couldn't have run aground.

Reefs. There were none in the area. *Rocks*. That was impossible, too, as the yacht was well away from the actual islets. I glanced again at the sky overhead, impossibly clear and calm. Weather couldn't be blamed, either, then.

"Fire?" Mal asked. "Maybe an engine explosion?"

I peered through a pair of binoculars I'd thrown into my bag and shook my head. "There's no smoke. Underwater currents, maybe?" I mused aloud. "Maelstroms? Everyone knows it's a turbulent stretch of water."

According to my prefieldwork research, Li Galli had been problematic for hundreds of years. A vortex of ocean currents converged here, amplified by the area's irregular seabed topography. Surviving mariners often blamed their ill-fated journeys on unforeseen maelstroms near the islets.

Still, there was something strange in the data I'd reviewed: the early nineteenth century saw a spike in Li Galli shipwrecks, one after the other through the 1820s and 1830s. Nearby villagers couldn't explain the uptick in incidents, though some speculated a sinkhole had altered the topography around the islets.

The phenomenon had been dubbed the Amalfi Curse and, for more than eighty years, mariners avoided Li Galli altogether.

Then, in the late 1920s, a few uninformed boaters traversed the area, experiencing no issues. It seemed that whatever oceanic vortex had plagued the area had all but disappeared. I suspected that seismological activity, or even climate change, had something to do with the shift. For me, the curse theory was ludicrous.

Mal gave me a skeptical look. "A superyacht like that, taken under by a whirlpool? Even a violent one. It doesn't make sense."

I couldn't disagree with her. The sea that lay before us was serene, motionless. Not a whitecap to be seen. I let out a long exhale and handed her the binoculars. "Jesus. The women on deck, look." I paused, short for words and feeling sick. "They're panicking."

On the sundeck, several women in swimsuits motioned frantically toward the coast guard. One woman fell to her knees sobbing, while another leaned over the edge of the boat, making a futile effort to reach one of the portholes. Brightly colored objects bobbed around the vessel, life jackets and flotsam that had either fallen, or been tossed, overboard.

And the vessel itself was taking on water. *Quick.* The cabins were most certainly flooded by now.

"This is terrible," Mal whispered.

My eyes welled with tears. I was witnessing, in real time, an event that would most certainly result in casualties.

But it didn't make sense, and this left the scientist in me further unsettled. By all appearances, this was a perfectly seaworthy yacht. There was no weather, no wind. The seas were easy and smooth. On the nearby islets, I spotted a few onlookers, people close to the water watching the scene unfold.

The yacht, rolling moments ago to one side, was now going down by its stern. Another two to three minutes, and she'd be completely underwater. I felt helpless from this vantage point, though reassured by the rescue boats within proximity.

Mal glanced at me, her expression hesitant. I knew exactly what she was about to say, much as I didn't want to hear it.

"The Amalfi Curse," she muttered.

I kept silent. The science-minded part of me wished badly I could counter with a better, more reasonable explanation.

But truth be told, I had none.

3

**Letter from Matteo Mazza
to his younger brother, Massimo**

Wednesday, April 11, 1821

My brother Massimo,

I have just come by your residence to find you not in. Forgive my passing along such news in this manner, but it is of great importance.

In this envelope, you will find a letter I received this morning from a gentleman in Positano. He remarks upon the suspiciously good fortune of that tiny, trifling village—the sort of place we have no interest in, barring the one thing that brought us there years ago.

I thought we'd stripped that village of her value. But what if there is something else, something we overlooked the first time?

He has asked for money in exchange for information. I am willing to agree to this, and I will send him a response immediately. In the interim, however, I would like to see the village, to scout around and explore for myself.

Will you join me? We can take the overland route by horse from Naples. I can leave as soon as tomorrow morning.

Come to me the moment you've finished reading this. We have much to discuss.

Fondly,
Your older brother Matteo

4

MARI

Wednesday, April 11, 1821

Mari walked home with two other *streghe*: Paola, her nineteen-year-old stepsister, and Cleila, her stepmother. After the loss of her mother twelve years ago, Mari's father had swiftly married Cleila, a widow who lived not far from the De-Luca family.

Now Mari couldn't help but wonder if one of these two would be voted in as the next leader. Neither was a *strega finisima*, but they were related to Mari by marriage, and that counted for something.

Back at the family villa, the women stepped into the dark foyer. Mari let out a loud yawn, badly desiring a few hours of rest. But then, she swallowed hard: Corso—a distant cousin, the man she was supposed to marry—and her father were awake, even at this ridiculously early hour. Corso had been in the village for the last several days, visiting from Rome as he often did. The two men were sitting side by side in the *salotto* with a lantern lit on one of the tables. Its light glinted off the cool terra-cotta floors.

Mari's father wore dark trousers and a simple white linen shirt. Corso, on the other hand, wore a perfectly pressed morning suit, bespoke and of a vibrant blue hue. In the humble village of Positano, no other man dressed in fabrics so expensive or in colors so bold.

At the sight of Corso, Paola ran her fingers through her hair, pulling a few strands around her face. She'd always made much of his fashionable attire, his babylike skin.

Mari, on the other hand, preferred a less civilized look. She wasn't bothered by a shirt with a few tears. A scar or two.

She touched her bosom, thinking of the letter tucked against it.

At the sight of the women, the men stood. "*Le mie ragazze,*" Father said. *My girls.* "Did the tide wash in anything interesting?"

Like the other men in the village, these two had no knowledge of sea witchcraft. They believed the women were out gossiping, or searching for shells, or swimming naked, all of them huddled together in the frigid sea.

They were good men, in their own way, these husbands and fathers and growing sons. Hardworking, well-built. Many in the village were fishermen, their arms lean and rippling with scars. Their hands were nimble, too, and quick to work the fishhooks, the nets.

Industrious as they were, the men of the village—and everyone else in the world, for that matter—were terribly unaware, and this was just how the *streghe* liked it. For if the village men got word of the truth, there would be complications. They would tell their friends, and their friends would tell their friends, and soon the entire coastline would be moving to town, monetizing and exploiting the women and their gifts.

"A few things," Mari said, "but nothing exceptional." The bag slung over her shoulder dug into the soft flesh, weighed down by the heavy rope still laden with seawater. Next to her, Paola shifted. They were far from the best of friends, but they had this secret-keeping in common. "You're both awake early," Mari added.

"A few of us are planning a morning watch." Father checked the clock next to him. A mug of something hot sat on the table behind him, sending up tendrils of steam. "Another hour or so and we'll go out. You didn't see anything unusual tonight, did you?"

He meant the pirates, of course. Mari shook her head. "No sign of anything." *Nor will there be.*

Corso nodded to the bag on Mari's shoulder. "May I have a look?" he asked. "Something to add to your collection of *chincaglieria*?"

Chincaglieria. Trinkets. Curios. That's what Corso always called the things the women brought home, though it was mostly just Paola now, for Mari no longer gathered things from the sea. All she wanted from it was the two people it had taken from her. Still, over the years, Corso had occasionally asked to see her old collection, and she'd shown him a few things: her comb made of a sawfish jaw, and the jar of dried kelp powder, good for applying to blemishes. Mari had made a point of explaining that everything in her collection had some purpose or function—that a woman could do more than gather useless trinkets.

"They are like gifts from the sea," Corso had once commented. "Little offerings."

At this, Mari had clenched her jaw. If only he understood how cruel the sea had been, how cruel *life* had been. Her plan to someday marry him was proof of it.

Mari's father had once done quite well for himself as the owner of Positano's only net-making shop, selling wares the village men required every day: corks, weights, net needles, and hemp in a variety of lengths and weights. But after his wife's death, he became inattentive, even negligent, with the business accounting records. One of the shop employees began discreetly stealing from the shop, ultimately making off with an extraordinary sum of money, never to be seen again. If not for the dowries that Father had set aside for Mari and Sofia, the family would have been left bankrupt, even homeless. Even after many years, he was still working to get the business back afloat.

Corso, an affluent cousin of Mari's father, had always paid regular visits to the family. Several years ago, as Mari developed from a spindly adolescent into a well-endowed young woman, he began to convey his interest in her, often bearing lavish gifts for Mari and a small purse of *ducati* for Father. Aware of the family's financial struggles, Corso made it clear that he expected no dowry. On the contrary, he wanted to help provide for them, and even offered to restore Sofia's emptied *dote*.

Though she felt no attraction to Corso, Mari knew this arrangement would at least give her dowry-bearing sister a chance at true love. It was decided that Mari and Corso would marry sometime after Mari turned twenty-one.

Of course, Mari had no way of knowing that Sofia would be dead a year after the arrangement was made. Her sacrifice had been all for naught and instead left her trapped and miserable.

Now, Mari shook her head at Corso's request to view what was in her bag. "Not now. Later, perhaps, once we've cleaned things up."

He paused, considering this. "Your hair is wet, yet your clothes are dry," he said, narrowing his eyes ever so slightly. Behind him, Father kept silent.

"I went for a swim."

Corso slowly dragged his eyes across her waist and breasts. *He is imagining me naked in the sea*, Mari thought, like she was another curio pulled from a bag.

"Will you join me on the terrace for a moment?" he asked her, absentmindedly running his finger down the edge of his vest. As he took a step closer, Mari was struck, as she often was, by his height. He towered over her, all lanky limbs and no muscle whatsoever. He was a terrazzo merchant who sat behind a desk in Rome, negotiating numbers while other men moved the heavy goods. He was as rich as he was repellent, at least in Mari's eyes. Everyone else seemed to worship the man.

Mari began to refuse, weary as she was. She wanted nothing more than to read her letter. "I'm so very tired, I—"

At once, Father pushed himself from his chair. "Mari," he said under his breath. A one-word warning.

Though their marriage had been agreed upon long ago, Corso had not formally asked for her hand, much less produced a ring. Might he be planning to propose now, on the terrace, as the sun slowly rose over the sea? She could imagine nothing more miserable—both the backdrop and the man.

Feeling her father's watchful eye, she placed a hand on her lower stomach and twisted her face into an expression of pain. "Just give me a few minutes, please," she said to the men. She pulled this trick every so often, feigning women's discomforts. "Ten minutes, Corso, and I will meet you on the terrace."

What did it matter if he proposed today, anyhow? They'd all believe her dead in a few weeks. Corso would grieve his almost-wife and, in time, he'd inevitably turn his attentions to Paola, who desperately wanted him for herself, anyway. Father would keep getting his *ducati*. It would all turn out perfectly well.

Without waiting for a reply, Mari raced up the stairs to her bedroom. She had not even shut her door before she had the envelope out. She lit the candle by her bed, withdrew the missive, and turned to the final page—the signature line—if only to lay eyes upon his name. *Holmes*. He'd signed as he always did, the tail of the *s* in a whimsical flourish.

A smudge of tar marred the bottom corner of the paper. Holmes's letters often bore marks like this, a result of his working with rigging and sails, which were regularly doused in tar to keep them waterproof. Mari felt no repulsion at the sight of such grime; if anything, it made her feel closer to him.

She rubbed her thumb over the smudge, letting it stain her skin, and began to read. The letter was dated March 22, several weeks ago.

Mari, my beauty. It is now more than three weeks since I last saw you. I am sure I cannot long for you any more than I do now, but I have been thinking that since I left Positano. Do you know that as we sailed westward, I could see you standing on your terrace?

Here, Mari paused. She remembered this exact moment: she'd watched him go, his ship in silhouette, the sky all pink and orange. She read on.

I look at our seashell every day. I have turned it over in my palms so many times, I fear I am dulling the ridges.
Promise we will go seashell hunting when I return?

Mari smiled. *Our seashell.* He'd found it the day that he and Mari first met, in May of last year. Holmes had been in port in Positano, and they'd found themselves on the seashore at the same time, walking very near one another. She'd known he was a sailor by his low ponytail, his wide-legged trousers, and the tar stains on his palms. He bent down to lift an object from the sand and held it up, consternation on his face.

"Something is unusual about it," he'd said, catching Mari's gaze. "But I cannot put my finger on it."

She'd caught a strange accent in his voice. "A sinistral shell," she explained, stepping closer. "It is like a left-handed shell. The spiral goes left, instead of right." She plucked a few other shells from the sand near her feet, showing him how their spirals differed from the one in his hand. "Sinistral shells are highly valued, rare as they are."

"Indeed. I have never found one before." He held it out for her.

She shook her head, indicating he should take the shell for himself. "I find them all the time. Keep it. It's good luck."

He smiled, dropping it into his pocket. "What else have you found?"

"All sorts of things," she answered over her shoulder, hoping he hadn't noticed the slight quiver in her voice. She felt feverish suddenly, despite the cool air. She dipped a foot into the shallow waves, and at once the water began to sparkle, tiny flickers of orange and pink. It reminded her of the luminescent sea creatures she'd marveled at a few times before.

They explored awhile longer, studying shells of various sorts. They made introductions, and at one point, she turned, pointing out her family's villa at the top of the hill.

When they parted a short while later, Mari thought she'd never see him again.

How very wrong she'd been.

She continued reading his letter, smiling every so often at his imperfect Italian, which he'd learned after spending the last two-and-a-half years aboard various Napoli merchant vessels. She'd never had a problem understanding him; if anything, she found his blunders endearing.

> Tomorrow, I will post this letter at the port of Anzio. We are anchored now, just off the coast. This might come as a surprise to you, as I should be farther north, near Livorno—but as these things so often go, there has been a change in vessels, a change in crew. I'd hoped to be done with the Fratelli Mazza, but I am back on another one of their vessels—the *Aquila*, a two-masted merchant brig. We are to run goods between Fregenae and Anzio through mid-May, after which we will return to the Amalfi peninsula. Seeing you again cannot come soon enough.

Mari placed her hand against her chest, hating this news for him. Everyone along coastal Italy knew of the Fratelli Mazza, Naples's richest—and least principled—shipping company. Matteo and Massimo Mazza had inherited the enterprise from their father. With a fleet of more than three dozen vessels, the brothers ran merchant routes throughout Italy. It might have made for an impressive establishment if they came by their success honorably. On the contrary, the Mazza brothers were known to collude with black-market malefactors and ocean-going thieves—pirates and privateers, in other words.

They also provided room for such criminals in their storehouses, making them traffickers, too.

Whether in spite of or because of their illicit associations, the brothers made good businessmen. Their rates were competitive, and their trade routes the fastest. Many in the community turned a blind eye to the brothers' degenerate behavior, caring for nothing but the fact that they had transformed coastal Italian merchanting for the better. People refused to call the brothers what they really were: thieves, most of the time. Murderers, some of the time.

And not to be trusted, anytime at all.

And as for the *gendarmerie*—the police? They could be bought off like anyone else. Many believed that the brothers made regular payments to secure impunity.

Mari continued reading.

> The *Aquila* is smaller than the vessel I was on a week ago. Only three decks—the main, the berthing, and the cargo. There are hardly two dozen of us on board. It is the usual scope of work: toiling with the rigging and sails, and four-hour shifts on watch.
>
> I didn't complain when they moved me to the *Aquila*, for they increased my pay slightly due to the extra work. But a few days have since passed, and it is clear the men on this Mazza vessel are of the foulest sort. My fellow sailors are half-witted, and the officers are bellicose, particularly the first mate, Quinto.
>
> Tonight, when we anchored, he and another officer called for us to ready the tender. As we did so, Quinto made no effort in hiding his plans for the evening: a visit to the bordello on Via Calipso.

Later, Nico—my only real friend on this brig—told me that this is Quinto's way. At every port, he slithers his way through the narrow streets in search of prostitutes and easy-to-pilfer merchandise. As I've told you before, the Mazza brothers have people all over, men who loot and thieve by land and sea. Quinto, I am certain, is one of the middlemen in these schemes. Nico says he often returns from his evening romps with boxes or canvas sacks that he takes immediately to the cargo hold. Stolen or black-market goods, certainly.

You know I'd escape them and go elsewhere, to another country altogether, but…there is you. They're worth tolerating, knowing that their routes keep me so close to my beloved.

Speaking of stolen goods, I think they are keeping something aboard the *Aquila*, hidden in the second mate's cabin. They kicked the officer out, made him bunk with Quinto. Now the cabin is padlocked. Whatever it is they're concealing in there, they don't want any of us crew to see it, to even know about it.

I might have thought it was only jewels they're hiding, if not for something I learned the other day. As I repaired a split panel outside the officers' quarters, I overheard Quinto and the captain bragging about the fact that they were, at that very moment, transporting the "most valuable asset the Mazza brothers have ever moved from port to port."

What, I wonder, could this be?

Surely more than gems.

Regardless, what a life they're all living, chasing women and stealing goods. I'd rather be here—in my cold, rattling berth—with a sheet of paper on my lap and your name at the top of it.

The candle is growing low, my beloved, and still I must write to my father in Boston. It is almost too good to declare on paper, but it is due time to inform him of what you and I have kept between us for so long: next time I see him, I intend to have a sweetheart in tow.

With all my love,
Your Holmes

Mari read the letter a second time, then she folded it back up and pressed it against her chest. How very far away Holmes felt now. His routes would keep him north of Rome for the next few weeks. At least he'd made a friend, Nico, aboard.

She took a deep, unsteady breath. The letter unnerved her, especially the fact that Holmes's new vessel was owned by the Mazzas.

And what of Holmes's mention about the padlocked cabin, the valuable goods inside? It was perplexing, indeed.

She sat on the edge of the bed, aware of the time: Corso would be waiting for her on the terrace. She opened the bottom drawer of her dresser, reaching toward the back, where she hid her most prized possessions. The coral bracelet Sofia had always worn. A tiny satchel of dried pits, which she'd kept from the olives she and Holmes shared after the first time they'd made love. And the bundle of letters he had written her over the months, tied up with twine.

After their initial meeting, she and Holmes had managed to see each other every few weeks. Between these visits, they wrote to each other. It was this bundle of letters that chronicled their falling in love, all of the stories and secrets shared between them.

It revealed their escape plans, too.

She added this most recent letter to the bundle and closed the drawer.

The day after their initial encounter on the beach, nearly a year ago, Mari had been surprised to find Holmes settled beneath a tree on the outskirts of her family's property. It was nearly dusk.

At the sight of him, she'd quickly wiped her eyes, cleared her throat. That day marked the one-year anniversary of Sofia's death, and she'd spent a tearful afternoon walking through the hillsides and citrus groves belonging to neighboring villagers.

"Hello again," Holmes had greeted her, speaking softly in Italian.

She did her best to look cheerful. "Hello."

"You have been crying," he said, frowning. He stepped toward her, studying the splotches on her cheeks, her neck. *Of course he would notice*, she thought, feeling foolish. He'd already shown his penchant for detail while on the seashore yesterday.

"Would you like to talk about it?" he asked her, pulling a clean kerchief from his pocket and handing it to her.

Mari glanced at the villa. A single lantern shone from within. Her father's office. He had told her, that morning, that he would be in his office all day, reviewing invoices. He would not like to be bothered. Mari hadn't pushed it: this, she knew, was a hard day for him, too. Work was how he grieved.

Meanwhile, Cleila and Paola were in Naples, shopping the markets, not minding the importance of the date.

"Yes," Mari said, surprising herself. Holmes was a stranger, after all. But she felt so lonely on this of all days.

She took a seat next to him and began to tell him all about Sofia. Her whims, her curls, her stubbornness. It was an especially painful loss, she said, given that the girls had lost their mother long ago, too.

Holmes had not asked questions. He'd simply let her talk. After nearly an hour, Mari shook her head. "You now know more than Corso does. Perhaps more than he ever will." She could never confide in him about such things. He'd grow bored in minutes.

"Corso?" Holmes asked, his jaw twitching. "Who is that?"

Mari bit her lip, recognizing her error. She hadn't meant to say his name. It had slipped out, safe as she felt with her new friend, Holmes.

"The man I am supposed to marry," she said. "Much as I do not want to. I do not want to be here at all, in fact."

"Not here as in, not in Positano?"

She nodded. "Have you ever felt destined for a life you did not want?"

A thoughtful look crossed Holmes's face. "Yes," he said. "As an adolescent, when I could not grasp a whit of anything scholarly, and I managed to frustrate every teacher I ever had. My father so badly wanted me to follow in his footsteps as a lawyer, but I knew a stack of contracts on a desk would not satisfy my sense of adventure. I wanted to see the world."

He shifted in the grass, stretching his legs out. "I fear he'd all but given up on me, but at age thirteen, even my father could not deny that I was destined for something else. With his approval, I made for the docks in Boston, seeking work. Plenty of other boys were there doing the same. None of us had any experience, only a hatred of restraint and a fear of boredom. I was hired as a sailor boy on a merchant vessel. My first journey took me to Havana. Later, I crossed the Atlantic. Eventually, I made it as far as China."

The lantern in Father's office suddenly went out. "I should go inside," Mari said quickly. "Will you write me?" She recited an address. "That is my friend Ami's house. She will make sure I get your letters." It would be too suspect if letters sent by another man began arriving at Mari's doorstep. "And next time you are in port, please come visit me again."

He promised he would.

They stood, ready to go their separate ways.

"Holmes," Mari said suddenly. He had seen the world. She wondered now whether his itch for adventure had been satisfied. "Has this life given you all you hoped for?"

He fixed his gaze on her. "Quite a lot more, in fact."

★ ★ ★

On the terrace, Mari approached Corso from behind. He leaned over the railing, looking out at the ocean. The sun had just lifted above the horizon, and the clouds were grayish-pink.

On the water, not a single boat could be seen.

Quickly, Mari checked to see if Corso had anything in his hands, relieved when she saw that his spindly fingers were empty.

When he did bring her tokens of affection, she nearly always threw them away. It wasn't that Corso was a terrible man, but even still, Mari didn't want her bedroom riddled with reminders of him.

A few weeks ago, Paola had caught her discarding his latest gift. Mari had been standing on the terrace. From her pocket, she pulled out a colorful silk headscarf, something Corso had just given her. She lifted it to the breeze and released her grip on it, watching as the scarf caught the wind and floated away, making directly for the ocean. The silk, spun by worms, would dissolve in the sea in a matter of days.

Paola came up behind her, eyeing the headscarf, its teal and pink design twisting in the wind. She said nothing at first, merely watching it drift away like a kite. Then she faced Mari head-on.

"You are a fool," she said. "You haven't any idea how fortunate you are." She glanced once more over the edge of the railing. "Marrying a man as handsome and rich as Corso. Everyone admiring you, or showering you with sympathy you don't deserve."

Mari frowned. "What do you mean by—"

She stopped short. Paola had turned to retreat inside.

Now Mari stepped to the railing, leaving some space between her and Corso. He slid himself along it until their shoulders were touching, then he dropped his lips to her ear. Mari closed her eyes, wondering what he was about to say. She knew she must play along, for rebuffing Corso would enrage her father and rouse suspicion. Besides, it was possible that Paola was watching from somewhere nearby.

"I'd hoped to have something for you today," he whispered, gazing down at her.

Mari's finger still bore a shadow of tar from Holmes's letter. She comforted herself with the fact that, even now, some part of him, some tiny molecule, clung to her. "Oh?" she asked, trying to sound interested.

"Yes. Only, it is taking longer than I'd hoped. A few more weeks, according to my friend in the city."

He meant Rome, of course. "Your *friend*?" she repeated.

"*L'orefice*," he said.

L'orefice. The goldsmith. The jeweler. Her hand went to her throat, and she stifled a cough.

"Think of it," he continued. "We will go back and forth between here and Rome. The city is infinitely more exciting, anyhow. The streets are paved. Everything is made of marble. The people are civilized. And it is not along the sea, so it is not as rough, teeming with sailors and the like." He rubbed his hands together, and Mari gazed at his pale, long fingers—as feminine as hers, really. How different he was than Holmes, who had calloused palms and wind-chapped cheeks. Yet it was Holmes's toughened hands that Mari imagined every night, breathing hard in the quiet darkness of her bedroom.

Mari toyed with her ring finger, imagining a sliver of metal wrapped around it. Such a small thing, but binding her nevertheless to man she had never loved.

She had a sudden urge to lean over the railing and heave.

Corso was right, that Rome was landlocked, and this should have excited her. But like everyone else, he believed she loved the sea. "Rome does not have an ocean," she half-heartedly countered.

"Ah, so it does not smell like fish, you mean? Besides, Fregenae is very close. I can take you there to collect little things from the sand. I've already spoken with a few other merchants. Those treasures you stumble across, the things you find during your swims—you cannot imagine the price they will command in a place like Rome. Sponges and oysters go for enough, but conch shells have sold for hundreds. Thousands. We will be even richer, Mari. So terribly rich." He turned to face her, but his look of exhilaration disappeared when he saw her morose expression. "Why, I can buy us a place along the water in Fregenae, then, with a view. You can look at the sea every day."

Mari could imagine nothing worse.

"I've been wanting another residence, anyway," Corso went on. "I have a great deal of money coming in soon."

Mari didn't give a whit for his money. "It is all sooner than I expected. We have plenty of time, don't we?"

He turned his face away, exasperation flashing in his eyes. "Your father has told me all about your mother," he said. "He wishes they'd had more years together. I won't let us be robbed of any more time." He gave a stiff, quick nod. "The jeweler said it won't be much longer. And I very much hope, Mari, that you understand how good this will be. Your father supports us. And your mother would, too, I think, if she were still alive."

Mari flinched at this, biting her tongue, swallowing her reply.

Nevertheless, everything Corso had just shared was irrelevant. He'd painted a picture of a life she wouldn't be living. He could be the richest, most handsome man in the world. He could own a thousand villas.

But he would never be what she wanted.

He would never be Holmes.

5

HOLMES

Sunday, April 15, 1821
2:20 a.m., somewhere near Anzio

I cannot sleep for having just woken from a terrible nightmare about Mari. I am lying here now in my berth, writing by candlelight. The sea is calm, but my hands are trembling.

I dreamed that our plan went awry—that I drowned in the sea before I could make my way back to her. We did not end up together at all. Another man—not Corso, but someone nameless, faceless—came for Mari and rowed her away from Positano.

Faster, Mari told this man in my dream. Row as hard as you can. Get me away from here. She sat behind him, her legs outstretched in the little boat. He was bigger and stronger than me, able to row quicker than I ever could.

Yes, my love, he told her, rowing harder. His Italian was perfect—no accent, nothing to be misunderstood. Mari bent forward, then she ran her finger between his shoulder blades and down his lower back, reaching toward the front of him…

By the grace of God, I woke before it could get any worse.

6

HAVEN

Monday

Mal's statement echoed in my mind. *The Amalfi Curse.*

"Absurd," I said quickly, not keen on giving it any credence. "It's just a legend."

"I'm not saying I believe it," Mal continued. "I'm only saying this is why the legend exists at all." She pointed to yet another rescue boat making its way toward the scene. "If people can't explain something logically, they'll resort to legends. The supernatural. Magic. Gods."

Looking through the binoculars, I watched as the rescuers pulled the women off the sundeck to safety with only moments to spare. The bridge deck slipped underneath the water, followed soon after by the yacht's exhaust pipes and, lastly, its navigational antennae. For all my time in and around boats, I'd never actually seen one sink. I was amazed now at how the ocean seemed to swallow the thing whole, like a snake with a rat.

Meanwhile, a trio of geared-up divers had just jumped into the water. Rescue divers, in a race against time.

Mal turned back to the Vespa. "Can we go?" she asked. "I feel kind of sick."

"Same. If they come up with—" I cut myself short, unable to finish the statement. If there were others onboard, this could be a rescue mission or a recovery mission, but I didn't have the stomach to watch and find out.

What were the chances? Despite the legend about the Amalfi Curse, no boats had gone down in this area for a decade. Yet this morning's incident had unfolded at exactly the site of our impending fieldwork. I couldn't decide if this was a case of bad luck or a self-fulfilling prophecy. We had, after all, selected the site *because* of the number of wrecks to be surveyed. Should I really be surprised that another boat went down in such a perilous waterway?

Yes, I thought to myself. *Because nothing about it looked perilous today.* And while the lives at stake were of utmost importance, there would be project considerations to think about later, as well. This would disturb our site, no doubt: news crews patrolling the waterways. Police monitoring the area. Disaster tourists wanting to see the area for themselves.

Feeling discouraged, I leaned my helmet against Mal's back and sighed loudly.

"You good?" she called back.

"I guess," I said, shaking my head.

She turned and grabbed my hand. "Look. The divers will do their best. Maybe they'll get them out alive. Think positive." Then, as if reading my mind, "And even if there's a delay, the project will go on."

But we were already on borrowed time. "Mount Vesuvius," I reminded her.

Mount Vesuvius, the enormous and very active volcano not far from here, was long-overdue for an eruption. Scientists monitored the volcano around the clock, knowing the eruption would be catastrophic, not only for the Amalfi Coast's residents and tourists but its historic ruins. Nearby Pompeii had been buried in ash for two thousand years after the Vesuvius eruption in 79 CE. The sunken relics in the Bay of Naples and the Amalfi area were also at risk of being lost to history when the volcano inevitably blew again.

Still, *long-overdue* was ambiguous enough to push aside in favor of more urgent crises.

Until six weeks ago, when scientists released concerning data showing that underwater hydrothermal vent activity in the area had taken a turn for the worse—without explanation.

Suddenly, Mount Vesuvius *was* the more urgent crisis.

Once this news hit, my team convened. We knew the change in hydrothermal vents might put the wrecks at risk of further deterioration. And an eruption? That could bury it all.

We unanimously agreed to expedite Project Relic—a fitting project name, now more than ever—by several months. After all, we already had our funding, our dive boat, and our jurisdictional approvals.

What we didn't have was time.

Project Relic was born two years ago, the product of a fortuitous conversation and a few espresso martinis.

I'd been attending a conference on advances in maritime technology. After the first day of sessions, sitting at the hotel bar, I'd struck up a conversation with another conference attendee—Sloane, the CEO of a software start-up firm working on ways to leverage their oceanic databases and AI in the field.

An hour passed, and we delved into my work, the archaeology side of things. "It's too bad we haven't found a way to reconstruct fragmented shipwrecks," I said at one point, taking a sip from my martini, "or wrecks stacked on top of one another."

Sloane furrowed her brow, popped an espresso bean into her mouth. "Draw it for me," she said.

I pulled a paper napkin out from underneath a bowl of mixed

nuts and reached for a pen in my bag. I drew two rudimentary shipwrecks, one on top of the other. It was a rather pitiful sketch, but she got the point.

"What do you need to know in order to reconstruct them?" she asked, pointing to the drawing.

"The age of the vessels. Ocean current patterns. The weight and salinity of the water. Composition of the seafloor in the area." I let out a long sigh. "To name just a few."

"We have that data," Sloane said, leaning forward. She took the pen, made a few markings of her own. "And if we had renderings, or photographs, our AI could use it to…"

I took out a second pen, both of us now furiously scribbling notes. We ordered two more martinis and got to work.

That very evening, at the hotel bar, Project Relic was born. We would combine my team's photographs of underwater wrecks with Sloane's slew of databases and her new software. Using AI, this would—hopefully—render four-dimensional, reconstructed images of each vessel.

It was photogrammetry on steroids.

The new software would not only be transformational in the field of underwater historic preservation but would also shed light on the Amalfi Coast's heritage, and it was crucial in strategizing excavation of the wrecks, too.

If we could get it done before it was too late, that was.

We built out a solid project plan, then began to seek funding. Conrad Cass was well-connected with HPI, an international heritage protection foundation, having once served on their board of directors. He set up a call between HPI and my team. The foundation was looking to venture further into the oceanic project space—James Cameron and his *Titanic* expedition had set enticing precedent—and after hearing our project plan, they committed one million dollars, contingent on their approval of our site selection.

This was where my father's extensive diving experience

proved helpful. A year before we hoped to kick off the project, and six months before his death, my father had gone diving in Li Galli. It was his first of two trips there. "It's stacked," he told me afterward. "Wreck upon wreck. I barely scratched the surface." He'd been so impressed that he'd hit Pause on his other planned dive trips, interested only in returning to Positano again as soon as possible.

Little did he know what would happen on his second, return visit.

Nevertheless, after that first awe-inspiring trip, he showed me a few photos. Even I was astounded: dense wreckage littered the area, and the site was less than thirty meters deep. This was important for air preservation, safety precautions, and photography.

With the exception of being situated in the danger zone of mainland Europe's only active volcano, Li Galli was the perfect site.

HPI liked our selection, and we signed a few final documents. They reminded me several times that they could exit or alter our agreement at any time, and their attorneys required a slew of confidentiality agreements, too. I wasn't so much as allowed to breathe the organization's name to anyone outside the project. I couldn't blame them for being tight-lipped: if Project Relic failed, it could sabotage the foundation's future opportunities.

Still, it was unthinkably exciting. If my team pulled this off, we'd be trailblazers. And when we spoke with HPI about scientists' concerns in recent months and our desire to expedite the project, they enthusiastically supported us. Underwater relics were seductive enough. But a race-against-time element made it all the more exhilarating.

The foundation's funding was more than enough to cover our expenses, like chartering a boat and paying my team. Not to mention I was given free rein to run the project as I liked, including handpicking my colleagues. In the end, though, I sensed HPI—particularly the CEO, Gage Whitlock, who was very close friends with Conrad—had mixed feelings about my selection. A team of five women was unheard of in the male-dominated field of nautical archaeology, and our partners at the software start-up were mostly women, too. I wondered if Gage thought we'd be spending the next year in Positano sunbathing and sipping limoncello.

I didn't let it weigh on me. I'd built a hell of a team, and if Project Relic could be done, we'd do it.

Back at the villa, I retreated to my bedroom, though I could only call it mine for a couple more days, as I'd soon be sharing it with another team member. I heaved my backpack on top of the bed and sat down next to it, thinking of the Li Galli islets. I envisioned the skeletal pile of wrecks scattered across the seabed. The layers of sediment—sand and pumice and biodebris. The mollusks clinging to ship fragments.

And somewhere among this, something else. The *something big*: the treasure my father had spotted.

I still remembered his phone call that day, the elation in his voice. It was his second, final trip to Positano. "A trail of pink and red gemstones," he told me, nearly out of breath. "Hard to see in the silt, but I reckon there were thousands of them."

"Do you think they're real?" I asked, wary of his years of bad luck.

"Yes," he urged. "I know they are. I have proof of it. I'm going back down tomorrow with bags. I didn't have any with me today, and I was near out of air, too."

Strange, I thought, how he'd been so convinced of their authenticity. *I have proof of it*, he'd said. It was unlike him to make such a declaration.

Later that night, however, he'd suffered a minor stroke. It upset his coordination so much that he could hardly use the stairs. Diving was out of the question until he'd recovered.

He returned to the States to rest, to rehab. For a couple of weeks, I stayed with him. He suffered frequent vertigo and weakness in his arms and core. Worse, he was beginning to fear that he'd never dive again, which was a grieving process I hated to watch. Diving was all he talked about. The deepest dives he'd done. The rarest sharks he'd spotted. The roughest currents he'd navigated. *I miss the ol' deep*, he said time and time again, his eyes downcast.

Still, he was sharp as a tack. His recollection of the second Li Galli dive was detailed and elaborate. He showed me a few grainy underwater photos he'd taken near the gems and an abovewater photo that was geotagged with the wreck's general location, so he could return to the site.

If I can't make it back to Positano myself, he said one morning, *don't let this go.*

I've always had better luck than you, I teased in return, trying to keep his spirits high. I gave him a kiss on his forehead. *I'm headed outside for a bit*, I told him. *Love you, Pops.* I would forever be a daddy's girl, and I made sure he knew it.

I put on a swimsuit and spent a few hours sunbathing on the dock. I had a strong margarita, then a second one. At some point, I dozed off.

Later that afternoon, when I went back inside, I found my father slumped over in his desk chair. I screamed and ran toward him, trying to shake him awake, but there was no use. He was already dead.

His cell phone lay on the floor next to him. When I opened it, it was evident he'd been confused: he had tried calling *9-9-1-1-1* several times.

He'd suffered a second stroke, and this one had killed him.

Remorse and sorrow I could have handled. Instead, I was filled with self-loathing, knowing I was mere steps away while my father died so completely and entirely alone. Had he called for me, shouted my name? If I hadn't had my headphones in, perhaps I'd have heard him. If I hadn't had a second margarita, I wouldn't have dozed off. If I'd invited him out for a drink with me, I would have been there to call the ambulance.

If, if, if. They've haunted me ever since. Mal tells me to go easy on myself. But I wasn't there when he needed me.

After my father's death, I realized that Positano now held more than just professional value. The team had selected the site for its preservation potential, but amid these wrecks lay my father's sunken, unfulfilled dream.

Whatever it was he'd seen, I wanted to bring it to the surface, just as he had intended to do. *Don't let this go*, he'd pleaded with me.

I might not have been there when he took his last breath, but that didn't need to be the end of the story.

I could still give him this.

I pulled out my phone to reply to Conrad's text earlier that morning.

Thanks for the nice message, I said. **How's Australia?** According to Conrad's social media, he was somewhere near Brisbane on a week-long dive expedition.

Hey, kid, he replied. **Wrapping up down here. Great week in the water. How's Positano? Find anything other than shipwrecks yet?** ☺

I paused, staring at the message. Something about it rubbed me the wrong way—like he was probing for information. Like maybe he knew something.

And the emoji? He never used emojis.

I shook my head, annoyed with myself. Conrad was a good guy. I decided I was being sensitive—defensive, even—because I had a secret, and I feared someone finding out.

Besides, I had every reason to trust Conrad. As a former helicopter rescue swimmer with the US Coast Guard, he was responsible for saving thousands of lives throughout his career.

Mine included.

★ ★ ★

I reached into my backpack and snagged my iPad, then I opened up the cloud folder containing the dozen grainy photographs my father had taken on his GoPro camera during his final dive in Li Galli. He'd shared the folder with me before he died. He'd named it *Li Galli Potential*.

The password? My middle name.

There was one other item in the folder, too: a Word document with a haphazard table of numbers and letters, presented in no rational manner. I'd stared at it countless times, trying to make sense of any pattern. I could find nothing. The only clue was the file's creation date as noted in the metadata, showing that my dad had compiled this list the day before he spotted the underwater loot—the day before the grainy photos were taken.

Most of the photographs in the folder were taken underwater, and though they were full color, the camera had not picked up much beyond murky shades of steel-blue. In a few of the photos, I could make out the hazy shapes of wood segments, though it was impossible to determine whether these were part of a stern or mast or porthole. Other photos revealed only indistinguishable plankton or the air bubbles emitted from my father's mouthpiece. And because these pictures were taken underwater, the metadata didn't include longitude and latitude. This made it impossible to trace their precise location.

The last photo was taken abovewater. It looked to be a sunny, warm day, a band of cottony clouds stretching their way across the sky. In the distance stood La Rotonda, the southwesternmost islet of Li Galli, which was rich with foliage, assorted shrubs and umbrella pine trees. A lone bird soared high above.

I right-clicked on this photo's metadata, as I'd done countless times before. The camera had recorded the longitude and latitude, and this geotag represented the best clue I had in locating my father's last wreck amid the mess of other ruins.

I jumped at the sound of a knock on my door—Mal. Quickly,

I flipped over my iPad. I hated hiding this from her, but it seemed the right thing for now. Yes, the team had selected the Li Galli site months before my father's discovery of the gems, but I still worried Mal or my team might question my motives for being here.

Besides, I didn't want to distract them from the project objectives we'd set. And though I trusted that Mal's values were in the right place, I didn't know the other team members quite as well. What if one of them decided she wanted to locate the loot herself? I'd have liked to think they'd prioritize our professional goals over anything else, but it wasn't a risk I was willing to take.

And worst-case scenario? Even with my professional ethics in the right place—I'd report any discovery to Italian authorities at once—if my team knew I was treasure-hunting on our off days, they might report the information to HPI. I'd read the contracts more than a few times, and I knew better than anyone that the foundation could back out of the project as easily as I could be kicked off it.

No, I simply couldn't find a good reason to reveal this secret to my team. Project Relic was important to me, yes: it would propel the five of us women archaeologists to the forefront of respected conservation circles, and if we succeeded, my career was set. But I reminded myself who had gotten me here in the first place: the adventurer who'd geared me up in my first dive kit at age eight. The teacher who'd scolded me for touching coral. The competitor who'd raced me in our dive descents. The friend with whom I'd developed a shared underwater language consisting of strange hand signals.

No matter what Project Relic might do for me professionally, fulfilling my father's final wish remained a priority.

And it was something I needed to keep close to my chest. Something I needed to guard.

Later that afternoon, Mal and I changed into our swimsuits. We packed a bag with sunscreen, water bottles, and some of the fresh fruit we'd bought at the roadside stand yesterday. We'd need to find a market later today and start stocking the kitchen.

Before we went outside, I checked the news for any mention of the yacht that had gone down in Li Galli. As I opened my phone, I smiled at the photo I used as my wallpaper: my father in a wet suit many years ago, his white hair disheveled and dripping, and his forehead indented from his dive mask. Smile lines creased his cheeks and eyes; he'd always been terrible about sunscreen, and anyone could guess he'd spent a lifetime on the water.

"Not much on the news yet," I told Mal, scanning a short article in English. "Just says a yacht went down west of Positano. Twelve people on board. Story still developing."

"Twelve people?" she repeated.

I gave a small nod, knowing we were thinking the same thing: we'd only seen three people get rescued. But we also hadn't stayed to watch what unfolded. For all we knew, the rescue divers could have gotten the others out just after we left.

"I'll check again in a bit," I concluded, leading us to the door.

Spiaggia Grande was only a twenty-minute walk, so we decided to forgo the Vespa. As we started our downhill journey, Mal called her longtime girlfriend, Megan, back home in Miami. They'd been together for years but never lived in the same city, and it seemed to work for them: they were two fiercely independent, career-driven women, satisfied with a daily phone call and the occasional getaway to Austin or Asheville. I'd met Megan a few times and adored her instantly. We bonded over a shared love of to-do lists and raw oysters, whereas Mal, with her spiked blond hair and a naked woman tattooed onto her collarbone, hated both, and we liked her all the more for it.

I listened to Mal's half of the conversation as I carefully navigated my way down staircase after staircase, one of Positano's claims to fame. It was a city built on a hill, and though the route down to the beach wasn't bad, I was already dreading the trip back up. On one side of us was a stone wall with natural vegetation—tiny ferns, interspersed with patches of white wildflowers—protruding from the gaps. An orange tabby cat had found himself a perfect hideaway in the wall, and I gave him a rub under the chin, glancing up at the colorful hillside above us.

When we turned a corner, I nearly ran into a man rushing up the staircase. He carried a box of what I instantly recognized as snorkel gear: masks, fins. His forearms glinted with sweat as though he'd been carrying boxes all morning. "*Mi scusi*," he said breathlessly, his eyes flitting briefly to my lips.

"No problem," I replied, then I chided myself for not using my rudimentary Italian. I'd been studying basic phrases for the last few months with a phone app. I turned around to give him a final glance, and I caught him looking back at me with a grin. Now was my chance. "*Va bene*," I called out, beaming back at him.

"Ah, very good!" he replied, disappearing into a doorway.

As we wound our way along pencil-thin sidewalks and stairwells dripping with bougainvillea vines, I began to ruminate on my love life...or lack thereof. I'd dated a few guys in recent years, all of them fellow dive researchers. But time after time, I grew bored, and for now, I was done dating anyone in the field. It made for too many date-night conversations about work or colleagues or research papers...and not enough good, plain *fun*.

I wondered how I'd fare in Positano. As we passed one *trattoria* after another, I couldn't help but notice all the tables set with pairs of wineglasses. Everywhere, couples walked hand in hand, while restaurant signage advertised fixed-price menus for two.

Sometimes, I envied Mal and Megan for what they managed to keep aflame: a *relationship lite*, of sorts, with minimal time commitment yet no shortage of devotion. But now I shook my head, feeling ashamed for brooding on it. I was thirty-five with a PhD, and I got to explore wrecks along the Italian coastline for the next year.

What more could I possibly want? And it wasn't as though I'd be alone here in Italy—or idle. Between managing Project

Relic and the work of four other nautical archaeologists, as well as making time to discreetly hunt down my father's last wreck, I'd be too busy to care about romance.

I sighed as we passed another ridiculously attractive Italian man, this one sweeping out a doorway without a shirt on. Maybe I wasn't too busy for *all* romance. A night or two of fun never hurt anyone.

"*Non lavorare troppo*," I said sweetly as he and I made eye contact.

Mal had just hung up the phone and looked at me mischievously. "*Troppo*-what now?"

"It means *Don't work too hard*," I said. "You didn't study much Italian before this trip, did you?"

"I'm here to work, not flirt," she teased, winking. "And God knows if one of us is having sex in Italy, it isn't me."

I gave her a playful slap on the shoulder, laughing along with her.

We turned a final corner, finding ourselves in a large plaza overlooking the beach. The sand here was rocky and ash-colored, different than the pebbly, pale sand in the Keys. Barefoot, we made our way to the sliver of beach available to people who didn't want to pay for an umbrella. We were perfectly happy lying on our towels.

As we searched for a place to settle in, two women walked past us, conversing in Italian. One of them pressed a tissue to the corner of her eye, her cheeks streaked with tears. Her friend gave her a gentle pat on the back, and I couldn't help but wonder what troubled her so.

I glanced at Mal through my sunglasses, reminded of my dad's birthday. I was grateful to have a friend by my side today, too.

We spotted an empty area close to the water and made our way through the throng of tourists, stepping over coolers and toy buckets and thrown-aside beach hats. Settling down, I fought off a feeling of disappointment: this beach was far more crowded than I'd have liked. Polluted, too. I glanced out at the small tenders queued up alongside the seawall, a sort of makeshift marina. Streaks of oil trailed behind several of them, glinting black and purple in the sunlight like bruises on the water.

Mal and I sunbathed for the better part of an hour. Just as I nearly dozed off, she reached into our beach bag, withdrawing a miniature bottle of sparkling wine and a pair of cups.

I frowned. "What's this for?" I hadn't seen her sneak anything out of the kitchen.

She uncorked the bottle and split it between the two cups, then she held hers up to make a toast. "To your dad. Happy birthday, Mr. Ambrose."

I might have taken a sip right then, if not for the sudden lump in my throat. "Thank you, Mal," I managed.

The crowd around us grew denser with no sign of letting up. A pair of English-speaking tourists settled in so close that our shoulders nearly touched. Mal and I were just about to pack up our things and leave when one of the women posed a question to her friend.

"Did you hear about the yacht?" she asked. Her accent was thick, British. I glanced over at her, hiding my gaze behind my sunglasses, and watched as she scrolled through social media. "Went down very near here, just this morning. Several passengers still unaccounted for."

Shit, I thought. Mal and I shared a sobering look. It was the worst possible outcome for those poor people.

This news, plus the crowded, littered beach, had put me in a mood. "Let's go and find something to eat," I suggested.

We didn't have to walk far; the plaza near the beach was home to countless restaurants and bistros. We chose a small pizzeria with an outdoor terrace overlooking the water. Despite the good view, a gloomy energy settled around us. Neither of us seemed keen on pulling up the news ourselves.

After our order was placed, my phone lit up with an email from Gage Whitlock.

Just checking in, he said. You girls make it okay?

I rolled my eyes. I wasn't a huge fan of Gage for a number of reasons, not the least of which was his tactless communication style. "He can be so condescending," I said to Mal, turning my phone to show her the beginning of his email.

"I'm just glad I don't have to deal with him. That's your job as boss, right?"

Mal and I played this game often. I was project lead, yes, but as the designated dive marshal and safety officer, she didn't rank far behind me. After every dive, she would download the data from the team members' dive watches and run a quick audit. If she found anything concerning—an uncontrolled descent, for instance, or inadequate air reserves—she could, quite literally, halt this entire project.

And if we encountered an incident on the water? She'd immediately be the one in charge.

"Yes," I said, as the server approached with our Aperol spritzes. "Doesn't mean I have to love the guy."

Still, no matter what I thought of him, Gage was CEO of the foundation paying for this project, and I needed to keep the peace.

Great to hear from you, Gage, I replied, tapping away with a bit too much force. **We made it just fine. Checked into lodging okay. No issues with anything s—**

I paused. *No issues with anything so far,* I'd almost written.

But that was a lie, wasn't it? A yacht holding a dozen people had gone down that morning in Li Galli, our exact project site. And they hadn't gotten everyone off the boat.

There were absolutely issues.

I just wasn't about to discuss them with the project's largest stakeholder.

I deleted the unfinished sentence and wrapped up my reply on a positive note, assuring Gage I'd check in again soon.

Nothing else will go wrong, I assured myself. Then I dropped my phone in my beach bag with a sigh and reached for my drink.

7

MARI

Monday, April 16, 1821

The pirates turned east, sparing Positano yet again.

Instead, they landed in San Marco, where—according to the newspapers—they pillaged a cluster of villas built along the coastline, before setting fire to the piazza at the center of town. They destroyed an ancient monument and made off with a few dozen casks of olive oil, but to everyone's relief, they left the women and children unharmed.

Soon after the news made its way to Positano, the village men gathered by their boats, praising providence and relishing, yet again, their good fortune. The *streghe* acted as surprised and delighted as everyone else, but privately they whispered words of commendation to the three women who'd successfully cursed the currents.

In this interim, Corso had left town, too, returning to Rome. He gave no indication when he would return, and though Mari might have breathed easier without a return date, instead she found herself uneasy about the uncertainty of it all. The next time he returned, he would very likely have a ring.

Thus, a few days after Corso's departure and the good news about the pirates, Mari woke again in a restless, uneasy mood. Today, she had promised to take Lia and another young *strega* out onto the water for a morning of instruction, but as she dressed, she found her agitation growing. She considered finding some excuse to call off the outing, but now more than ever, it was important to relay her knowledge to as many as she could.

Mari first stopped by the house of friend and fellow *strega*, Viviana—Vivi for short—to retrieve seventeen-year-old Pippa, then they made their way to Ami's house to get little Lia. As the three walked down one of the many crude staircases built into the cliffside, Lia paused, bent over, and began to whine about a pebble stuck between her toes.

On any other day, Mari would have sat with Lia and carefully pried the stone out with her fingers. But today, Mari ignored Lia's grumbling. She wanted to get this morning over with as quickly as possible.

At the shoreline, tied to a boulder and bobbing gently in the waves, was the small *gozzo* they would take out. As they approached it, Mari lifted her nose to the wind as she always did, her senses attuned to any threat: the musty scent of incoming rain, or the reek of rot, suggesting something gone wrong with the water.

But Mari smelled nothing. Just salt and good sea.

Next, she scanned her eyes over the waves. The tide was going out. A dry *scirocco* breeze blew from the south, and enormous bands of kelp drifted with the breeze. On the horizon, she could make out a few other *gozzi*—tiny fishing boats, the same ones that left her village every morning and returned a few hours later—but nothing larger. No merchant brigs. Nothing with sails.

It was, by all accounts, a very dull morning.

As Mari approached the water's edge, she bent down and placed her hands in the ocean, cupping them into a bowl. Although her hands were steady, the water held inside of them began to tremble of its own accord. Mari turned her body to hide this from the girls, but the quivers went on until nearly all of the water had sloshed out of Mari's palms.

Mari took a long breath. Though she was uneasy for a reason she couldn't quite place, still she'd never seen water tremble so violently in her hands. She tried again, quickly lifting her hands to her lips. As she sipped the water, her thick hair fell forward, grazing the sand.

Just salt, she thought as she tasted it, *and minerals*. She'd know if there was something foreign in this water, something like gunpowder or grease or the subtle tang of decomposition. She'd know if a nearby brig had jettisoned goods or if a pirate ship had dumped bodies.

She'd tasted these things in the water before.

Mari motioned to the two girls, indicating they should do the same as her. Side by side, they knelt down and cupped their hands. Pippa didn't so much as flinch, but Lia made a face when the seawater touched her tongue, spitting it out with a grimace. Mari couldn't help but smile.

Once in the boat, Mari tossed an extra length of rope to Pippa and instructed her to make a butterfly loop. Wordlessly, Pippa obeyed, forming a perfect knot in less than thirty seconds.

"Excellent," Mari said. Pippa had been practicing knots for months and was very good at them. *Strega* or not, Pippa wanted to go to sea in a few years, and Mari knew it would happen. There weren't many women on merchant ships, but there were a few. The ones with grit found a way.

Mari began to row and soon found herself subdued by the rhythmic, meditative pull of the water against the oars. Forward they went, the oars making perfect halos. Ahead, peeking out from the water, something glistened, the color of silver.

Mari knew just what it was. She smacked the oars several times against the water, then—to amuse the girls—she feigned surprise as several dolphins appeared either side of the *gozzo*.

They cried in delight as the dolphins surfaced and blew their breath into the air, showering them all with mist. Even Mari laughed; she knew this pod well. They liked to follow the boat a long ways, and she always felt a sense of safety with them so close. When she and Sofia were young, they would lie back and let their hair tumble over the *gozzo*'s edge. The flash of red against blue caught the dolphins' attention, and they would nose and nudge their way through the thick masses of hair, playing with it like they might strands of seaweed.

Times like that, the sea was not so loathsome.

As they rowed along the rocky coastline, Lia pointed. "A net," she said. Ahead, an enormous seine was wrapped tight around a boulder. Such litter was left by foreign mariners who cast traps like this along the delicate coastline, ensnaring entire schools of fish—sometimes hundreds and thousands at once. Far more than any village could eat.

"Good, Lia." Mari smiled, impressed as she often was with the child's keen eye.

The *streghe* knew the danger posed by these nets. They were traps for wildlife. Plovers, gulls, crabs. Mari had seen their carcasses countless times, caught up in dragnets just like this one.

They rowed toward the boulder. Together, using a small knife, Mari and the girls worked to remove the net. Mari rolled it into a ball and tossed it into the boat to discard later.

"Plenty of problems," she reminded the girls, "can be solved without *stregheria*. Magic doesn't solve everything."

After a few more minutes of rowing, Mari spotted the black mouth of a grotto ahead. This was their destination. It was a cave, only partially immersed, with enough light to see by, to teach by. The opening to the grotto was well-camouflaged; the cliffs jutting into the water were rugged, full of black pits and protruding boulders. Unless one knew precisely where to look, the grotto was all but invisible.

Before steering the *gozzo* into the mouth of the cave, Mari advised the girls to stay very quiet. She rowed the boat forward and back several times, taking close note of her surroundings. No one, not even a fisherman from her own village, was in sight.

Quickly, she rowed the boat into the grotto. The dolphins followed, playfully twirling. As they entered the cave's opening, the two young girls gasped in unison: the water inside was a radiant sapphire color.

Once she had the *gozzo* situated toward the back, Mari leaned over in the boat and plunged her hand beneath the blue depths, feeling for the cave wall. She touched something spongy and soft, bringing it to the surface. It was a clump of sea algae. She held it out for Lia, pointing to a cluster of tiny spheres, resembling yellow bubbles, hidden among the algae. Fish eggs.

"How many?" Pippa asked, leaning forward.

Mari squinted in the low light, counting. "Hundreds," she said, feeling pleased.

"Because of the *incantesimo dell'elemento*?" Lia asked, fumbling over the words. "The one where we use the dried-up fish snout?"

"Close," Mari replied, "but not quite. For this, there is no need to change the composition of the water. Only the temperature of it, which is the *incantesimo raffreddare*." Such cold-water spells resulted in good conditions for breeding. It also attracted tiny organisms, which meant food for larger fish. "Do you remember which tool that spell requires?"

Lia frowned for a moment. "The mermaid's purse."

"Right." Mari nodded. "The shark egg-sack." She lowered the clump of algae beneath the water, returning it to its dark crevice. "The water is still very cold. Much colder than outside the cave." She nodded at the girls to feel the temperature for themselves.

"I would not like it cold," Lia said, "if I were a little egg."

Mari smiled. "That is why you are not a fish. The fish love the cold. The colder it is, the more food there is."

"But what kind of food do the *eggs* eat?" Lia asked.

Beside her, Pippa stifled a laugh.

"The eggs do not eat," Mari explained. "But as soon as they hatch, they will be very hungry." She took Lia's hand in her own and pointed to a tiny, almost invisible freckle on Lia's thumb. "Beneath us now, in the water, are tiny living things we cannot even name. As countless as the stars, and too small to see. Smaller, even, than this freckle." At this, Lia's eyes grew wide, and Mari went on, "These things cannot swim; they merely drift where the currents take them. And once the baby fish hatch from the eggs, they will be ravenous, and they will eat the little floaters."

"How sad," Lia said, her face falling. When her tiny hand went limp, Mari gave it a good squeeze.

"It gets better," Pippa added, grinning. "The baby fish will get eaten, too. A shark, or maybe one of these dolphins, will devour it."

Mari threw Pippa a warning glance, but still, she was right. "That is how it works, yes," Mari said. "The bigger fish always eat the little fish. It begins with the invisible organisms floating around us, and ends with..." She paused, thinking of the village men trawling the coastline now. "Well, it ends with us, and the food on our plates. The fish are what sustain us, what keep us alive. And that," she whispered, "is why we three are here, ensuring the water is still very, very cold, so the babies will survive. So the village does not go hungry."

She'd almost said *our village*. Already, she'd begun to consider herself an outsider.

The three took the small boat around the cave, Mari testing the chill of the water in several more places. As a whole, she was pleased with what she found. It meant a good fishing sea-son ahead, yet again—though this time, she wouldn't be around to see it.

When they were finished, Mari rowed the boat to the outside of the cave and set the oars down. There wasn't much of a current along this part of the coastline, and the boat bobbed along in place. A few meters away, enormous slabs of limestone sloped gently downward, creating a natural beach. Before Sofia's death, Mari would occasionally row herself out here to lie on the rocks and sunbathe, daydream. Sometimes, others had beat her to the spot: above this natural beach was a narrow, steep pathway leading upward to the road.

The natural stone beach was empty today. Done with their task inside the cave, Mari withdrew a few lemon candies from a bag and gave them to the girls. She heard the beating of wings nearby, and a pair of cormorants flew past as though spooked, their long necks stretched eastward.

So near the beach, Mari wondered if they should disembark and have their candies on land.

She jumped as Lia suddenly threw her skinny arms into the air. "Spin for us in the water!" she exclaimed. "*Ruota!*"

Mari looked over the side of the boat. The sea was as beautiful as it had ever been—crystalline blue, studded by glints of diamond-white, reflections of the sun above—yet Mari still had no desire to get in. "No," she said softly.

"Please," Lia said now. "Just once, for—"

"Yes!" Pippa interjected. "It is almost Lia's birthday, anyhow."

Mari looked at the girls' pleading expressions and felt her chest tighten. Moments like this were numbered. Or perhaps this was the last of them entirely.

She would try one more thing, testing the girls. "I don't have my bag of *attrezzi*," she playfully argued.

"Nice try," Pippa said. "*Incantesimo vortice* doesn't need any."

Mari huffed. "You are too good," she conceded.

The girls cheered as Mari readied herself to put on a display.

Standing only in her undergarments, she stepped off the boat and into the ankle-deep water. She walked deeper and deeper, and then, knowing precisely where the underwater drop-off began, she dove in with a swoosh.

At first, she let herself sink. She knew this part of the sea: there was nothing here to fear, and besides, the two dolphins had followed her into the depths and now flipped playfully just below her. She kept her eyes open, for she'd grown used to salt water many years ago. Here and there, she caught the silvery flash of a young fish.

Reciting a few words, Mari stretched out her arms and fluttered her fingers, feeling the water around her begin to spin. It whirled slowly at first, then faster and faster, and Mari let it twirl her around a few times, like she was a dancer doing a pirouette.

After a few moments, she lowered her arms and let the whirling subside. Then she blew air out of her mouth, watching as the bubbles floated upward to the surface. For all the sea had taken from her, she could appreciate moments like this: the weightlessness of water, the soundlessness of it.

Suddenly, Mari felt a whoosh of water nearby: Pippa had just dived in, too. She did a few somersaults, a grin of delight on her face. Mari expected Lia to jump in any moment—even at her young age, she was an excellent swimmer—but when she didn't, Mari began to kick for the surface. Meanwhile, the dolphins suddenly darted away, making for deeper water. Mari thought it strange, how quickly they'd gone.

As she kicked for the glinting, crystalline surface, she heard a muffled cough. It was not the sort of noise Lia herself could have made; it sounded like a man. Pippa must have heard it, too, for they glanced at each other underwater, eyes wide.

Mari's blood went cold. She gave a final kick, finally breaking above the water. Then she smelled it, something pungent and foul.

Sweat.

A man with shoulder-length curly hair was crouched on the limestone slope only meters away, looking ready to lunge, to attack. How long had he been watching them? Long enough, Mari feared, to see her dive into the ocean and twirl the water with her hands...

But Lia. Where was Lia? As Mari touched her feet to the rocky bottom—she was standing now, in hip-high water—she looked frantically around. Lia was not in the boat, not on the beach. She looked for bubbles, wondering if Lia had jumped in elsewhere, but saw nothing.

"Where is she?" Mari cried, vaguely aware that the water around her was growing colder with each passing moment. She saw no other boat, which meant the man must have come down the narrow trail, leading from the road.

Horrified, Mari could only reason that the man had yanked Lia from the *gozzo* when she and Pippa had been underwater. Or had the girl somehow escaped? Perhaps now she was hiding behind a boulder or even scrambling up the cliffside. Mari hoped so—hoped little Lia had done whatever it took to put distance between her and this stranger.

"Get over here, both of you," he demanded, running his eyes over Mari's sodden undergarments. A knife flashed on his hip. As he stood, he stumbled forward a step, visibly drunk. A flask lay discarded on the rocks.

Mari was struck with a feeling of vague recognition. She had seen this man before, she felt sure of it.

She turned to Pippa, whose wet hair was plastered to her shoulders. "Go," she demanded with a whisper. "Back into the water. Swim as deep as you can."

"What are you saying to her?" the man called out. Fear glimmered in his eyes as he watched Pippa slip backward into the shallow water, then quickly disappear, leaving only a few ripples.

Mari ignored him and waded forward. The water around her

had grown so cold, like ice, that she could barely feel her feet. "Lia!" she screamed, darting her eyes back and forth. "Lia!"

There was no reply. Not a rustle, not a soft cry. Mari didn't understand. How had the child disappeared so quickly, so completely? "Where is she?" she demanded again.

He bent down for his flask. "Don't worry about her." He uncorked the flask, pressed the metal to his lips. "We'll take good care of her in Naples."

Mari's lower belly churned. *No. No, this cannot be.* She felt heat prickling in her hands, her feet. Instinctively, she reached for her *cimaruta*, delicately fingering the tiny piece of coral.

In a flash, she lunged for him, surprised by her own speed and agility. Though he saw her coming, the man was intoxicated, his reactions slow. Mari went for his groin and gave him a hard kick. He doubled over, fell to his knees, and cried out. When he lifted his hand, Mari saw that he'd cut it on the rock when he fell. Blood trickled onto his forearm.

She kicked him again, this time in his lower belly, and he wheezed, short of air.

She didn't waste a moment. Knowing he would be disoriented only momentarily, she wrapped her arms underneath his shoulders and dragged him into the shallow water. His weight posed a challenge at first, and he flailed his limbs, digging his fingernails into the flesh of Mari's thigh, leaving her with a bloody scratch. She nearly lost her balance. If this man somehow overtook her or pinned her arms against her sides, she'd be useless, as good as a fish in a net. Pippa and Lia would be left to watch as he hauled Mari onto the rocks to do God-knew-what, then he'd drag her back to Naples. His newfound loot.

No. Mari would not let it happen.

She regained her balance and pulled him deeper into the water. Soon, he was buoyant, easier to manage. Here in the ocean was exactly where she needed him—here, she could do what she needed to get him out of her way, so she could go find Lia.

With the man halfway immersed, Mari released him. He began to flail his arms again, the blood from his hand mingling with seawater. He tried to keep himself upright, his head above the surface, but his feet slipped on the slick rocks. Quickly, Mari waded a few steps away and plunged both of her hands into the water.

Softly, she began to recite the *incantesimo vortice*.

The water around the man began to spin. It intensified quickly, sucking his body into its rotation, pulling him under. He made a futile effort to plant his feet, to steady himself, but when he realized the maelstrom's power, he turned his attention to breathing. Eyes wide, he gulped for air. He'd begun to drown.

Mari could stop it now in an instant—could, quite literally, pull the water from this man's lungs if she so chose. She had never killed a man before, but nothing in her hesitated now. She was tired of losing everything she held dear.

She ran her fingertips across the surface of the sea, her lips moving. With the natural ebb of the tide, the underwater cyclone began to shift out, deeper into the center of the small bay. This man would die momentarily, leaving any passerby to put the puzzle together for themselves: the discarded flask, his abandoned coach on the road above. They'd assume he'd drowned from being too drunk. Too dehydrated. It happened all the time. This cliffside coastline was dangerous, and people often met hazards they couldn't have prepared for.

As the whirlpool moved deeper, the man reached his hand out, as if grasping for the sky. There came a gurgling cry, something like an underwater wail, and Mari lifted her fingers from the water.

The whirlpool slowed, ceased. The man's body had been sucked under.

All fell silent and still, not so much as a bubble.

He was dead.

Eventually, maybe in a few days, his body would wash ashore. And to think this morning had been so dull when it began...

The water around Mari began to warm again. A moment later, something small and narrow glimmered in the water, right where the man's body had gone under. The object made a slow arc toward Mari, still propelled by the whirlpool's rippling remnants. Mari frowned. It was solid and cool, like metal, but one side was abrasive—a man's nail file.

She spotted a tiny inscription and lifted the nail file closer. *Aut inveniam viam aut faciam*, the first line read. And beneath this, *Massimo Mazza*.

Mari gasped, the nail file slipping from her fingers and sinking at once. She clasped her hands over her mouth and shook her head back and forth.

She had not just killed any man.

She had just killed one of the Mazza brothers. One of the most powerful, wicked men in Naples.

Now the two brothers were only one.

She briefly thought of Holmes. He held nothing but disgust for the brothers and would be unaffected, at least emotionally, by Massimo's death. Nevertheless, she wondered about the Fratelli Mazza as a company, and whether this might affect Holmes's employment, his future.

No matter. It was a minor worry compared to the present crisis—finding Lia.

Mari needed to get away from this scene, and quick. She heard a splash and turned to find Pippa's eyes just above the waterline; she was treading deep water a few meters away. The two shared a silent nod before swimming frantically for the shore.

"Lia!" Mari called out again now, wondering if she had witnessed the drowning. If she had, she could come out of whatever hiding spot she'd been in. Mari called for her three times, four times.

Still, nothing.

A few seconds later, Mari and Pippa reached the shore. They began to scramble up the beach, but—

"Wait," Mari hissed, holding Pippa back. She'd just spotted something—a flash of red—above them, on the trail leading up the cliff. There, near where the trail met the road, stood a man.

In his arms, with a canvas sack tied over her head, was a child. *Lia.*

How had Mari not considered it? There'd been two of them—one to snag Lia, one to distract Mari. While Mari had been addressing Massimo, this second man had been silently traversing his way up the hill with Lia.

Mari could only guess that Lia was gagged and unable to scream out. Her disheveled hair jutted out from the sack's bottom, strands the color of apple blossoms. From this vantage point, she looked exactly like Sofia, with her small frame and light hair.

Sofia. Lia. And this time, Mari could not even blame the sea.

Her horror intensified as she got a good look at the man holding Lia. He was the spitting image of the man she'd just killed—the same broad shoulders, the same pointed chin.

He could only be the second Mazza brother. Matteo. The older, more wicked of the two.

Mari knew, instinctively, that he'd seen it all—what she'd done to his brother. How she'd harnessed the sea. How she'd killed a man without so much as touching him.

She might have chased him down, but there was no chance she would make it in time. Matteo was but steps from the road, where his horse would be waiting. Even at a sprint, it would take Mari several minutes to maneuver her way up the rocky trail.

If only she could fly. If only she could kill a man with a stare. If only the sirens had bestowed upon the *streghe* more than seven curses, all for use on the sea and the sea alone.

Mari fell to her knees and let out a wail. *Lia,* she thought, watching the man roughly tug the child along for the last few steps. *Lia has been seized, and it is all because of my carelessness.*

Over and over and over, she kept failing the people she loved.

Pippa stood next to her, breathing hard, an anguished look on her face. Pippa wasn't the sort to cry—she was too tough for that. Still, Mari had never seen her wear such a tormented look. "It is my fault," Pippa whispered.

Mari glared at her. "No—no. Do not say that."

"I jumped in after you. I left her alone."

"I shouldn't have jumped in at all. I shouldn't have left either of you." It occurred to Mari, then, how close she might have been to losing Pippa, too. What if each of the men had snagged one of the girls? "You will not take the blame for this," Mari insisted. She grabbed Pippa's hand, pulled her toward their *gozzo*. "We need to go tell the others. We'll gather the men, go to Naples—" Her voice cracked. She couldn't manage another word. Naples was a day away by horseback, which felt impossibly far.

And… *Ami.* Her best friend, and Lia's mother. How on earth could she break this news to her?

Back in the boat, Mari pulled at the oars as hard and quick as she could. Sweat pricked at her brow, and her forearms burned. She'd never rowed so hard. Her palms stung with blisters, splinters.

When she'd rowed a short distance away, she turned. Matteo still stood at the top of the trail. A small horse-drawn coach was just behind him. In front of him, Lia stood pitifully motionless, frozen with fear, the sack still over her head. The poor girl wasn't a fighter, not like Pippa.

Matteo stood tall on the precipice, a predator satisfied with his catch.

He called out a single, slow word. It echoed off the cliff side, ringing in Mari's ears.

Her blood ran cold.

"*Tornerò*," he shouted. *I'll be back.*

8

HAVEN

Monday

After a simple dinner of sliced tomatoes with fresh burrata, I was nearly about to crawl into bed with a book, but Mal knocked on my bedroom door and let herself in. Her eyebrows were knit together, her mouth set hard. "Hey, you need to hear this." She reached for the remote on my nightstand and flipped on the television.

She found a news channel in English and scooted back against my pillows. Together, we watched as a weatherman behind a desk sifted through a stack of papers.

"The weather?" I said. "God, you're that bored?"

"Shhh," she said, no hint of a grin.

Chastised, I returned my attention to the TV.

The meteorologist held up a piece of paper: it was a graph, covered in erratic lines and indecipherable symbols. "We received this a few moments ago from our oceanography team," he said, a grave expression on his face. "Additional data indicating increased carbon dioxide levels observed around several key offshore hydrothermal vents." He checked his notes for a moment. "Sorrento, Amalfi, Positano," he added. "All are showing significant increases. The data has been unusual for the last six weeks, but this is..." He shook his head. "This is a notable spike."

Mal turned the television down a notch. "There were a few articles posted this morning," she said, "about the correlation between increased CO2 seeps—basically carbon dioxide from underwater vents—and imminent volcanic eruptions." She put her elbows on her knees. "They'd issue formal warnings if we needed to be worried about this, right?"

"Did the articles say anything about the Vesuvius steam vents? Or earthquakes?" Both were far more concerning indicators than oceanic CO2 readings.

"No," she conceded.

"Okay, then." I grabbed the remote and muted the television. "We have enough to worry about, Mal. I can't deal with something else."

She stared at me for a moment, looking unconvinced.

I put up my hands. "I promise: if there are warnings, *real* warnings, we'll do what we need to do to stay safe." I motioned to the television, which had flipped to a commercial break. An enormous cheeseburger stretched across the screen, grease dripping down its side. "Look," I said and pointed. "They don't play cheeseburger commercials during real emergencies, right?"

"I guess so, yeah." She turned the television off. "I think I just need to get out."

I remembered seeing an ad for Positano's world-famous nightclub. "How about Music on the Rocks? It isn't open yet, but we could get ready, go somewhere for a drink beforehand."

She pursed her lips, then said, "I could dance, yeah."

We made plans to head that way in an hour. Yet just as I dug a short blue dress out of my suitcase, my phone rang. *Gage.*

I didn't have the energy for him tonight. I hit *Ignore*, making a mental note to call him back tomorrow.

★ ★ ★

Music on the Rocks, nestled inside a cave on the eastern edge of the village, undoubtedly made for a good distraction.

Pink and blue neon lights illuminated the low concave ceiling, while patrons stood along the cave walls, marveling at the craggy stone interior. The dance floor was already packed when we arrived, and I scanned the room, feeling more upbeat than I had all day. The vibe was not only chic but wildly unlike any place I'd been before.

We went to the bar and ordered a couple of beers, then we made our way to a white leather sofa situated near the dance floor. I tugged down my short blue dress, while Mal looked much more comfortable in her ripped black jeans.

She and I toasted to our second night in Positano, but as we both took a drink, I felt my phone buzz in my purse.

"What the hell," I said aloud. "It's Gage. Again."

"Again?"

"He called me earlier, just before I started getting ready. I ignored it."

Mal grimaced, a hate-to-break-it-to-you expression on her face. "If he's calling again, you need to take it."

"I know, I know." I stood, eyeing the doorway. "I'll step outside. Don't get into any trouble while I'm gone."

"No promises."

I rushed out the main club door and onto a terrace built into the cliffside. A few men leaned over the railing, smoking cigarettes. One of them had his phone open, showing off a text. "They canceled their flights," I heard him say.

"Because of Vesuvius?" his friend asked.

"Yup."

I flicked open my phone, answering Gage's call. "Hi, Gage," I said.

"Haven." His voice was solemn, serious. "I tried calling you earlier."

"Yes, I saw. Mal and I are out for the night. I think I mentioned we arrived a few days early."

"Right." He cleared his throat. "So, Haven, we have a situation." I stayed silent, alarmed by his tone. Cigarette smoke wafted in my direction, and I took a few steps away, trying to get fresh air. "You heard about the yacht sinking today?" he asked.

"Yes," I replied. "We saw it this morning, as it was happening."

"Oh," he said. "Do you have any idea what caused it? The media isn't saying much."

"No. There was no smoke. And it seemed a perfect day for boating." Nearby, the men along the railing glanced at me.

"Did you see the news a couple hours ago? Where they announced the casualties?"

I hung my head. This must have been why he'd called a couple hours ago. "No, I didn't. I knew there were people they hadn't yet located. But nothing beyond that."

Maybe, I thought, Mal and I had avoided checking for updates as an unconscious way of avoiding what we already knew.

Gage exhaled. "Eight people died."

I closed my eyes, brought my hand to my mouth. *Eight*.

"This is unbelievable," I said into the phone, feeling dazed. "I can't—"

"Conrad's calling," Gage interrupted. "Let me take this and call you back."

"Conrad?" I said.

My question was met with silence. Gage had already hung up.

I rushed back inside, maneuvering through a throng of people to get back to Mal. I cursed as a woman in high heels backed into me, spilling her entire drink—something dark, like soda—onto the front of my blue dress.

"Hey," I said to Mal, raising my voice above the DJ's music. "Come outside for a minute."

With a wary look, she followed me out. We made our way

past a line of people waiting to get into the club, neither of us speaking. Finally, we emerged onto a wide, empty walkway running alongside the main beach.

"Eight people died in the yacht sinking," I said softly.

Her mouth dropped open. *"Shit."*

"Yeah. Gage told me." I paused, wondering what he and Conrad were discussing at that very moment. Given their close friendship, it could have been anything—but still, I had a bad feeling about this. "He's talking to Conrad about something now, then will call me back."

Mal ran her hand across the back of her neck, exhaling hard. I spotted a nearby bench, and we took a seat, suddenly bone-tired. I kicked off my heels, and Mal did the same, then I glanced miserably at my dress, wet from the woman's spilled drink. Already, the stain was setting.

What a sight we must have made: not even eleven o'clock, and already we looked like we'd had a rough night.

While I waited for Gage to call me back, I pulled out my phone and googled *positano yacht sinking*. It was the headline story on countless news outlets, so I clicked the first one.

As Gage said, eight people had died—but this wasn't the headline. The headline was *who* died: Asher Vice, a well-known TikTok influencer boasting thirty million followers, and his swimsuit-model girlfriend, Julie Jensen. As the boat went down, Asher had been trapped in one of the berths belowdecks with his girlfriend and four other women, all swimsuit models who featured regularly on his social media platforms. A few surviving passengers had tried to break through the door to save them, as well as Asher's friend in another berth, but they were unable. The bodies would undergo autopsy to determine whether drugs had been at play.

The cause of the sinking was to be determined, the article stated. There was no indication of fire. No bad weather. Seas were calm. All of it, just as Mal and I had observed this morning.

The comments below the news article varied. Some expressed

condolences, some were unashamedly insensitive. Most were speculative. I read through a few quickly, my fingers trembling as I scrolled.

@jforge23: How tragic. I know his little sister. She must be crushed.

@kch_forthewin: There's something they're not telling us. No fire, no bad weather? Boats don't just sink.

> @craterhunter99: I think it was a sinkhole. Check out the news about the carbon dioxide levels in the same area. Scary stuff given Vesuvius.

>> @cruzecpl: Heard a new steam vent formed in the crater. Already canceled our trip to Isle of Capri. Not worth it.

>>> @kch_forthewin: Vent activity varies by the day. Means nothing. Volcano's not gonna erupt.

@jp1104: Five girls in the same room? Someone, teach me the way.

@reliccollector: Probably a drug-induced coma. Don't even feel bad for them.

@tears_n_lore: The Amalfi Curse strikes again.

> @kch_forthewin: Say what now?

>> @tears_n_lore: Google it. Said to be the reason behind lots of sinkings in that exact area.

>>> @kch_forthewin: Old wives' tale. Fake news.

>>>> @tears_n_lore: Do you have a better explanation?

I might have kept reading, but my phone rang again. It was Gage calling me back.

"Here he is," I said to Mal, cringing as I answered.

"Sorry about that," Gage said.

"No problem. How's Conrad?" I crossed my legs, squeezing them tightly together, everything in my body tense.

"He's fine. Look, Haven, we need to have a conversation about this."

I gazed out at the beach. The tide was out, making the water feel far away. "Absolutely," I said. "Probably best to delay the project a beat—let the police wrap up their investigation, stay out of their way. We can use that time to do some work at the archives in Naples, try to get a feel for the existing inventory of vessels downed in the area."

This was met with silence. All I could hear was a faint tapping sound, as though Gage were nervously drumming a pen against his desk.

"We don't have time," Gage finally said. "We've never had time, but now more than ever, every hour counts." He let out a heavy sigh. "This isn't easy to share with you, but HPI has decided to reassign the project."

I swallowed hard, shaking my head. I must have misheard. "I'm sorry?"

"It's for your safety, Haven. You said yourself you couldn't determine why the boat went down. The only explanation is the currents—the maelstroms. The area is known for them. And with the strange data, the hydrothermal vents, we just don't know what's going on down there. I can't pay to put a group of women in the water, Haven. Should something happen, think how that would look."

Think how that would look. Always worried about optics, this one.

"So if not me, then who?"

Another pause. "Conrad," he finally said.

I frowned. Had I misunderstood? "But Conrad is in Australia."

"His dive trip is done, apparently," he said. "Look, I know you two are close, and there's a lot of history there. You can stay involved with the project in a remote consulting capacity. And with his diving abilities, his safety record—I don't care what the hell those waters do. I trust Conrad can get himself and his team out safely if needed."

"His team?" I repeated.

"Right. He sent me a short list of names. They're working on travel arrangements now."

"Hang on," I said, my mind reeling. This was all happening so fast. "Whose idea was this? The foundation's, or Conrad's?"

He let out a sigh. "Look, Haven, I'm gonna shoot you straight. When your team opted to expedite the project, we at the foundation were supportive—but we were nervous, too. Things have only gotten worse over there, and I've been losing sleep over it, quite literally. Conrad called me early this morning and pitched the change in plans. I gathered my leadership team and the board. We all agreed this is for the best."

I clenched my jaw, furious that I'd been excluded from these meetings. "Am I on Conrad's list of names? His team?"

Gage hesitated. "No."

I thought I might scream. "So none of you trust me in challenging waters," I said flatly. I glanced at Mal. "Or my dive marshal."

Gage spoke quickly now. "It's not a matter of trust, Haven. It's a matter of experience. Conrad has a lifetime of incident management under his belt. You're newer to this. A lot newer."

"I've been diving my entire life."

"Fair." He took a breath. "How many dive accidents have you handled?"

I bit my lower lip until I tasted blood. "None." Actually, one, and it was my own, but I wasn't about to share this.

Or the person who saved me.

* * *

Despite having logged more than fifteen hundred dives, I'd only had one significant incident underwater, when I was sixteen years old. It was nothing short of a miracle that Conrad, who had only joined my father and me for a few recreational dives over the years, was there when it unfolded.

We meant to explore an underwater arch trail, a series of swim-through rock and coral formations off Key Largo. During the dive, I spotted an arch a few meters away from the trail and made my way toward it. As I swam underneath, admiring a moray eel hidden in a tiny crevice, I felt a snag and then a pop against the back of my head.

At once, a rush of cold salt water flooded my eyes, my nose. The strap on my face mask had caught on the rocks, snapping it. My mask, no longer secured, broke its seal and floated away.

As divers, we train for moments like this, but we rarely expect to use that training in real life. I'd removed my mask countless times in pools and even shallow ocean water. I knew well how to replace my mask on my head and clear it of water.

But I'd never practiced that snag and pop. I'd never had my mask strap split in two. And nothing had prepared me for the violent sting of salt in my eyes, the instant blindness, the water flooding my nose, and—worst of all—the immediate onset of panic.

All of this, thirty feet beneath the surface of the water.

I remained as calm as I could for ten, maybe twenty seconds. I still had my regulator—my source of air—in my mouth. My eyes quickly adjusted to the sting of salt water, though all I could see was the blur of blue, a shadow here or there. I fumbled around as best I could to get my bearings, but as I waved my arms frantically, my hand caught the hose attached to my regulator and inadvertently yanked it out.

Now I was without a mask, without air, and hidden beneath an archway without a dive buddy.

A calmer, more mature diver—a diver like Conrad or my father—might have considered this predicament yet another training exercise. I should have gone for my air first: even if the regulator slips from a diver's mouth, it's attached to the tank and always there to be found, if only a bit out of reach. Even without a mask, I could have then taken a few deep breaths to calm myself, then made a safe, slow ascent to the surface.

I did none of these things.

I panicked, inhaling exactly when I shouldn't have.

Even to this day, I'm not sure how much time passed after this. The story was pieced together in fragments offered by my father and Conrad, beginning with the moment they noticed I was no longer behind them on the original trail.

When Conrad spotted bubbles rising to the surface a short distance away, he swam toward me, realizing something was awry: my mask was off, but the regulator hadn't yet slipped from my mouth. Just as he came up behind me to assist, I yanked the regulator out.

Which meant that in the exact moment I needed help, I had a rescue diver mere inches away.

This was easy work for Conrad. He released the weights attached to my dive gear, put my head in a neutral position, hooked his arm around me, and took me to the surface.

At some point during the brief ascent, I lost consciousness.

Once on the surface, Conrad performed CPR. As I came to, he blew on his whistle to alert the boat's driver, who had anchored a short distance away. They say my father surfaced about this time, too, his eyes ablaze with so much fear they thought he'd suffered an incident of his own. Someone called for an ambulance to be waiting upon our return to shore.

This was the day we all decided that where my father was lacking in luck, I was getting his share of it. Conrad's quick thinking had saved my life, and it was part of why now—even after my father's passing—he and I stayed in touch. I wasn't sure how I could ever repay him.

No matter Conrad's yachts and high-rolling associates and flashy nature, so in contrast to my upbringing. He'd been one of my father's lifelong friends; a fervent supporter of my career; and the man who'd breathed air back into my lungs.

I trusted him completely.

Until right this very moment, on the phone with Gage.

"Why can't Conrad and I lead it together?" I disputed. "Why let him bring in a new team? My crew has been studying our approach for months."

"I'll make sure he gets all the documentation, but there won't be much of a learning curve. He could do this in his sleep. He's got his own camera equipment, too, including some new proprietary tech. He can send his images directly to the software start-up. We'll make sure they get what they need."

I felt Mal's reassuring hand on my knee, though she could only hear half of the conversation. Tears burned in my eyes, but still, I refused to let this man make me cry. "Sounds like the two of you have it pretty well figured out, then."

"We'll need to have a few handoff calls, make sure the docs are transferred to him, et cetera. I'm having my admin draft up a new contract for him. It will be ready by morning. Conrad can be out in two days. He already booked his flight."

"He's lucky he got a flight this late," I said, making no effort to hide my irritation.

"From what I hear, cancellations are off the charts. My wife's travel agency handles a lot of Italy bookings. She said nearly a quarter of next week's reservations have postponed. Premature, in my opinion. There have been no official warnings."

For once, something Gage and I agreed on.

Stunned, I bent forward and put my head in my hands. I thought of Conrad more than a year ago, referring me to HPI and setting me on track for professional success.

I thought of him pulling me from the water nineteen years ago, saving my life.

I thought of his kind text message only hours ago, acknowledging my father's birthday.

And yet he and Gage had just yanked me from the project. And Conrad hadn't put me on his team.

What the hell was this about? Conrad had done so much for me in years past, but now I felt betrayed. He'd been stealthy about it, and now he was making Gage do the dirty work of delivering the news.

This wasn't the Conrad I'd known for most of my life.

I looked at Mal. Her eyes were downcast, resigned. "What about my team?" I asked Gage.

"We just talked about that. Conrad wants—"

"No, what my team is *due*. Their earnings. Three of them, my dive marshal included, left jobs or transferred projects to make this happen."

Gage let out a little laugh. "Well, we obviously can't pay them for work they won't be doing." I heard him shift a few papers around. "Of course, the foundation will cover everyone's expenses incurred thus far, your trip home, and so on. And I'd be willing to honor the team's living stipend through, say, end of next week."

I stood and paced the sidewalk in my bare feet, my heels dangling from one hand. "My dive marshal *quit her job*, Gage." I had nothing to lose now. "She sublet her apartment in Miami. This isn't just a staffing change. My team has upended their lives for the next twelve months. This was to be our work, our income. I'm not even over my jet lag and you're already calling it off? None of us can just fly home and pick up where we left off."

"Haven." Gage lowered his voice. "Today's incident could very well be your blessing in disguise. I don't know what's going on in those waters, okay? I can't have you dead at the bottom of the ocean."

I had one last idea. "Then, we'll shift sites. We'll go back to OBX." In early project-brainstorming days, it had been a contender: North Carolina's Outer Banks, particularly the wreck field around Cape Hatteras, was dubbed the Graveyard of the Atlantic. "We'll need a bit to reframe our approach," I continued, "but we can keep my team intact. And we'll be out of harm's way."

I wouldn't be able to search for my father's discovery, but at this exact moment, I was more worried about my team and their ability to pay their bills.

Gage paused, let out a resigned breath. "I'm sorry, Haven. We can't shift sites, not this late. We *can* shift people. This is just business. You can't take it personally."

I thought of the rudimentary napkin drawings I'd sketched at the hotel bar a couple of years ago—the birth of Project Relic. This entire idea had been mine, so of course I was taking it personally. If it weren't for me, we wouldn't be here at all. But I supposed Gage could say the same. If it weren't for his organization's funding, we wouldn't be here, either.

And that was where he had me beat.

"How about this," Gage continued. He'd lowered his voice, probably suspecting I wasn't alone. "You stay put. Just you. Assuming Vesuvius doesn't do anything drastic, I'll find a way to secure your living stipend through the end of the twelve months. Call it a year-long vacation. Will that make you happy?"

Was this a joke? Did he consider me shallow enough to take such an offer and send my team home empty-handed? "No," I said. "For one, I'm not taking an incentive that leaves my team with nothing. And two, I don't want a vacation. I want to work."

He exhaled hard, and I knew our conversation was finished. "Then, I can't help you," he concluded. "We'll be in touch tomorrow about the handoff."

I didn't acknowledge this, nor did I give him the courtesy of a goodbye. I ended the call and shoved my phone into my purse.

Mal stood to the side, eyes downcast. I wrapped my arms around her neck and held her close. "I'm so sorry. Gage said—"

"You don't need to recap it for me," she said. "I heard enough."

I nodded, and we embraced for a long minute. With my head on her shoulder, I looked off into the distance, beyond the ocean's edge, to where the water grew deeper, darker. The waves lapped rhythmically along the sand, easy and slow.

I thought again of Conrad. He'd once been a friend to me. Now, he felt anything but. What had changed with him?

I remembered his strange text message that morning. Find anything other than shipwrecks yet? ☺

Was it possible, somehow, that Conrad knew about the loot my father had spotted? Could that be behind this unexpected shift in…everything? I didn't think my father had shared his discovery with anyone else. But Conrad was an experienced guy, and I supposed my father might have wanted to seek professional or technical guidance on recovering the gems.

Regardless, Conrad had been the one to initiate this change in plans. If he knew about the gems, he could have gone after them anytime on his own. But with HPI sponsoring the project? That gave him a free ride.

As Mal and I began the uphill walk back to our villa, I couldn't shake the possibility of it. Maybe, to Conrad, this last-minute journey to Positano wasn't about Project Relic at all.

Maybe he wanted the loot. Maybe he wanted someone else to pay for the expedition.

And maybe he wanted me out of his way.

Gage had made it clear: there was no negotiating this decision. The project wasn't mine anymore. He had given me the choice to remain in Positano for a year with the living stipend we originally agreed upon, but his stipend could go to hell. I didn't want the foundation's money.

Still, I hadn't come here with only one objective. And Gage couldn't pull the plug on finishing what my father had started.

"What will you do?" Mal said.

We'd just ascended yet another staircase, and we were both breathing hard. I paused, turning to sit on the top step and catch my breath. "I guess I need to email the others," I said, pulling out my phone. I hovered my fingers over the screen, hating the news I was about to share. The rest of my team was supposed to board their flights the day after tomorrow. I imagined their suitcases, already half-packed on their bedroom floors.

I kept the email short and sweet, telling them the project had been reassigned and they needed to cancel their flights. We could hop on a team call to discuss details at some point tomorrow. After I hit Send, Mal took a seat next to me. From this vantage point, we could see much of the village. Toward the center of town was an ancient church, its facade glowing blue and violet. Beyond this, a few lights bobbed on the water—small boats, anchored for the night. From somewhere nearby, I could hear the faint thumping of music.

"I can't believe we have to leave," Mal said, admiring the view. "I guess I'll stay with Megan until I can undo my sublease situation. *If* I can undo it."

"We already paid the first month on the villa, so we have it for a few more weeks, if you want to stay." I sighed. "But, still. I'm so sorry."

"I don't want to hear you say that ever again. You did nothing wrong, Haven."

"What about income?" I asked her. "What will you do?" I had a modest savings account, thanks to what I'd inherited after my father's death. Mal had no such thing.

She chewed her bottom lip. "My boss was pretty understanding. She said if I changed my mind in the near future, I could come back. Not sure what she meant by *near future*, but if I head home like, ASAP, I think I'll be okay."

This, at least, gave me a measure of relief.

"What about you?" she asked. "What will you do?"

I held my breath. Now was the time.

"I'm not going home," I said.

She was silent a moment, frowning at me. "What?"

"I'm not leaving." I looked her in the eye. "I never told you this, but my father's last dive was Li Galli. He located a wreck with something valuable. Gemstones. He didn't retrieve them—didn't have what he needed. He intended to go back the next day, but…"

"His stroke."

"Right. He couldn't return. He made me promise I'd come back in his place."

Mal eyes were wide. "Why are you just now telling me this?"

"A lot of reasons. Mainly, it wasn't my secret to share—it was my father's. But also, I didn't want to divert the team's focus with mention of anything valuable among the wrecks. And I didn't want you all…" I sighed, splaying my hands. "Well, even though we chose this site before his discovery, I don't want anyone to think my motives for being here are misaligned."

"So no one else knows," Mal said.

"Not on the team, no. And I want to keep it that way."

But Mal was shaking her head. "No, I mean, does anyone else know about the wreck and the loot? Besides you and your dad?"

I exhaled. "I'm not sure. Conrad, he said something strange earlier." I showed her the text with the wink emoji, and I told her about the few clues my father had shared: the grainy underwater photos, the abovewater image with longitude and latitude coordinates, the strange list of numbers and letters I couldn't decipher. All of them were digital and uploaded to the password-protected cloud folder. "I don't know what, if anything, my father shared with Conrad. But his text seems strange, doesn't it?"

Concern spread across Mal's face. "Totally. I mean, I've never met the guy, but I've listened to some of his interviews. He goes on and on about how much untapped value is sitting on the seafloor. And I'm one hundred percent sure he doesn't report his discoveries."

I stood, ready to keep walking back to the villa. "Which is why I'm not going home. I'll find somewhere cheaper to stay. I'll tap into my savings. But I'm sure as hell not letting Conrad beat me to it."

We resumed walking up the steps, and my phone buzzed. Erin, one of the women on my team, had replied. *I'm so sorry, Haven,* her email said. *I'm crushed and can only imagine how you feel. Is it because of Mt. Vesuvius? I've seen the news—people are worried. This sucks, but our well-being comes first. Get home safe. XO.*

"She's right," Mal said, "about our well-being." She tripped on a step, cursing under her breath. "What are you going to do about a boat? Air tanks? A dive buddy? It's clear you won't be diving with Conrad."

"I guess I'll find a local dive shop," I said. For Project Relic, we'd arranged all of this with a private dive outfitter in Sorrento, but that was off the table now.

"You'd trust a stranger with what could be a massively valuable discovery?"

The more questions Mal asked, the more my plan began to slip from my fingers. "Depends on the stranger. Maybe I will. Maybe I won't." I felt myself growing defensive, even combative. I hadn't prepared for any of this.

She side-eyed me. "I'm on your side, Haven. Remember that."

Our villa, with a single lamp illuminating a window, stood just ahead. "I don't have all the answers," I said, "and I know this endeavor isn't necessarily safe." I turned the key, swung open the door. In front of us lay our half-unpacked items, a mess of groceries and luggage and dive gear we'd intended to organize in coming days.

"But I'm not going home," I reiterated. "Not yet. I'm not letting Conrad take this from me, too."

9

MARI

Monday, April 16, 1821

As Mari and Pippa made their way to the village in their *gozzo*, they spotted a group of fishermen ahead, toiling on the docks, unloading their nets and hanging them over wooden racks to dry. Wisps of street-vendor smoke curled into the air. A group of boys stood at a long table near the water, gutting and weighing fish. Later, they would salt and smoke it, and whatever didn't stay in the village would be shipped out.

All of these people, and indeed the very welfare of the village, were now at risk because of Mari's mistake. Matteo had said he'd be back. He'd come for her, undoubtedly, but what about the others? If they got ahold of the other *streghe*, the village of Positano would never be the same.

Mari should have heeded her instincts: she hadn't wanted to go out at all this morning. She thought of the water trembling in her cupped hands as she tasted the sea, and the spooked cormorants flying past, and the dolphins darting away. The signs had been there. Why hadn't she been more careful with the girls, more attuned to her surroundings?

It had been reckless to do her underwater pirouette in broad daylight. She'd known this, but she'd done it anyway, wanting to make the girls happy. And she'd been careless last week, too. Instead of leading the women to the cove to perform their spells against the incoming pirates, she'd brought them to the seashore. There, she recalled, was where she'd spotted that strange shadow on the dock...

Was that, perhaps, related to what had just unfolded?

As they rowed, Mari glanced at her reddened hands. They were blistered now, and she dunked one of her hands into the ocean, hoping the cool water would ease the pain. But not a moment after her skin touched the sea, an enormous swell rose from beneath them. Pippa screamed, nearly falling over the edge of the boat as it pitched to one side.

Mari yanked her hand from the sea, instantly realizing her error, but it was too late: the sea sensed Mari's fury, and after the swell had nearly rolled their boat, it joined the current and made its way to shore—a single rogue wave, steadily building in size. It must have been three or four meters high.

On one of the docks, a fisherman looked up and shouted in alarm. "*Onda! Onda!*" he screamed, dragging his friends onto land. A moment later, the swell struck the dock, its force snapping the wooden frame into pieces. The dock itself, along with the nets and the fresh catch, tumbled into the sea.

The men looked at the place their dock had just been, visibly confused. Then, their eyes fell on Mari's *gozzo*.

They waited for her to approach. "You are all right?" one of them asked Mari as she crawled out of the boat and onto the sand. "*Onda anomala*," he was saying, over and over.

"Yes," she managed, "a rogue wave. We are all right." The dock would need rebuilding, but the men were safe, at least.

She and Pippa pushed past them, running for the hillside.

They would go first to Pippa's—Mari wanted to get her home, to safety—then Mari would break the news to Lia's mother.

As they went, they retraced a portion of the route they'd taken that morning, when Lia had complained about the pebble stuck between her toes. Now, Mari regretted not sitting down with the child to help her, not showing her more compassion.

At Pippa's *casetta*, Mari asked if Vivi was home. She was not, meaning Pippa would need to be the one to share the details about Lia's kidnapping with her mother. Still, Mari trusted Pippa; unlike some of the other village women, Pippa was not the sort to gossip or embellish details.

"Keep the doors and windows locked," Mari told her before she left. She thought again of the man vowing to return. "And keep a knife on you," she added.

A short while later, at Ami's house, Mari beat her hand against the door, knowing Ami didn't go into the bakehouse on Mondays but instead stayed home, preparing her ingredients for the week.

Ami answered the door in her apron, her hands covered in flour. She was known around the village for her *crostata di frutta*, a dessert tart made with local fruits Ami handpicked herself—apricots and figs—and lemon rinds glazed with sugar. Now she wiped her palms on her apron, her expression one of unease. "What is it?" She peered outside and glanced behind Mari. "Where is Lia?"

Mari tried to catch her breath, dabbing at the sweat on her upper lip. "Something has happened," she said between breaths. Her mouth felt full of grit, dry and tasteless. She could not look Ami in the eye.

"Where is Lia?" Ami repeated, louder this time. On the road, a young boy with his dog stopped, turning to look at them.

"She is…gone," Mari choked out.

Ami grabbed her, roughly, by the shoulder. "What do you mean, she is gone?" Her nails dug into Mari's skin, and Mari wished she'd dug harder, wished she could exchange this pain for the return of the child.

"Pippa and I were in the water by the cove. Lia was in the boat, watching us. I heard a scream, and when I surfaced, a man was there. Lia, she was—" Mari's knees buckled, and she fell to the ground, there on Ami's doorstep. "She was gone. Matteo Mazza. He took her, stole off with her."

Ami's face twisted in anguish, and dark red splotches formed on her neck. Suddenly, she leaned over the tiny garden bed at the front of her house and began to vomit.

"Why did you not go after her?" she cried between heaves.

"We did," Mari insisted, still kneeling. "But Massimo Mazza was there with a knife, and he—"

"A *knife*? You are the most skilled *strega* in Positano, and you let my daughter go because you could not fight off a man with a *knife*?"

Mari shook her head, held out her bloodied hands. "I killed him. I killed Massimo so I could get past him, go in search of her." Then, she grasped Ami's hand, giving her a grave look. "Matteo saw everything."

Ami stood, wiped her chin. A moment later, her husband, Dante, appeared behind her, rubbing salve onto his knuckles. Mari recognized the small tub of balm from her father's shop. Dante was one of the better mollusk-trappers in Positano, and his cracked and calloused hands showed it. The lime the men used to prevent net rot was terribly harsh.

Dante glanced at Mari on her knees, then studied the pallor on Ami's face, the dampness on her forehead. "What's wrong?"

Even now, in such circumstances, a lifetime of secrecy was not so easily forgotten. The women needed to choose their words carefully.

"Lia was taken," Ami whispered. "She is gone. Kidnapped, by Matteo Mazza." Suddenly, she let out a wail and fell into him. He wrapped an arm around her, trying to hold up her weight.

Dante's mouth fell open. "Of Fratelli Mazza?" At her nod, he let out a cry. He fixed his eyes on a small wooden doll that lay discarded near the door. Mari recognized it as a toy Lia often carried. "My girl," he whispered, his voice thick with disbelief. "My sweet girl."

He released Ami and went to the doll, clutching it against him. Suddenly, his face hardened; he looked ready to kill someone. "I will go," he hissed. "What was he wearing?"

"He was at a distance," Mari said, "but he wore a dark green hat. He had broad shoulders, a sharp chin. Dark hair. He will be taking her to Naples."

"How do you know?"

She paused. "He was accompanied by his brother, Massimo, who told me they would take Lia there."

"Did Massimo make off with them?"

"No. Dante, you cannot repeat this, but I—" she lowered her voice "—I killed him." She didn't elaborate further, and to her great relief, Dante did not ask.

Dante placed his hands over his lips. "Mari. They will—" He shook his head, correcting himself. "Matteo will come for you."

"I know."

Dante unwrapped his arm from around Ami's shoulder and ran inside. A moment later, he came out with a pair of boots and a satchel, from which jutted the butt of a revolver. He sat on the front step, pulling a boot on. "How long ago did this happen?"

Mari paused. "An hour and a half ago, I'd say."

"Was he in a coach? Or on horseback?"

"A coach."

He pulled his second boot on. "He'll have a good head start, but if he's looking to return to Naples, there is only one overland route. Pray an axle has snapped. I will take one of Leo's horses and track him down." Leo was Pippa's father and a very good boatbuilder. He owned a small plot of hilly land just north of the village, with plenty of room for livestock and *gozzi* undergoing repair.

Dante took off up the road at a sprint. Ami remained on the ground, a faraway look in her eyes. "I fear what they will do to her," she said. "Why do you think they took her?"

Ami deserved the truth, much as it might shame Mari to admit it. "We cannot know for sure," Mari said, "but the other night on the shore, I saw a man hiding near the docks. I worry he saw the group of us women. Perhaps he has been following us since then..." Mari then told Ami about the pirouette she'd done for the girls a short while ago. "If he took Lia because he suspects she is a *strega*, he will want to keep her safe and well, so he can see what she is capable of."

"She's a child," Ami said, face streaked with tears. "She isn't capable of anything. Not yet."

"Matteo doesn't know that."

"He will learn soon enough. She will be useless to them. She can control nothing, divine nothing. He may kill her when he realizes it."

"He said, '*Tornerò*,'" Mari told Ami. "Just before he took off. If he comes back, I will insist on trading places with her. He has seen, firsthand, what I am capable of. He will want me in her place."

"You're a fool to think he will want only one of us," Ami snapped.

Mari knew she was right, and it was this reality that horrified her most. What, she wondered, would become of all of them?

"What about Massimo's body?" Ami asked.

"It drifted out to sea. Anyone who finds him will think him drowned."

"Until Matteo tells the officials what he saw."

Mari shook her head. "Telling the officials would mean revealing that he has seen a woman practice *stregheria*. He will want to keep that secret close to his chest, so he can exploit it, if he can manage." She reached for Ami's hand, grateful when she let her take it into her own. "I vow to find Lia," Mari said. "I will die trying if I must. But I will find her, and I will bring her home."

10

HOLMES

Friday, April 20, 1821
9:15 a.m., port of Terracina

At port since half two in the afternoon yesterday. Weather is fair. Eastward breeze at 7 kts. The cabbage stew we ate last night did not settle with me, and my stomach has been in knots. Nico, good soul that he is, gave me his last ginger lozenge, which helped tremendously.

It seems we have a thief among us. One sailor's silver snuffbox has gone missing. Another insists his box of candied orange slices were taken from his sea chest. A few of us were inclined to blame Quinto, until he revealed that a bottle of his brandy had disappeared overnight. I have resolved to keep my diary hidden even deeper in the seams of my mattress, lest someone try to snatch it.

Tacking all morning; a day hardly worth noting in my diary, but for the fact that we have been issued a strange shift in itinerary. We are not to remain north of Rome any longer. Instead, the captain has advised we will make straightaway for Positano, much earlier than planned. According to Quinto, it relates to some urgent errand on behalf of the Mazza brothers. En route, we will stop in Naples—the Mazza docks at Castellammare di Stabia. Quinto did not expand or elaborate on the reason for this, either.

I will try, if I can, to get a letter off to Mari once we're in Naples. I need to tell her we will be reunited much sooner than anticipated. Still, sending notice by post may be inconsequential. If we are not tied up in Naples for long, it will be a race between the postman and the Aquila. How stunned Mari will be if I arrive before the letter! She will think me an apparition, a dream.

I would feel exuberant about all of this if I did not have the nagging feeling that something is amiss.

11

MARI

Friday, April 20, 1821

Four days passed, and still Dante had not returned from Naples with news on Lia.

It had been a disheartening few days, filled with difficult conversations. Everyone in the village now knew about Lia's abduction, though Mari and the other *streghe* had kept the story very simple.

It wasn't the first time the Mazzas had kidnapped someone, but usually it involved a ransom. Lia's family wasn't wealthy or renowned. Why, the villagers asked, would they have gone after her?

There was no mention of teaching the girls magic.

There was no mention of the brother Mari had killed, his body now at sea.

Mari did, however, warn the villagers of Matteo's intent to return. *They must have something against us*, a few of the men surmised.

The village vowed to remain vigilant, difficult as it would

be: Mazza-owned vessels were all over the area. They traversed the waters offshore every day.

Further, the Mazzas' men might not even come by sea. They might take the overland route, just as they'd done the day they kidnapped Lia.

Evading the Fratelli Mazza seemed an impossible task, so the village men kept themselves well-armed.

During this time, Cleila and Paola were an unexpected source of support, encouraging Mari not to wallow in remorse. "You couldn't have known they would follow you when you took the girls out," Cleila reassured her one morning.

Mari kept silent, too ashamed to mention the shadow she'd seen on the dock the week prior.

If she'd heeded her instincts, none of them would be in this predicament.

On Friday evening, Mari lay in the olive grove for more than an hour. In the darkness, the sea was hidden from view; she could almost trick herself into believing it was not the sea at all but instead an expanse of dark land, void of lamps and villas, stretching indefinitely into the distance.

She looked up at the stars, tracing shapes in her mind, just as Holmes had taught her to do on the nights she could not sleep for anxiety or grief.

Inhale, he'd taught her, *and count five or six stars. Imagine they form a shape, that they are something altogether different than stars. Just as you are different than your feelings, your pain. They do not make you who you are.*

For all the effort Mari had put into pushing aside her sadness over the years, nothing had been so effective as Holmes's counsel. He reminded her that few were as intimate with sleepless nights as men who sailed the sea, and he had used this method many times himself.

Now Mari counted stars and imagined they formed owls or

towers or swords. Her pulse slowed, her breathing calmed. She marveled at what he'd taught her—the ability to exit her own tumultuous thoughts and turn to imagination.

It was one reason she'd fallen in love with him. Holmes had softened Mari, peeled back the hardened layers of her heart. At times, he even unburied a childlike spirit within her.

She smiled in the darkness, thinking of the time they snuck into the domed church at the base of the village. It was last fall, on a night when the temperature had dropped quickly. They managed a way in through an unlocked door at the back, giggling as they made their way through the darkened nave.

Mari eyed the delicate-looking sculptures situated throughout the church. "We shouldn't be here," she said. They could easily break something—a sculpture or any number of rules posted outside the building.

Holmes ignored her. "Dance with me," he whispered with a mischievous smile.

Mari had only ever danced with Sofia when they were girls. "I don't know how to dance," she objected, "and we have no music, anyhow."

A clavichord sat at one end of the altar. Holmes walked toward it, clumsily pressing on a few of the keys. The resulting noise was shrill, discordant, and so loud Mari felt sure an angry clergyman would arrive any moment. She'd never been so nervous in all her life, and yet the thrill of doing something improper made the tips of her fingers tingle.

She clasped her hands over her ears, laughing. "That is not music at all."

Holmes left the altar and approached her in one of the pews. "Then, we will dance without it," he said, wrapping his arms around her lower back.

Mari couldn't resist. She leaned into him, tucking her head against his chest, breathing in the earthy, salty smell of him as they swayed back and forth in silence. Once, she caught him eyeing the low, flat pew beside them. She knew what was on his mind. She chuckled, giving him a little shake of the head.

Not yet, she remembered thinking, *but soon.*

Now, as Mari lay in the olive grove, she decided she wanted to walk to the church. She wasn't tired yet, and perhaps that same back door would be unlocked. She liked the idea of standing in the exact place where she and Holmes had danced. Maybe it would make her feel closer to him.

She stood, wiping off her skirt, but before she could make her way down the hill, something dark caught her eye on the watery horizon—a shadow, something even blacker than the sea.

A ship.

It shouldn't have been anything out of the ordinary, except that it was very close, it was the middle of the night, and—most alarming—the vessel was enormous, the size of a *fregata*.

Squinting in the dark, Mari made out a few of the ship's details. Three masts. Two gun decks. And—to Mari's horror—the cannons were pushed out, ready to fire.

This ship looked ready for war.

With the church forgotten, Mari ran for the house. Inside, she went to Paola's room and began to hammer on her bedroom door. Paola opened the door, eyes bloodshot. Cleila was behind her; the two often shared a room because Mari's father snored so loud.

"A ship has arrived," Mari whispered, lantern swinging in her hand. "They are anchored just offshore. Their guns are out."

Cleila covered her mouth with her hands, anguish in her eyes. "Do you think the Mazzas have come back already?"

This was exactly what Mari feared, and she said as much.

Paola turned, began to gather a few things. "Who knows how long they've been anchored. They could be creeping through the village now. Should we hide? Gather the others and leave?"

Mari glared at her. "*Leave?* For all we know, Lia is on the ship. I…" She felt unable to believe what she was about to say.

"Well, I intend to go to them. You can do whatever you want, but I intend to confront them. I will turn myself over if they will give Lia back."

"You cannot go alone," Cleila said. "I won't let you go alone."

Mari felt a rare surge of affection for her stepmother.

As the women slipped out of the house and made their way down the hillside pathway, Mari listened closely for the sound of footsteps, in case men sent by the Fratelli Mazza—or even Matteo himself—were already dispersed through the village. But to Mari's surprise, it wasn't a man they encountered, it was—

"Pippa," Mari hissed, spotting her on the road a short distance from Pippa's house. She was wearing canvas breeches, her hair tucked into a flat cap. It was safer, she probably thought, to disguise herself as a man if she intended to go for a late-night walk. "What are you doing out here?" She felt a moment of irritation with her younger friend: yesterday, she'd warned her against leaving the house.

Pippa's eyes grew wide; she'd been caught. "Mari," she said. "Please don't tell my mother. I snuck out. I was—" She stood fixing a few loose strands of hair. "Well, I have not been able to sleep since Lia was taken. I was only taking a walk."

For this, Mari could not blame her. "There's a ship anchored off the beach." She nodded at Cleila and Paola. "We don't know who it is, but we're going to find out. Perhaps they have Lia."

In an instant, Pippa's face turned hard. "I'm coming with you."

"*No, assolutamente no*," came a man's voice behind them. They all turned to see Leo rushing forward with a scowl. "Where have you been, Pippa?" He looked her up and down. "Are those my clothes?"

"I couldn't sleep," she blurted out.

A moment later, Vivi ran up. She and Leo had both been out looking for their daughter. Relief crossed her face, and she bent over, breathing hard. "You had us terrified," she told Pippa. "We thought they'd come for you."

Briefly, Mari told the newcomers about the ship.

"We'll go," Vivi said, nodding to Leo. "Pippa, go straight home. Now."

"No," Pippa said. "I'm old enough. I'm seventeen. Mari is only three years older than me. And Paola, only two years older."

"You haven't a choice," Leo said. He pointed at their house, a short ways away. "Go."

Pippa huffed, saying nothing more, and headed for home.

Together, Mari and the others raced their way through their village, making their way down the steps on the fastest route to the beach. The village was empty, shutters pulled closed over windows.

Leo ran in front, taking steps two or three at a time. There were countless winding routes down to the beach; after a few moments, the women lost sight of him. He was faster, more agile. He also had a small revolver on him, though this didn't give Mari much comfort. The men who'd arrived would undoubtedly be better armed.

Moving quickly down a narrow set of steps between buildings, Mari steadied herself with her hand on the stone walls either side of her.

A sudden gunshot rang out ahead, around the corner of a building. Mari, Cleila, and Paola froze in place, but Vivi let out a cry. Either Leo had just shot someone, or someone had shot him…

"Leo!" Vivi shouted. She jumped the last three steps and cried out in pain when she landed. "Leo!"

"Viviana, no," Mari hissed. None of the women knew what lay around the bend. But Vivi raced ahead, continuing to shout her husband's name. Mari was tempted to run after her, but to do so could be a death sentence. "In here," Mari said, grabbing Paola's and Cleila's hands and pulling the women into a recessed doorway. They tested the doorknob, finding it locked. Together, they huddled in the corner, breathing hard.

A few seconds passed in silence; Vivi had ceased her shouting. Mari leaned her head out and whispered Vivi's name a few more times, to no avail. At least there were no shouts, no more shots. If Leo had been hurt, Vivi would be screaming now. Perhaps Leo had been the one to fire his gun, and now he and Vivi were taking cover...

Then, footsteps sounded above them, in the direction from whence they'd come. This could be anyone—a villager, or a man sent by the Fratelli Mazza. Fearing the latter, Mari darted back into the doorway, placing her finger over her lips as though to say *Keep quiet*. The footsteps grew closer, and Mari's heart began to thud impossibly hard. Whoever was on the stairs would be passing their doorway in a matter of seconds.

Mari pressed her body against the wall, not daring to breathe as a shadowy figure flew past them.

"Could you tell who it was?" Mari asked the others, once the unknown person had gone.

Both Cleila and Paola shook their heads. The women held still a minute or two, listening for anything else. Finally, Mari could wait no longer. "Let's go," she said.

They tiptoed their way down the final staircase, approaching the beach. It wasn't an open expanse—net-drying racks and wooden huts were interspersed throughout—but Mari managed to spot Vivi ahead. She and Leo stood at the waterline, engaged in what looked like tense conversation. Just beyond them, a smaller boat bobbed in the waves. "There," Mari said, pointing. "She and Leo are there, just ahead."

Suddenly, Cleila drew to a stop. "Mari," she said solemnly. "That's not Leo."

Cleila was right—the man with Vivi was taller and heavier than Leo. And as Mari studied him, she realized that he and Vivi were not holding hands; instead, the man was restraining her.

Mari's mouth went dry, remembering the gunshot.

Protected from view by one of the huts, the women began to run forward, but suddenly Paola fell to the side, crying out in pain. She'd stepped into a small hole, turning her ankle. She clutched it now, her eyes instantly welling with tears.

Mari glanced again at the men by the waterline. To her relief, they hadn't heard Paola cry out. Nor had they spotted the women approaching in the darkness.

"Go with Mari," Paola begged her mother, her voice thick with pain. She pointed to another nearby lean-to, a place the fishermen often congregated to eat lunch. "I'll stay over there. As soon as the pain subsides, I'll come help with—" She cut off, crying harder now.

Mari knelt down, feeling Paola's ankle. It was hot to the touch, quickly swelling. Her pain wouldn't be subsiding anytime soon.

Mari cursed under her breath. She wouldn't let Paola remain alone. "Take her over there," she said to Cleila, pointing to the lean-to. "You stay with her. Get her back to the villa as quickly as you can."

Cleila gave a stiff nod. "Be safe, Mari."

Then, alone, Mari ran for Vivi.

She hated this stretch of beach, tucked on the far east side of the village. It was a cursed place, the very spot where she'd lost her mother. Still, she pressed on, shoving memories aside in favor of courage.

As she got closer to the shoreline, she noticed a small tender fighting against the waves, making its way toward the enormous ship anchored offshore. In the boat, a pair of men rowed forward, but it was clear there were one or two others of smaller stature with them. Whether they were *streghe* or not was unclear, but they were most certainly women.

Mari kept running, but her feet sank into the sand, slowing her movement.

She was ten meters, five meters, from the water...

Suddenly, a body slammed against hers. She screamed and fell to the ground, getting sand in her mouth. She tried to push herself upright, but whoever had knocked her over was kneeling over her, his knee in her back. He grabbed her hair, yanking her head up. She turned toward him best she could, blood draining from her face.

It was Matteo.

"Where is she?" Mari cried. "Where did you take the child?"

He ignored her and instead shouted to his friend. "This is her," he yelled, hauling her upright. Mari tried to writhe out of his grip, but he kept her arms pinned behind her back.

"Mari," Vivi called out, her cheeks streaked with tears. "They shot him."

Mari felt her throat tighten. "Leo?"

Vivi replied with a sob. "They took the Fontana sisters, too," she said, nodding toward the tender rowing away.

The Fontana girls, both teenagers, occasionally worked along the shore overnight, scrubbing the filthy docks. Inevitably, each evening the docks were covered in dried fish guts left behind after the men cleaned their catch. It was a task that took a few hours, even with a pair of workers, but each week the fishermen pooled funds to pay whoever completed the unpleasant chore.

And there was one thing that made the Fontana girls stand out: though they weren't *streghe*, they had naturally vibrant red hair.

"You don't want them," Mari now told Matteo. "The Fontana girls, they only clean the docks, that's it. They're not like—"

"Quiet," he said. Gripping her waist, he produced a rope and tied Mari's arms behind her back. The knots pulled tight against the tiny bones of her wrist. She winced but refused to cry out.

She glanced toward the lean-to; on a nearby staircase, she could make out the dark forms of Cleila and Paola slowly ascending the steps. Paola was hunched forward, managing a slow hobble. Seconds later, they turned a corner, out of sight. Mari was glad for it: the situation on the beach was even worse than she'd imagined.

A shout rang out. "Matteo!" a man said. "I've got another." Beside him, a young woman—gagged and blindfolded—stumbled along.

Vivi screamed.

It was Pippa.

"Found her a few minutes ago," the man said, wearing a salacious grin. "She was coming down the stairs, over there…" When he pointed toward the west end of the village, Mari understood: it hadn't been one of these men, nor another villager, who had rushed by when the women were hiding in the doorway. It had been Pippa, looking for them.

If only Mari had been braver, had dared to peek out of the doorway. She would have spotted Pippa, might have prevented her capture altogether…

This beach is cursed, Mari thought at once. *This entire village is cursed.*

"No, no," Vivi was saying now, fighting hard against the man restraining her. "No, please no, take me, anyone but—"

"We're taking all of you," he snapped. "Red hair or not, I'll get every woman in this pathetic village, if I can manage. Can't trust the lot of you."

Every woman. Mari bent forward, her stomach cramping. She thought of the Fontana girls, certainly confused and terrified.

"There are only a few of us." Mari pointed at Pippa. "And she's too young," she lied. "Both she and the girl you took from me the other day, they can't do anything. Take me instead. I can show you this very moment what we're able to—"

The distant clang of a heavy bell interrupted her. Someone on the ship had just sounded it, and now, the men glanced uneasily at the vessel.

"We need to go," Matteo shouted.

Vivi began to sob, while Pippa remained stoic, perfectly calm. Mari had never seen courage like the sort Pippa displayed now.

Quickly, the men with Pippa and Vivi forced them into the boat, while another man lifted the oars. Mari wanted to get as close as she could to the water and her friends, but Matteo remained in place, his arms tight around her torso.

"What is it?" the man with Pippa demanded.

Matteo hesitated. "This is the woman who killed Massimo." He eyed the water, advancing and receding in steady, low waves. "I am worried about taking her on the water."

Mari decided to use this in her favor, pointing at Pippa. "Let her stay, and I will cooperate. She cannot do anything, anyhow." Then, with as much intimidation as she could muster in her voice, she added, "Otherwise, I assure you, you will be making a very grave mistake."

The men eyed each other, and Mari caught a glimmer of fear pass between them. One of the men untied Pippa, removed her gag and blindfold, and pushed her out of the tender. "Go," he said. "Get out of here."

For once, Pippa obeyed. She was outnumbered, anyway, and the men were well-armed; for Pippa to use her magic now would be reckless—a death sentence for all of these women.

When Pippa ran off, Mari's shoulders fell in relief. They put her in the front of the boat with Vivi toward the back. From the corner of her eye, Mari caught Vivi's wrists and hands writhing in her binds. She was trying to loosen them, to escape. Mari hoped that Vivi's *cimaruta*, hidden beneath her gown, would lend her extra dexterity as she aimed to work her way out.

Mari's own binds were far too tight, and she could not shift her hands one bit, much less loosen the knot. She, too, still wore her *cimaruta*, but the necklaces weren't cure-alls.

One of the men pulled at the oars, heading for the larger vessel anchored offshore. What—and who—awaited them there?

Mari hoped Lia was somewhere on the ship. If nothing else, they could be reunited.

She lay on her back on the floor of the boat, a tear slowly crawling down her cheek. Her hands were twisted in a painful position, and one of the men pushed his knee hard into her shoulder to keep her supine.

Above her, Mari could see nothing but sky, studded with bright, blinking stars, the same stars she'd been gazing at just an hour ago in the olive grove. *How safe they are*, Mari thought to herself, *year after year, hour after hour, while the rest of the world shifts and shudders.*

She closed her eyes, too terrified to imagine any star shapes now.

She hadn't any idea what the rest of the evening would bring. She only knew that here among these men, restrained and out of the water, her powers—her magic—were as good as dead.

12

HAVEN

Tuesday

The morning after my call with Gage, I stood in front of Positano's only scuba outfitter, a tiny stand-alone building not far from the main beach, with a faded stucco facade and a beat-up sign reading *Positano Underwater Adventures*. The fact that it was written in English told me most of its customers were tourists.

I paused a moment before going in, gazing at a few of the items in the shop's display window: a snorkel set that looked to be half-melted from UV rays; a poster advertising a discount on lessons that had expired months ago; and a collection of plain white oversize T-shirts. One of them had come loose from its hanger and lay in a messy heap beneath the others.

If this was the storefront, I could only imagine the condition of the shop's gear.

Grimacing, I opened the door, a bell clanging against the glass to announce my arrival. The shop was empty of customers, and no one stood behind the counter, though the lights were on and hip-hop music played from somewhere in the back. I inhaled the all-too-familiar scent of neoprene and sunscreen, then I glanced around at the merchandise, which wasn't any better than what I'd seen in the window.

"Hello?" I called out.

This was met with a loud hissing sound, then an ear-piercing crash, like someone had dropped a metal tray. A man's voice in back muttered, "*Cazzo.*" I knew what this meant; I'd studied up on a few Italian swear words, too.

A moment later, footsteps.

"I'm so sorry," I called out, about to come face-to-face with whatever employee I'd startled. But when he turned the corner, I was relieved to see a wide grin.

"*Ciao,*" he said.

"*Ciao,*" I replied. He looked about my age, maybe a few years older. "I'm sorry if I startled you." Then again, he didn't seem the sort to be easily disturbed: he wore board shorts and a long-sleeved rash guard, and his wavy, almost-black hair was rumpled and half-wet. He looked like he'd just gone for a swim.

He also looked familiar. "Did I see you yesterday morning?" I asked him. "Walking up the steps with a box of snorkel masks?"

He laughed. "Indeed. You tried your Italian on me. It wasn't terrible." He leaned forward, resting his elbows on the glass counter. His skin tone was a beautiful, Italian bronze, and as the sleeves of his shirt inched up, I caught the bottom edge of a tattoo on his forearm: a pair of sea turtles surrounded by a few abstract-looking waves.

"And you didn't startle me," he said in a thick Italian accent. "The hoses on our air tanks, they can be a pain in the ass. Uncooperative."

I might have found the statement troubling, if not for his very intense gaze, which left me fumbling for words.

"Right," I said, approaching the counter. "I, uh, well, I'm a scuba diver, and I thought I'd stop in to ask about a few things."

I nearly cringed as I said it. He probably thought I'd come for a bottle of mask defogger or maybe a spare pair of water shoes. Little did he know all that had transpired in the last day and how very much I needed help. "Do you do dive excursions?" I finally asked.

"*Certamente*," he said. He handed me a brochure. Now, closer to him, I could make out a few days' worth of unshaven stubble on his jawline, and his dark, coffee-colored eyes. "We have a spot open this afternoon," he said, "and several tomorrow. Luca's leading the dives. She's *top-notch*, as you Americans like to say." At this, he winked.

He was being a bit forward, but I didn't dislike it. I forced my eyes back to the brochure, trying to concentrate on the map within. Out of the corner of my eye, I caught him checking my left hand.

"Thanks," I said, handing back the brochure. I wasn't interested in exploring underwater grottos or looking for barracuda. "These excursions look great, but I'm actually not here to dive recreationally. I'm a researcher, and I'm more interested in a private boat charter."

"Oh? Do you have a dive site in mind?"

"Li Galli."

He grimaced. "You heard about the—"

"The yacht, yes." I sighed. "Terrible timing." I didn't want to dwell on it, so I moved on quickly. "I need to rent air tanks, too. Does Luca do private charters?"

He pressed his lips together and shook his head. "Sadly, no. We've just got the one boat, and we only use it for group dives."

I nodded, instantly deflated. "I see." I gazed aimlessly at the counter, trying to think of an alternative. "Can you recommend any private boat charters around here?"

"*Sì*, we have hundreds of them in Positano," he said. "But being a diver, you know…"

"Most boats don't make good dive boats."

He shifted his weight from one foot to the other. "Exactly."

Dive boats had brackets to keep air tanks safely secured in addition to special ladders and swim steps. Freshwater tanks, too, for dunking wet suits and expensive gear. I thought of the precious equipment I'd brought, some of it costing thousands of dollars—particularly my camera lenses. The lenses needed to be submerged in fresh water as soon as possible after using; salt water was terribly corrosive.

Suddenly, an idea struck me. "What time are your group excursions?"

"We do two a day," he said. "Eleven to one, and two to four."

"So before eleven, or after four, no one is using the boat?"

He was silent a moment, studying my face. "That's right," he finally said. The edges of his mouth twitched like he was holding back a grin.

"Would I be permitted to charter the boat during those hours, then? Of course, I'll pay whatever it costs, including fuel."

He looked away, drumming his fingers on the glass. "I don't know," he said, furrowing his brow. "I will have to check with the owner, see if he approves."

"Of course," I said quickly.

"How many open-water dives have you done?" he asked, his head tilted to one side.

"Thousands. I've been diving since I was four years old."

He went still, then. "Give me one moment," he said.

I nodded, expecting him to go to the back and have a word with the owner, whoever he was. But instead, he remained at the glass counter, spending a few moments needlessly tidying the brochures and organizing them into a neat pile.

Suddenly, he looked up. "The owner approves."

I gave a little laugh. "Sorry?"

"I am the owner, and I'd be glad to agree to this." He held out his hand. "Enzo Rossi."

My hands had suddenly gone damp, and I fought the urge to

fidget with my hair. I put my hand out, too, praying he didn't notice how sweaty my palms were. "Haven Ambrose," I said, looking him straight in his dark brown eyes.

"Four o'clock today, then, for our first dive?" he asked.

I paused. Even when Project Relic had been squarely my own, I hadn't planned to make my first dive until next week. I hadn't even unpacked my gear yet. But nothing about this trip to Positano was going as planned. And I worried that if I didn't accept Enzo's offer this very moment, he might reconsider.

And—Conrad. He was en route and would be landing in Naples tomorrow. How quickly would he don his scuba gear and deploy his team? If I were in the water this afternoon, well, I would beat him to that, at least.

"Yes," I said. "Four o'clock. I'll be ready."

"I cannot let you go down alone, you know."

"Of course," I said. "Will someone else be coming along, then?" A third person to man the boat wasn't imperative, but it was certainly best practice.

"No," he said. "We will drop anchor and put up our flag."

I nodded, pretending this did not worry me at all. Mal would be furious with me for agreeing to this.

"Meet me at the main dock." Enzo gave me one last smile, before coming around the counter, stepping to the door, and propping it open for me. "Have a beautiful day, Haven Ambrose," he said, his voice low.

I thanked him, giving him a quick, light touch on his arm. It was unlike me to be flirtatious with someone I'd just met, but with this Enzo, I simply couldn't resist.

13

MARI

Friday, April 20, 1821

When the tender slowed next to the imposing hull of the ship, Mari could hear laughs and shouts from the men aboard, as well as the clatter of metal and rope.

All of this, interspersed with the sound of Vivi's soft weeping. She had not managed to escape her binds.

Mari sat up, glancing toward the ship, a maze of shrouds and taut lines. The vessel's name, *Lupo*, was painted in enormous black letters on the hull. On the upper gun deck, a young man peered out from one of the gun ports. He couldn't have been but sixteen. He looked lanky and underfed, the whites of his eyes reminding Mari of something dead.

At least, Mari thought briefly, her little sister, Sofia, wasn't alive to face this.

Someone on the main deck threw down a rope ladder, and one of the men in Mari's tender scampered his way up, his limbs moving deftly, like an insect. Once aboard, he and another deckhand threw down a pair of ropes with heavy, iron hooks. Mari's captors quickly secured the hooks to their small boat.

She jolted as the pulley engaged. Upward they moved, out of the water, a sense of unsteady weightlessness seizing her. Soon, the tender was level with the ship's main deck.

The deckhands pulled Vivi from the boat first, steadying her as she took a long step over the gap from the boat onto the ship. One of the men whistled and groped the front of her, but once she was securely on deck, he cried out: Vivi had just slammed the heel of her shoe onto his toe.

A moment later, limping, he whisked her away.

"Where are you taking her?" Mari cried out, watching as her friend disappeared into a hatch leading belowdecks. In the distance, the village of Positano was dark, silent. Amid the hillside, Mari caught a flicker of light: a lantern, probably, still lit in someone's window.

No one answered her. Instead, Matteo yanked her upward from her seated position. She slipped, crying out as she fell against his broad, bony shoulder. She'd hit her nose, and it began to bleed profusely.

She glanced over the edge of the tender, now hovering about five meters above the water. Beneath her, the sea rolled, black and menacing. And yet, for the first time in a long time, Mari longed for the water, the relative safety of it.

She heard a muffled scream: Vivi, somewhere inside the ship. Were the Fontana girls there, too? Or Lia? Though she desperately wanted to reunite with them, Mari couldn't be sure these men would send her down the same hatch as the others. She was not willing to gamble with such unknowns. She had sacrificed herself for Pippa on the beach, and she was glad she'd done it: she'd choose this peril for herself over Pippa any day. But admittedly, Mari had not considered what would come next—what she would do when faced with the predicament of captivity.

I cannot save any of these women if I am locked in a cell in the hold,

Mari thought, eyeing the ship. She swallowed, tasting iron as her nose still bled heavily.

She discreetly shuffled her feet a few inches, getting a better look at the water. How deep was it, anyway? Deep enough for this large ship to drop anchor, so at least twenty, thirty meters. At this depth, there would certainly be sharks, jellyfish. The water would be frigid. And her hands—they were still tied tightly behind her back. The temperature, even the threat of sharks, she could tolerate. But the knots binding her? That proved another challenge entirely. She would need to hold her breath a very long time and remain underwater as she attempted to work her way out of the ropes.

Now more than ever, she was grateful for the *cimaruta* around her neck. She would need all the help she could get.

Mari eyed the chasm. In a single, fleeting moment—after Matteo had let go of her, but before the man on deck had grabbed her—she took a long breath and pitched herself over the side.

She heard the men's shouts, their belligerent curses, before she even hit the water.

A moment later she felt the shock of frigid water, her body fully immersed. Water this cold triggered an instinctual urge to gasp for air. It would pass, if only she could calm herself and let her body adapt.

Using only her legs, she propelled herself sideways, toward the front of the ship, so she would not float to the surface in sight of the men. Suddenly, she felt the tickle of stones against her neck: her *cimaruta* had come undone. Mari cursed as it slipped from her neck and began to sink. With her hands bound behind her, she gave a little spin and reached for it with fumbling fingers, grasping the coral fragment at the last moment.

Several gunshots pierced the water very near her. With her *cimaruta* in her hand, Mari kicked deeper, staying well below the surface for as long as she could manage. A steady, thudding sound in the water surrounded her, like someone beating a drum underwater.

It was the ocean, pulsing in rhythm with Mari's heartbeat.

★ ★ ★

When the shots and shouts had grown distant, she dared to kick her way up and lift her head above the waves.

She was beneath the long, copper-sheathed bowsprit, hidden from view. The air now felt colder than the water, and her nosebleed had ceased, too. But with her arms still pinned, treading water was difficult. As she struggled to stay afloat, she considered her options, any way to use her magic to save the women she'd just left behind. But the women were now deep in the bowels of the *Lupo*; conjuring a whirlpool that endangered the ship would do more harm than good.

Mari coughed, swallowing a mouthful of seawater. She needed to save herself first, then decide on another plan. She eyed the village, took another deep breath, and went under again.

Underwater, she made for the direction of the village. It was difficult, at first, to swim with only her legs, but as the seconds passed, she understood it was like being a fish, and she could pin her legs together, using them as one to effectively propel herself forward. The current, too, was favorable: the tide was going in, and while swimming against it would have been a great effort, swimming with it was not so bad.

All the while, Mari tugged at the rope tied around her hands, encouraged when a few of the wet hemp fibers came loose. After a few more minutes of pulling and twisting, the knots gave way, and Mari's hands were free. They were numb on account of the cold, although by now Mari had swum so hard, this minor discomfort hardly bothered her. She merely longed for the shore.

She lifted her head above the water every minute or so to check her location and ensure no one had followed her. Had the men assumed her drowned and dead? To her great relief, they had not lowered the tender back into the water, and she didn't see any shadows moving on the main deck.

Forward she went, growing calmer as she neared the village. If the men had intended to catch up with her, she would know it by now. But it was very silent, just Mari and the dark sea. The ocean's pulsing, thudding sound had not ceased, but it had grown slower and softer.

Finally, her feet touched bottom. She stood up, exhausted, and began to wade her way to the shore. Had an hour passed? Twice that? Her legs shook, her head throbbed, and still she could not feel her hands. But she was safe. She was alive. She could now get to work on devising a plan to save the women who had been captured.

As she stumbled out of the water, it dawned on Mari that she had not used any magic at all tonight. Much had worked in her favor: the water had been cold enough to stop the blood seeping from her nose. The direction of the tide had lessened the work of swimming. And, most importantly, the ocean—dark and ominous as it was—had kept her well-hidden, cloaking her in darkness. If it had been clear and warm, surely the men on the *Lupo* would have jumped in after her.

And during all of this, her *cimaruta* had been clutched in her hand, not tied around her neck. She hadn't needed its protection at all.

Mari could not deny it: the sea, for all she resented it, had taken great care of her tonight.

Stumbling to the shore, Mari turned to gaze out at the waves. She squinted, searching for the ship she'd just escaped. But it had turned, now headed southwest.

The men sailed off with their three new captives in tow.

Mari collapsed, exhausted and bereft, into the sand.

14

HAVEN

Tuesday

Enzo was late.

Not five minutes, not ten or fifteen, but twenty-six minutes late. I sat in the sand waiting for him, growing less patient—and more discouraged—by the minute. I'd give it four more minutes before I returned to the villa, which now was empty. Mal had taken a shuttle back to Naples around lunchtime. She hadn't been able to book a flight home yet—flights out of the area were sold out, and many were on a standby list in front of her—but in the event a seat opened up, she needed to be near the airport.

At least she'd gotten her old job back. Her former boss had been more than understanding when they spoke over the phone.

Before she left, I told her about my visit to Enzo's dive shop and his agreeing to help me. She'd had mixed feelings. Not because Enzo was a stranger but because she didn't like the idea of an unmanned boat when we were underwater, which meant one less person to handle an emergency. But Mal had known me long enough to know that I would do what I wanted. And if she couldn't stop me, the very best she could do was advise me.

"Have you tested your mask for leaks?" she'd asked.

Yes.

"And your regulator?"

Yes.

"Your dive watch is charged?"

Yes. All of it, I'd assured her, was good to go. I'd been in the water since I was four years old, I reminded her. She'd given me a defeated look before grabbing me by the shoulders, telling me she loved me, and kissing me square on the forehead.

"Then go find what your dad left behind," she said. "And give Conrad the middle finger while you're at it."

Sitting in the sand waiting on Enzo, I wondered if I'd get the chance to do either. But then, I spotted him or, more accurately, his boat. It was blue and white, *Positano Underwater Adventures* printed on its side. I was surprised by its good condition; given the state of his shop, I'd expected the boat to be somewhat ramshackle.

He stood at the helm, waving at me. Exhaling in frustration—I'd nearly begun to pack up my things—I stood, brushed myself off, and walked down the dock.

"*Mi dispiace*," he said over and over. "So sorry, Ms. Ambrose, so very sorry. My mother, she needed help with her Jet Ski. The battery was dead, and she was quite distraught."

I wanted to be mad, but this, if true, was somewhat endearing. I'd have done the same for my dad. "It's okay," I said. "And please, call me Haven." I tossed my gear bag over the boat's aluminum railing and onto the padded bench.

"New boat?" I asked, admiring the flooring, void of dents and scuffs, and the underwater sonar screen tucked in the center console.

"Brand-new boat." He held out his hand to help me on. He wasn't wearing a shirt or shoes. Just a pair of aviators and black swim trunks which, I couldn't help but notice, fit him quite snugly. "The shop is worn-down, I'll admit, but this—" he waved his hand around "—this is what matters."

Enzo slowly backed away from the dock, then leaned forward, turning up the dial on the speakers. A rhythmic beat kicked on—some sort of Italian house music. I leaned my head back against the boat's railing, marveling at the fact that yesterday, I'd been pulled from Project Relic, but here I was now, with an outrageously good-looking Italian man, making straightaway for Li Galli. I smiled, the sunshine overhead turning my cheeks warm. I was pleased with my resourcefulness and thoroughly enjoying the views, too.

To our right, the cliffs outside the village were riddled with eerily dark grottos and ancient stone structures. As Enzo drove, I pulled my gear bag toward me and withdrew a few items. I hadn't brought my camera equipment today, having decided that this would be an acclimation dive. This water was cold, low sixties. Even with a wet suit, it wouldn't be comfortable.

I needed to acclimate to the visibility, too. I'd been spoiled in the Keys, with its diamond-blue water. Some days, visibility was so good we could see a hundred feet or more. But the water alongside Enzo's boat was dark blue, almost black. I couldn't even see fish, much less the ocean floor. Once in the water, I'd have a better sense of the lens filters my camera would need.

I caught Enzo watching me. He turned down the music and slowed the boat, quieting the motors. "So, Haven, here is the little I know about you. You are a researcher. You have nice gear." He eyed the mask I'd just pulled from my bag. "And you want to dive Li Galli."

My heart began to race. It always did before I entered the water—adrenaline, eagerness—but now, I had even more to navigate.

"That's right," I said, choosing my words carefully. "I'm involved in a project to photograph underwater wrecks." This wasn't a lie—I was still technically involved in Project Relic, even if that meant I was handing over a number of files to Conrad. "Ideally," I added, "before Mount Vesuvius erupts again."

"Unlikely to happen in our lifetime," he said.

"Many scientists would vehemently disagree."

"Fair," he replied. Maneuvering us closer to the islets, he motioned to where the yacht had gone down. "Does your project include the newest wreck?" he asked. "The yacht?"

"No," I said. "I'm interested in the older wrecks. Eighteenth- and nineteenth-century."

"I can't imagine there's much left of anything."

"You'd be surprised," I said. In fact, there were an untold number of wrecks throughout the world that were well-preserved despite their age. Especially those partially buried in silt or sand. It was not uncommon for archaeologists to retrieve entire rudders, chains, stoneware jugs. Sometimes, enormous wooden hulls remained intact, even the words engraved on them. Photographs of such things were precisely what Project Relic aimed to compile and render into four-dimensional images. "Every site is different," I told Enzo, who'd begun to rub sunscreen on his lower abdomen. I cleared my throat. "We'll see what this one has to offer."

He nodded, and a pensive expression came over his face. "You have heard of *la Maledizione Amalfitana*?" he asked. "The Amalfi Curse?"

Despite the warm air, a chill came over me. "Of course," I said. "Impossible to research the wrecks in this area and not stumble across a few references." I cocked my head. "What do you think about it?"

"I don't believe in any such thing," he said. "I consider myself more of a realist." Then, quickly, "I hope that does not offend you."

"Not at all," I said. "I feel the same."

He pointed to my gear bag. "Will you be taking photos underwater today?"

I shook my head. "Today, I just need to get in the water—get a feel for the temps and visibility and make sure my gear is good. But next time, yes, I'll bring my camera."

"Next time," he repeated, grinning. "So my being late has not scared you away entirely."

"Not entirely, no." I began to pull on my wet suit, then smiled back at him. "Besides, if your mother is the reason you were late, I suppose I can excuse it."

He pointed back toward land. "See that hilltop, and the villa at the crest of it? She lives there, with a close friend of hers."

I nodded, spotting it easily. "Beautiful," I said. "How long has she lived there?"

"Just a couple of months. She used to live outside Venice, where we—" He stopped himself, cleared his throat. "Where I grew up. The villa has been uninhabited and will take years of renovation." He shook his head. "Much of it to fall on me, I fear."

He hadn't said anything about his father, or any other family for that matter, but I didn't dare pry. "I'm sure it will be lovely, someday." I glanced once more at the house. "The views must be spectacular, too."

"She claims on a clear day she can see Palermo from the terrace. I do not believe her." He smirked. "I was there yesterday. Plenty clear, and I could not see Palermo for shit."

We were approaching the islets, and Enzo turned to the screen on his console, which displayed a sonar map.

"Where in Li Galli would you like to go?" he asked. "The depth is a bit shallow for us in some places, but we can anchor elsewhere and drift-dive our way in."

I withdrew my phone, returning to my father's photos. I navigated to the one with the abovewater GPS coordinates, then pointed to the sonar screen. "Can I give you some coordinates?"

He raised his eyebrows. "Even better." He plugged in the longitude and latitude, steering the boat toward the easternmost islet.

As we approached Li Galli, I spotted a few boats, including, to my dismay, yet another coast guard vessel. Even though the rescue and recovery had been completed, I figured there was still much ahead for them, not the least of which was determining the cause of the yacht's sinking. I wondered if they had found the voyage data recorder yet, the boat's black box.

Enzo brought the boat to a stop, killing the engine and turning off the music. His sonar said we were at a depth of eleven meters. He dropped anchor, then put up the red-and-white Diver Down flag, meant to inform passing mariners that a diver was underwater. I kept my eye on the coast guard vessels, wondering if they would approach and ask us to leave. But after a couple of minutes, it was clear they weren't interested in us.

We bobbed along for a bit in silence. I suspected Enzo might have been quietly paying his respects to the victims, but all I could think of was my father.

He hadn't died here, but still, this dive site had been his last. He'd breathed in this same air, gazed out at these same tiny islets, and immersed himself in these same cold, dark waters. I felt a wave of fresh determination, a desire to fulfill what he couldn't, but the reality of the task at hand wasn't lost on me: I might be within meters of the loot he'd spotted, but this was the ocean. Things moved and shifted and swayed and collapsed. The sea promised nothing. It was possible my father had only spotted the gems because the silt had shifted; the gems could have very well been obscured mere hours later.

Suddenly, my phone dinged—Conrad.

Hiya, kid, he'd texted. Gage said you two talked. Hell of a change in plans, isn't it? But we need to keep you out of harm's way. Your dad would want that.

"Jesus Christ," I muttered to myself. I suddenly hated his pet name for me, *kid*.

His comment about my dad's wishes didn't sit well, either. Would my dad indeed have wanted me off the project? Or would he have trusted me to handle the tumultuous waters? I couldn't decide.

Enzo turned to me. "Did you say something?"

"Sorry, nothing," I said, as another text buzzed.

We need to go over the site plan, Conrad said. Lunch tomorrow, after I land?

I hammered away at my phone's keyboard. **Busy, I said.** Then I silenced my phone and threw it down on the seat next to me.

Wet suits on, we donned the rest of our gear. It wasn't the most glamorous of getups, especially once the fins were on. We made our way toward the swim platform at the back of the boat.

"*Andiamo*," I said. "Ready?"

"After you," he replied, his voice nasally, thanks to the dive mask. I couldn't help but laugh at the youthful look of exhilaration in his eyes. After years of working with subdued divers of the academic sort, Enzo's energy and playfulness were refreshing.

I stepped off the platform. A moment later, I shrieked, cold water instantly flooding the foam pores of the wet suit. It would take a few minutes for my body heat to warm the innermost layer of water within the suit, but even then, wet suits didn't keep you *warm*, they just made cold water feel slightly less miserable. Slightly.

After Enzo had jumped in beside me, we exchanged the Okay sign and began to descend. Instantly, I was disappointed: I'd expected a few meters of good visibility at the very least, but the plankton and floating sediment were so dense I could hardly make out Enzo's form. I scrubbed the outside of my mask with my finger. I'd forgotten to spray it with antifogger before jumping in, but I realized now it hardly mattered.

I stayed close to Enzo, so close I could nearly touch him with my arm extended. The cold, murky water was unnerving. Still, I gave Enzo the Thumbs-down signal, indicating I wanted to keep descending. We were only a few meters deep, and because plankton liked to hover at the ocean's surface, it was possible the water would be clearer once we went deeper. Unfortunately, deeper also meant colder, so we'd be trading one inconvenience for another.

We descended quickly, and I felt Enzo's hand reach for mine. We might have merely clasped hands, but instead, I intertwined my fingers in his.

The visibility improved somewhat, and soon I could make out the hazy seafloor. I pressed the inflator button on my kit to vent air into my vest, slowing my descent. Enzo did the same, and we hovered, weightless, in the dark water.

He pointed to something behind me, and I turned. Just a few meters away lay a pile of wooden boards. I began to swim for it, knowing Enzo would follow me, but upon closer inspection, I frowned. It looked like fragments of a wooden pallet, maybe made of oak. I got closer, squinting at the markings on one of the boards, which appeared to be spray paint. This was recent, then—probably something washed out to sea.

For a few minutes, we traversed a zigzag route underwater, my dive watch tracking our movements. At one point, Enzo did a couple of somersaults next to me, his eyes wide in delight. I couldn't resist, and I did one, too, relishing the little flip in my belly. I hadn't done an underwater somersault in years. And certainly never on a research dive while under the watchful eye of colleagues.

We explored a few other debris piles but found nothing interesting or even very old. Knowing we were right below the coordinates of my father's abovewater photo, I couldn't help but feel a sharp pang of disappointment.

I reminded myself that this dive was about acclimation, nothing more. Besides, according to my watch, we'd only covered an area the size of a tennis court.

I began to tremble, the chill of the water no longer tolerable. I would need to ask Enzo about a thicker wet suit for future dives. We swam back to our starting point, and I gave Enzo the Thumbs-up signal to ascend. Together, once again holding hands, we made our way up, doing a brief safety stop before breaching the surface. My dive watch showed we'd been under for only twenty-two minutes, and the water temperature had gone as low as the midfifties. I'd used a lot of air, too, on account of my nerves and trying to retain body heat.

If these conditions held up, the search for my father's discovery could be brutal, indeed.

Back on the boat, Enzo and I removed our wet suits. With goose bumps and chattering teeth, I wasn't disappointed when he stepped up behind me with a dry towel and draped it around my shoulders, letting his hands linger a moment. Nor was I disappointed when he retrieved a thermos of hot *caffè amaretto* from the center console.

"Not a popular drink with most summer tourists," he said, handing me the thermos. "But then again, most of them aren't diving to the bottom of the Tyrrhenian Sea."

I took a long drink, and my teeth ceased their chattering in an instant. "Thank you," I said, leaning my head back, letting the sun warm my forehead. I still had goosebumps. "That was… cold. Like, *fucking cold*."

He laughed. "Good for your circulation," he said, taking a drink himself.

"Do you have a thicker wet suit at the shop?"

"Of course." He ran the back of his hand over his lips. "When do you want to go back out?"

"When would work for you?" I asked, somewhat sheepishly. I hated to overstep; Enzo had been incredibly generous so far.

"Tomorrow morning? Tomorrow afternoon? I don't get into the water enough. Any excuse I can find…"

"Either would be great," I said. "Either or both. I'd feel guilty asking, but given your somersaults, it's clear you were having a good time down there."

"Of course," he said. "I don't take anything too seriously, Haven. I worked too hard for my business, my freedom. I want to enjoy it."

Using his towel as a cover, he slipped off his wet swim trunks, replacing them with a dry pair. He turned the music back on and took a seat next to me. "Did you bring a change of clothes? There's a small cabin, and bathroom, below."

With so much on my mind, I'd completely neglected to bring something to change into. "I forgot," I said. "I'll warm up on my walk to my villa, though. More than four hundred stairs. I counted." I handed the thermos back to him, our fingers brushing.

He paused a moment, his cheeks flushing. "Could I take you to dinner later?"

Given my streak of bad dates with fellow scuba divers, I nearly said *no*. But nothing about Enzo reminded me of my previous dates, what with their seriousness and preoccupation with academia. On the contrary, Enzo was doing somersaults and whipping out thermoses of spiked coffee.

"Yes," I said, eyeing his lips as he took another long drink. "I'd love that."

"*Bene.*" By the expression on his face, I thought him pleasantly surprised I'd accepted. "Seafood? Pizza? Mascarpone gelato?"

"All of the above." I checked my watch; it wasn't even five thirty. "I'll just clean up, then meet you wherever you'd like."

"Excellent." He passed me the thermos once more, then reached for his phone and sighed loudly.

"What is it?" I asked.

"My mother, again. She broke her key inside one of the exterior locks." He made for the console and turned on the engines. "Don't tell her I said this, but sometimes she frustrates me to no end. The Jet Ski battery she asked me to fix earlier? I could find nothing wrong with it. It started right up." He turned to face me. "The villa, though, it's something else. Any interest in seeing it before dinner?"

I widened my eyes. "Your mother won't mind a visitor?"

He threw his head back and laughed. "Oh, not one bit. She loves showing it off. It has a belvedere terrace unlike anything you'll find in town. We can hop on my scooter, swing by your place to change, then head that way. Maybe have an aperitif while we're there?"

It sounded divine. And when else might such an opportunity present itself? "I'd love to see it," I said.

With a nod, Enzo flipped the music back on and put the boat into gear. Already, the hot amaretto had left me feeling light, giddy.

But as he drove us back to shore, I gazed upward at his mother's villa, high on its hilltop, overlooking the ocean. I was sure I spotted someone standing on the terrace, looking toward Li Galli. Another chill came over me, and I wrapped my towel more tightly around my shoulders, forcing my gaze away.

15

HOLMES

Sunday, April 22, 1821
Bay of Naples

On Sunday evening, aboard the *Aquila*, Holmes wrote a short letter to Mari informing her of their shift in itinerary and his expedited arrival into Positano. Quinto had just come by, advising all men to have their mail ready by seven o'clock the next morning, for a dispatch boat would be taking any letters, and a few of the captain's documents, into the city.

Later that night, something woke him: the hiss of ropes, the groan of straining wood. He thought he heard the cry of the pulleys, too, as though a tender had arrived with newcomers.

He lay awake for the better part of an hour, trying to fall back asleep. One of the men near him snored and panted in fits. With a sigh of frustration, Holmes gave up on sleep, lit a candle in his berth, and reached for his diary.

He considered writing down a few thoughts, but his pen was nowhere to be found—it must have slipped between the wall and his thin mattress—so instead, he occupied himself with reading old entries. He turned to an entry from December of last year, during a stopover in Positano, when he'd known Mari for nearly seven months.

It has been weeks since I last saw her, he'd written. *I waited for her in the grove, eating a few fat olives I'd plucked from a laden branch.*

She knew to look for me there; I'd sent a letter telling her when I'd be back. Finally, I spotted her approaching, a mischievous grin on her face. She carried a basket and a thick blanket in her arms.

As she came close, I opened my mouth to speak, but then she pressed her lips to mine in a way she has never done before. Her breathing was quick, her nails sharp against the back of my neck. She took my hands, put them low on her waist, and whispered a few things I have never in all my life heard a woman say.

We tumbled our way to the ground, our lips interlocked, our hips pressed close.

After two hours, finally we managed to say hello. We shared the figs she'd brought from the house, talking all the while. She told me her father had taken Cleila and Paola to Sorrento but, having received my letter, she feigned an illness in order to stay home.

A short while later, she began to giggle. My hands had left a smudge of tar on the softest, highest part of her inner thigh. I offered her a kerchief at once, but she refused. "I hope it never washes off," she whispered, before placing my hand there again.

We made love a second time. "Already," she said afterward, "you are learning me."

Later, Mari spotted the olive pits I'd spit onto the ground. She collected them one by one, dropping them into her bag. She told me she wanted to keep them, to remind her of this night.

Holmes read through a few more entries as his shipmate's snoring droned on. Eventually he could stand it no longer, so he heaved himself out of his berth, tucked a cigarette behind his ear, and climbed the ladder to the deck.

As he went, he passed the second mate's cabin. The padlock hung from the door, unlocked. Was someone inside the room now? Though curious, he didn't dare approach—he shuddered to think what would happen if he were caught peeking inside.

He continued on his way. It was very dark on the main deck,

early as it was. Holmes made straight for the stern, thinking he might tuck himself under the shrouds and have a smoke. Ahead, port side, lay the city of Naples, wrapped in fog.

Midship, Holmes heard whispered voices near one of the hatches leading to the officers' cabins. Quinto's unmistakably raspy growl was one of them. Ducking behind a capstan, Holmes then heard another voice: the captain's.

Holmes paused, not wanting to be caught. He wasn't doing anything wrong, but he was not in the mood to engage with anyone at this hour, least of all the officers.

Massimo, Quinto was saying over and over. *Massimo Mazza, Massimo Mazza.* It almost sounded as though he were crying.

And then, *Il mio amico è morto.*

My friend is dead.

He went on to explain that Matteo Mazza had informed him of it not an hour ago.

"Matteo?" the captain exclaimed.

"Indeed. He boarded a short while ago. He is in the second mate's cabin, sifting through some of the maps. He does not want to be bothered."

Holmes *had* heard the arrival of a tender, then. It had been Matteo with the news of his younger brother's death. That explained why the cabin's padlock was undone, too.

"What happened?" the captain asked. "Who killed him?"

"A woman," Quinto spat. "Nearly a week ago. Matteo was some distance away, but he watched her do it, watched as she drowned him."

"Massimo could not fight her off?"

"She used the water against him. As if the sea were at her command. And Matteo said her hair was…impossibly red."

Holmes held his breath. *Impossibly red*. Mari fit this description.

"Red hair?" the captain repeated. "Why, that's—"

"Yes," Quinto interrupted. "Precisely. She was with a young girl, also. Matteo managed to seize the child."

The two men shuffled their feet, and Holmes prayed they

would not come any closer. Stalking the empty deck for a smoke was not a crime, but eavesdropping on officers certainly was.

"Matteo thinks they were mistaken long ago," Quinto went on. "The village may be full of these redheaded *puttane*."

"My God," the captain said. "Think of it..."

"Indeed." Holmes heard a thlunk, as though one of the men had just kicked something. "We are under directive to seize them all," Quinto said. "Every last one."

At this, Holmes stumbled forward a step, suddenly off balance.

"Where are we to take these captives?" the captain asked.

"Ischia," Quinto said quickly. "Castello Aragonese. The child—six or seven years old, they think—is already there. According to Matteo, another woman, and two sisters, were delivered to the island only yesterday, via the *Lupo*."

"Is one of them the woman who killed Massimo?"

"No," Quinto said. "They nearly had her on. At the last moment, she threw herself from the tender into the water."

"Do they believe her dead? Escaped?"

Holmes held his breath, waiting for Quinto's answer. If this woman was indeed Mari, he was encouraged by the fact that she had jumped into the water. Mari had always been an exceptional swimmer.

"Not dead," Quinto said. "They think she stayed under and swam back to shore. We are to make our way to Positano even quicker now, if we can. Before they all flee."

"Damn the winds," the captain hissed. "Had they not shifted last night, we could be there in a day."

The winds, yes. Gusts had been strong from the north for the last week, but yesterday evening they had altered, now coming from the west. And the winds were strong.

A storm was on its way, they all suspected.

"And once we arrive in Positano? What then?" the captain asked.

"We seize any woman with red hair. Though we are looking, especially, for the woman who killed Massimo. Matteo heard the other women calling to her the night they almost got her onto the *Lupo*. It seems her name is Mari."

Holmes squeezed his eyes shut tight, his suspicions confirmed. Mari had killed a man. And not just any man—one of the most powerful men in the region. She must have been in grave danger if she had resorted to violence. She must have been terrified.

How brave you are, my Mari, he thought.

And what of the letter he'd just written to her? He might as well toss it into the sea. It would not be going to Mari, not in light of all he'd heard. He needed to hurry back down to his berth and pen her a new letter telling her all he knew: Matteo was on this brig, and they were coming straight for her.

She needed to flee.

Quinto and the captain spoke for a few more minutes. The captain asked whether any more thefts had been reported among the men.

"No," Quinto assured him. "Not to my knowledge."

Finally, they parted ways. Once all was silent and clear, Holmes made his way back belowdecks.

Fingers trembling, he tore his letter to Mari into tiny pieces and began to write her anew. He could hardly hold his pen steady; his sloppy, shaky handwriting betrayed the turmoil inside of him. Mari would spot it at once; before even reading a word, she would know something was wrong.

He dropped his new letter into the mailbag a short while later, in plenty of time for the dispatch boat to take into town at seven o'clock.

But still, something inside chewed at him. He was not willing to gamble Mari's life on a race against the postman. He needed to guarantee—not merely hope—that his letter got to her before the *Aquila* arrived in Positano.

He had a very good idea in mind—but it was a dangerous one. If he were caught, Quinto and Matteo would think nothing of flogging him or tying him to the mast.

Despite this, his mind was made up.

It was what must be done.

16

HAVEN

Tuesday

Back at my Airbnb, Enzo parked his Vespa. I rushed inside to change, throwing on an ankle-length pale pink sundress with an open back. I thought it equally tasteful and flirtatious, though it proved a challenge when I tried to get onto the scooter, as I had to pull the dress to my knees in order to sit properly. Enzo seemed not to notice—or at least he did a good job pretending he didn't.

"Does your mother know you're bringing a guest by?" I asked him.

"I texted her, yes," he said, starting the motor. "She's thrilled to have a visitor. Her housemate won't be there. She's in Sorrento for the day."

Enzo expertly navigated the scooter between narrow rows of moving traffic. Soon, we were outside the village, heading west on Amalfi Drive. It was the same road Mal and I had taken yesterday morning.

"Wait," I said, spotting a roadside flower stand ahead. I motioned for Enzo to pull over, then I quickly hopped off the scooter and bought a burlap-wrapped bundle of tiny white wild roses. It was the least I could offer Enzo's mother while showing up unannounced with her son.

I hopped back onto the scooter. "What's your mother's name, by the way?"

"Savina."

"How beautiful."

"It is, yes." He paused. "She's somewhat...challenging, though. You know how mothers can be."

Actually, I didn't. I'd never been close with my mom. She lived in Manhattan, and we rarely saw one another. I'd long ago made peace with it, and besides, my growing-up years never felt short on love.

Keeping this to myself, I wrapped my arms around his waist as he pulled onto the street. "Does she speak English?" I shouted over the motor.

He nodded. "Of course. Though, she will be very touched if you try your Italian on her."

"Got it," I said, trying to remember a few basic pleasantries. I couldn't seem to think straight, not with my face so close to the back of Enzo's neck and my bare thighs wrapped around his hips.

Eventually, he slowed the scooter and pulled onto a narrow gravel path hardly wide enough for a small car. Trees stood all around us; we were in a thicket of sorts, and an old wrought iron gate, closed and latched, loomed just ahead.

"The villa was abandoned for a long time. We aren't even sure, really, when anyone last lived here." Enzo hopped off the scooter and unlatched the gate. "Some of the walls had graffiti on them. People love abandoned places, especially kids and tourists. My mother is still worried about trespassers."

"Do you know when it was built?" I asked as we passed through the gate. Though the pillars on either side were crumbling, the detail on the gate itself was extraordinary. A motif consisting of flowers and snakes lent a haunted-mansion feel.

"Mid-1700s, we think," Enzo said. As we began to drive up the wooded hillside, the scooter's motor whined in complaint; it was steeper than it looked. "And parts of it still look that old. The terrace is the highlight of the property, but don't get too excited about the rest of it. It has a long way to go."

He wasn't wrong about this. After we made our way out of the trees, the villa appeared in all its Old World glory: the stucco facade had peeled away in some areas and crumbled entirely in others. A few of the second-story windowpanes were broken or missing altogether.

No wonder Savina had been messaging Enzo for help with the place. It didn't even seem safe for habitation.

An enormous bumblebee hovered near my hand, and I gently swatted it away. "Does it have..." I didn't want to offend him or sound judgmental. I was merely curious. "Does it have electricity and water?"

He laughed, turning the motor off. "Yes. Both were installed before she moved in." He pocketed the keys and helped me off the scooter.

"Well, it's stunning," I said, and I meant it. This wasn't the touristy Positano of below, riddled with knickknack shops and hordes of tourists. And while I couldn't yet see the terrace, I suspected the view would be breathtaking.

A woman's head popped out of one of the broken upper windows. "*Il mio Enzo!*" she called out with a grin. She wore bright red lipstick, and her ash-colored hair was pulled aside in a long braid. She struck me, at once, as warm and spirited.

Something about her also struck me as familiar.

She asked Enzo a question in Italian, which I couldn't comprehend. "*Ciao, Mamma,*" he replied, then he began to speak to her in rapid-fire Italian, likely about me, the unexpected visitor. Feeling somewhat embarrassed and exposed, I gazed around the property, admiring the many purple and pink wildflowers adorning the perimeter.

Inside, I was able to have a closer look at Savina, and I realized where I'd seen her: on the beach yesterday. She'd been the woman walking the shoreline with her friend, crying. I wondered if that friend was her roommate.

Briefly, I thought of Mal. She was still in Naples, waiting on a flight out.

I gave Savina the bundle of wild roses, which she fawned over for a few moments before setting them on the countertop, next to a framed photo of a young woman who looked remarkably like Enzo. "My daughter, Bria," she said.

I did my best to say a few words to Savina in Italian—*Lovely to meet you* and a slew of thanks—but to my relief, she responded in English, releasing me of any obligation to speak to her in her native language.

They spent a few minutes giving me a tour of the villa's sparse interior. It was clear renovations were underway: buckets of paint sat against one wall, and a not-yet-mounted chandelier dominated the floor of the main living space. There was almost no furniture beyond a chaise lounge and a small table. It gave me a curious, sudden sense of gloom.

The terra-cotta tile floors were one of the villa's most magnificent features. I asked if they'd been newly installed, but Enzo insisted they were original. "Just last week," he said with a discreet roll of the eyes, "I polished them to within an inch of their life."

"I don't need much," Savina added. "But thank goodness my friend and I have Enzo to help with these tasks. My husband, Enzo's father, died many years ago." Her expression turned wistful, and I understood now why Enzo had not mentioned his father. This was something we had in common, and I made a mental note to ask him about it when the time felt right.

"Let me show you the terrace," Enzo said.

"Ah, the terrace, yes!" Savina echoed.

Together, the three of us approached a pair of glass doors at the villa's south end. Sheer curtains hung in front of them. At once, Enzo pulled them aside and threw the doors open. I gasped, clasping my hand over my mouth.

I had expected a good view, but I had not expected *this*. Looking west, I could see as far as the Isle of Capri, and looking east and south, Enzo pointed out Salerno and San Marco. He explained that a belvedere terrace like this one was designed with the landscape in mind: the white limestone railing was hip-high so as not to obstruct one's view. The word *belvedere*, he explained, meant to look upon something beautiful, and indeed I could think of no fairer sight than the one in front of me now. It was as if the entire Amalfi Coast were spread out before us.

"But where's Palermo?" I whispered into Enzo's ear, remembering how we'd joked about this earlier.

He turned to me, all dimples and brown eyes. "You're a quick one, Ambrose."

No one had ever called me by my last name, and I quite liked it now.

I turned to Savina. "How amazing that you were able to buy property in such a desirable area. I'd think the hotels would have made strong bids on a property like this."

"Oh, this was never for sale," Savina said. "It's been passed down through many generations of friends, family. We Italians, we're very close, you know." She placed her hands on the railing. "The hotels never had a chance. I'm glad for it, too. Positano has seen enough. If it goes on like this much longer, why, I think its charm will be altogether lost."

Enzo stepped up behind us, three shot glasses perched in his palm. He must have retreated while we were talking. Within each glass was a bright yellow, almost neon, liquid.

"Limoncello?" he offered.

We both took a glass, and Savina went on, "I, for one, am not terribly disappointed by what I've heard on the news recently."

I remembered what Enzo had said about his mother and her challenging manner, yet I couldn't help but balk at the callousness of her comment. "The yacht sinking, you mean, or the concerns about Vesuvius?"

She gave a stiff nod and took a sip of her limoncello. "Both," she said. "I heard there have been an unprecedented number of flight cancellations this week."

"I've heard the same. Are you worried about Mount Vesuvius?"

"Not a bit." Then she lifted her glass. "*Salute.*"

I reluctantly lifted my glass and took a sip, anticipating the bright, sweet citrus flavor. Instead, it tasted flat, almost bitter.

"That is the olive grove," Savina said, pointing to a grove of trees extending down the hillside. "If you weave your way down the hill for some time, you will come upon Amalfi Drive, and then below that, a *stairway to the sea*, as we like to call it. We have a pair of Jet Skis at the base of the steps. Enzo and I have gone out a few times." She took a step away. "Come, let me show you the olive grove."

"Of course," I said, glad we'd changed topics.

Enzo busied himself with the broken door lock his mother had mentioned earlier, while Savina led me down the terrace steps and into the grove. It was in as much disrepair as the house itself. "I have quite a bit of tidying to do," she said, "but most of these trees are still alive. Olive trees live for hundreds of years." She pointed to a small cluster of them in a nearby wooded thicket. "Strange that a few of them also managed to sprout over there." She continued walking. "I'll plant citrus, too. Someday, I'd like to be able to make my own limoncello." She held up her glass and tossed it back.

Feeling vaguely unsettled, I did the same.

We wove our way through the grove, Savina examining a

few wild shrubs. Suddenly, she turned to me, her face newly flushed—though, whether it was from the alcohol or the bright sunshine, I wasn't sure. "Enzo is thirty-nine, you know, and not getting any younger."

This surprised me: given Enzo's adventurous spirit and his near-flawless skin, I wouldn't have guessed him older than thirty-five.

"He doesn't look it," I replied. "And how about your daughter—is she older or younger than Enzo?"

Savina gazed up at the house. "Bria passed away last year. Very unexpectedly. She and Enzo, they were...twins."

"Oh," I said, putting my hand over my mouth.

She plucked a couple of yellowing leaves from a bush. "I've lived a harder life than most," she said. "I thought I'd endured it all—losing my husband, struggling financially for so long—but then, *Bria*." She reached into her pocket and pulled out a mascara-stained tissue. "Sometimes, I feel cursed. How much more can I sustain?" she asked, dabbing at her eyes. "Bria wanted to marry someday, to have children. I cannot say the same for Enzo. All he thinks about is work. If not for the help I need here, at the villa, I am sure I would not even see him." She let out a long sigh. "I desperately hope for grandchildren, but as of late, I've begun to fear it is not in the cards. Enzo has not brought a girl home in many years," she said. She tucked the tissue back into her pocket, put on a smile. "Which means I am so very pleased to see you."

Oh, I thought. *Oh, no. She thinks we are...a couple.*

"We're n—" I stammered, shuffling my feet. "Well, we're just friends. We only met this morning. I'm a scuba diver, and he took me out on a dive this afternoon."

A flash of worry crossed her face. "He took you out on the water?" When I nodded, she gazed up at the terrace. "He told me he stays in the shop and lets his employee take divers out."

"It was a special favor, I guess."

Savina resumed walking through the grove, stepping her way carefully over a few exposed roots. We talked about underwater photogrammetry and my research in the nautical archaeology space. I tried my best to keep my explanations simple, not knowing whether some of the more technical aspects might be lost in translation.

"Very interesting," Savina finally said, though her face was not so convincing. "How did you get into the field?"

I told her about my late father and his interest in shipwrecks, treasure-hunting. At this, she turned to me, her eyes bright. "Reminds me of Giuseppe Ferlini. You have heard of him?"

I laughed. "Heard of him, yes." An Italian treasure hunter in the 1800s, he plundered more than forty pyramids in Egypt and died a rich man. "Truthfully, I'm more interested in the wrecks themselves, but certainly, there are rumors of sunken treasure that do intrigue me."

"Especially for someone like you, who has the skill set to explore the wrecks."

I smiled to myself. If only she knew.

As we continued talking, Enzo approached.

"Quite a few archaeological ruins in the Bay of Naples," Savina was saying as her son walked up.

"Yes, there are," I said. "But no need to go so far. Turns out, there are plenty of wrecks here along the coastline. Especially around Li Galli."

"Li Galli?" Savina said, voice tight. Then, she turned to Enzo. "Is that where you two went today?"

We nodded simultaneously, and Savina bristled. "That is not safe, Enzo," she said, shaking her head. She began to talk at him in rapid Italian, waving her hands in the air. I thought, for a moment, she might begin to cry again.

"It's fine, *Mamma*," Enzo said, trying to settle her. "The currents were fine, and we were nowhere near where the yacht—"

She interrupted him, spouting off more Italian. I didn't need to understand what she was saying in order to gather that she was horrified by our choice of dive site.

I caught the word *Vesuvius*. As she said it, she used her hands to mimic a volcano erupting. And yet she'd just said she wasn't worried about an eruption.

Savina, I was beginning to realize, could be a bit dramatic.

"Okay." Enzo held up his hands. "I hear you. I hear you."

Savina eyed him for a moment as if she weren't ready to concede, then she began to walk again. Behind her back, Enzo shot me an I'm-sorry glance.

Beautiful as the villa was with its panoramic views, I was ready to leave. After the mention of Li Galli, Savina's mood had shifted so suddenly that now I felt uncomfortable, like I'd intruded on a family argument.

I was relieved when Enzo said he'd fixed the lock and it was time to leave for our dinner reservation. We said goodbye to Savina, and I wished her well with her renovations before hurrying my way back to the scooter.

I was glad we'd come, for the views from up here were indeed outstanding.

But truth be told, I had no desire to return.

17

MARI

Monday, April 23, 1821

On Monday, Dante returned from Naples. He'd been gone for a week.

Lia was not with him.

When Ami saw that he'd returned alone, she fell to her knees sobbing. Mari had been sitting with her in the kitchen, the room dim despite it being midday: they had the curtains pulled closed, for Mari was secreted away at their house. Only her father and the other *streghe* knew she was here.

As Ami composed herself, Mari told Dante all that happened since he'd been gone: the arrival of the *Lupo*. The additional kidnappings. Leo's murder.

The news had made its way quickly around the village. Through households and merchant shops, down the hillsides and around winding avenues, the whispers could be heard: *Three more kidnapped, and a man killed, too.*

Lia's abduction, they all knew now, had been a glimpse of what was to come. Some of the village men wept in broad daylight, lamenting that their good fortune had, at long last, come to an end.

Signs of the incident were still visible, too. Grooves cut through the sand where the women had been dragged to the waiting tenders, and a fat bloodstain marked the place where Leo had fallen on the stone pathway after being shot.

The villagers felt helpless. The police in Naples would favor the Fratelli Mazza, as they always had. The brothers had too much money, too many friends in the right places.

To most, there seemed no explanation. The four women seized from the village—a child, a well-loved baker, and the Fontana sisters—were of varying ages and social classes. While some villagers speculated the assailants had been after a specific family—unpaid debts, perhaps—others thought the men would hold the women for ransom.

Only the other *streghe* knew this was not true. This had nothing to do with a ransom.

Despite the many questions circulating, there was only one question that mattered. Where were the women? Everyone wanted to bring them home.

Upon learning the most recent news, Dante sat down at the small table in his kitchen, placing his head in his hands. "I don't understand," he said, shaking his head, his words muffled behind his palms. "So long as I can remember, Positano has prospered. Our fishermen, our children. We have been blessed with all we need. More than. And we have been *safe*." He looked up at Mari, desperation in his eyes. "My child is gone. My friend is dead. What have we done to deserve this?"

He began to weep.

"I wish there was something we could do," he went on, despite his tears. "Some way to protect these waters forever. The sight of the sea has always comforted me. Never again. From now on, I will be watching for their ships."

There is a way to protect the waters, Mari thought, *for a very long while, at least.* She watched Dante swipe away a tear with the back of his hand. *It is the* vortice centuriaria, *and any of us women would die if we recited it.*

Mari turned away, shamed at the pain she'd brought upon him and Ami, the pain she'd brought upon this entire village. What an impostor she felt, too. No one, not even Ami, knew that Mari intended to abscond from this place with Holmes. If the other women knew the real Mari, they would not want her as their leader or even their friend.

In all her life, Mari had never felt so ashamed, so alone in her inner turmoil.

At least, she thought, Holmes was far away from all of this. It was a small comfort, even if it meant their plan to escape together had come to a sudden, unforeseen halt.

They'd settled on the details in early March when they'd last seen each other.

During Holmes's next visit to Positano, they would meet on the beach in the middle of the night. Mari would leave a change of clean clothes in the sand to give the appearance that she'd gone for a late-night swim, but really, Holmes would be waiting in a *gozzo*, ready to row her to nearby Praiano, where no one knew her. From there, they would take the overland route to Naples.

Her friends and fellow villagers would wait for her. As the hours passed, they would grow worried, wondering if Mari had swum to a nearby grotto or rowed her way toward the turbulent waters around the Li Galli islets.

Soon, they would begin to search for her. Someone would be assigned the unenviable task of rushing to Mari's home to share the news with her father, but even he would be unable to find her.

Eventually, they would assume she drowned. They would wait many days and weeks, grieving, wondering if her bloated body might wash ashore. Wondering if the sea might give her back.

They would call it fate, someday. The ocean had taken her mother, her sister. It was Mari's destiny to fall victim to it herself, wasn't it? Those who longed for her—Ami and Lia, especially—would comfort themselves with the belief that Mari was in a happier place now, looking down upon the sea for endless days.

Mari and Holmes, meanwhile, would be making their way north. They didn't know where exactly they would settle, only that it would be someplace far away where the sea could not wreak havoc on Mari's life any longer.

But now, the plan would have to wait. Mari had brought too much upon her village; she was determined to set it right.

And she would never stop looking for Lia.

After Dante composed himself, he informed Ami and Mari that he, too, had news to share.

He began by recounting his trip to Naples, telling the women about his futile efforts to recover Lia. Though he'd ridden his horse hard after leaving the village, he never managed to catch up to a man matching the description Mari had given him, leading him to wonder if Lia's captor had taken her to Naples at all.

Once in the city, he'd stalked the establishments where the Mazza brothers were known to do their business. Not only their offices, but their docks along the Bay of Naples. He'd hoped to spot Matteo and, having brought a gun, he was ready to take any measure necessary to gather information on his daughter's whereabouts.

He never found him. He did, however, encounter a young stevedore unloading cargo on the Mazza docks. Handing over a pocketful of coins, Dante begged for any information about Matteo Mazza.

The stevedore took the money and shared a few interesting pieces of information.

First and foremost, he said that the night prior, he'd helped load a case of clothing onto a small Fratelli Mazza boat destined for the nearby island of Ischia. It was women's clothing, he said, and there were a few children's frocks, as well.

"They are alive, then," Ami sputtered, reaching for Dante's hand.

He nodded. "I believe so. I asked the boy if he knew of any boatmen I could hire to take me to Ischia. He told me the Fratelli Mazza were not permitting anyone onto the island, and that only a few days ago, their men shot and killed a fisherman who got too close to the rocks." He shook his head. "I might think the young stevedore a very good tale-teller, if not for the fact that a few others were discussing the fisherman's death, too."

Mari and Ami shared a somber glance, speechless.

"That is not all," Dante said, his voice grave. "There is another Mazza vessel en route to Positano at this very moment."

Mari went still. Could he be referring to Holmes's brig, the *Aquila*?

"It is in Naples now," Dante continued, "and expected to arrive in two days' time. Maybe less, depending on the incoming storm and the favorability of the winds."

It wasn't the *Aquila*, then. Holmes was well north of Rome, many days or weeks away.

Dante paused, taking a long breath. "The stevedore told me that Matteo Mazza himself is aboard. We need to leave the village," he concluded. "All of us. It is the safest thing to do."

"I am not leaving without Lia," Ami disputed. "What if Vivi and Lia manage to escape? This will be the first place they go."

"They may find us dead," Dante argued, "given all these men have done to us so far."

"Dead or not, I'm not leaving," Ami said to her husband, resolute.

"Nor am I," Mari added. Not with another vessel, and Matteo, en route. She wouldn't dare run from the very peril she'd brought upon this village.

Besides, she had begun to settle upon a very grave idea.

★ ★ ★

Late that evening, the ten remaining village *streghe* gathered in Ami's tiny one-room bakery, tucked at the far end of one of Positano's many inconspicuous alleyways.

They arrived one by one, their faces grim. Many of them, Mari included, had dressed in men's attire, with their hair tucked up in hats.

The bakery was cool inside; its stone walls were impervious to the day's warmth, and Ami had not done any baking for days, given all that had happened. Candles lined the edges of the room. The women lingered in silence, waiting for Ami to explain the reason she'd gathered them all on Mari's behalf. The flagstones were slick with flour, and the crowded room smelled of rotting lemons and stale almonds.

Ami sat next to Pippa, her arm protectively around the girl. One had lost her daughter; the other, her parents. Now, Pippa was staying with the oldest of the *streghe*, Emilia, who lived only a few houses away with her husband.

Mari walked to the front of the room. She could hardly look at any of them.

Just before Mari began to speak, Emilia raised her hand into the air. "Mari," she said, "Pippa and I saw something strange last night. We think you ought to know."

"Of course." Mari frowned.

"Someone was by the side of the house, going through my garbage can," Emilia explained. "It was after dark. My dog alerted us. When we went to the window with my husband, the person ran off."

Strange, indeed. In Positano, no one locked their doors or worried about trespassers. "Did you get a good look at him?" Mari asked.

Pippa interjected. "We aren't sure it was a him at all. They were slight in stature. And slender." She wrung her hands together. "My mother complained of something similar a couple of weeks ago," she said. "She thought she saw someone skirting the back of our house, peering in through a window."

Mari frowned. "She never said anything about it to me."

"She convinced herself it was nothing. She'd had a terrible headache all day. She thought she'd merely imagined it."

Across the room, Cleila let out a frustrated sigh. "When will this end?" she asked. "I am tired of living in fear." She put a protective arm around Paola, who kept her gaze locked on the flagstones.

Mari might have thought the trespasser a Mazza scout, if not for the description of the culprit, slight and slender. And Vivi's sighting was strange, too. It greatly unnerved her. The Fratelli Mazza had given them enough to worry about. But a villain so close to home, someone in the village?

She shivered involuntarily, wondering who she could trust anymore.

She forced her attention back to the task at hand. "Today we learned that another Mazza vessel is making its way for Positano," she began. "And Matteo Mazza is on it. It could arrive tomorrow, or the day after."

Emilia leaned forward. "We must go," she said, looking frantically about the candlelit room. "Why are we still here? Why are we not gathering our families to leave?"

"No," Mari said, holding out her hand. "We will not run from them."

Emilia pointed at Pippa. "They took her mother and killed her father," she said. "You're a fool if you think we can protect ourselves against them."

The statement stung, but Mari forged on. She lowered her voice. "I have another idea."

Around the room, silence.

"What is it?" Ami asked, brow furrowed.

Mari took a long breath, then said, "We sink the ship."

A few of the women drew in sharp breaths. As far as they knew, no *strega* had ever sunk an entire vessel.

A few of the women began to whisper, but Mari held up her hand. "The Mazzas, cocksure as they are, have always taken the dangerous Li Galli route instead of the longer, safer path south of it."

Indeed, only the most overconfident of captains ran their routes close to Li Galli; most merchant ships avoided the islets and their invisible whirling eddies, choosing instead to sail well south, around Capri, thus approaching Positano directly from the south.

She went on, "They are fortunate they have not had any issues around the islets. Not yet, anyhow. We will recite the *incantesimo vortice*." Its potency was dependent on the number of women reciting the curse, and the number of times they recited it. Once would generate a small whirlpool, as Mari had done with Massimo. But several of them, reciting the incantation over and over and over? It would be tremendously powerful. "Three of us will recite the curse. We will generate a *vortice* wide and strong enough to upset the ship's ballast, to toss her about before pulling her under."

Murmurs of unease rippled through the room.

"Remember, we are not cursing the vessel herself," Mari went on. "We are cursing the water upon which she sails. Given they will be going through Li Galli, the men will blame the currents. And if we are successful—which we will be—there will be no survivors to say otherwise. Everyone will believe the ship another unfortunate victim of the islets."

Mari felt encouraged by the few nods around the room. She wanted to exploit the ocean's existing danger—its unpredictable underwater maelstroms—and use it to their advantage. To trick the men with the sea.

"We will wait for them near San Pietro," she said, "tucked away in one of the caves."

"Why can we not simply shift the currents away from Positano?" another *strega* asked. "Like we've always done. Like we did last week."

Mari had already considered this, deemed it insufficient. "These men want to seize us." She peered around the circle of women. "They have taken four of us and killed one of our husbands. If they make landfall in Positano, it will be devastating. We cannot let them do it. And with Matteo aboard?" Mari clasped her hands together. "Think of the evil these men have brought upon the region. This will be the end of the brothers. Without them, the Fratelli Mazza, their associates…they will not prosper. Not as they have been."

"We don't know when the ship is coming, though," Paola countered, "and San Pietro is a ninety-minute walk from here. How will three of us get there in time?"

"Beginning tomorrow midday," Mari explained, "we will keep a watch from the cave overlook." The *streghe* had a number of secret meeting locations, but the one near San Pietro was particularly well-suited given its panoramic view of the Amalfi coastline. This cave, like the others, already had several lanterns and floor mats. Mari and Holmes had passed more than a few evenings in the cave; the women would only need to bring food and oil for the lanterns. Mari would bring a blanket or two. "I'll stay there as long as needed. The rest of you can join me in pairs. Every twelve hours, you will switch. That way, we'll always have three of us in place."

"And when we see the ship?"

The room fell silent.

"When we see it," Mari said, "the three of us on watch will wait until it is passing by Li Galli. We will go down to the water, and once it is in position, we will perform the curse."

Pippa made a sound of agreement, and then Ami, too. At once, the murmurs around the room began—*sì, sì*.

Mari seized on this. "Let's take a vote," she said.

These assemblies, few and far between as they were, consisted of minimal protocol. There was no formal calling of the meeting to order, and certainly no one took notes. But there was one rule, long-standing and highly revered, that the women adhered to: in the event of a vote, the majority prevailed. Given the nods around the circle now, it was clear that Mari's idea had garnered favor among the women.

Besides, with Pippa and Ami urging the idea forward, what else could the women say? Those two had lost more than any of them in recent days.

All voted in favor.

The Mazza ship would never make it to Positano at all.

18

HAVEN

Tuesday

For dinner, Enzo took me to a *trattoria* tucked away on the outskirts of the city. "The city is very quiet tonight," he mused. "Even for a Tuesday."

I nodded. Had I not known any better, I'd have thought we were in a town well off the beaten path.

According to Enzo, this restaurant was known in particular for its *zuppa di cozze*—fresh mussels in tomato broth. "It's almost impossible to get a table in here without a reservation months in advance," he said. "Lucky for us, the owner is a good friend."

But when we stepped inside, Enzo frowned. It was eight o'clock, yet only two patrons were dining.

A waitress took us to a small, L-shaped booth toward the back of the restaurant, and a few minutes later, she brought us a bottle of wine and an enormous bowl of steaming mussels.

"Thank you for introducing me to your mother," I said to Enzo, dipping bread crust into the broth. We sat side by side, mere inches apart. "She seemed to think we were a couple. She said it's been a while since you introduced anyone to her."

He smirked. "A long time, yes. I moved here a year ago to open the shop." He pried open a mussel, using his teeth to pull out the flesh. "I really haven't been interested in dating," he said. "The shop, my work...they take a lot of time. If I'm being honest, this is my first *first date* in two years. Maybe more."

"My record isn't much better." I leaned back in the booth, crossing my legs toward him. "I've had a lot of first dates, but unfortunately, most of them have been last dates, too. I think I've been fishing in the wrong pond. Too many academics and researchers, not enough—"

Heat. I thought of my very first encounter with Enzo, when we'd passed each other on the outdoor stairwell. He'd been busy hauling snorkel equipment, but we'd both done a double take. That chemistry—whatever strange energy field drew strangers together—had been white-hot before we'd even exchanged names.

"Well, just not enough interest to warrant a second date," I concluded.

We both fell silent. I wondered if we were thinking the same thing—*so we're both single, then*—and I took a sip of my wine, acutely aware that Enzo had just shifted his legs another inch toward mine.

"Have you always wanted to own a dive shop?" I ventured, willing myself to think about anything other than the warmth building in the lower half of my body.

He turned toward me. "I grew up very poor," he said. "After my father passed, my mother and sister and I, we really didn't have much." I swallowed, wondering how much he would share about his late sister, Bria. "We lived in a one-bedroom apartment in a rough part of town," he went on. "Some nights, there was nothing for dinner. Other nights, our mother was gone working. I think she barely covered our most essential needs. Always down on her luck, it seemed. She could never catch a real break." Enzo frowned, as though this were a tough topic for him.

"Watching her struggle like that, I knew I didn't want a traditional job. I wanted to work for myself. I've always loved the ocean—I started diving with friends when I was fourteen—so I decided I'd own my own scuba shop someday. I started working odd jobs, saving every penny I could." He smiled proudly. "The shop, the boat—they're what I worked for. I can only afford one employee right now, but I hope to hire another soon, someone to run the shop so I can do more diving. Today, with you, was my first dive in months. I've missed the adventure of it. The adrenaline. The unexpected surprises."

A pang of melancholy struck me: my father and Enzo would have made the best of friends.

"To me," Enzo concluded, "the sea means freedom."

What an incredible perspective, I thought—to not resent his childhood struggles but instead use them as an example of what he didn't want for his own life.

"I'm proud of you," I said, daring to give his hand a squeeze. "I've only known you for a day, so maybe it's strange for me to say, but I mean it. I'm proud of you."

He went silent a moment, glancing down at the table. "I—" He swallowed hard, cleared his throat. "Well, I don't hear that much these days. Thank you, Haven." He gave a sad smile. "I wish Bria were here to see it. She always joked that she wanted to go into business with me. I wonder if we'd be working together, here in Positano."

I was curious about their relationship—which sounded like a good one, given Enzo's statement just now—as well as what had happened to her. "Your mother said she passed about a year ago?" I asked, as delicately as I could.

He nodded. "Last year, at the end of the London Marathon. She went into cardiac arrest, very near the finish line. My mother was there, standing by as the paramedics loaded Bria onto a stretcher. She died en route to the hospital."

"I am so sorry," I said. I'd always considered my dad's death abrupt, but this was even more so. I ached for Enzo and his mother, the suddenness of it all.

"The worst part," Enzo went on, "is that even to this day, we don't know *why*. They did an autopsy afterward. No sign of heart disease, nothing congenital. They deemed it idiopathic. I made peace with it, eventually. Every day, bad things happen to good people for no reason. But my mother doesn't see it this way. She is convinced that bad luck trails her like a shadow."

This explained Savina's comment earlier today in the olive grove. *Sometimes, I feel cursed.*

Enzo shook his head and reached for his wine. I sensed he was done—with this topic, at least.

I wanted to bring the conversation back to his mother and Li Galli. Perhaps her fervent opinions were a matter of upbringing. Italians were known for being firecrackers, weren't they?

"It's clear your mother feels strongly against Li Galli," I said.

Enzo nodded. "Ever the worrier. Especially after what happened to Bria. She's very protective of me now, in a way she never was before."

"Do the currents around the islets worry you at all? Especially after the yacht incident?"

"The currents don't worry me, no," he said. "As for the yacht, they'll figure out why it went down. Just a matter of time."

In a corner of the restaurant was a mounted flat-screen TV. A news station played helicopter footage of Mount Vesuvius, panning into a narrow band of steam emanating from one section of the crater. Seeing this, I raised my eyebrows. "Have they gotten worse?" I asked. "The steam vents?"

Enzo followed my gaze, studying the television for a moment. "No. The steam vents have always been there. They're only showing the footage to get viewers." He pried open another mussel shell, then caught the eye of the restaurant's owner standing near the front door and waved him over.

"Where is everyone?" Enzo asked him in English.

The owner pointed to the television. "Scared away."

The news broadcast flipped over to images of Asher Vice, the influencer who'd died in the recent sinking. The three of us watched in silence as the words *La Maledizione Amalfitana* came up across the bottom of the screen, followed by a video montage that was taken not from the Li Galli area but from the Bermuda Triangle, east of the Caribbean. The news segment was making a comparison between the two areas and their unexplained phenomena.

After the owner left, Enzo leaned in, swirling his wine in his glass. "Italians love their legends." He glanced around the empty dining room. "Unfortunately, all of this happening at once is having real implications. I have never seen Positano this quiet."

The television still showed footage of the steam vents, which reminded me of the oceanography data I'd seen on the news yesterday. "What about the *underwater* vents?" I asked him. "The carbon dioxide readings that have gotten worse in the last few days?"

I'd known Enzo less than a day, but he seemed pragmatic enough, levelheaded. After all, he didn't give any credence to the Amalfi Curse, and he'd just said the Li Galli currents didn't worry him.

His answer, then, alarmed me.

"The underwater readings do worry me somewhat," he said, "because they're new—and they can't figure out what's causing it." He tore a piece of bread from the loaf and turned his gaze on me. "You should have a plan in case you need to fly out," he said. "Just to be safe."

For all the news broadcasts and chatter I'd seen online, it was this—Enzo's warning and his sudden somber expression—that scared me the most.

I set my fork down. I'd lost my appetite.

He read the sudden shift in my mood. "Hey," he said gently. I turned my face to his. "In this very moment," he said, "we're safe, right?"

I nodded.

"And we're enjoying ourselves."

I nodded. *Very much so.*

"And we have an entire bottle of wine to drink."

I couldn't help but crack a smile at this. "Yes," I said.

"Then, worry not, my Haven." He leaned in slowly, eyes on me all the while, and touched his lips to mine. They were softer than I expected, tasting subtly of wine. I leaned into it, gripped by the sensation of free-falling.

After a few moments, he pulled back. "All we're promised is now," he concluded.

How very much I needed to hear it. I reached for my wine and gave him a warm smile, terribly glad that despite all we'd both lost in the last year, we were with each other tonight.

I woke the next morning with a blazing headache.

After dinner, Enzo and I had holed up in an open-air bar, sipping meloncello and talking for more than two hours. We'd agreed that a morning dive wasn't in the cards, but an afternoon dive most certainly was.

Now, I turned over in bed, happy to see that he had already messaged. Good morning, Ambrose, he'd texted an hour earlier. How you feeling?

Terrible, I replied. What exactly do they put in meloncello?

Cantaloupe. Sugar. Vodka. All the necessary food groups. A few minutes later, he asked me about our afternoon dive. Come by the shop around four? I'll get you set up with a new wet suit. 2 mm? 3 mm?

I smiled at his thoughtfulness. 3 mm. That water is COLD.

Gotta toughen you up, he replied.

In spite of my headache, I couldn't help but laugh. **See you then.**

A moment later, another text came through, and my smile fell. It was Conrad. **Landed in Naples,** he said. **We need to transfer docs. I'm making my first dive this afternoon—need the site plans asap. Where's your hotel?**

Shit. He was diving this afternoon? I loathed the idea of running into him on the water.

I'd already put him off once. I didn't want him to come to my villa, so I gave him the name of a café Enzo had mentioned last night, telling him to meet me there in an hour. I showered and dressed, then begrudgingly gathered up everything I'd need to hand over, including a large binder containing the site plans, which I'd printed and marked up in recent months. There were topographic maps riddled with annotations as well as my ideas for surveying the debris field. There were also bathymetric charts, with my analysis of depth, salinity, the composition of the seafloor sediment, and how these factors might impact the location and condition of wreckage.

The charts and site plans themselves—without my analysis—were also on a one-terabyte thumb drive. I tossed that in my bag, along with the documentation and approvals from various Italian authorities, including the coast guard.

But when I was nearly ready to go, I hesitated, looking down at my bag. Did I really owe Conrad the binder? The raw data and site plans were, after all, on the thumb drive. The binder contained *my* notes, *my* research, *my* strategies.

I wavered but a moment before yanking the binder from my bag and tossing it onto the bed. Let Conrad take his own notes, I decided. I was under no obligation to give him months' worth of my analysis.

When I arrived at the café, Conrad was already there, sipping a black coffee at a corner table. He looked exactly the same as he had at my father's funeral months ago: sun-soaked, every inch of him a perfect bronze, apart from the rings around his eyes from wearing sunglasses. And a full head of thick gray hair.

He stood to greet me, bringing me in for a hug. I held back a moment before reminding myself that he and my dad had not only been schoolmates but long-standing friends. And that Conrad had once saved my life.

Still, as badly as I wanted to give him the benefit of the doubt, my guard was up.

"Coffee?" he asked after I took a seat. "On me."

I shook my head. "No, thanks." The thought of it now, on a queasy stomach, wasn't appealing. "I brought everything you need," I said, withdrawing the thumb drive. I wanted to get this meeting over with.

Conrad didn't even look at it as I set it in front of him. He kept his gaze on me. "Haven," he said, and I thought I caught something sad in his eyes—memories, maybe, of the ways things were before my father died: the three of us sharing fresh-catch dinners at a dive bar in Key West. Conrad and my father having one too many beers and belting out the words to "Fly Like an Eagle." A late-night dive several years ago, all of us searching for bioluminescent plankton and parrotfish cocoons.

I paused, fighting the sudden urge to cry. So much had been lost. "Why didn't you tell me yourself that you were taking over the project?" I asked. "Why did I have to hear it from Gage?"

"Gage's foundation is paying for the project."

"But you're the new lead. You should have called me yourself. Also, why didn't you put me on your team?"

"We don't know what the hell is going on in those waters, Haven." Reaching into his back pocket, he pulled out his phone. "Look at this," he said, showing me a web page littered with numbers and symbols. "Hydrothermal vent activity nearby," he explained. He scrolled down to display a graph, manipulating the axes several times. It was undeniable: the vents had grown markedly more active in the last few days.

"Now, you know I'm not an alarmist," he continued, "but even working with guys I've had in the field for ten, twenty years, well, we're taking greater precautions than normal. I would never forgive myself if—" Conrad's voice cracked. "Losing your dad has been tough on me, Haven," he went on. "Not as tough as it's been on you, I get that. But not easy, either. Imagine how I'd feel if something happened to you, too."

Chastened, I leaned back. Maybe I was wrong about him. Maybe this had nothing to do with the treasure and everything to do with keeping me safe. Just as Gage had said.

Now, I almost wished I'd brought the binder of marked-up maps for Conrad.

Almost.

"Here," I said, placing the thumb drive in his palm. "This has the documented approvals and the information on the boat charter. The site plans, too. Everything you need."

He gave a nod, his lips pressed tightly together. "Thank you, Haven. We're gonna do the best we can to get the photos we need."

"You're headed out onto the water today?"

He nodded. "This afternoon. Two of my guys are here already." He checked his watch. "Next one should be landing in Naples anytime. Hope to be on the water midday to do a little preliminary exploration. How about you?" he asked. "Headed home soon, or planning to stay in Positano for a while?"

I hesitated. Only Mal and Enzo knew I was here for the foreseeable future. "I'll head home," I said. "Not immediately, but soon."

It was vague enough.

"Good for you. Might as well do some sightseeing while you're out here."

"Yeah," I said, "something like that." I gathered my things and stood. "Keep in touch, Conrad." I paused, part of me wanting to say *Good luck*, and another part wanting to say *I hope your project fails*.

I settled with, "Be safe."

That, at least, was an honest sentiment.

By four thirty that afternoon, Enzo and I were on the water again. Given his mother's dismay about our diving Li Galli, we agreed we wouldn't tell her about this return trip.

As he drove, I stood next to him at the helm with my arm wrapped around his waist, his arm draped around my neck. Since our first kiss at the restaurant last night, we'd hardly passed a minute without finding some excuse to touch one another. Enzo kept the music low today, and I found myself closing my eyes as I stood next to him, listening to the sound of the boat cutting through the water. Every so often, he planted a kiss on my temple.

As we drove westward, he pointed to one of the nearby bluffs, along the water. "See that staircase there, and the small dock? That's where my mother keeps her Jet Skis. Looks like she's out on one of them."

"Funny," I said, "because she didn't really strike me as the water adventure type."

"She's got a wild side to her," he laughed.

He turned back to the helm while I reached for my camera gear: a digital Nikon with dual-grip housing, plus an assortment of strobes, lenses, and filters.

"Wow," Enzo said, glancing at my scattered equipment. It was far more than any lay person needed. "You really are a professional, aren't you?"

If only he knew I'd just been yanked from the biggest project of my career. "You'd be surprised what the right filters can do underwater," I said.

He nodded toward the nearby islets. "Where to today?"

I pulled my binder out of my bag. Earlier, I'd taken a highlighter and marked up one of the maps with the area we'd covered yesterday, making a few notes about depth and the lack of shipwreck debris. "A bit farther north than where we anchored yesterday," I told him.

"Got it," he replied. As we closed in on our new dive site, I monitored the depth on his boat's sonar equipment and cross-checked it against my own nautical maps, pleased to find that they mostly matched. The water had almost no chop; it was as calm as I could have hoped.

"Surface currents are good," I said. "I'm thinking we go in right about here." We were smack dab in the middle of the three islets—the eye of Li Galli.

Enzo dropped anchor, raised the dive flag, and began to pull on his own gear. Meanwhile, I affixed a wide-angle lens to my camera and snapped a handheld strobe around my wrist. Once we were ready, we gave each other a quick nod and took a long step off the back of the boat and into the water.

At once, I knew this would be a better dive than yesterday. Not only was the water calm, but I was much warmer, thanks to my thicker wet suit. The visibility was better, too. Even from a couple of meters away, I could clearly read the yellow Cressi logo on Enzo's wet suit.

I checked my dive watch. We were at fifteen meters, and then twenty, and then twenty-five. I slowed my descent, wary of touching bottom too quickly, and then gasped into my mouthpiece.

Just a few meters below me, protruding from the ocean floor, was the unmistakable form of a ship's bow. *A wreck.* Scattered around the debris were enormous segments of wood and oxidized copper sheathing. A long black eel slithered around beneath me, before tucking himself into a tight crevice.

I readied my camera to take a few shots. But suddenly, I heard a soft metallic sound. Enzo was a few meters away, clinking a small metal instrument against his air tank. I followed the direction of his pointed finger and squinted at something solid and dark. Swimming closer, I spotted the object that had caught his attention: the hull of another ship, this one lying on its side like a child's bath toy, the keel exposed.

I smiled around my mouthpiece: despite being pulled from Project Relic, I'd just discovered my first Li Galli wreckage field.

Still, I wasn't foolish enough to believe I was anywhere close to discovering the loot my father had spotted. This was only two wrecks of many.

But at least we'd found *something*.

I quickly strategized. I'd take photos of the wrecks, and then later, I'd load the images onto my computer, comparing them to my father's grainy images.

As I always did during my dives, I took a moment to slow my breathing. I nearly always returned to the surface with more air in my tank than my dive partners, something of which I was proud. I could only hope that Enzo could make his own tank last, too.

I gave him the underwater signal to stay close, then I began to take photos of both wrecks. I hovered over an area of copper debris near the first wreck; often, the hulls of sailing ships were sheathed in copper beneath the water line to protect them from shipworms and other biological damage. Thankfully, copper was one element that could endure the seabed relatively well for centuries, and it was often this metal that led scientists to shipwrecks in the first place.

I moved next to the second wreck, feeling especially drawn toward the sharp edge of this one's exposed keel. Clinging to it were thousands of mollusks, a few starfish. Parts of the hull were covered in sea lichen, dull orange in color. I snapped images of everything, as well as a few large holes along the keel.

I searched both wrecks for anything resembling a cannon or a bell, which might be stamped with an identifying maker's mark. Seeing nothing of the sort, I ventured away from the area in search of more debris, aware that I'd gone through half of my air supply already.

I thought I might lead us farther north, but in the last few minutes, the underwater currents had grown noticeably stronger. Not wanting to swim against the current—this was the fastest way to go through an air tank—I led Enzo east. My frustration at the deteriorating conditions dissipated when, moments later, we discovered yet another pile of rubble. This wreckage looked older: the wooden fragments were largely decomposed and generally more dispersed. It seemed possible this pile contained two, three, even four shipwrecks, tangled and twisted up in one another. On one debris segment, I spotted the number *13*, which was most certainly a draft marking affixed to the hull. These were often made of lead, which was almost impervious to salt water.

Enzo nudged me on the shoulder, and I turned to find him tapping his air gauge. He had 700 psi left. *Dammit*. We'd have to ascend at 500 psi. Given how quickly Enzo had gone through his air, I gave us five, maybe seven, more minutes underwater.

I took as many pictures as I could from a variety of angles, using the strobe light in places where the ambient light was insufficient. I couldn't resist snagging a few pictures of the marine life, too: orange polyps clinging to wreckage and swaying in the current; a school of grouper, their silvery skin reflecting the light of my strobe; and a lone green sea worm crawling in the sand.

As we swam through the debris field with only a few minutes left, I found myself expending more effort against the underwater current. I was breathing harder now, not from nerves or excitement but from the effort of trying to keep myself steady as I took pictures. The muscle in my left calf had started twitching; if it began to cramp, I would need to pull off my fin to stretch it out.

Finally, I decided to call the dive. I got Enzo's attention and gave him the Thumbs-up signal.

Back on the boat, Enzo and I debriefed. He asked if I wanted to drop a line and buoy to find the location more easily when we returned, but I declined. We already had the coordinates, and I didn't want to give anyone—most of all, Conrad—any overt clues to this exact spot.

I pulled out my binder, furiously jotting down what I remembered about the placement of debris. I recorded the longitude and latitude of our current position, which would be important when I was back at the villa analyzing the site maps on my computer.

"Currents really picked up at the end," Enzo said, tugging his wet suit off.

I finished making a few notes, then snapped my binder shut and tossed it onto the seat. "My calf almost cramped, trying to swim against it." I glanced at the ocean, noticeably choppier than it had been forty-five minutes ago when we'd begun our dive.

Enzo offered me a beer from the cooler, which I gratefully accepted before pulling off my own wet suit—cold, stiff, and sodden with seawater. He retrieved a pair of binoculars from a hatch beneath the helm, handing them to me and pointing toward Positano. "Have a look," he said.

I marveled at the level of detail. I could see children playing on the flat rooftop of a building toward the center of town—a school, maybe, or a daycare—and trellis walls of orange and magenta bougainvillea throughout the village. I spotted Savina's stairway-to-the-sea, too. She was still out on her Jet Ski.

I was almost ready to hand back the binoculars, but before I did so, I used them to look at a few nearby boats, adjusting the focus knob.

And then, I saw him: Conrad, standing at the front of a nearby dive boat, staring right at me. Through the magnified lens, he looked impossibly close.

"Shit," I said. *"Shit."* I turned to Enzo. "We need to go."

Before I could explain myself, the driver of Conrad's boat had throttled the engine. They'd spotted me.

Briefly, I explained to Enzo that one of the guys approaching was a colleague. "Not even a colleague," I clarified. "It's complicated. We're not on the best of terms right now." I might have said more, but Conrad's boat pulled up alongside us, its wake tossing our small dive boat back and forth on the water. Enzo wrapped a protective arm around me, keeping me steady.

"Haven." Conrad pulled his sunglasses off, perched them on his head. "Good seeing you again. Though, I thought you were...sightseeing." He glanced at the tossed-aside wet suit and dive mask, then he studied my binder for a moment. None of this was damning on its own. But the assortment of expensive camera gear? That was sure to draw some questions.

Quickly, I threw a towel toward the gear, hoping to cover it, but it slipped onto the floor. "You know me," I said, trying to act nonchalant. "I'd rather go sightseeing underwater than above it."

Our two boats bobbed parallel on the water only inches apart. Conrad introduced us to his driver, Gio, and a few of his fellow divers—his team, I presumed. They were too preoccupied with readying their gear to greet me.

As Enzo and Gio began to chat in Italian like old friends, I nearly groaned. I'd hoped this encounter would be brief, but Gio had already killed his engine.

Conrad opened his phone, pointing the camera around Enzo's boat and our immediate vicinity. "See anything good down there?" he asked.

"Not much," I lied. I squinted in the sunlight. The temperature had warmed in the last few minutes, and I was hot, thirsty, and in need of a shower. Much as I loved the ocean, I hated the way my skin felt sticky after a dive. I felt a headache coming on, too, which occasionally happened after an especially cold dive.

He nodded slowly. "And the photos, they're for...what now?"

"I always take my camera underwater," I replied, giving him a small smile. "Worry not, Conrad. I'm not sending my pictures to the software team in the hopes of running the project behind your back."

He chuckled. "You inherited your dad's feisty side, Haven Marie."

It wasn't the first time I'd heard this. "How's Project Relic going?" I asked.

"Project Delfino," Conrad corrected, now pointing his phone toward the water, seemingly taking pictures of the surface. "We renamed it."

Of course you did.

"So far, so good," he said. He set his phone on the center console and walked toward a large black case on one of the boat's seats. He unlatched the top, then pulled out a variety of instruments and handed them to his team members. I recognized a few—high-frequency sonar equipment, and a camera twice the size of mine—but one was completely unfamiliar. It resembled a speaker, or an echo-sounder, nearly a foot in diameter.

I couldn't resist. "What's that?"

"Proprietary," he said, fiddling with a few of the buttons. "A prototype camera."

"Did HPI loan it to you?" I asked, feeling the heat rising in my neck. "Or Gage Whitlock himself?"

He jerked his head upright, glanced at the people standing around us. "Jesus, Haven," he muttered under his breath. "Neither. My buddy heads up a tech company." He paused, looking up at me. "You sure there's not something else you're looking for out here?"

He held my gaze just a beat too long.

He knows, I thought to myself. *He fucking knows. But how?* I still couldn't accept the idea that my father had told him.

"No," I said, my mouth dry. I pointed at the black case. "Is it for image-rendering? Photogrammetry?" If so, I'd have been disappointed he didn't tell me about it in the lead-up to Project Relic.

He shook his head. "Not imagery, no. More like...*detecting*. It finds anomalies. Inorganic material on the seafloor, for instance. Best for small things, really. Makes that needle in a haystack just a little bit easier to locate."

I couldn't believe it. He was saying it without saying it, this brave bastard. The primary goal of Project Relic—or Project Delfino, now—was to photograph wrecks. And shipwrecks weren't *small things*.

Conrad was searching for the loot.

"We've come a long way from paper and binders," he went on, motioning his hand toward mine. "Though, I find it curious you didn't bring that when we met earlier. Anything good in there?"

Dumbfounded, I could only shake my head.

Conrad gave the black case a pat, then tucked his phone into a bag before turning to his fellow divers. "We ready, boys?"

One of the divers grunted in reply and pulled his mask on. I felt sick, knowing they might find something down there that I hadn't. In this precise location, which I'd inadvertently brought them to.

"Now, remember," Conrad said loudly to his partners. "No one get into any trouble today. If I have to save your life, you'll owe me big."

My throat went dry. I knew exactly what he was alluding to.

Conrad approached the back of his boat, ready to jump into the water. He turned back to face me once more, calling out over his shoulder, "'Round here," he said, "if I scratch your back, you scratch mine." He cocked his head. "Best of luck to you, Haven."

With that, Conrad jumped into the water and slipped beneath the surface.

Under the guise of leading Project Relic-turned-Delfino, he had begun his search for the very thing my father had begged me to find.

19

HOLMES

Monday, April 23, 1821
Bay of Naples

The eastern edge of the storm was upon them.

Several hours ago, they'd spotted the low, dark front to the west. The men had begun preparations at once. A pair of sailors had climbed the masts—a nerve-wracking task for even the bravest of seamen—and furled the topsails and mainsail to protect them from the violent gusts they'd soon face. A few sails, like the flying jibs in the fore of the ship, remained set to keep the brig as steady as possible during the storm.

Holmes himself was instructed to close and latch the hatches, while another sailor secured a rope from the *Aquila*'s helm to her stern, giving the men something to hold on to once the waters grew rough.

And rough they were. Now the *Aquila* pitched and tossed amid the heavy swells. It was near impossible for Holmes to hear the shouts of his officers over the screeching wind and the clamor of wet canvas catching the squalls above him. Rain and sea spray pummeled his face, blurring his vision. The brig shuddered several times as she careened into the troughs between swells. More than once, Holmes was thrown to his knees.

Every man kept a spare hand on something—a railing, a post, a rope—lest he slip on the deck and go overboard. These waves would take a man under at once; there would be no saving anyone, not today.

A few swells came over the main deck. As water seeped through the closed hatches, a pair of men began to work the bilge pumps. Others eyed the masts, which undulated back and forth with the *Aquila*'s rolling.

Lightning flashed all around them, and Holmes sent up a quick prayer: bad as the sea was now, a lightning strike would be worse. This vessel was made of wood, after all.

The brig plunged into another trough between waves. Amid the deafening gales, Holmes heard shouting toward the bow. It was Quinto, pointing toward the flying jib at the very front of the ship.

The rigging meant to keep it taut had—snapped.

In an instant, the sail collapsed in on itself. It began to shred apart at once.

"We've lost it!" Quinto shouted, a flash of panic in his eyes. Fore sails such as this one were imperative for keeping a ship sound in turbulent weather.

Holmes's stomach lurched. Indeed, the flying jib was now little more than a torn kite flapping in the wind.

It was all happening just as he'd intended.

That morning before the storm, while briefly docked in Naples, the officers had disembarked, but not before giving the crew a slew of tasks to perform aboard the *Aquila*: swabbing the deck with linseed oil, stuffing oakum into cracks between planks.

Holmes and several others were instructed to tar the standing rigging, which protected the lines against rain, seawater, salt, and the like. It was the least pleasant task of all: the tar itself reeked, the buckets were heavy, and it required climbing the masts to reach the uppermost rigging.

After more than two hours of work, Holmes took a long stretch, a drink of water. His tarring was finished, but he kept the bucket and brush with him. He made his way to the front of the ship, keeping a furtive eye on the activity around him: the officers had not yet returned, and the other sailors had retreated to the berthing deck, their work complete.

Now was the time.

Quickly, Holmes went to the bow, portside. He attached his paintbrush, now doused in wet tar, to the end of a pole. Leaning over the railing, he extended the pole and quickly painted a circle of black tar, roughly twelve inches in diameter, inside the yellow band stretching across the *Aquila*'s hull. From any distance, it would resemble a porthole.

With this done, Holmes set down his tools and crawled onto the base of the bowsprit, slick on account of its copper sheathing. The Fratelli Mazza insisted on copper-sheathed bowsprits on all of their ships. Vanity, Holmes surmised. A display of affluence.

At the end of the bowsprit, the flying jib was furled. This sail would be deployed as soon as they were underway. Especially with a storm coming.

Holmes reached for his knife.

A gift from his father when he first went to sea, Holmes always kept his rosewood-handle knife on his hip, tucked in a taut leather sheath.

Over the years, he'd used it to cut through old rigging; to gut tuna; and, once, to defend himself against a drunk who'd crawled his way up a rope ladder during the midnight watch.

More recently, though, he'd used it to peel oranges for Mari or cut loose threads from her gowns.

Always, Holmes used his knife for good: protection, or repair, or sustenance.

Until now.

He glanced at the storm building to the west. Grabbing a few of the lines that would be necessary to deploy the flying jib, Holmes quickly began to saw away at the rope. He didn't cut wholly through any of the lines; rather, he shaved away at the hemp fibers, greatly compromising the integrity of them.

The gales would take care of the rest.

Finished with this, he sheathed his knife, retrieved his bucket of tar, and made for the companionway. On the cargo deck, rather than returning the tar bucket to its storage chest, he carried it toward the bags of clean, dry canvas, meant for repairing sails. Next to these were neatly coiled piles of spare rigging—meter upon meter of perfectly functional rope.

None of it was locked or hidden away, for what sailor would dare assault the very things keeping his vessel aloft? It would be like throwing food overboard, or rum.

With a quick glance over his shoulder, Holmes lifted the bucket, turned it upside down, and poured the tar into the bag with the clean canvas. Like warm butter, it slowly seeped between the layers of fabric. In a matter of minutes, it would thicken into a sticky, coagulated mess. There would be no fixing it.

He might have gone for a second bucket—he hadn't had enough tar to pour over the coiled rope—but he heard voices somewhere above him. The officers were back onboard.

Holmes put the empty tar bucket into the storage chest, wiped his hands clean, and returned to the main deck.

Steadying himself against the *Aquila*'s rolling, Quinto reached for one of the snapped lines. He brought it close to his face, inspecting the place where it had failed.

"Frayed," he muttered to himself. With the back of his hand, he wiped rain from his brow. "Dare I say, *cut*."

He led a few of the men, Holmes included, to the cargo deck. "We'll need fresh rigging," he yelled as they descended the ladder, "and the damned sail needs replacing, too. As soon as we can."

Together, the group approached the bags of spare canvas, the coiled piles of rope. Holmes walked with an unsteady gait on account of the storm, his nerves. In a matter of moments, Quinto would look into the bag of canvas and find it doused with tar.

His throat tightened. He kept his eyes low, so better to keep his expression in shadow.

Quinto pried open the bag. He fingered the fabric and pulled his hand away, frowning at the gummy black tar on his thumb. He lifted a corner of canvas out of the bag, his expression aghast.

"Who did this?" he said, eyeing the men. Then, as though remembering the frayed rigging on the bowsprit, he said, "Show me your knives. All of you."

One by one, they unsheathed their knives to let Quinto inspect. When Holmes handed his over, Quinto gave it a long look, grunting when the blade caught the light. "Clean as I've ever seen a knife," he hissed.

Perhaps, Holmes thought, he should not have polished it so well after his misdeed.

Suddenly, another swell rose beneath the brig, and they were all thrown forward, landing on their hands and knees. A crack of thunder followed. Quinto left everything as it was and motioned for the men to follow him up.

As they returned to the main deck, Holmes's heartbeat slowed. Quinto hadn't assigned blame. And how could he? All of the men had knives on them. All of them had access to the cargo deck. Any one of them could have done this.

The storm went on, unrelenting, and the *Aquila* continued to list from side to side. One sailor stood at the stern, clutching the railing, trying to keep his balance as he vomited over the edge.

The captain ordered two of the men, including Holmes's friend Nico, to go aloft and unfurl the mainsail. It wouldn't compensate for the lack of a flying jib, but it would steady the brig somewhat.

In the minutes it took to deploy the sail, the *Aquila* drifted closer and closer toward land, which was precisely where they did not want to be. In such a storm, deep, open water was safest, for a vessel like the *Aquila* could handle swells, so long as nothing threatened her hull. But the shallower they got, the more likely their keel would run aground. The waters off Naples were beset with shoals and reefs and sunken Roman villages.

At the helm, the captain loosened the rope looped around his waist, which had kept him secure against the brig's thrashing. He threw the loop to a nearby sailor, commanding him to the helm. Holmes knelt close by, trying to fix a broken latch on one of the hatches now letting in water.

The captain spotted Quinto. "Christ," he shouted. "Where have you been?"

"Belowdecks!" Quinto yelled. He slammed the heel of his hand against a barrel as he approached him. "Someone has ruined the sails below—poured tar over the lot of them."

The captain frowned, mouth agape. He didn't speak for a moment, then, "When did you intend to tell me of this?"

Quinto glared. "What the hell do you think I'm doing now?"

The captain looked ready to give him a good blow across the face for his insolence, but something must have caught his eye, for he began to run toward the forecastle, yelling unintelligibly. Holmes followed him, a pair of pliers in hand.

Then, through the cold, blinding rain, he saw it. *Blood.* Bright red blood intermingled with rain and seawater, seeping toward the edges of the brig. Holmes followed the trail of it, his stomach lurching as he recognized Nico lying immobile on the deck, just beneath the mainmast. He bled from his mouth and nose, and his leg was bent at an ugly angle, turned outward at the hip.

"My God," Holmes whispered, falling to his knees alongside his friend. He began to openly weep as he surveyed the injuries.

Holmes knew, at once, Nico's pelvis was broken. Perhaps even his spine. His eyes were closed, and he groaned unintelligibly. He wasn't dead, much as he probably wished he was. The captain knelt beside him, clearly anguished. He reached for Nico's hand, where a deep red rope burn stretched across the length of his palm.

"He fell?" Quinto bellowed through the rain. He rushed to join the men, but his bowlegged gait slowed him down.

Another sailor stepped forward, shaking rainwater from his hair. "From the very top." He pointed at the heavy, wet canvas mainsail. Sailors often fell from masts during storms, but usually the outcome was not this grisly.

Quinto went pale. He glanced at Nico's buckled leg again, then turned to Holmes. "Get him belowdecks. Find him some whiskey."

Suddenly, the vessel shuddered.

"Have we—" the captain went still "—have we just run aground?"

A few men began to shout, and panic crossed Quinto's face. If they had indeed run aground, it was not a question of whether there would be damage to the hull, but how bad it would be. And if the storm continued on…

Holmes glanced westward, glad now to find that the sky had lightened, even if just by a small measure. The ship had suffered enough damage—more, even, than he'd hoped. If this storm did not let up, the *Aquila* would soon be a mess of splinters and sea chests, and they'd all be swimming for their lives.

Holmes steeled himself. He threw Nico over his shoulder, doing his best to ignore his friend's cries of agony. Nico's injured leg swung awkwardly as they went, leaving Holmes to suspect that the fascia and tendons within were severed, as useful as the ropes he'd sliced through with his knife. A heart-shaped locket necklace slipped from Nico's shirt. Within, Holmes knew, was a lock of his young daughter's hair.

If not for Holmes's tampering with the flying jib, the captain wouldn't have needed to deploy the mainsail at all. Now his friend was gravely injured because of it. *Perhaps*, Holmes thought with a deluge of deep remorse, *I ought to have thought on a different, better plan.*

He laid Nico on the floor of the berthing deck and went in search of the cook, who was vomiting profusely into a bucket, swearing he would never go to sea again. Cook supplied Holmes with some whiskey, and no sooner had Holmes given it to Nico than the brig ceased her rolling. The rain let up, and the vessel began to move again; she had loosened from whatever had caught her below.

Holmes took a long breath for what felt like the first time in hours. Nico was in very bad shape, but not all had been a failure: the *Aquila* had been rendered impotent, her progress toward Positano greatly hindered. Though Holmes could not hear any water gushing into the vessel, there would surely be hull repairs, and Quinto would need to call for a tender to bring fresh sailcloth onto the brig.

And most importantly, Mari would get his letter before the *Aquila* arrived.

Still... *Nico*. Had Holmes's plan been worth it given what had happened to his friend?

Someone lifted the hatch, and slow footsteps descended toward him. It was Quinto, alone. Kneeling, he placed his hand on Nico's forehead. Nico had gone pale, his skin like ice. He was unconscious. Holmes suspected—hoped, even, for Nico's sake—that he was unlikely to survive the hour.

"I vow to find who caused this," Quinto said, true compassion in his voice. "And when I do, I won't give him the courtesy of dealing with him myself. Matteo can decide what to do with him."

He shook his head and stood to go, leaving Holmes to stand vigil over the only friend he had on the *Aquila*—a father, a husband, and an innocent man he'd unwittingly sent to an early grave.

20

HAVEN

Wednesday

As Enzo steered us back to Positano, I pulled out my phone to text Mal. She'd told me earlier she remained on standby at the Naples airport. Unable to get home, she'd grown progressively more frustrated.

I was about to add fuel to the fire.

Ran into Conrad on the water, I hammered away at the keyboard. He's 100% after the gems.

A moment later, she replied. F* him. How do you know?

He has some new techy camera. Wouldn't tell me exactly what it was. But his implication was enough.

You're going to prove him wrong, she said.

I have no idea how. Went down today—great wreckage field. Perfect for Project Relic, but not so much for finding long-lost treasure.

Mal didn't reply, but I needed to off-gas my frustration, so I kept going. He told his guys that if he needed to save one of their lives, they'd owe him big. Then he looked at me and said, "If I scratch your back, you scratch mine." WTF.

He wants you out of his way, Mal finally replied.

I don't plan on giving him that.

Atta girl. Then: *You need to think outside the box here, Haven.*

I stared at my phone a few moments, then shoved it into my bag and turned my gaze to the cliffs. These same weathered bluffs had existed for millennia, and I couldn't help but wonder what, exactly, the faces of this mountainside had witnessed. Thunderstorms and torrential rain. Rogue waves and rough seas. People slipping to their deaths. Children learning to swim. Lovers sneaking away for a night. Ships listing, snapping, sinking.

You need to think outside the box, Mal had said. I could make some phone calls, try to commission my own state-of-the-art equipment. I could invite Conrad to sit down with me and beg him to give up his search for my father's discovery. I could tell Enzo to turn the boat around, then dive back under and turn off the knob on Conrad's air tank.

Or I could give this entire thing up, go home, and try to restore some dignity.

I hated every idea more than the last.

As we approached the dock and disembarked, I blew out a sigh, glad that Enzo hadn't asked me about my foul mood.

"I'll check in with you a bit later," I told him. "For now, I need some time alone."

He didn't argue. Instead, he gave me a slow, gentle kiss on my bottom lip, then he told me to take as much time as I needed. "Li Galli isn't going anywhere. Everything will remain just where we left it."

I appreciated his sentiment, his kindness. But someone else was searching those wrecks at this very moment.

Enzo had no idea how very wrong he might be.

Back at the rental, I downloaded that day's photos from my camera onto my Mac. Given their high resolution, the file transfer went slowly, and I perched on the edge of the bed, tapping my foot impatiently. I'd captured more than a hundred and fifty images during the dive.

Once the images had transferred, I took a quick look through them. Some were dark or underexposed, so I manually adjusted the photo settings to better view the subjects. It was quick, easy work, a task I'd been doing for half my life. Besides, I much preferred looking at shipwrecks this way, when I was dry, warm, and under a blanket. On my computer, I could zoom in and out or apply helpful filters.

With the photos organized, I began a more thorough review, searching for something, anything, that might resemble my father's grainy images: the shape of a cannon or bell, the pattern of wooden planks, or even a recognizable cluster of coral. If something matched, I'd spot it at once.

An hour passed, but nothing caught my eye. Many of the photos were very good otherwise—sharp, well-composed. The images of marine life, in particular, were outstanding. I created a separate folder for these images, in the event I wanted to print and frame them someday.

I'd seen an interesting type of orange lichen, or algae, on the second wreck—the one lying on its side, keel up. I revisited these images, zooming in to get a closer look. I'd seen the same bright-colored lichen on one of my father's photos; it must be common around here, I reasoned, if we'd both captured it in our images.

Yet as I studied the image, I frowned. This supposed lichen was not clustered, like most underwater algae. Instead, there were a few sharp angles, as though someone had taken a knife and cut shapes from it.

I frowned, using the trackpad on my computer to zoom in on the images. It was indeed orange lichen, but it was clinging to something else—three raised letters spelling *AQU*. I guessed the letters were made of lead, same as the draft markings affixed on hulls, and the lichen must have found this a suitable element on which to live.

Quickly, I navigated to my father's cloud folder, skipping past the list of indecipherable codes. I clicked on a photo I'd never given much thought to: a wreck segment, lying flat on the seafloor, with a cluster of the same orange lichen. Again I zoomed in, but the cluster didn't appear to form any letters.

Until I rotated the photo ninety degrees.

Viewing it from another angle, I could make out what the lichen had clung to: three letters reading *ILA*. And the shape of the letters—or the font, for lack of a better word—seemed to match.

But what about the size?

My dad hadn't used a scaling rod; he often didn't on his recreational dives. Instead, I found objects in each photograph that could be used as measurement tools: a starfish in my image, and a half-buried beer bottle in my father's. Knowing the general size of both, I approximated the size of the letters in each image.

To my delight, they matched.

"*Aquila*," I said aloud, letting the word roll slowly off my tongue.

Though my father and I had photographed different segments of the same wreck, this almost certainly confirmed that the spot Enzo and I had explored today was *close to* the right place. Now I knew where to concentrate my search—which wreck, even. I nearly yelped with excitement, knowing I was, at last, on the right track.

At once, I thought of Conrad. He might have had proprietary

equipment to search the seafloor, but I had something he didn't have: the name of the ship that had gone down. We were, now more than ever, head-to-head.

I needed to know more about the *Aquila*. If I could get my hands on a blueprint of the vessel, its specifications might help me determine where on the ship any loot had been hidden. A cargo manifest would also be helpful.

Newly encouraged, I opened up my binder, where I'd kept a list of local maritime archives and resources to assist with Project Relic. The most extensive of these archives was in Naples, the Archivio Marittimo di Napoli, which housed more than two million documents, including shipping logs, sailors' voyage diaries, vessel blueprints, and the like.

It was a long shot, but maybe they had something I could use.

21

HOLMES

Tuesday, April 24, 1821
Bay of Naples

It was the captain's idea to interview them all, to perform a methodical inquisition. He pulled aside each sailor, asked them the same questions: Who saw who, and when? The officers then weighed these responses against the watch schedule and the list of tasks that had been assigned to each sailor the prior morning.

This narrowed it down to four men, Holmes among them. It was then a mere matter of exclusion.

With the four men corralled, Quinto demanded they pull out their knives again. With these in hand, he went to the front of the ship where the damaged rigging still lay. He began to saw away at the lines, just as Holmes had done. He then held the ropes close, examining the way each blade cut through the threads.

In the end, it was undeniable: Holmes's knife had done it. It was so obvious, even Holmes could not deny the charges.

"Have you been the one stealing from the men, too?" Quinto asked him. He'd sent the other men to the berthing deck. "The snuffbox, my brandy..."

"No," Holmes spat back. "If so, you'd have seen me drunk by now."

Quinto narrowed his eyes. "Why'd you do it, then? Why'd you cut the rigging?"

Because you intend to capture and kill the woman I love, Holmes thought to himself. But he didn't dare reveal this or anything else he'd overheard when eavesdropping on the conversation between Quinto and the captain. Instead he stayed silent, praying his journal—which he'd tucked against his lower back in the event he was caught and banished from the ship—did not come loose. He shifted his weight from one leg to the other, feeling the book's waterproof oilskin sleeve chafe against him.

Holmes's silence only infuriated Quinto further. Quinto pushed him against one of the masts, put his hand against his throat. "Do you know about the—"

But then he stopped, eyeing Holmes suspiciously.

About the what? Did he mean the plan to seize Positano's women or something else?

Quinto released his hold, and Holmes bent over, gulping for air. "I'd kill you if I could," he said. "But I think Matteo would prefer to do it himself."

"Kill me?" Holmes said. "For cutting some lines? Hardly seems worth it."

Quinto spit out a laugh. "He doesn't give a whit for the rigging." He tucked Holmes's knife into his back pocket. "You haven't any idea what else is on this brig, you fool. If I let it sink, why, they would never forgive me."

He grabbed Holmes by the arm and led him to the cargo hold, as far aft as they could go. The space was dark and dank, hidden by wooden crates.

Ahead, Holmes spotted their destination: an iron cage built into the very beams of the ship. His prison cell. And next to it, something wrapped in a dark canvas shroud. It was six feet long. Motionless.

Nico's dead body.

★ ★ ★

The vessel remains impotent, Holmes wrote in his diary a short while later. *It will be some time, I think, before we begin to move.*

I hear the constant sloshing of the bilges below the cargo deck where I'm imprisoned—a mix of seawater, festering excrement, tar, and food scraps. I smell it, too, piss and fish guts.

A rat has crawled through the iron bars. He sits at my feet, gnawing on the sole of my shoe.

It is very dark, for only the faintest light comes through a few cracks between planks. It is bitterly cold, too.

I will never sail again. This I know. After they arrest me, they will kill me.

I do not think I have fully grasped the reality that I will never lay eyes on my Mari again. I cannot breathe if I even begin to think of it. Instead, I occupy my mind with trying to unravel the puzzling comment Quinto made earlier today, moments before he imprisoned me.

You haven't any idea what else is on this brig.

22

HAVEN

Thursday

The next morning, when I called the Archivio Marittimo di Napoli to inquire about the *Aquila*, a young woman answered. After an awkward exchange in which I told her, to the best of my ability, that I knew only elementary Italian, she reluctantly resorted to English. I gave her my name, and she gave me hers, Chloe.

"How can I help you?" she eventually asked, her tone cool and curt. In the background, I heard her nails drumming.

I got right to it. "I'm looking for information on a ship that sank off the coast of Positano, near Li Galli. The vessel's name was *Aquila*."

"When did it sink?" Chloe asked.

"I—I'm not sure."

There was a long pause on the other end. "Do you know what…century? Or the name of the shipbuilder, or owner, or any of the crew?"

I placed my hand over my face, glad she couldn't see me. "No," I replied. "None of that. Just the ship's name."

"One moment." I heard Chloe typing away. "Well," she said, "there are fourteen vessels with the name *Aquila* in our records."

"Fourteen?"

"Right. A few records from the late 1700s, a handful from the 1800s..." She continued typing. "The rest from 1912."

"Do your records indicate whether a ship was retired or scrapped or sank?" I asked.

She huffed. "Our database is somewhat limited. I'd need to pull the records for each vessel to see what information we have."

"I see." I paused, hesitant to ask more. She was one of the more irritable archivists I'd encountered. But the *Aquila* was important—the very wreck, I thought, that my father might have been diving when he'd spotted the loot. And I wouldn't forget his sage advice: *Sometimes the answers aren't in the water, but out of it.*

"Can I come into the archive, then?" I asked. "I'm perfectly happy to sort through the records myself."

Her tone softened, albeit not by much. "Of course. We're open until five o'clock on Tuesdays, Wednesdays, and Thursdays."

Today was Thursday.

"So," Chloe continued, "if you can't make it in today, we can make an appointment for next week."

I scratched the back of my neck, disappointed. I'd have much rather gone on another dive today, particularly since Conrad would be out there. But I didn't want to wait another four days to learn about this ship.

"I'll be there in a couple hours," I told her, already reaching for my bag.

From Positano, I took a bus into Naples. During the trip, I'd texted Enzo, telling him I couldn't make our afternoon dive. When he asked what I was up to in Naples, I kept it vague. Visiting a few archives, I said, and if there's time, Museo del Mare—the Museum of the Sea.

The Archivio Marittimo di Napoli was located in central Naples, a few blocks north of the main shipping port, down a narrow cobblestone side street. It was two stories high, with a peach-colored stucco facade and a few barred windows. I approached the arched stone doorway, twice my height, and pushed open the door.

Sitting at a desk in the low-lit front room was a woman. The small placard in front of her read *Chloe*. "Hi," I said, hoping she was a bit more friendly in person. "I'm Haven. I called earli—"

"Yes, hello," she interrupted, pulling her gaze from the screen.

Chloe was small-statured, with platinum-blond hair and piercing blue eyes. She invited me to sign into the visitors' log, then she slid a form across the desk—the front was in Italian, but the back was in English—and asked me to fill it out. Afterward, she took me through a door and down a hall. The deeper we went into the building, the darker and cooler it became. I fought off a chill, wishing I'd brought a sweater.

Eventually, Chloe opened yet another door, and into the archive room we went.

"Oh, my God," I whispered, coming to a standstill.

She smiled, her first sign of warmth toward me. "We hear that a lot here."

I was not in a single room, not really. Instead, it was a deep row of adjoining rooms, each separated by an archway. Along the walls were enormous floor-to-ceiling metal shelves crammed with books and manuscripts wrapped in brown kraft paper. A ladder was mounted to each wall for ease of accessing the upper shelves.

A quick glance at a nearby shelf told me the archive was well-managed. Security cameras were mounted throughout, and a digital thermostat read nineteen degrees Celsius.

Chloe led me to the next room, which was identical to the first, with the exception of a large vent mounted to the ceiling.

A dehumidifier, Chloe explained, before leading me to the last room, where a pair of outdated computers sat on a wide desk. After showing me how to use the database—which was entirely in Italian—she left me alone, reminding me that the archive closed in three hours.

I sat down at the computer, watching the cursor blink above an entry field. When I'd studied Italian before this trip, I'd worried mostly about conversational phrases—how to get around, what to order at restaurants. I hadn't learned anything as technical as this. Sighing, I pulled out my phone and opened the Google Translate app, trying to make sense of the database.

Eventually, I managed to plug the word *Aquila* into a search field, and I was relieved when the number of records returned: 14. Just as Chloe had said on the phone.

The record identifiers were, I assumed, tied to the actual documents in the archive rooms. I'd been to many archives before, but I had to admit, this felt a bit foreign: I was surrounded by documents in a language I didn't know, tied to a database I couldn't understand, with a single unfriendly employee I wasn't keen to ask for help.

For each of the fourteen records, I jotted down what seemed to be the room number, the cabinet code, and the shelf identifier. I went in search of the first record, climbing a ladder to reach the uppermost shelf. I was thoroughly delighted when I spotted a brown paper bundle bearing the code I'd been searching for.

I brought the bundle back to the desk. After untying the cord wrapped around it, I discovered it was a manifest of more than two thousand passengers, dated 1912. There was no way the hull I'd spotted was this large. Even a crew of a hundred would be pushing it.

I rewrapped the bundle and returned it to its spot.

I pulled a few more records from various rooms, discouraged when they, too, related to the 1912 *Aquila*. As well-labeled as the archive seemed to be, I would have thought they'd put all records relating to a single vessel in one place. Still, I worked quickly down my list, determined to make this visit worth my time.

As I worked, I wasn't thinking of Conrad or Enzo or even Project Relic. Instead, I thought of my father. He'd be proud of me for digging into this. Mal would be proud of me, too, for thinking outside the box.

Finally, I unwrapped the records for a different *Aquila*. This next bundle consisted of blueprint and shipbuilding plans, nearly three dozen of them, all dated 1798. Though written in Italian, they detailed the vessel from various angles and cross sections. But tucked behind the blueprints was a certificate indicating the ship had been retired and scrapped in the mid-nineteenth century. In Gothenburg, Sweden.

It wasn't a match.

I pulled a few more records. Two were in German; another was in Spanish. In one of the bundles, I found an illegible journal and a tiny comb, both marked with a label bearing the word *relitto*, or flotsam. This was briefly encouraging, as this indicated the ship had sunk, but after a few more minutes, I put my elbows on the table and bent forward, frustrated. This particular ship had sunk in the Adriatic Sea. Another nonmatch.

I began to mull on the very real possibility that the *Aquila* I'd spotted underwater did not have any records, at least at this particular archive. There was only one record left to pull.

Fighting a sense of defeat, I brought the last bundle of documents to the desk and untied it. It was just after four o'clock, and with the way things were going, I'd be headed back to Positano in a few minutes' time.

I was shocked, then, when what I saw first was a leather pouch with a thick overlay of tar and a tiny, faded engraving on the front:

Voyage Journal of Holmes Foster
Boston, Massachusetts

A few folded documents were also in the bundle, but I went first for the pouch. I carefully pried it open, withdrawing the leather-bound journal inside. Both pouch and journal were badly stained, the leather bleached and rigid in places. Heavy water damage.

Like the engraved title on the cover, it was written in English, though in many places, the handwriting had faded so badly, the words were illegible. Still, many of the passages were clear, and I quickly gleaned that the author—Holmes—had been a sailor on a brig called the *Aquila* in 1821. I chose an entry at random, learning that he hated his fellow crew, whom he thought belligerent and unprincipled. There were multiple references to the *Mazza brothers*—I jotted this down in my notebook—and their bad business dealings, which Holmes called *deplorable*.

I set the journal aside, then studied the other document in the bundle, a newspaper article laminated in a thin plastic covering. It was dated May 1, 1821, and written in Italian. *L'Aquila Affonda*, the headline began. *Causa Sconosciuta*. I pulled out my phone, navigated back to Google Translate, and hovered it over the article. Instantly, the app translated the headline: *The Aquila Sinks, Cause Unknown*.

I tried this same technique with the rest of the article, but the typeset was small, and the laminated cover caught the glare of the lights overhead. Still, I was able to glean that the *Aquila* had gone down in precisely the spot I'd gone diving: the doomed waterway skirting the Li Galli islets.

I sat back in my chair, feeling confident—albeit not positive—that this article related to the wreck my father and I had both found.

I skimmed what little else the app had translated. Twenty-five men had perished in the sinking. One sailor, Nico, had been gravely injured before the sinking—but how news of this had reached the mainland was unclear. His injuries, the article stated, were the result of an incident blamed on another crew member.

And then, my jaw fell: the guilty party, according to the article, was none other than Holmes Foster. He'd been imprisoned in the brig's hold, with the intention of placing him under arrest upon disembarkation in Positano.

A feeling of excitement rose in my chest. This ship had sunk in precisely the right location. The *deplorable* bad business dealings, the incident onboard... I couldn't help but wonder if all of this had to do with the goods onboard.

Goods or...*loot*. Gems.

I glanced back at Holmes's diary. Guilty or not, he hadn't even made it to Positano. None of them had. They'd gone down, along with whatever else was on that boat.

I touched the waterproof pouch again. A few flakes of black waxy coating dislodged and stuck to my fingers, but otherwise it had sufficiently protected Holmes's journal within. It must have been recovered as flotsam, eventually—the tales of a man lost at sea. I was overwhelmed with a sudden urge to curl up on a chair and read every last page.

I glanced at my phone. The archive would be closing in less than half an hour. It wasn't enough time to read the journal, and I didn't want to make multiple return trips to Naples. I couldn't photograph every page, either—that would take hours, not to mention the added headache of sorting through hundreds of images.

So I did the next best thing. I hit the Record button, held my cell phone over the journal, and began to turn the pages. Later, I could rewatch the video, pausing as needed to read the journal at my own pace.

An automated recording played overhead, announcing the archive was about to close. I snapped a few additional photos, including the waterproof pouch and the news article, then I carefully rewrapped the bundle and returned it to its place.

When I returned to the entry hall, Chloe was gathering her

things to leave. She gave me a nod. "Find what you were looking for?"

"Yes," I said. "I think so." I took a few steps toward the door, then paused, remembering what I'd written down in my notebook. "Have you ever heard of the Mazza brothers?" I asked. "I came across their name in one of the records."

She chuckled. "Every historian in Naples has heard of the Mazza brothers. In the early 1800s, two-thirds of the ships in and out of Napoli were owned by them."

"Wow," I said. "Impressive."

"Eh," she said, cringing. "They were bad men—ran around with thieves, corsairs. Always packing their ships with stolen goods. They were swindlers, too, known for pulling tricks and planting decoys." She grabbed her purse, flung it over her shoulder. "They often stuffed their real goods in unexpected places." She shrugged. "Entertaining for us archivists, to be honest. We have plenty of records on the Mazzas, should you need them."

I thanked her, said goodbye, and stepped outside.

Always packing their ships with stolen goods, she'd said. I glanced at the azure sky, thinking of my father.

I was onto something, I felt sure of it.

23

MARI

Tuesday, April 24, 1821

On the morning the women intended to begin their watch, while Mari was at Ami's preparing her things to leave, there was a knock on Ami's door. With a small revolver in his hand, Dante rushed to the window, peering through the closed curtains.

"Corso," he said, frowning.

The blood drained from Mari's face. She hadn't expected him back so soon. She wondered if her father had sent him notice of all that had transpired in Positano.

Or perhaps this was about the engagement.

Dante opened the door.

"Your father said I would find you here," Corso said to Mari. "May I speak with you privately outside?"

Only a few people knew Mari's location. Now she felt a surge of irritation with her father for telling Corso where she was. She eyed the pathway leading up to the house. "It isn't safe," she said. "Surely he told you what happened."

"He told me about the kidnappings, yes." He turned to Dante and Ami. "I am very sorry to learn of Lia. I trust she will be found soon and returned home."

"Thank you," Dante said, his jaw set hard. "You two are welcome to speak in the cellar at the back of the house, if you'd like." After waiting for Mari's nod, he opened the door to let Corso slip inside.

The cellar was damp, sparse. Corso lit a candle near the entrance. In the flickering light, Mari could make out a few bottles of wine and a pair of boxes holding bruised fruit and wilted lettuce.

Corso reached into his pocket, and Mari braced herself as he withdrew a small box. "The jeweler finished the millegrain just two days ago," he said, prying it open.

The ring was lovely: a thin band of yellow gold, with intricate filigree wrapped around the entirety of it. The center of the ring bore a cluster of purple amethysts set in a marquise shape.

Mari fought an almost uncontrollable urge to pry the ring out and crush it beneath her shoe.

"What do you think?" Corso whispered. "It is unspeakably valuable, given the custom fil—"

"I think I want Lia home," she interrupted. "Viviana and the Fontana sisters, too. I want Leo to be alive. I want all of this to disappear."

Corso paused, studying her, then he snapped the ring box shut. "Come to Rome with me, Mari." He placed his arm around her shoulder, grazing his fingers along her skin. "Let me take you away."

Mari flinched, remembering the time Holmes said this exact thing to her—on the same night he'd taught her to trace shapes from the stars. They'd been tucked away in one of the many cliffside caves, looking out at the wide expanse of night sky.

"A mountain," Mari had said, pointing west. "I see a mountain just there. And another, right next to it." For a moment, mountains were all she could see among the stars.

Holmes nodded, tucking himself closer to her. He kissed her shoulder, watching her as she watched the sky. "Have you ever been to the mountains?" he whispered.

Mari shook her head. In fact, she had never left the Amalfi region. "No. I have always wanted to go. I've heard the peaks north of here, in Austria, are made of stone so white, it hurts to look upon them."

"The Pale Mountains," Holmes said. "I've met men who have climbed them." A falling star shot across the sky, then seemed to plunge into the sea. "Let me take you away. We'll travel there and see the mountains together."

Mari turned her face to his. "You promise?"

He pushed himself to his feet and walked deeper into the cave. With his knife, in the near total darkness, he carved a tiny, upside-down *V* into the cave wall.

A mountain.

And beneath this, their initials: *M&H*.

"I promise," he said, sitting down beside her again.

How distant that night felt now. Mari wished she'd appreciated it more: a sky full of star mountains. Holmes's breath on her skin. Their easy, childlike promises to one another.

Mari ducked away from Corso's embrace, making for the stairs. How interesting, she thought, that for all his money and friends in high places, he hadn't spent a moment contributing to the effort in locating Lia.

She had only one thing left to say to Corso. "No," she told him. Then she turned, leaving him at the base of the cellar steps, the ring box clutched tightly between his fingers.

That afternoon, the women began their watch from the hidden hollow tucked between two bluffs, very near the village of San Pietro. This cave was the best place to look westward, toward Capri: any ships coming from the west or north—like Naples—would be readily visible.

The women took twelve-hour shifts, scanning the horizon for the shadowy, slow-moving form of a ship. Anytime they spotted one in the distance, they kept a close eye on its heading, its speed, its flags.

Two days passed. By Thursday afternoon, Mari and Ami began to wonder whether Dante had been misinformed by the young stevedore on the Naples docks. The ship should have arrived by now. Mari decided they would wait a few more days, at least, before making the decision to give up their watch. After all, a storm had come through the region a few days earlier; perhaps that had hindered whatever vessel was on its way.

That evening, as Mari sat alone at the mouth of the cave, a gentle breeze kicked up, and a white-and-gray feather landed softly at her feet. She smiled, taking the feather in her hand. It reminded her of Holmes—he'd once shared a story about saving a young plover from a boatswain who intended to keep it as a pet—and she tucked it in her gown, tight against her breast.

She glanced westward—still nothing—and wondered what tomorrow might bring. The Fratelli Mazza? News of the kidnapped women? Or yet again, nothing at all? From what she'd been told, several more villagers had gone to Naples to inquire about the tiny island of Ischia and why the Fratelli Mazza were keeping it so closely guarded. These men had returned frustrated and empty-handed. They hadn't been able to track down any new information and certainly not the missing captives.

The mood in Positano, then, was grim. Many anguished over the kidnapping of four women. All anguished over the inevitable arrival of another Mazza vessel.

24

HAVEN

Thursday

That evening, Enzo and I lay on my bed. "How was the Museo del Mare?" he asked. We were on top of the duvet, propped up against pillows.

I had all but forgotten about the Museum of the Sea. I'd been too preoccupied with the archive. "I didn't go, actually. I ran out of time."

He faced me, smiling. "An entire afternoon at the archive, then?"

I smoothed the bottom edge of my thin pajama shorts, then crossed and uncrossed my legs. I couldn't seem to sit still, not with Enzo lying next to me. Even fully clothed, he left me light-headed. "I'm an archaeologist, remember. I love archives."

"Find anything good?"

I reached for my cell phone on the nightstand next to me. "Let me send you this picture of an article," I said. "Can you translate it for me?"

"Maybe." He scooted closer. "Depends."

I playfully swatted his arm and AirDropped the photo to him. While he read, I toyed with my own phone, begrudgingly peeking through Conrad's Instagram. He'd posted a story that morning, the video taken as he stood at the boat's helm next to his driver, Gio. Their dive boat cut through the waves, throwing sea spray into the air. Though I couldn't see Conrad, I could hear him laughing and hollering. They were making straight for Li Galli.

I glanced over at Enzo. "Done reading yet?" I asked. When he didn't reply, I threw a long, bare leg over his. "Psst. Hello. Hi."

He put his hand on my bare thigh, squeezing it. "Just finished," he said, his voice hoarse.

"Can you read it to me?" I asked. "The article?"

He paused a beat, all but eating me alive with his eyes. "Yeah," he finally said, situating himself more comfortably against the pillows. "All right, so—"

"Wait." I reached into my bag, grabbed my notebook and a pen, and then nodded. "Okay."

As he read, he repeated much of what I already knew: twenty-five men had perished on the *Aquila*, including a Holmes Foster, who was a prisoner onboard. But Enzo did share a few details that Google Translate hadn't picked up, including the brig's owners—the Mazza brothers—and assorted technical details about the vessel. Two-masted. One-hundred-eleven feet long. Two-hundred-fifty tons.

I tapped my pen on my notebook, disappointed. There was nothing useful here. And nothing gleaned about its cargo.

"Why this article?" he suddenly asked. "Do you think the *Aquila* is one of the wrecks we saw yesterday?"

I didn't think it was. I *knew* it was.

Still, I deflected. "I came across it while searching for info on Li Galli. Trying to understand why there are so many wrecks in the area."

Seemingly satisfied with this answer, he glanced at the bedroom door. "Care if I grab a glass of water?"

"Not at all."

When he left, I viewed Conrad's final Instagram story, posted six hours ago—when I was tucked away at the archive.

The image loaded, and my stomach dropped. Not only had they returned to Li Galli, they'd returned to the same location we'd left them at yesterday. It was further proof, as if I needed it, that Conrad wasn't taking pictures for Project Delfino at all. If so, they would have dropped anchor elsewhere.

"Goddammit," I said aloud, tossing my phone aside. I had to get back in the water tomorrow, no matter what. No matter the conditions.

Enzo returned, a glass of water in each hand. He took one look at me and raised his eyebrows. "Everything okay?"

I exhaled hard. "Yeah. Just work stuff."

He settled in again, facing me, propped up on one elbow. He toyed with the string on my pajama shorts.

"Can we go on another dive in the morning?" I asked. "Same spot as yesterday?"

He paused, his fingers hovering near me. "Is there something more to all of this? You seem…in a rush. These wrecks, they aren't going anywhere." His brown eyes searched mine. "We have time."

He didn't understand. I didn't have time. But I couldn't blame him for the statement: he didn't know the full story. And looking at him now, his expression full of both concern and desire, I felt more frantic than ever. About *everything*.

I set my water glass down, untied my pajama shorts, and kissed him with a week's worth of urgency and frustration.

The next morning, I shot a quick text to Mal. At last, having spent three nights at a hotel near the Naples airport, she'd finally been able to book a flight home for later that evening.

Can confirm, I said, Italian men make the best lovers.

Details, girl, she replied, with a flame emoji.

Walking to the kitchen for coffee, I eyed the countertop and flushed: last night, Enzo and I had frantically pushed everything to one side. I could make out the outline of a handprint, still visible on the glossy marble countertop. Then I glanced out at the terrace, the railing bright white in the morning sun, remembering how I'd clutched it last night, Enzo's hot breath on the back of my neck.

He's very adventurous, I texted back. If there's a solid surface in this place, I think we christened it.

Three little dots as Mal typed her reply. That's my kind of sex.

I laughed. Before last night, I'd never had sex on a kitchen counter or a terrace partially within view of an entire village. And yet, I'd loved every second of it. I hadn't been worried about breaking rules or being seen. I craved him so bad—even now, making coffee in the kitchen—that I thought I might ignite. **I think it's my kind of sex now, too, I replied.**

Enzo had gone home at three in the morning. Every last inch of me was tender, so I took a couple of Advil and a hot shower. Then, with plenty of time until I met him at the dock, I retreated to the terrace with my coffee and phone, ready to dive into Holmes's diary.

I started at the beginning. Holmes's first entry was made in July of 1817, and it recounted his excitement about an impending cross-Atlantic voyage from his home, Boston, to Sicily and then on to Naples. It was clear he'd been working on boats for much of his adolescence and early adulthood, and his journal entries revealed that he knew a little of everything, from repairing sails to carpentry to basic navigation. His knowledge of rigging was clear, too, and although I thought I knew a decent amount about sailing, I was quickly lost in Holmes's detailed descriptions of reefing lines, pulley systems, and intricate knots.

Entries of this nature went on and on. I kept my eye on the

clock—I needed to meet Enzo in half an hour—and I began to skim the pages, anxious to reach the part about Holmes's arrival in Italy. Only then, I suspected, would I find the topics that interested me: the Mazza brothers and their black-market loot.

Still, I found myself liking this Holmes more and more. Some entries revealed his compassionate side—like the time he'd pried a lure from a cormorant's mouth, despite his shipmates wanting to leave the bird for dead—and others were humorous, like when he once duped his crew with a seashell stew.

In December of 1817, on his twenty-second birthday, Holmes finally arrived in Naples. Yet just as I began to read the entry, Enzo texted.

Can't make our dive today, he said.

I frowned, feeling the brief sting of rejection, but then I began to worry he was ill or something had happened to him. You okay? I asked.

It took him a few minutes to reply, which only furthered my concern. Vesuvius headlines everywhere. I've been making calls all morning. Meet me for coffee?

"Shit," I whispered. "What now?" I went online to CNN where the leading headline was *Threat of Mt. Vesuvius Eruption Halts Amalfi Tourism*.

The beginning of the article quoted a leading travel agency. According to their spokesperson, more than seventy percent of their bookings to the Amalfi region for the next two months had been canceled in the last ninety-six hours.

"Some have changed their travel plans to Santorini or Ibiza," the spokesperson said. "Others have canceled outright. We're staffing extra agents around the clock to keep our customers happy."

Forget hype. The archaeologist in me wanted actual *data*. Toward the bottom of the article, as though an afterthought, a volcanologist had gone on record discussing his concerns. The underwater CO_2 measurements in the area had worsened overnight, he said. Certain water temperature recordings had shifted, too, and they didn't correlate with seasonal currents.

And yet, Mount Vesuvius herself—the actual crater, well inland—wasn't demonstrating anything out of the ordinary. No tremors. No dried-up vegetation. No change in the steam vents.

I went back to my text message with Enzo. **Coffee sounds good**, I typed out, my hands shaking. **When and where?**

We met at Dall' Alba al Tramonto, a café Enzo's mother had recently recommended to him.

The shop was mostly empty inside, just a pair of employees standing behind the counter. The news played out on a corner television. I couldn't understand it, but the subject of the story was evident enough, as the camera crew filmed live from Positano's Spiaggia Grande. The reporter waved to the half-empty beach behind him.

Enzo sat at an outdoor table, his hands folded in his lap. The terrace had a magnificent view of the ocean, but Enzo's expression was morose as he looked out at the water. Two cappuccinos sat in front of him.

I snuck up behind him, kissing him on the cheek. "Good morning."

He smiled, not letting me sit down until he'd pulled me in for a longer, deeper kiss. The brim of my hat mussed up his hair, and a few tables away, an elderly couple scowled at us. I fell heavily into my chair and reached for my cappuccino.

"So," I said, motioning toward the ocean. I didn't have a good view of the beach from here, but somewhere down there was the reporter I'd just seen on TV. "What do you make of it?"

"What I think doesn't matter much anymore." Enzo tapped his fingers on the table and exhaled hard. "When I got to the shop this morning, I had a voicemail from our insurance company."

I closed my eyes. I knew where this was going. "The decision isn't up to you anymore," I offered.

"Right." He showed me his phone, the list of outgoing calls. "Luca and I spent this morning calling everyone with open reservations. Updated our website. For the time being, we're—" he took a sip of his coffee "—closed."

"I'm so sorry," I whispered back, feeling terrible about his predicament. He'd told me how tight his shop's margins were. Without any divers for the foreseeable future, the shop would most certainly be in a deficit. And to think how hard he'd worked for all of this…

I couldn't help but think about myself, too. "Does this mean you can't take the boat out at all?"

He nodded slowly. "Unfortunately, yes. I'm so sorry, Haven."

So our diving was done. "Don't say that. None of this is your fault." I pushed my cappuccino away, my spirits as low as they'd been all week.

"It's so frustrating," he said, his jaw set. "The data, it doesn't—"

"Make sense," I finished for him. "There should be earthquakes, or geysers, or something else, if Vesuvius was about to erupt."

"Exactly. I don't know whether to be scared or not. Whether to leave or not."

"Do you know people who are leaving? Locals?"

"Quite a few, yes."

This surprised me. "What about your mother? Is she staying?"

"She's staying. She insists everything is fine." He shrugged. "Everyone is jumping on the bandwagon. But tourists are how my business stays afloat. No tourists, no work."

I mused on all that had gone awry in recent days. "What a shit week," I finally said.

Enzo reached for my hand. "Not everything about this week has been terrible."

My memory flashed to last night—the clean smell of his skin, digging my nails into his shoulder blades, resting my head in the crevice of his collarbone—and felt myself grow warm.

"Not everything, no," I agreed. "Meeting you has been the complete opposite of terrible."

Enzo's face was solemn. "I just don't understand why the world works this way. I meet the first amazing woman I've met in years, and in the same week, my business—and the entire town—go to shit."

I gave his hand a squeeze, but his phone buzzed and he pulled away. "I need to get going," he said. "People wanting refunds on their deposits..."

I ached for him, wondering if his business even had the cash on hand to issue refunds.

After Enzo left, I checked my Instagram again. Conrad had posted a new story, and I clicked on it, wondering how he was dealing with the latest news.

Apparently, he wasn't.

He was ignoring it entirely, given that he'd posted a video of himself on a boat only a few minutes ago. *Making great progress!* the caption read. *I've got a good feeling about the next few days.*

I could read between the lines: this post was meant for me. He wanted me to know he was getting close to my father's discovery. Had his equipment picked up an anomaly of some kind?

I felt helpless. Without Enzo, I didn't have a boat. I didn't have a dive buddy. I didn't have air tanks. And even if I had all of those things, did I want to dive in such precarious conditions?

Not for the first time in recent days, I began to wonder if I should simply accept defeat. Conrad had the tools and the skills to brave these waters. I didn't. Simple as that.

I called Mal, who picked up on the second ring. "Everything okay?" she asked, her voice higher-pitched than normal, laced with concern. Indistinct voices chattered in the background. She would be at the airport now, getting ready to head home. "I've seen the news."

"Yeah," I said. "Well, no. I mean, I'm fine. I'm not in any danger." I spun my empty cup on its saucer, annoyed with everything. "I just feel…hopeless. Frustrated. Part of me is tempted to throw in the towel and come home."

There was a moment of silence. "Wow," Mal finally said. "I did not expect you to say that."

I hadn't expected it myself, either, but nothing about this trip had gone right. Professionally, at least. And I didn't think a budding romance with Enzo was reason enough to stay. Better to cut my losses, I thought, and head home before I fell even further for the guy.

"Hold on," Mal said. I heard footsteps, then the background noise on her end quieted. "Haven," she said. "Don't do anything rash. You need to think on this. You're not the quitting type."

"Conrad is on the water right now," I reminded her. "I'm not. I don't even have access to a boat anymore."

"Did things go sour with Enzo?"

"On the contrary. I'm crazy about him."

"That's unlike you."

"I know. But his shop's insurance company called. No diving for the foreseeable future. I can call up other dive shops, but they're probably in the same predicament." I found myself spewing words at Mal, telling her about the last couple of days. Photographing the *Aquila*. The archive. Diving with Enzo, sleeping with Enzo. "I feel like I'm so close to putting a few puzzle pieces together. But I need more dive time." I stifled a yawn. "And I need a full night's sleep."

"That's on you, girl. Take a nap. No one told you to stay up all night having sex."

"And for the love of God," I went on, ignoring her, "I need a dive buddy. I can't go down there alone."

"Let me make some calls," Mal suddenly said. "Go take a nap. I'll text you soon."

"Calls? Who do you plan to call?"

"I know people."

"What do you—" But I stopped short, interrupted by loud chatter on the other end of the call again.

"Talk soon, love," Mal said.

She hung up before I could reply.

Having resolved to accept Mal's suggestion about a nap, I grabbed my purse to leave. Two women had just stepped onto the terrace, coffees in hand. They took a seat beneath a potted wisteria tree, bursting in blooms. I glanced at them with only minor interest, but then I did a double take: one of the women looked very much like Enzo's mother, Savina. And hadn't he said she recommended this café to him?

I studied her for a moment behind my sunglasses. That bright red lipstick—it was undoubtedly her. And she was accompanied by another woman, the one she'd been with on the beach the other day.

I wavered for a moment. Saying hello might open the floodgates to questions about me and Enzo, a conversation I didn't have the energy for. Besides, Savina herself seemed preoccupied, sitting close to her friend as the two of them looked over a stack of papers.

Pulling the brim of my hat down, I planned to make a quick exit. I already wore sunglasses, so I felt certain Savina wouldn't recognize me.

Then I heard it—the name of the influencer whose yacht had gone down. *Asher Vice.*

The women were speaking in fast, hushed Italian, but I caught a few more words, including *Vesuvius* and—at this, I nearly tripped—*la Maledizione Amalfitana.* The Amalfi Curse. Savina's friend said the word *streghe* several times, and I made a mental note, thinking it vaguely familiar.

Everyone was talking about the hydrothermal vent data and the yacht sinking. But still, I found it strange how the women hovered over the pages in front of them. What were the printouts, anyway? I badly wanted a peek.

Throwing my purse over my shoulder, I quietly stood. As I moved toward the door, I paused, pretending to rummage through my bag while eyeing the papers spread out on the table.

I was only able to glance at them for a second or two, but it was more than enough. The papers were covered in data—tables—that I recognized, instantly, as oceanography readings. A couple of days ago, the news broadcaster had displayed charts looking just like this. And these pages were riddled with annotations and highlights, like something out of my own research notebook.

I remembered Savina's concern about Enzo diving Li Galli, and now I understood why: obviously, she was fixated on its strange occurrences. Obsessive, even, given the marked-up data tables. It reminded me of the way my father used to mark up his site maps, his depth charts. And now, as I walked past, she tapped a pen against the pages. She mentioned the word *Asher* again, and *memoriale*.

This woman was even more peculiar than I'd thought.

I'd nearly made my way to the front door of the café when I felt a hand lightly touch the spot between my shoulder blades.

Shit.

"Haven," came Savina's voice. I turned, feigning surprise, and greeted her. "I saw you walking out," she said in her thick Italian accent, "and my friend, Renata, was just leaving. Have a few minutes?"

It would have been terribly inconsiderate to refuse. I returned to the patio and took a seat, making brief small talk with Renata before she left.

To my relief, Savina steered clear of talking about Enzo. We discussed her villa renovations—next week, a contractor would be installing the chandelier I'd seen sitting on the floor during my visit—and then she asked me more about my schooling and some of my favorite wrecks in the Keys.

The conversation began to wane. "Before we go," Savina

said, motioning for me to stand. Fallen wisteria petals dotted the ground around us. "I was thinking about something you told me at the villa."

As we stepped into the sunshine, I was better able to study her face. I noticed, now, the lines etched deep in her forehead, the shadows under her eyes. She looked sleep-deprived, strained. I knew that look well—grief, wallowing its way through the body—and I empathized greatly with her. Losing Bria...well, I couldn't fathom the toll it had taken on her heart.

"You said there are rumors of sunken treasure that intrigue you," Savina said. "Is there anything specific you're looking for?"

I tried to keep my expression neutral. Her question was a bit too on the nose. I traced back through our earlier conversation, wondering if I'd accidentally revealed *why* I was diving Li Galli. I felt sure I hadn't.

I gave a weak shake of the head. "Not really," I lied.

"Hm," Savina said, opening the door for me. I sensed my response had disappointed her. She leaned in to give me a quick hug. "Well, have a lovely day, Haven."

With that, Savina slipped out of the café before disappearing into the narrow and winding streets of sun-riddled Positano.

25

MARI

Friday, April 27, 1821

The vessel arrived, at last, in the twilight hours of Friday, April 27.

Mari was on watch with Emilia and Pippa. They had been awake all night, practicing the stanzas of the *incantesimo vortice*. Their aim was not to draw a deep, slow current from the sea but rather something fast and impossibly turbulent—something unsurvivable—in a small area of the ocean.

The women could not err, not with so much at stake.

Trying to stay alert, Mari had just taken a half-hearted glance through the brass eyepiece of a scope that had once belonged to her mother. Her eyelids were heavy, and as she rubbed at them, her vision blurred.

She could not quite believe it, then, when she spotted the hazy shape of a vessel in the distance, cloaked in sea mist.

She handed the instrument to Pippa, then she heard someone crawling down the steep, shrubby hillside outside the cave—Ami and Paola, arriving for their shift.

Mari pointed at the silhouette in the distance. "Look," she said to the women.

As the others peered out at the sea, Ami discreetly reached into her bag and withdrew a letter, tucking it into Mari's hand.

Mari frowned, confused for a moment. Yet the moment she spotted the handwriting on the envelope, her stomach lurched. *A letter from Holmes.*

While the four others took turns looking through the eyepiece, Mari stepped outside the cave and tore open the envelope, reading it by the light of her lantern. It was dated Sunday, April 22.

The missive was short, his handwriting sloppy.

I heard what happened, the letter began. *How you killed Massimo. How you escaped the* Lupo.

Mari's brows knit together in confusion. How could Holmes, seabound aboard the *Aquila* north of Rome, have possibly heard this news?

You must flee the village, the letter went on. *Matteo and his men intend to find you and seize you.*

This Mari already knew. If all went as planned, Matteo would never have the chance.

But what Holmes revealed next horrified her.

Two days ago, they shifted our itinerary, and we began a southward route. As I write this, we are very near Naples. It is my brig—the *Aquila*—that has been assigned to make its way, with haste, to Positano. Matteo is on board.

If you have not left already, you must leave the moment you get this letter. If you cannot, then at the very least keep vigilant: I will paint a circle of tar very near the bow, portside, on the hull's yellow band. From afar, it will resemble a porthole. Remember, we are two-masted. No guns.

When you are safe, send a letter to Ami, telling her where I can find you.

Please keep well, my dearest.

With all my love,
Your Holmes

Mari placed her hand against her chest. He'd written this five days ago, near Naples. They should have arrived by now, but the storm would have held them back.

Slowly, Mari tucked the letter into the small bag slung across her chest and looked out at the horizon, the shadow of the brig growing infinitesimally closer.

This could not be real.

This could not be true.

"Mari," Ami said, her voice grave. "Mari, the vessel is flying the Mazza flag."

Her knees grew weak. She glanced out—the sea mist had begun to lift—and she could make out the dual masts of the brig, its lack of cannons.

And—the yellow band of paint. From so far away, she could not yet make out a painted circle of tar. Still, she sensed this could only be the *Aquila*. With Matteo onboard. With Holmes onboard.

And to think this had all been Mari's idea.

"It's them," Paola said, her face flushed. She eyed Mari suspiciously—had she seen Ami pass her a letter?—then pointed. "Let's go down to the water."

"Are we sure about their heading? They're coming this way?" Pippa asked.

If the brig were headed south, they would be gazing now at the side of the vessel, and the sails would look like oyster shells, shallow arcs as they caught the wind. But these sails were spread high and wide, rectangles seizing almost the full width of the vessel, which meant it was headed—

"Yes," Paola said. "It is coming right for us." She lifted her *cimaruta* to her lips, giving it a light kiss.

"It's a long way off yet," Mari managed. She crossed her arms, so better to hide her trembling hands. The brig was still well beyond the Li Galli archipelago and moving quite slowly. She estimated it would be an hour at least before it passed the islets.

"There are five of us," Paola said suddenly. "We had planned for only three. Think of it. How quickly we will take it down."

Mari's mind could not comprehend what she was seeing, what she'd just learned. As the women gathered their things, readying to leave the cave, her stomach sank with dread.

What, she wondered, *am I to do now?*

26

HOLMES

Friday, April 27, 1821

In the very early hours of the morning, Holmes woke from a restless slumber to the sound of something scratching nearby. He thought it might be the men making more brig repairs. Yesterday, he'd overheard them announcing the arrival of a few tenders with fresh stores of sailcloth and wood. This had been followed by hours of hammering, thumping.

Eventually, they'd begun moving, though Holmes had no sense of their speed, nor their heading.

A few men had retrieved Nico's shrouded body, too. Holmes wept when they took him away. He hoped that Nico's body would, somehow, make it back to his family.

Now he shifted in his tiny cell, his shoulder aching terribly, as the scratching went on. He'd heard footsteps for days now, the back-and-forth clamor of men walking the berthing deck. And yet, this noise sounded so terribly close. Directly above him, in fact.

His prison cell consisted of four iron-barred walls; the ceiling and floor were merely planks, which separated him from the bilges below him and the berthing deck above him.

He looked upward, curious about the noise.

Suddenly, he jumped.

In a narrow gap between the wooden planks above him were *eyes*. He thought it an animal at first, but their voyages were too short for livestock; they hadn't any need for pigs or chickens, as they were in port often enough to keep their food stores well-stocked.

The eyes blinked. They were very dark, almost black, and the eyelashes thick and long.

Holmes wrapped his arms around himself, feeling exposed. He contemplated his precise location on the ship; he must be directly beneath the second mate's cabin—the same cabin where the officers were keeping something of unspeakable value.

Matteo. According to Quinto, Matteo had been in the second mate's cabin a few days ago, looking through maps. Was it the older Mazza brother looking down upon him now? Spying, maybe?

"What do you want?" Holmes asked, louder than he intended.

"Hush," came the soft reply. "You fool. He'll return for you if he hears you talking to me."

Holmes's mouth fell open. It was a woman's voice.

She peered directly at Holmes through the gap. Given her gaze between the planks, Holmes thought she must be lying facedown on her belly. He clamped his hand over his mouth in surprise: while he was accustomed to chafed skin and noxious bilges and the ceaseless swaying of a vessel, he was not accustomed to this—women on his ships.

He studied her eyes more closely. "Who are you?" he whispered. The second mate's cabin had been locked, except when Matteo had been inside. Was this woman imprisoned, too, then, in the cabin? He wondered if she'd lifted a rug, or moved a piece of furniture, to peer down at him.

"Who are *you*?"

He hesitated a moment, then: "Holmes Foster."

"You're not from here," she replied in magnificent Italian. Her dialect sounded familiar.

He shook his head. "Massachusetts."

"And what did you do to get yourself locked up?"

Holmes might have thought her one of Quinto's prying accomplices, if not for the fact that Holmes had all but admitted to the crime already. "I took a knife to the rigging," he said, "and tarred the spare sailcloth. I hoped to sabotage the voyage. Perhaps I've done so. I've delayed it, at the very least."

"Hmm." Her eyes narrowed, and she shifted on her belly. "Did Quinto or the captain do something to anger you?"

He wouldn't dare tell the truth—would not so much as breathe Mari's name. He kept silent.

"Ah, so he's a man of secrets," the woman said, giving a small laugh. "Well, I cannot say I am surprised. It is a Mazza vessel. I fancy every man here has a motive different than what he's stated aloud."

Whoever this woman was, she wasn't new to this brig, nor the dealings of these men. He tried again. "Who are you?"

"I do not trust you enough to tell you," she said.

Holmes picked at a hangnail, feeling himself grow frustrated with her. "We were told the second mate was thrown out of his cabin. They wouldn't tell us why, but they installed a padlock bigger than any I've ever seen." He narrowed his eyes, tried a new tactic. "What do you have up there with you? Black-market goods?"

"Nothing worth anything," she said.

"*Who*, then?"

"No one now."

"Someone was with you earlier?"

"They have been in and out for weeks, yes."

Holmes considered who she might mean. "Quinto," he ventured, "or the captain, or Matteo?"

"All three," she said, "though, mostly Matteo."

He felt certain, then, that she was a prostitute. It wasn't uncommon to bring them aboard. But still, the secrecy around her—and the padlock, too—didn't make sense.

The woman's eyes disappeared, and Holmes heard footsteps as she shuffled away. It seemed she had free reign of her cabin.

She must have left a lantern on the floor, for a faint light seeped through the planks into Holmes's cell. It was more light than he'd seen in days. He opened his diary, feeling the urge to write or draw. He hoped he had not frustrated the woman, and he waited impatiently for her to return. He busied himself by half-heartedly sketching an illustration of the *Aquila*.

The woman did finally return, a few minutes later. "Here," she said, dropping half a hazelnut through the planks.

Holmes popped it into his mouth as she continued to drop hazelnut pieces, one by one. His stomach ceased its growling for the first time in days.

"The other Mazza brother is dead," he volunteered, hoping to keep her interest, earn her trust. It was maddening, her refusal to share her identity.

Her fingers hovered over the slit, a tiny nut perched between them. "What did you just say?"

"The other Mazza brother is dead."

"Massimo," she offered.

"Yes."

"What happened to him?"

"Someone killed him," Holmes said.

She gasped. "Serves him right. They are evil men."

Holmes paused. She wouldn't have called them *evil men* if Matteo were within earshot. Perhaps Matteo was now in the officers' quarters.

How uninformed he felt, secreted away in the bowels of this brig.

"Yet here you are, hiding—or imprisoned—in the second mate's cabin," he said. If he could not get her to tell him *who* she was, he could at least try to understand her purpose here.

"Imprisoned," she muttered.

"Are you someone's mistress, then?"

"Absolutely not," she hissed. "I would not touch one of these men—not the officers, not the brothers—if my very life was at stake."

A flash of silver caught his eye. The woman was trying to squeeze a narrow container—a snuffbox—between the gaps, but it would not fit. Instead, she pried open the container and dropped a few pinches of tobacco through the crack.

Holmes held out his hand, letting it fall into his palm. But then, he frowned. A silver snuffbox had been reported missing earlier in the voyage. "Did you steal this?"

"I did," she admitted, the hint of a smile in her voice.

"How," he asked, "if you are locked in?"

"The louver at the bottom of the cabin door," she said. "I slide the privacy cover off, take out the wooden pegs, and remove the louver. It is just wide enough for me to slip through."

So she is the thief among us, Holmes thought, eyeing his prison cell for some ingenious exit, as she had. He could find none.

"How have you not been caught?" he asked. "You must be sneaking out very late. And even still, you're lucky you haven't run into anyone on the night watch."

"Lucky, indeed," she said. "Though, don't forget, I have a closet full of men's clothing at my disposal. In the middle of the night, I'm not nearly as conspicuous as you might think."

Holmes popped another nut into his mouth.

"What is that book, anyway?" the woman said, nodding at Holmes's journal.

"Many of us sailors keep a log," he said.

"That is far from a record of headings and weather observations, though. A diary, then?"

"I suppose," he relented. "Sometimes, I tear out pages and write letters." He gave a shrug. "No way to send any letters now, though."

"I could send a letter for you," she said. "There is enough of a gap between these wooden planks for you to slip me a piece of paper."

"I appreciate the offer." He leaned back against the iron bars and sighed. There was nothing else to send. He could only hope that Mari had already received his warning and left Positano. "There is only one person I would write to, and she is—" Holmes paused. "Well, I don't know where she is. I hope she is not in Positano any longer." He felt no hesitation about sharing this with a stranger. He was lonely—terribly so—and scared, too. Even the most hardened of seamen longed for friends.

"Positano?" the woman repeated, her voice rising. "A sister?" she asked. "A friend?"

"Not a sister. But not really a friend, either." He thought of his time in the olive grove with Mari, the glances and stories exchanged between them. The ways they'd touched each other, too.

"A lover, then."

He paused. "A lover, yes." Though, even this felt terribly inadequate.

"Tell me about her," the woman said.

Without thinking, Holmes said the first thing that came to mind, perhaps because he was surrounded by it himself. "She hates the sea. She lives in a villa overlooking the ocean, but she keeps the curtains drawn over her bedroom window. She would rather sit in the dark."

Or go to the mountains, he mused. He'd vowed to take her. It was a promise he wouldn't be able to keep.

"What does she look like?" the woman asked.

"Her hair is very red." *And there is a tiny mole on her left palm,* he didn't add, *and my thumb fits perfectly in the little dip behind her earlobe.*

"There are not many women in Positano with red hair..." He heard a shift in the woman's voice, something like surprise or hesitation.

"Nor in Italy at all," Holmes agreed.

"I used to know many women with red hair," the woman said. "But they all adored the sea."

"Well—" Holmes stopped Mari's name from slipping from his tongue "—she once told me she used to adore the sea, too."

"What changed her mind?"

"Her mother drowned," he said, "and her younger sister, too. She feels she has lost everything to the ocean."

"When did her mother drown?"

Holmes frowned, thinking on the math. "Twelve years ago."

"And what about her—" the woman's voice caught "—her sister?"

That was easier to remember. Mari spoke of her every time they met. "Two years ago."

The woman fell silent, her breathing so quiet he thought she might have fallen asleep. But then, as the moments passed, Holmes heard her weeping. He waited patiently, giving her space to purge whatever burdened her so.

Finally, she said a name he recognized. "Sofia."

Mari's little sister. Holmes sat up very straight. "You know of Sofia?"

"Yes," she said. "Sofia and Mari, they are my daughters. I am...Imelda. I am Mari's mother."

27

MARI

Friday, April 27, 1821

From where she stood, high on the bluff, Mari gazed out at the water, wringing her hands. The *Aquila* grew closer.

"We ought to go down to the water now," Paola said to the women. "They are furling their sails."

Mari knew what this meant: if the officers had ordered the furling of the sails, they intended to slow the vessel, to ready her anchor.

"Let's go," Emilia said.

Though the others nodded, Mari stayed put. She felt numb, unable to move forward.

"Mari," Paola said, a chill in her voice. "You seem unsure about something." Suddenly she lunged forward, thrusting her hand into Mari's bag. She pulled her hand away, Holmes's letter clutched between her fingers.

"What's this?" she demanded.

"Give it to me," Mari cried. But Paola turned her back, ripping the letter from the envelope while using her body to deflect Mari's reach.

"Paola," Ami interjected, voice trembling, "it's not something we have time to discuss. Please, give the letter back to Mari. The two of you can talk about it later."

"Talk about what?" Pippa asked. She and Emilia stood to the side, confusion on their faces.

Paola held up the letter. "It seems Mari has a lover." She glanced out at the brig. "He's on the *Aquila* at this very moment." She turned to Mari. "How long have you known this man? And does he know about Corso?" Then, under her breath, so only Mari could hear, "I shouldn't be surprised. Not with everything else you've lied about."

Mari snatched the letter back. "This has nothing to do with you," she hissed.

"It has everything to do with me. Corso would ask for my hand if he didn't intend on asking for yours."

"*Intend* on asking?" Mari spat back. "He already has."

Paola's mouth dropped open. "When?"

"A few days ago, at Ami's." Mari stuffed the letter into the pocket of her dress. "I told him I don't want his proposal or his filigreed ring. I just want to find Lia."

"I don't understand," Pippa said, clutching her *cimaruta*. "Are we still planning to go down to the water, to sink the vessel?"

Mari couldn't reply. Her knees buckled, and she fell to the ground with a sob.

"Leave us a minute," Ami told the others. She knelt next to Mari, brushing her hair away from her face. "We must," she said. "We must sink it."

"I know," Mari said through tears. She fixed her mind on Matteo instead of Holmes and thought of all the pain the Fratelli Mazza had brought upon the village. If the women let the *Aquila* make landfall, the men would ravage the village again. Who would they seize—or kill—this time? Mari could not bear to have more blood on her hands.

She considered what Holmes would want. He would insist she go forward with her plan. He would, in fact, be furious if he knew she'd considered otherwise, even for a moment.

"Holmes would want me to do this," Mari concluded, grief-stricken.

She pushed herself upright, clearing dirt and leaves from her gown. She wiped her hand across her face, blinking back tears. There was no time for it now. She had a lifetime to grieve the loss of a dream, the loss of being Holmes's wife.

Right now, however, there was a task at hand.

"Let's go," Mari said, motioning for the others to make their way down the hill. She took her place at the back but, after a few moments, Paola slowed to walk in step with Mari.

"How many other secrets are you keeping?" Paola hissed.

Mari's breath caught. "I'm sorry?"

Paola came to a halt, faced Mari head-on. Ahead, the other women continued down the hill. "You've been living a lie," Paola said, "but I know the truth. I know what really happened to your mother."

Mari's heart lurched. *No.* This must have been what Paola meant a few moments ago when she'd said, *Not with everything else you've lied about.*

For an instant, Holmes was forgotten. It was just Mari and Paola. And this long-buried secret, blasted wide-open.

"We both know she didn't drown," Paola added. "I was with my mother along the water that night, too. We saw it all."

That day twelve years ago, in the early hours of the morning, eight-year-old Mari had woken to the sound of hurried footsteps. Glancing out the window, she caught her mother leaving through the gate, a bag slung over her shoulder.

Earlier, Mari's mother had been particularly affectionate with her and Sofia, embracing the girls for a long while, planting kisses all over their foreheads. Mari remembered feeling so safe that night, so very loved.

But after seeing her mother rush through the gate, young Mari's curiosity got the best of her. In her thin nightgown, she wasted no time discreetly following after her. Down staircase after staircase she went. Once on the beach, Mari watched in horror as her mother crawled into a *gozzo* with two strange men. For a moment, she thought she was not awake at all but in a strange dream.

Just before the men began to row her mother away, Mari started to run.

"No!" she screamed, her bangs sticking to her face. She nearly slipped on the pebbled beach.

Her mother looked up, startled. "Mari!" she yelled. "What are—"

"Where are you going?"

Imelda's eyes were wide in horror. "You were not supposed to see this. You were not supposed to know." She nodded at one of the men. "She is my cousin. Move. Now."

Young Mari frowned. Cousin? That didn't make any sense. The man thrust his oars into the water and began to row, but Mari threw herself against the side of the boat, pulling at it with weak fingers. The edge of the *gozzo* dug into her palms; later, her father would pick out a half dozen splinters.

"Please, no, where are you—"

Suddenly, a forceful current pulled her backward. She glanced up; her mother's fingers were trailing on the surface of the ocean. The current grew stronger, and as Mari fought against it, the boat floated farther and farther away.

Mamma, she whispered, up to her waist in the sea. *Mamma*.

There was nothing more she could do.

Her mother had left, willingly so.

Mari returned to the house in anguish, her legs shaking. She'd vomited twice on the road. She went to Sofia's room first. Nudging her four-year-old sister awake, she prepared to tell her that *Mamma* would not be coming home. But as Sofia turned over in bed, bleary-eyed and looking terribly fragile, terribly naive, Mari found herself unable to admit that their mother had just abandoned them.

It seemed easier to say she was...dead.

And so that was the story Mari told her father and Sofia, and the villagers, and Holmes, too: that she'd followed Imelda to the ocean in the middle of the night and watched as her mother went for a swim—but after diving in, she never emerged from the water. Mari, being so young, hadn't had the strength to rescue a grown woman from the sea.

The *streghe* asked Mari if Imelda had been wearing her *cimaruta* when she drowned. Mari said yes, for her mother never took it off. Even still, the sea had been too much. The women nodded in understanding: they all knew that the talisman was a source of strength, but it did not make a *strega* invincible.

Everyone believed Mari's story, then.

The sea *had* taken her mother.

That part, at least, was true.

Now Mari held Paola's gaze, astounded that she and Cleila had known the truth all along. "Why were you on the beach that night?" Mari asked. "It was the middle of the night."

"Neither my mother nor I slept well in the months after my father died," Paola replied. "We often took late-night walks along the water."

Paola's revelation explained much, including why Paola had recently accused Mari of being showered with sympathy she didn't deserve: Mari's mother wasn't actually dead. Paola's father was.

It also made sense that Cleila and Paola had kept the secret. If the village knew that Imelda was still alive somewhere, it would illegitimatize Cleila's marriage to Father.

"Anything else?" Paola hissed now. "I know the truth about your lover, your mother... What else haven't you shared?"

Mari thought of her covert plan to escape Positano, to forgo a life with Corso in favor of one with Holmes. But what did that matter now? It had been just that—a plan. One that would not be coming to fruition. It was as good as dead.

"Nothing," Mari said. "There's nothing left at all." She turned on her heel and began to walk, leaving Paola behind her.

Mari rejoined the women as they made their way down the narrow, rocky trail. Though they'd used this path a few times before, it was overgrown, and Paola cried out as sharp branches slapped against her legs. Ami nearly slipped twice.

By the time the five women arrived at the bottom, the *Aquila* loomed not far ahead; it would be crossing by Li Galli in half an hour, Mari thought bleakly.

They could begin *le incantesimi*—their incantations—shortly.

Emilia suddenly began to cry. "I do not think I can do it," she muttered, shaking her head. "Those men, they are brothers and fathers and..."

Lovers, Mari thought to herself.

"They are *captors*," Pippa shot back, hands splayed. It seemed any talk of Holmes had been forgotten. "They took my mother and killed my father. They mean us nothing but harm."

"Let's get into place. It's time," Mari said, her bottom lip trembling. She bit down hard, willing herself to focus, though her thoughts still circled the conversation she'd just had with Paola.

She'd never been able to understand why her mother had abandoned her and Sofia. As a child, Mari wondered if she and Sofia had driven their mother away for simple reasons: their ever-sandy feet, their mess of shells in the garden, their repetitive questions about the sea and its watery mysteries.

Yet as Mari grew older, her suspicions matured. Like prying a mussel shell open with a knife, Mari eventually understood that some people—women, especially—tucked away their most tender secrets.

Secrets like greed. Had the simple life as a villager's wife not been enough for Mari's mother? She might have wanted bigger, grander things or a more luxurious lifestyle.

Or had it been love? Perhaps Imelda had kept someone on the side. Had she been in love with one of the men who took her away?

It didn't give Mari peace, exactly, to consider that these might have been the reasons her mother had left, but anything was better than the idea of her and Sofia driving their mother away.

Now Mari forced her attention back to the sea.

This part of the coast formed an arc roughly twenty meters wide. Mari directed Paola to the far end, then arranged herself and the other women so they were evenly spaced apart along its remaining length. This way, the cursed tract of water encapsulated a narrow strip extending from the coastline right into the eye of the Li Galli islets.

Once in position, the women bent down, each placing her hands in the sea. Mari heard faint whispers as the other four women recited the first stanza of the incantation.

At once, the water began to pull away from Mari's hands, as though it wanted nothing to do with her. Small waves lapped outward from her fingers, creating a concave indentation in the water.

She was filled with resistance, and this was the sea's expression of it.

The *Aquila* grew near. Mari wondered about Holmes. Was he on deck or in his berth or elsewhere? Did he see the strange whirlpool building just ahead? Did *any* of the crew see it?

Keeping her head low, Mari began reciting the incantation. She kept her gaze on the water, the reflection of her blood-red hair shifting and swaying in the newly incensed current.

28

HOLMES

Friday, April 27, 1821

At Imelda's revelation, Holmes froze. "Impossible," he said. "Mari, she—"

He searched his memory for the details of her story, what Mari had seen when she was only eight years old. She had never shared her mother's name. "Mari said the sea took you from her—that she watched you drown."

"The first part is true," Imelda said. "The sea did take me from her. But I did not drown, and Mari knows it."

There came a rustling sound above Holmes, and then through the gap, several long, red hairs floated downward. She had either run her fingers through her hair, or she'd plucked them out. He lifted one of the strands, trailing it across his palm. Even in the low light, he could make out its blood-red color, just like Mari's.

He began to think this a trick. Swindling was the Mazza way, after all. Had Quinto some idea that Holmes was in love with Mari? Perhaps he had put him here, just beneath the second mate's cabin, for a reason—instructing this actress of a woman to sniff out whatever information she could glean.

"What happened, then?" he asked. In a matter of moments, his feelings about her had turned from curiosity to disdain. Either this woman had abandoned her two daughters, or she was lying and pretending to have done so.

"I left to protect them," she said. "I fooled the Mazza brothers into believing I was the last *strega*. They did not know I had two daughters. I turned myself over before they could learn that Mari and Sofia even existed."

Holmes shifted to get a better angle, his back aching. "*Strega?* I've never heard the word."

"Mari has not told you?"

"No." The air around them had grown silent. The brig seemed to have slowed somewhat.

"There are women in Positano with special…abilities. We practice something known as *stregheria*. Witchcraft. Have you heard about it?"

Nico had once said something about his sister and her odd interests—kitchen spells with herbs and pastes, prayers over babies, olive pits turned to beads—but he hadn't called it witchcraft.

"I don't know anything about it," Holmes concluded.

"Some call us witches of the sea," Imelda went on. "We can decipher the ocean's secrets—its strange movements, its seemingly inexplicable behaviors. We understand what it is saying about the things that lie beneath the surface. Things like wrecks, treasure. The ocean reveals it all," she went on, "though in a language few understand."

Holmes wondered if *stregheria* explained some of the more perplexing things about Mari, like her ability to hold her breath underwater for long stretches of time or her skill in finding rare seashells.

"Many years ago," Imelda continued, "the two Mazza brothers were in the village, and they caught me performing a simple sea spell. I'd been searching for a small silver bracelet Sofia had lost in the shallow waters, very near the beach. I placed my strand of hagstones in the water, reading it, letting it guide me. Within moments, I found the bracelet."

"Did the bracelet have a tiny seal charm affixed to it?"

Imelda held his gaze. "You have seen it."

He nodded. "Mari showed it to me once."

"Does she wear it?"

"No. She is terrified of something happening to it. She keeps it safe, elsewhere."

"Ah." Imelda nodded. "Well, little did I know the brothers began to follow me—for days, I later learned. Thank God, they only caught me doing spells on my own. They never saw me with my daughters, nor the other *streghe*."

"So Mari is a *strega*, then?"

"Of course she is," Imelda said quickly. "And I suspect a better one than I ever was." She let out a long exhale. "Eventually, the men confronted me at knifepoint. They asked if anyone else in the village had such abilities. I said no, for I was not about to risk the welfare of my daughters or my friends. The men instructed me to come with them, else they would kill me. I convinced them to let me return home for a few hours, so I could gather some things to leave by the shore, which would give the appearance I'd merely gone for a swim. This, I said, would prevent my husband from searching for me, asking questions." Imelda swiped away a tear. "It was not about my husband at all. I just needed to see my daughters once more. To kiss their foreheads once more.

"Mari, clever girl that she was, followed me out of the house. She was not supposed to see me leave. She, like everyone else, was supposed to think some dreadful accident had befallen me. I'd left my clothes in the sand, wanting to make it look like I'd drowned." She breathed out slowly. "Based on what you've told me, it seems this is the story she used."

Now more than ever, Holmes wished he had Mari in his arms, she and all her heartaches, her secrets. All these years, she'd hidden behind this tale about her mother's death. He could hardly believe the truth she'd locked inside, sharing with no one—not even him.

His mistrust of Imelda, too, had dissipated in an instant.

Imelda went on, "After Mari chased me down to the water, I had no choice but to lie to the men. They asked who the girl was, why she was following me. I told them she was my cousin, and they believed it. They believe everything I tell them, for I've led them to countless piles of sunken loot. Much of what they have is because of me. This is why Matteo visited me earlier. He and I convene regularly. He moves me from ship to ship, whatever suits his fancy."

Finally, Holmes understood what Quinto had meant when he said, *You haven't any idea what else is on this brig.*

He hadn't meant jewels at all.

He'd meant this woman, this witch.

"How do you do it?" Holmes asked. "How do you find sunken treasure?"

"We were born with this witchcraft in our blood," she said. "A strand of hagstones—stones from the sea, with a small hole in them—is all I require. It guides me. Pulls me, quite literally."

Far more interesting than herb pastes and olive pits, Holmes thought.

"The men believe me immune to the wrath of the sea—*al contrario*, able to harness it. And if I am being honest," she went on, "I sometimes think they seized me for more than just the riches I could lead them to. The sea has always been the domain of men, an instrument in their aims of domination. Once they realized who I was, I suspect they were scared. Isn't that why men fear witches, anyway? A woman using her powers to destroy them? Perhaps they worried if they didn't hold me captive, I could manipulate the sea against them or disturb trade routes or consort with one of their competitors." She gave a little laugh. "They wouldn't be wrong, either.

"I cannot tell you," she concluded, "how relieved I am that the men never discovered I'd left behind two daughters, both of whom held as much power over the sea as I did."

"Well," Holmes said, knowing Imelda was his only ally on the brig, "they know it now."

She sucked in a breath. "What do you mean?"

"Mari is the one who killed Massimo. She drowned him. I did not say it earlier, but she drowned him from afar, apparently. She somehow had control over the water."

"My foolish girl," Imelda whispered. "I wonder if she recognized him from that night I went away. But then again, twelve years is a long time to remember a face."

"I wrote Mari a letter several days ago," Holmes said, "telling her to flee. It's why I took a knife to the rigging, too. To slow our voyage, so she could escape."

"You are a good man," she said. "And I hope she's gotten the letter, for we are but an hour from Positano."

Holmes froze. "An hour?" He'd known they were sailing again after repairs to the brig, but he hadn't any way of knowing how far they'd gone.

"Yes," she said gravely. "I overheard the officers discussing it a short while ago."

Holmes's heart thumped harder inside his chest. He might have been a good man, as Imelda had just said, but he was a criminal. A dead man, once he was back on land.

The *Aquila* shuddered beneath him, inching forward.

29

HAVEN

Friday

My strange conversation with Savina had left me unsettled. Walking back to my rental, I pulled out my phone and returned to my camera roll, finding the newspaper article from the archive, the same article Enzo had translated in full for me.

I skimmed it quickly, then spotted it at the bottom—the word *streghe*, which I'd overheard Savina and Renata discussing earlier. The article also contained a related word, *stregheria*. I frowned, not remembering how Enzo had translated this, so I plugged the word into my browser, then hit Enter.

The results were not at all what I expected.

Stregheria was the Italian word for *witchcraft*, and *streghe* meant *witches*.

When I'd first read Google's translation of the article about the sinking, I'd been so stunned by the mention of Holmes Foster that I hadn't given the end of the article much attention. And even when Enzo translated the article for me, he hadn't said anything about witchcraft.

Why, I wondered, would he have omitted this piece of information?

Once home, I grabbed my laptop and got to work, painstakingly translating each sentence.

The end of the article discussed rumors of a group of women secretly practicing *stregheria* in the area. The author called these women *streghe del mare*—witches of the sea—and reported that while the women had not been identified, they would be pursued by officials to determine any potential involvement in the sinking.

I sat upright on the bed, feeling both intrigued and a bit unhinged. Witchcraft? Seriously?

In spite of this, I spent the next hour reading everything I could find online about *stregheria*. Its existence was a pervasive legend through Italy, particularly in the Napoli region: the first *streghe* were believed to have originated in medieval times in Benevento, while the sea witches specifically had originated in the Positano region.

As a whole, the women were known for reciting strange incantations and venerating various amulets, the most important of which was a *cimaruta*, a sort of talisman necklace meant to protect the wearer. It featured tiny branches, like coral, and charms such as hearts or moons.

These women, I learned, were largely practitioners of benevolent kitchen magic: they worked with babies and herbs and gemstones. Today, many women still practiced forms of *stregheria*, though they were taken about as seriously as other practitioners of the esoteric, like mediums or Reiki healers.

Which was to say, not very seriously at all.

On an obscure website about the legends of the *streghe del mare*, I stumbled across a register of sea-spell incantations and their associated tools. I thought the list seemed rather ludicrous—mermaid's combs and century-long spells?—but interesting, nevertheless, and I found myself googling images of hagstones and shark egg sacks.

Eventually, I could find nothing more on the *streghe del mare* or any evidence that the historical *streghe* used their witchcraft in malevolent ways. As I ran out of research threads to pursue, I pushed my laptop aside and went to the kitchen, suddenly starving.

As I stood there at the counter, nibbling the corner off a block of pecorino cheese, I began to laugh at myself. I'd come to lead Project Relic and find my father's sunken treasure, yet I'd spent only a fraction of my time here in the water. Instead, I'd been bent over my phone reading about witches, the Mazza brothers, and influencers on yachts.

Still, so many of the threads intertwined. Everything came back to Li Galli. Everything came back to the legend of the Amalfi Curse.

I had to keep digging.

Last night, I'd stopped reading Holmes's log at the point of his arrival in Naples. Now I picked up where I left off, determined to read more slowly this time. I'd overlooked the *streghe* mentions in the newspaper article, and I didn't want to overlook something important again.

Soon after his arrival in Naples, Holmes mentioned the Mazza brothers.

I met with Matteo this morning to sign my papers, Holmes wrote in one entry. *He had a yellowing bruise around his eye, and his arm in a sling as if fresh from a fight. He sucks constantly at his teeth, trying to dislodge food. Still, we're all a rough sort, those of us who choose life on the sea. And he's the one responsible for my wages, so I'll stay in his good graces, teeth-sucking or not.*

But as Holmes worked voyage after voyage—most lasting only a week or two—he began to resent the Mazza brothers and the way they ran their business. *I've never witnessed such abuse from of-*

ficers, he wrote. *Flogging the crew for minor infractions. There are even rumors of tying men to the transom and dragging them. Where do the Mazza brothers find such barbaric men? Our wages are late, too, sometimes by as much as a week, when I've already left on my next voyage.*

I had all but made up my mind to leave for Marseille or Nice, Holmes wrote, *but there is my beloved, Mari...*

Here, I paused, thinking of Enzo and how my situation paralleled Holmes's in some ways. I, too, knew what it meant to grapple with romantic feelings for someone who lived in a place I was better off leaving.

I read on, anxious to learn more about what seemed like a budding love story.

Holmes and Mari met when he was in port at Positano. He described the village as a place of *upstanding fishermen and their well-off families, all of them warm and welcoming. The village enjoys cold, fruitful waters and seems impervious to the challenges faced by other nearby fishing villages.*

Then, Holmes relayed the moment he first laid eyes on her.

We had anchored offshore and moored our tenders along the rocks, then we walked along the beach. Some of my fellow sailors began to shout, insisting there was a naked woman frolicking in the water ahead. One or two of them broached the idea of going after her.

I had not seen the woman myself, and as we stood there waiting for her to reappear in the water, I wondered if the men—who were drunk—had merely imagined her. They finally gave up the wait, making for the village. I stayed back, walking slowly along the low waves, collecting a few shells and dwelling on how I should spend my evening.

It was then that I caught a flash of skin. Bare shoulders, bare neck, and hair the color of cherries.

I looked away, ashamed. But I am a man, am I not? I had to glance once more. When I did so, she was coming out of the water, and she was not naked at all. She wore a muslin swimming frock, tied just above her breasts. Her hair hung down to her waist, clinging to her wet skin. In her hands was a small turtle, a hook protruding from his mouth. She looked dismayed—I thought she might even be crying—as she worked to remove the object.

I thought her straight out of a book. A painting. A dream. Who, I wondered, was this woman that had just emerged from the sea?

I jumped at a knock on the door. *Enzo.* He must have finished up his calls. Setting my phone down, I quickly checked myself in the mirror, swiping on a pink lip gloss and brushing back a few stray hairs.

"Hiii—" I said, swinging it open.

I stopped short. It wasn't Enzo at all.

It was Mal.

"I know you're not leaving here without finishing what you've started," she said. "I can't do the dirty work for you, but I can try to make sure you don't hurt yourself while you're at it."

"Well, hello to you, too," I managed.

"You're the most stubborn person I've ever met in my life." She dropped her bag, and it hit the floor with a thlunk.

"What about your flight?" I asked.

"They actually paid me to give up the seat," she said. "Cash mon-ay."

"What about your other job?"

"Like I said, my old boss is a badass. She gave me a bit more time."

I remained frozen. "You're seriously here."

"Yup." She slipped past me and into the kitchen. She made for the fridge, pulling out the cheese I'd put away a short while ago. "Who eats the corner off the cheese?" she asked, holding up the block. She glanced at me, then snapped her fingers. "And why are you still standing there? We have shit to do."

I closed the door, smiling. This was the best thing that had happened to me in days. Weeks. Maybe ever.

"First things first," she said, reaching for a plate. "Let's find ourselves a boat."

"No. First things first," I echoed. "I have a *lot* to show you."

* * *

I spent the afternoon, and well into the evening, telling Mal about all I'd learned in the last two days. I also showed her the article indicating the little-known circumstances surrounding the *Aquila*'s demise.

"This," I said, pointing at the word *stregheria* in the article. "Ever heard of it?"

Mal frowned. "I can barely say *bathroom* in Italian. So no."

"It means *witchcraft*. There were rumors of it after the sinking, since no one could explain how it went down. And here's something else. The article talks about a prisoner on board, Holmes Foster. Check this out." I pulled up the video of his journal, showing Mal the inside cover. "I have his journal. Though, it's more of a tell-all diary."

Mal's eyes widened. "How the hell did you find all this?"

"A little luck, and a whole lot of Google Translate."

She nodded to my phone. "Have you read his journal?"

"Some of it. Listen to this." I navigated to where I'd left off. *"Who, I wondered, was this woman that had just emerged from the sea?"* Then I looked at Mal. "Isn't that…poetic?"

"Beautiful," she agreed. "So who was it? Who was the woman?"

I continued to read aloud.

So as not to frighten her, I kept my distance, pretending to pay her little attention as she walked onto the beach and squeezed the water from her hair.

She bent down, still working at the hook caught in the young turtle's mouth. With her brow furrowed, she studied its angle, its way in, and then very gently, with great tenderness, she eased it out.

At once, she returned the turtle to the water. He floated for a minute as though disoriented.

"Ti ringrazierebbe se potesse," I said. He would thank you if he could.

Together, we watched as the turtle thrust his tiny flippers into the water, at last making for open sea, for freedom.

I studied the woman more closely. She had a deep dimple on her upper lip, and I was struck, at once, with the urge to run my thumb along it. "You are quite fond of the ocean?" I asked her.

She gave a little shake of her head. "In fact," she replied, "I hate it." She nodded toward where she'd just returned the turtle. "But it was a matter of life and death for him."

I was not quite sure how to reply, so I stayed silent. Then I knelt down, a seashell having caught my eye. I couldn't place my finger on it, but something about the shell seemed unusual.

I continued reading Holmes's account out loud, learning that he had stumbled on what Mari called a *sinistrale* shell. Such shells were, according to her, quite rare.

It was evident that Holmes had been touched by this early encounter.

Knowing the shell was so rare, I asked if she would like to keep it. She insisted she found them often, so she let me have it. I dropped it into my pocket at once, and I have not parted with it since.

Eventually, the woman introduced herself as Mari DeLuca. She pointed to the villa on the hillside. "That is where my family lives," she said.

I gazed at it, wondering why she told me this. There seemed no reason for it, apart from her having some desire to see me again.

"Hell of a meet-cute," Mal said. "Almost enough to make me straight. Shame the poor guy dies at the end."

I glared at her. "Mal. This isn't a novel. This is some guy's real life."

"Sorry," she said, cringing. "You're right, that was rude. How did the journal survive the wreck?"

"Flotsam," I told her. "Lots of the documents at the archive were water-damaged. Recovered from shipwrecks or washed in."

I flipped to the next entry. We learned, much to our delight, that Holmes had made straight for Mari's villa the next day.

It was evident from his log that in the weeks and months to follow, Holmes and Mari fell desperately in love. And no different than reading a romance novel, I was both enchanted and tortured by Holmes's agonizingly short account of the first time they made love, in December of 1820—the smudges of tar he'd left behind on Mari's thighs, and what she whispered to him after the second time they made love: *Already, you are learning me.*

I smirked as I thought of Enzo—he was a quick learner, too—then I continued reading the December entries, very glad this journal hadn't sunk to the bottom of the ocean.

As we gathered up our things to part for the evening, she asked me when I set sail.

"Tomorrow, midday." Only, I must have mispronounced something, because she smiled and bent forward to kiss my forehead, as she always did when I tripped over my Italian.

"And where are you headed?" she asked.

"To Naples. A short voyage, I hope, even accounting for the tramontana. It will depend on the currents, too, of course. They have been pulling us south."

Mari gave a slow nod. "Yes," she said softly.

Here, Holmes had drawn an arrow to a small note in the margin. I turned my phone screen to read it more closely.

As it turned out, the tides were very much in our favor when we set sail for Naples the following day. They had shifted northward, and we made it to Naples in half a day. According to Quinto, it was the fastest this little ship had ever sailed.

Not one of us could explain it.

A chill overtook me. I was about to ask Mal what she thought, but when I looked up, she'd just reached for her phone, her brow furrowed.

"What's up?" I asked.

"Megan just texted." She flicked through her phone notifications for a second. "What the actual—" She trailed off.

"What?" I said again.

"The influencer who died, Asher Vice. There's a memorial for him tonight, on the water. Megan texted, said the memorial is on the news right now. Two boats collided en route, right near Li Galli. One lost control, something about an eddy in the water."

My chest tightened. At the coffee shop, when I'd eavesdropped on Savina and Renata, I'd caught the words *Asher* and *memoriale*.

I threw myself off the couch. "I think I'm going to be sick." I stood, feeling the blood drain from my face.

"Let me get you some wa—"

"No," I interrupted. I took a few deep breaths. "Get your things. We're going for a ride."

30

HOLMES

Friday, April 27, 1821

As the minutes passed and the *Aquila* neared Positano, Holmes felt himself growing sick with dread.

Imelda had been very quiet for the last fifteen or so minutes—Holmes wondered if she'd snuck out of the cabin again—and this left him to muse on his bleak future. Upon disembarkation, Matteo would come for him, then—what? Arrest, torture, death?

He wondered if he could talk his way out of things, if he could lie about his reason for cutting the lines. *Better start thinking up a damned good story*, he thought miserably to himself.

Footsteps. Imelda was back. There was a rustling above him and then a hollow grating sound, followed by a soft shower of wood dust.

"What are you doing?" he whispered as a serrated metal blade slid between the planks, coming dangerously close to the top of his head.

A saw. Had she snuck out just now to retrieve it?

Imelda continued to work, and after a few minutes, she had

cut a hole in the planks wide enough for Holmes's forearm. He coughed, sawdust lodged at the back of his throat.

Soon, their faces were only inches apart.

He wiped away a thin layer of grit on his lips, taking a good look at his new friend. She and Mari closely resembled each other: the sharp, sloped nose, the high cheekbones, the dip above their upper lips.

Imelda pulled her face away, and Holmes spotted what she held in her hand: a compass saw, tapered and narrow. "Help me," she said. "Pull the blade in farther, just there." She nodded to a tight gap between the next two planks.

Gripping the edge of blade with his thumb and forefinger, Holmes helped pull it into place. Imelda resumed her work. Within a few minutes, she had removed another section of plank. Holmes could now fit his entire arm through, even his shoulder.

His heart began to race. *My God*, he thought, *she is helping me escape.*

"Wait," he said, breathing in air fresher than anything he'd breathed in days. "We must think through this. Before someone sees what you are doing."

"We haven't the time," she hissed. "We will be there soon."

His mind raced for an escape plan that felt feasible. Even if he emerged through this hole into the second mate's cabin and slipped out of the louver, just as Imelda had been doing, he'd have to get to the main deck, somehow jump over the railing.

If he was spotted by one of the officers, he'd be shot.

For a brief moment, remaining imprisoned seemed the more fitting choice. To stay alive for the next few hours, at least.

"Imelda," Holmes whispered, "how will I get out without being seen?"

She paused her sawing and wiped her upper lip with the edge of a blue scarf tied around her neck. "I am getting you out of this prison cell," she said. "Admittedly, I have not considered the rest." She began to saw again, harder this time.

"Even in disguise, there are so few of us on board," he said, thinking out loud. There was no anonymity, no hiding. Not on the *Aquila*.

She ignored him, still working away. "Once you're on the main deck, throw yourself overboard. We are not far from land. A ten-minute swim, if that." She looked at him with a new intensity. "You must be quick about it, though, and swim harder than you've ever swam before." She reached for his hand, clutching it. "Promise me you will swim as hard as you can."

He hoped he would be so lucky. If he could even make it to the water, he knew he'd be free.

He nodded, his throat too tight to reply. Imelda was saving his life.

Soon, she had cut enough wood away for him to slip through. Using what little arm strength he could muster, Holmes heaved himself up and through the hole.

Finally, he found himself sitting right next to her, panting with the effort he'd just expended. A pair of glass prisms were installed in the cabin, which let in the faint morning light from above, on the main deck. "She looks so much like you," he whispered.

"You should have seen Sofia," Imelda replied, giving him a sad smile.

Holmes touched his chest, checking for his journal. It was still on him, snug in its oilskin pouch. Quickly, Imelda gave him some brandy and food—dried beef and the sweetest candied orange slices he'd ever tasted. As he ate, he looked around the cabin, finding it rather less interesting than he'd imagined all this while. A few sea chests. Spare clothing, used dishware. A rope ladder, neatly folded and set aside.

"Shall I put on different clothes?" he asked her, eyeing a pair of men's trousers draped over a chair. His own clothes were bloodied, thanks to Quinto's fist, and hung loosely off his body.

He was barefoot, too, though there was no need for shoes. They would only weigh him down in the water.

"I see no use," she said. "You won't be on the main deck but for a few moments." She put her ear to the door, listening for a moment, then she slid the louver's privacy shield out of its track. Slipping her thin fingers between the slats, she took out the four wooden pegs affixing the louver to the door.

Then, very quietly, she removed the louver. The dark, gaping hole in the door—a perfect escape—lured Holmes forward. He knew the layout of the berthing deck well, knew exactly how to get to the main deck.

He turned to her. "Once I am safe, how can Mari and I find you?"

Imelda's gaze was unreadable, but Holmes felt sure he saw sorrow. Grief, even. Perhaps she intended to keep working with the Fratelli Mazza. She'd turned herself over to them once; knowing that Mari's life was now in danger, Holmes wouldn't be surprised if Imelda tried some new tactic to keep Matteo happy.

Ignoring his question, Imelda checked her small pocket watch. "There is one more thing," she said, handing him a glass flask, about six inches long and stoppered with a cork. It appeared to be filled with seashells. "Do not open it," she instructed. "Give it to Mari when you find her again." She glanced toward the gap in the door. "Go, Holmes."

Holmes placed his hand on Imelda's shoulder and looked her hard in the eye, seeing only Mari. Already, his thoughts had turned to her—finding her, protecting her, stealing her away to a place where they could not be discovered. "Thank you for saving me," he said, then he dashed off, making straight for the gaping hole in the door. As he went, he unbuttoned one of his pockets, tucking the glass flask inside.

Outside the cabin, he went left. He rushed up the ladder, encountering no one, and emerged onto the main deck.

Imelda had been right: the shoreline was not far off. A thin mist hung in the air, giving the coast the appearance of a looming, dark shadow. The faintest tease of salvation.

He rushed toward the taffrail, ready to heave himself over. Yet as he took a long step, he slipped. The fog had left the deck slick, and Holmes went down hard, his right knee twisting beneath him. He heard a tiny pop within the joint. He wasn't sure if he'd broken something or merely sprained the joint, but he didn't have time to investigate.

He threw one leg over the railing, then the other. He sat on the taffrail for a moment, eyeing the shore, dreading the swim toward it on account of his throbbing knee.

Behind him, a shout. Then footsteps and the click of a revolver's hammer being cocked.

Holmes did not turn around to see who held the gun.

At last, he jumped.

31

HAVEN

Friday

"Where are we?" Mal asked.

I turned off the Vespa and grabbed my cross-body bag. "Enzo's mom's house," I said under my breath. "Savina is her name." Above us, a canopy of trees hung ominously low.

"Is Enzo here?"

I eyed the driveway, not seeing his scooter. "Doesn't look like it. And if I'm being honest with you, I hope he's not. He'd ask too many questions."

"Haven," Mal said, grabbing me by the elbow. "What's going on?"

"Look," I said, relenting. "I know this sounds absurd. But his mom, she's—" I stopped, not knowing where to begin. "Something about her unnerves me. The other day, she was horrified—angry, even—that we'd been diving in Li Galli. She begged us not to go again. Then earlier today, at a coffee shop, I overheard her and a friend talking about the yacht going down. They mentioned the Amalfi Curse. And *streghe*. And they were looking at…" I grimaced, feeling more foolish by the moment. "They had printed out a bunch of oceanography graphs. Highlights and notes everywhere."

"And this is unnerving…why? Everyone is talking about the yacht, about Vesuvius."

"The article about the *Aquila* sinking," I went on. "The end of it mentions *stregheria*—witchcraft—twice. I asked Enzo to translate the article for me, and he completely left this part out. Just glossed right over it."

"So you think Enzo's mom is a—" Mal laughed, looking away. "I can't even say it. My God, what has Positano done with my rational, science-minded friend?"

"I know, I know," I said, turning away and walking toward the villa. "But at the coffee shop, Savina and her friend also mentioned a memorial for Asher. And now there's been another incident in Li Galli, during the memorial?" Twigs and leaves crunched beneath my feet as I walked. "Maybe it's nothing. Maybe it's something. Just humor me."

My pulse quickened as we neared the house. Ahead, through the trees, I could make out the light of a single lamp in the main living area.

"Follow me," I told Mal, making my way along the side of the villa. I peeked in through one of the windows. An open bottle of wine sat on the counter, alongside a half-eaten plate of antipasti.

I grabbed Mal's hand, pulling her forward. We kept close to the exterior, approaching the terrace from behind.

As we walked, I pulled out my phone, navigated to the audio-recording app, and clicked Record before tucking my phone back into my front pocket.

Then, hearing a voice, I stopped where the terrace met the house.

"What the hell," Mal whispered, running into me.

I placed my fingers over my lips, shushing her. We'd paused

behind a trellis exploding with plum-colored clematis. Through the gaps in the lattice, I spotted Savina. She leaned over the railing, whispering into her cell phone.

Behind her, in the shape of a circle, were more than a dozen pillar candles flickering in the night. Beyond the terrace, with its extraordinary view of the Tyrrhenian Sea, the silhouette of the largest Li Galli islet rose up from the sea.

Countless boats bobbed in the water, red lights flashing. Police boats.

Around Savina lay a few books and disorderly piles of paper. Every so often, she reached to touch something against her collarbone.

I wanted badly to tell Mal what I'd read last night about the *cimaruta* necklaces. But I couldn't breathe a word now, not so close to Savina.

Not knowing what was at stake here—not knowing what I was seeing, if anything at all—I couldn't watch, or wait, a moment longer.

"What are you—" Mal reached for me, but I moved quickly toward the stairs leading up to the terrace.

"Savina," I said, forcing a wide smile as I took the last stair. "Pardon my trespassing, but I was just showing my friend your villa, then I saw you standing here. I thought we'd say hello."

Savina whispered something into the phone, then hung up. She looked back at me, her expression a mix of shock and dismay.

"Haven," she said slowly. "Is Enzo with you?"

"He's not," I said, "but this is my dear friend, Mal." The two nodded at one another while I motioned toward the candles, keeping my voice cheerfully oblivious. "What's this?" I asked her.

"Ah," Savina said, fumbling for words. "Well, I..."

"Excuse me," Mal said, "but Megan has called me six times. I'll be right back." She slipped off quickly. Though, knowing Mal, she would be only steps away, keeping a close eye on us.

Savina knelt down next to the candles, and I was able to get a better look at a few other objects around her. Including, to my surprise, a strange-looking comb, resembling a saw or teeth.

I'd seen this on the website I'd perused earlier, with the register of sea spells. I couldn't be sure, but I thought this saw-looking object was the tool required for the incantation that altered the composition of water.

This could not be a coincidence.

"This is nothing," she said, finally answering my question. She tidied a few of the papers while I looked out at the water, the flashing lights.

"It's not nothing," I disputed. *Here we go.* "The hydrothermal vent readings, the changes in the carbon dioxide levels." I nodded to the comb. "This is one of the tools needed. I know all about *stregheria*, Savina."

She raised her eyebrows. "There's only one reason you would have researched that," she said, voice hoarse. "You're looking for something in Li Galli."

If I wanted her honesty, I needed to do my part, too. "Yes."

She stepped close, placing her hand lightly around my wrist. "Then let me help you. I can read the water—the ocean." She pointed to the black expanse of ocean beyond. "I can make the sea…do things. I can make it reveal things. I can lead you to precisely whatever it is you're searching for."

I kept silent. Only hours ago, this would have seemed an absurd notion, the claims of a lunatic. If not for all I'd uncovered.

Savina took my left hand in both of hers, toying with my empty ring finger. "Haven," she finally said, "you are a beautiful, accomplished young woman. Why have you not married yet?"

I balked at the affront. "I've been focused on my career," I replied, even though it was none of her business. "And I haven't met the right person."

She leaned in. "Might my Enzo be the right person?"

I didn't see where this was going, what Enzo had to do with

stregheria or the flickering candles around our feet. "I only just met him."

"Ah, but think how perfect it could be," she said in an urgent whisper. "My son, owner of a dive shop." She stepped to the terrace railing, gripping it with both hands. "My Enzo has what is needed to get you into the water, into the wrecks. You have the skill required to explore them, to search them for riches." She paused. "And I, well, I can lead you right to them. This is how it is supposed to be. The moment he brought you to the villa, Haven…it was all the proof I needed."

I peered at her in the darkness. "Proof of—what?"

"Proof that what Renata and I are doing is working. The misfortune following me around for my entire life, well, I finally know *why*. And, more importantly, I know how to fix it."

"I'm not following," I said. "Fix what?"

"We are *streghe*," Savina said, "much as Renata and I wish we weren't. Growing up, my grandmother and mother tried to teach me about it. They shared the legends and lore passed down through history—everything about Li Galli, the mythological sirens, the women who lived here for thousands of years. They taught me the incantations, too."

She lifted one of the books at her feet, showing me the open page. It was a diary, written in a child's hand. *Incantesimo di riflusso* read one entry, next to a sketch of a bullet-shaped fossil.

"I refused to listen to my mother and grandmother," Savina explained. "I wanted nothing of such silly stories. Renata, too. We were friends even then, as our families have long known one another. Her mother had been teaching her the same things, but like me, Renata was more interested in dolls and boys than seashell spells."

I looked around, peered in through the tall glass windows. "Where is Renata, by the way?"

Savina motioned to the water. "She took one of the Jet Skis out."

I suspected as much.

Savina went on, "As I grew older, my mother told me that by rejecting my lineage, my inborn powers, I would be haunted by misfortune. Even on her deathbed, when I was eighteen, she pleaded with me to accept the truth, to accept who I really was. *This is dark witchcraft*, she said. But still, I refused. I scorned the whole idea of it. We Italians are mostly Catholic, you know. My friends, their parents, a potential husband—what would they have thought of me if they knew I practiced witchcraft?"

Savina closed her childhood journal, clutched it to her chest. "I nearly burned this but decided to stash it away in a closet. And as the years went by, I became convinced that bad things happened more often to me than they did to others. My husband, Enzo's father, died in a car accident. I was dismissed from job after job, despite working diligently, always showing up on time. Our apartment was burglarized, twice. For years, Bria dealt with ear infections, and Enzo, I swear he broke every bone a young boy can break. Still, I refused to believe any of this was related to my rejection of *stregheria*. Until the very worst happened…"

"Bria's passing," I said.

"Exactly." She nodded. "That, at last, convinced me that what my mother had said was true. If I did not embrace—and more importantly, *use*—my powers, this curse would continue to weigh upon me. She once told me that rejecting my gift was like cutting circulation from my limbs. My lineage, whether I like it or not, is my lifeblood. Cut it out, and every part of me will perish. Including my own children, it seems." She gently set her journal on the ground. "This dark witchcraft has made me victim enough. I lost Bria. I will not let it take anything more from me."

How strange, I thought, that she called it *dark witchcraft*. Given the research and incantations I'd uncovered online, it didn't seem that *stregheria* was inherently sinister. "What about Renata?" I asked. "Does she believe this witchcraft is tied to misfortune in her life, too?"

"Yes," Savina said, nodding hard. "When I reached out to her last year—she and I had remained acquaintances over the years, though she'd moved to Milan—I told her about my theory. She was speechless, then she broke into tears. All she ever wanted was to have children, she told me, but she could never conceive. Not once. Now, it is too late for her, but when I told her what happened to Bria—and so suddenly, too—she swore she would help me. Neither of us want to resist the curse of this lineage any longer. Neither of us want to lose anything more than what we already have.

"I dug up my childhood diary with the incantations, then Renata and I uprooted and moved here, together. This villa has always been shared between our two families, though, as you know, it has been uninhabited. As it turns out, we have done very well practicing as a pair. This location is perfect, too, overlooking Li Galli. With its history of maelstroms and sinkings, it is not a waterway likely to rouse suspicion. It is witchcraft," she concluded, "masquerading as natural forces."

She watched my reaction for a few moments, then, "You do not believe me, do you?"

I didn't know how to answer this. It all seemed so farfetched. But then again, I'd been the one to drag Mal out of the house and onto Savina's terrace to investigate further.

"Let me show you," she said. She pulled out her phone once more and dialed a number. "Renata," she said into it, before sputtering off something in Italian.

"Watch the waterline," Savina said to me then, "just there."

I followed her gaze, eyeing the place where the waves met the vertical cliff side. At once, the surf in that place began to swell and spin in a counterclockwise motion.

"Make it stop," I challenged her.

"*Fermate*," she said into the phone.

At once, the water grew still. *Impossible*. I placed my fingers over my lips.

Savina hung up the phone and turned to me. "Now every sea spell we perform gives me great comfort—like I am chiseling away at a lifetime of ignorance."

"The yacht," I said. I motioned to the circle of candles behind me, then turned to face her head-on. "You two are responsible for it, aren't you? And whatever else is happening out there tonight."

She looked away as though ashamed. "It was not what we intended. Had they not been *ubriaco*, on drugs and in a stupor, they would have gotten out…"

"Eight people died," I reminded her, feeling disoriented. "You will be found out. The police, they will get to the bottom of it, someday."

Savina shook her head. "No, they won't. They will attribute it to the currents around Li Galli, which have always been unpredictable."

Unless they hear what I'm recording on my phone at this very moment, I thought.

I bent down and picked up the sawfish comb. "What about this?" I asked. "Is this related to Vesuvius concerns, the hydrothermal readings?"

"Yes," she said, taking the comb in her hands.

"So there is no risk of eruption at all."

She shook her head. "No. None at all."

I ran my hand over my forehead, astounded at her selfishness, her cruelty. She and Renata were responsible for the yacht sinking and whatever boat incident had unfolded tonight. They were the reason why tourism to the Amalfi region had plummeted overnight. And why Savina's own son was now at risk of losing his business.

She was also why I'd been yanked from Project Relic, and

why Conrad was but an inch away from finding something that was never his to find.

"I've seen the list of incantations," I said. "Spells as simple as making water ebb or flow. Why sink a yacht, then, or terrorize an entire region? Why not sit by the water and perform the spells privately, safely?"

"Because I am making up for a lifetime of denial," Savina said, her voice louder now. I'd angered her: she clutched the comb so tightly between her fingers, her knuckles were white. "I will not *sit by the water*, as you say, and do little hexes like a child might. I have much to prove, to fix. I am years behind. I don't know how this witchcraft works, but now I'm listening. Now I'm on its side."

Her gaze on me had turned cold as ice. "I lost my daughter," she hissed. "She is dead because of me, her entire life cut short because I would not heed my mother's warnings. What about Enzo? I cannot lose him, too. I will do anything to keep him safe—even witchcraft."

She tucked the comb into her pocket, huffed a breath of frustration. "You aren't a parent, but if you understood this pain, you'd do it, too. Any mother would."

32

HOLMES

Friday, April 27, 1821

Holmes hit the water as a gunshot rang out. His body slipped under. He kicked and kicked, flailing his arms, cursing the weight of his wet clothes. He tore off his shirt, being careful not to lose the diary, though he wondered, now, how well the oilskin pouch would work against such complete immersion.

He swam a few paces. The cold water, despite leaving him short of air and on the verge of panic, had all but numbed the injury to his knee. For this, he was grateful.

Another gunshot. He spun around in the water. On the main deck, Quinto aimed a revolver toward him. He pulled the trigger again and again.

Holmes took a deep breath and slipped beneath the water again. Blindly, he swam as hard as he could, just as he'd promised Imelda. But at the hollow crack of another shot, he winced.

Quinto had shot him in the lower right leg.

Holmes did his best to keep propelling himself forward, but it was no easy task with one leg all but useless. Unable to hold his breath any longer, he had no choice but to surface. He felt sure this was it: Quinto would spot him, fire the gun again, and this time he'd be going for his head.

Surfacing, he turned to look back at the *Aquila* heading eastward. Quinto stood there, trying to reload his gun.

Suddenly, the *Aquila* listed sharply, as though some enormous wave had just pummeled her larboard. Quinto hit the deck, the gun falling out of reach.

Holmes made a quick circle, frowning: the rest of the sea— including where he tread water now—was relatively calm. He eyed the horizon; there were no whitecaps to be seen. The revolving turbulence seemed confined to a small area, precisely where the *Aquila* now listed.

He continued to pull himself toward shore, but he swallowed a mouthful of seawater, coughing and sputtering. He glanced again at the *Aquila*. She had righted herself, but the water around her churned viciously, and her bow now faced Holmes. She'd turned one hundred and eighty degrees. The brig groaned loudly, her hull audibly straining against something invisible.

It made no sense whatsoever. He must be imagining it all.

He considered, briefly, that perhaps he'd already died.

Holmes closed his eyes, drifting with the current for an untold amount of time while the *Aquila* faltered in the churning sea. Several times, her masts swung almost parallel to the water.

The brig's spinning hastened, and then came a loud crack as a fissure in the bow split open. The sea made quick work of filling it, and Holmes thought of Imelda in the second mate's cabin.

The *Aquila* continued to break apart, spinning and bobbing as he looked on. The brig lurched starboard, and the foremast snapped in two. Ropes and rigging swung from the snapped mast.

And then he heard the screams.

The men had begun to leap from the doomed vessel. Presumably, they thought they could make their way to land, but it was clear these efforts were futile, for just as the vessel could not resist the maelstrom, nor could they.

By jumping from the front of the brig when he had and swimming northward, Holmes had managed to escape all of this.

The other men began to drown one by one, Holmes's last sight of them nothing but an arm, a hand, reaching for the early morning sky.

He could not stand to watch it. Yet just before he averted his gaze, he spotted Quinto in the water. Accustomed to his menacing countenance, Holmes hardly recognized him now. He looked like a child—a little boy, flailing in a pond too deep for his tiny legs. With his mouth agape, Quinto gulped for air and cried for help. "*Aiutami*," he shouted. "*Aiutami!*" Over the clamor of snapping wood, his cries were unmistakable.

Holmes felt no pity.

Moments later, the sea swallowed the *Aquila* whole.

There were no more shouts. The sound of splitting wood had ceased. Treading water, Holmes could still see a strange swirling maelstrom where the brig had gone down. Flotsam began to drift toward him: fragments of splintered oak, a canvas sack, a rope ladder he recognized from inside the second mate's cabin.

And then, a bright blue scarf.

Imelda.

Holmes reached for it, knew he would never let it go. He wasn't sure what had just befallen the *Aquila*, but he ached for Imelda, who had shown him so much kindness.

In a state of shock and fatigue, he did what one must do when they cannot swim any longer.

He turned on his back. With a great deal of effort, he tied the scarf around his knee to slow the bleeding of his gunshot wound. Then, he surrendered to the sea and let himself float.

He had escaped the *Aquila* and whatever had happened to her, but he thought it very unlikely he would make it to shore in this condition.

He felt himself grow dizzy, warm.

Just moments before he lost consciousness, he smiled to himself. The *Aquila* and its men had gone under. Matteo had gone under. The Mazza brothers—they were both dead.

At least, he thought, *they will not get to my Mari, nor the other women...*

He closed his eyes and began to sink.

33

MARI

Friday, April 27, 1821

Mari bent forward along the shoreline, heaving for air. She could not breathe. She could not think. Her arms trembled violently as she attempted to keep herself from collapsing.

They had ceased their incantations.

The women had sunk the *Aquila*.

Holmes was dead.

She glanced at the water, tempted to swim toward the place the brig had gone down. Already, the curse would be lifting, softening. Perhaps she could shout for him, call Holmes's name in case he had somehow escaped the floundering vessel. But she knew this was mere fantasy: she'd watched the ropes snap, the hull buckle. She'd heard the screams, men begging for their mothers before being sucked under. She'd smelled the salt on the air, watched as the sea mist was expelled upward from the revolving whirlpool.

Mari felt a hand on her back. She turned to find Ami standing behind her, sympathy in her eyes. "Come," Ami said. "Let's go home."

"It sank so fast," Mari replied, dazed, still kneeling next to the water. "Faster than I could have imagined…"

Ami used both arms to heave Mari up and off the ground. "I agree," she said sadly. "It was quicker, and more powerful, than any of us expected." She pointed to the hillside behind them; the other women had already retreated, making their way back to the village.

"And gunshots…" Mari frowned, thinking of the loud pops she'd heard just moments before the *Aquila* had entered the cursed tract of water. "Did I imagine it?"

Ami shook her head. "I heard gunshots, too." She gently tugged Mari by the hand, leading her away from the water. "Perhaps there was an altercation of some kind."

They shared a glance. *Not that it matters now.*

Mari couldn't resist. She turned back to the sea once more, searching for any sign of life: an arm protruding from the waves or flotsam bearing a still-moving body.

There was nothing.

She let Ami lead her away from the shore and up the hill. Mari was grateful to have a friend as her guide, helping her navigate the rocky footpath home.

She was crying too hard to see any sort of path at all.

Not two hours after watching the *Aquila* perish, Mari quietly opened the door to her family's villa and slipped inside.

It was no longer dangerous to be here: Matteo was dead. No one would be coming after her. Now, she merely wanted to go to her bedroom, bury herself under her covers, and cry. Perhaps for a lifetime.

As she made her way there, she passed her father's office. The door was closed, which was unusual. Even when he was inside working, typically he left the door open.

She paused, hearing low voices inside. She leaned in closer, pressing her ear to the door.

"...the four captives," her father was saying. "This all got terribly out of hand."

The four captives. She knew exactly who he was referring to.

"I didn't intend for this," came the reply.

Mari frowned, recognizing the voice at once. *Corso.*

"I only wanted to scare the women," Corso continued. "If the Mazza brothers began meddling in whatever it is the women are doing, I thought it might dissuade Mari from wanting to stay here. Rome, perhaps, wouldn't seem so distasteful to her then. And of course, I hoped to make some money in exchange for the information."

"You are a businessman, after all. I hope Matteo paid you as well as you hoped, given all that has unfolded?" Father asked, a hint of eagerness in his voice.

Corso made a sound of disgust. "After I sent my initial letter, he promised he would compensate me for any information I could give him. I wrote him back as soon as I could, telling him what I'd seen that Wednesday night by the water, the way the women went into the sea, shifted the currents. I told him about their strange comings and goings. Their red hair. The little objects they insist on carrying around. I was hoping to have something tangible for him—I've gone through the garbage piles of a few of Mari's friends—but I couldn't manage anything."

Mari's mouth dropped open. The day she and the women had cursed the water against the incoming pirates had been a Wednesday. She thought of the shadow against the dock that night. And then, when she'd returned to the villa, Corso and her father had been awake—despite the very early hour. But she hadn't dreamed it had been Corso down by the water.

And it had been *him* sneaking around Vivi's and Emilia's houses. Mari could understand how, from a distance and in the dark, Corso's lithe stature might be mistaken for that of a woman.

Everything began to make sense. This was why the Mazza brothers had been in the village that day she went out with Lia and Pippa. They'd been scouting, looking for what Corso clued them in on.

Corso exhaled hard and went on, "The worst part is that I've yet to receive any money from Matteo. I feel a fool, especially having promised you a cut of it."

Mari steadied herself against the wall, dazed by this additional detail: her father had hoped to profit from this plan all along, too.

"Stay on him," her father urged Corso. "Make yourself a nuisance, and I'm sure he'll pay you what you're due."

No, Mari thought, *Corso will never get paid because Matteo is dead.*

"I'm not so sure he will pay me," Corso replied. "I spoke with him just last night, in Naples."

Mari frowned. She must have misheard.

"Pardon?" her father exclaimed. "How on earth did you manage to find him? None of the village men have been able to."

"I caught him leaving via the rear entrance of the Fratelli Mazza headquarters, at the Castellammare di Stabia shipyard. I'd waited there for some time, wondering if he might be coming and going from another door." Corso cleared his throat. "The moment I introduced myself, he waved me off. The money would come, he said, but now was not a good time. He was headed to the docks on an urgent errand. He asked me to return another time, then he rushed off.

"I followed him to the docks," Corso went on, "wondering about this urgent errand. He boarded a ship—*La Dea*. A dockhand told me it was headed for Positano and should be arriving late this morning. He was supposed to be aboard another vessel arriving today—the *Aquila*—but she has no artillery, and *La Dea* has forty-four guns."

"Does he intend to blow us all up?"

"The cannons are not loaded. It is all for show."

"Unsurprising."

"Indeed," Corso said.

Mari fought the urge to sink to her knees. Matteo had not been on the *Aquila*?

"Tell Cleila and Paola to stay home today," Corso told Father. "I will go to Ami's to ensure Mari does not leave the house, either. I don't know what else Matteo is planning once they drop anchor," he said, "but I cannot fathom it is anything good. I only hope that this is the last straw for Mari. That after today, she'll agree to join me in Rome."

Sure she was about to be sick, Mari slowly backed away from the door. After the sinking of Holmes's brig only hours ago, she couldn't have imagined this day getting any worse. And yet it had.

Matteo was alive and well. It was a living nightmare, the worst possible news: she had sunk the *Aquila* and killed Holmes, thinking she was protecting the village.

She rushed through the house and out onto the terrace. She looked out at the horizon and let out a cry.

In the distance, approaching from the west, near the cape, was another ship. Its heading, so close to the perilous coastline, meant this could only be the Mazza-owned *La Dea*.

There was no time for Mari to gather the other *streghe* for a second attempt at the incantation: by the time she managed to do so, *La Dea* would be here. But if Mari alone recited the *incantesimo vortice*, it would not be powerful enough to take under an entire ship.

There was only one other way for Mari to fix this. The *vortice centuriaria*. The most powerful incantation, requiring the greatest of sacrifices...

She needed to leave at once. She estimated she could row her way to *Li Galli* more quickly than *La Dea*, which was still a long distance off.

She rushed to her room. She went to her desk first, penning a short note to Ami. Mari trusted that, in the days to come, Ami and Dante would pursue the captives' recovery from Ischia as vehemently as anyone.

We sunk the wrong ship, Mari scribbled in her note, *and I must make it right. After this, you will all be safe. Do not go near Li Galli again.*

Ami would read this and understand, in an instant, what Mari had done.

She then went to her dresser, reaching for the bottom drawer. Here, she pulled out the things she'd hidden away: the bundle of letters from Holmes. Sofia's bracelet. The little pouch of dried olive pits.

She would take them with her to the sea.

Noiselessly, she slipped out the front door. Instead of taking the road that led away from the villa, she made her way through the olive grove, pausing a moment to take a final, long look at the tree under which she and Holmes had passed many an hour. The olive pits in her pocket had come from the fruit of that very tree.

She pulled out the tiny pouch, turning it over in her hand. These pits, at least, held something inside of them, some promise of hope or a future. As she walked away from the grove, she skirted the edge of the woods and tossed them underneath a shrub. Perhaps they would embed in the dirt and sprout. Perhaps something about her and Holmes would not be lost entirely.

After dropping her letter on Ami's doorstep, Mari went to the water and untied a *gozzo*. Into the boat she tossed a pair of oars and a long length of rope. Lastly, among a mess of nets and corks and chisels, she found a heavy anchor. She heaved this into the boat, too.

With these things, she began to row. She touched her *cimaruta* every few minutes, sure it was helping her row faster. She wondered if she would spot flotsam from the *Aquila* the farther out she went. She only prayed she wouldn't see bodies. She could not withstand it, not after everything else.

Strange how this was the deception she'd planned all along: drowning, a victim to the sea. And yet, how very different her intentions were now. This was not about escape or running away with Holmes. This was about saving the village. Ending the Fratelli Mazza, once and for all.

There were no dolphins alongside her, no seabirds to escort her out. It was only Mari and the black waves below her, luring her, like the sirens had done centuries ago to unsuspecting sailors. She felt betrayed by her lineage, by every circumstance leading her to this moment.

She'd begun to sweat. She dipped her hand into the sea, then ran it along the back of her neck to cool herself. But after doing this several times, she paused, looking at the water either side of her boat. Despite her utter despondence, her heartsickness, the sea remained unchanged. It had not turned black, nor had it begun to churn. It did not throb in time with her pulse, nor did it ebb away from her fingers. The surface of the water was perfectly serene.

This, Mari believed, was the sea's final abandonment of her. No longer did she and the ocean share any connection at all.

North of the islets, she crossed through the tract of water the women had cursed. The incantation had lifted, and the swells around her were low, steady. Momentarily, she would row her small *gozzo* into the eye of Li Galli.

But first, she readied herself. She tied the anchor to the rope, pulling it as taut as her weak hands would permit. Into the knot, she tucked the bundle of Holmes's letters. She clasped Sofia's bracelet in her hand.

She removed her *cimaruta*.

Then she began to wrap the rope once, twice, thrice around her waist.

34

HAVEN

Friday

Savina might have been furious with me moments ago, but now she began to cry. She took a few steadying breaths and reached for me. "Forgive me, Haven," she said, eyes wet and glinting in the candlelight. "I never wanted this burden. I never wanted any of this. But what am I to do now?"

Standing there stiffly, I let her hug me, thinking of Bria and my father. Like Savina, I still wavered precariously between anger at my dad's passing—it seemed unfair, losing him when I was so young—and sorrow at all the opportunities robbed of him. All the things he'd never experience, never discover. Which made me think, again, of the *Aquila*.

A few minutes ago, Savina had said something about the legends and lore her mother had taught her.

"Do you remember," I asked, "your mother mentioning a ship called the *Aquila*?"

Savina's eyes widened. "The *Aquila* is why we—the *streghe*—left Positano. How do you know about it?"

I felt my heart thrum harder in my chest. "It's one of my open research leads," I said. "What do you know about it?"

"It was a Mazza ship, for one," she said. "They were powerful shipowners living in Naples in the early 1800s. They kidnapped several *streghe* from Positano, vowing to return for more. They intended to use us for their own benefit. Control of the tides, protection from enemies, discovery of sunken treasure. They sent the *Aquila* to seize more women, but the brig sank, just there." She pointed to Li Galli.

Savina went on, "The foremost *strega*, a woman named Mari DeLuca, was rumored to have been in love with one of the men on the vessel."

Holmes. I could hardly keep from exclaiming aloud.

"My mother said Mari DeLuca resented her witchcraft, too. She shunned her powers over the sea, and look how it turned out for her. Mari's mother abandoned her. Her little sister drowned. Her lover floundered on the *Aquila*. Then Mari drowned herself." Savina raised her hands and let them fall, as if to say, *It isn't any big surprise to me now*.

A rush of air left my chest, like I'd just flipped to the last page of a novel only to find that the story ended in tragedy. Only hours ago, I'd been immersed in the beginning of Holmes and Mari's love story, their early days of growing attraction.

I knew Holmes had gone down with his ship, but Mari's fate? What a heart-wrenching end for her.

"After Mari died," Savina continued, "the *streghe* left the village one by one. Most went north, making for San Marino or Venice, and never returned to the Amalfi region. These other women were my ancestors, and Renata's, too. Sadly, though, my mother said Renata and I are the last of the living *streghe*." Suddenly, she gave me a curious look. "Enzo would be a great father someday, you know. Until this week, I'd nearly given up on him."

I wanted to defend him—to remind Savina that Enzo had spent the last few years building his business instead of worrying about marriage, something I admired greatly—but given all she'd just revealed, defending him seemed a minor worry.

"Enzo's daughters," she went on, motioning to the villa, and then the sea, and then the items at her feet, "would inherit this power, too."

She held my gaze, her implication now painfully obvious. If Enzo and I were to fall in love, to marry, to have children... well, they would carry this lineage forward.

"My daughter, Bria, badly wanted to marry and start a family. She was our best hope at carrying on the line. Now she is gone. A legacy stretching back thousands of years, and we are the last of it. Except for..."

"Enzo."

At her slow nod, this suddenly felt a lot more personal. But she must have thought me a fool if she believed I'd give her grandchildren—an arsenal—to help her carry out her atrocious schemes.

"Does Enzo know about *stregheria*?" I asked.

She let out a soft laugh. "No. Every Italian has heard of it, but most think it's a hobby, a diversion for women with too much time on their hands. Just what I thought of my mother, in fact. Enzo believes I have some odd habits, a few strange totems around the house, but what son does not think his mother's behavior somewhat peculiar?" She motioned to the sea. "He would never suspect this. Never."

In spite of everything, I felt a surge of relief, knowing Enzo hadn't lied to me when he'd translated the article. He'd probably just spared me details he considered utter nonsense.

"As I told you," Savina added, "you are proof this witchcraft is already working. Enzo is not only safe and well, but in the last week, he has been happier than I can ever remember seeing him."

Did she mean to imply that her powers, her curses, had somehow drawn me to Enzo? How absurd. The mere idea of it was offensive, nonsensical—

Or was it? I'd gone to Enzo's dive shop precisely because of the strange things going on in the region. Because Gage kicked me off the project and I needed a boat. I'd been instantly attracted to Enzo, unusually so. And just last night, we'd had the hottest sex I'd ever had in my life.

Still—*witchcraft?*

I spotted Mal coming up the terrace steps. "Haven," she said, "I think we ought to get going. I—"

"Just one minute," I called back, interrupting her. "I'll be right there."

After glancing over her shoulder, Savina leaned in, putting her lips close to my ear. "I'm not sure what you're looking for," she whispered, "but I can lead you right to it." On the ground, she retrieved a strand of smooth gray stones, each with a tiny hole allowing the cord to feed through.

Hagstones. I remembered this from the register of sea spells. Intrigued, I took the stones from her, feeling their cool, silky surface. The strand must have weighed a few pounds. I peered at one of the stones, spotting a tiny starfish fossil embedded within.

With a reluctancy that surprised me, I handed them back to her.

"I can find the greatest undiscovered riches," Savina said. "Whatever you want to achieve, personally or professionally, can happen if you will let it."

If you will let yourself fall in love with Enzo, she might as well have said, *and become his wife and the mother of his children.*

"What if I…don't?" I asked her. "What if I leave Positano in a few days, never to see your son again?" In truth, no matter my feelings for Enzo, I wanted no part of any of this. Even if Savina could lead me to the most valuable shipwrecks in the world.

I wasn't as shallow as Conrad, after all.

"Renata and I will not quit," Savina concluded. "I will do whatever it takes to protect what I have left."

I felt a chill run down my spine, thinking of all that was at stake. The well-being of the region's residents and its economy. Enzo's business. The lives of those on the water.

I realized now that what had begun as Project Relic and the

hunt for my father's sunken treasure had transformed into something much more consequential. This wasn't about my career anymore. This wasn't about my father anymore.

I couldn't walk away from this, not knowing all I knew.

If I did, I'd be as guilty as Savina.

Mal and I trudged carefully back down the hill in the darkness. Once we were well out of earshot, I recapped our conversation in a frenzied rush of words.

"She made the water…move?" Mal asked in disbelief.

"Twice," I nodded.

"She creeps me out. Her and all of this."

"I swear to you, Mal, I'm not making this up. You know I'm as skeptical as they come."

"And she wants you to…join her?"

"Not *join* her, really, but—" I turned the key in the scooter's ignition "—well, she wants a grandchild to carry on her line. She's desperate for someone to marry Enzo. And she all but told me that if I did, she'd help me however I wanted. Personally and professionally."

"I'm not following."

"She says the *streghe* can find things. They read the water. Sunken loot, and the like."

"In that case, why isn't she a billionaire?"

It was a fair question. "Right now, she's more concerned about using her powers to undo what she thinks is a lifetime of misfortune. Maybe money will matter to her later. Right now, she's just worried about Enzo."

We made our way down Amalfi Drive and back toward our own villa. "Well, *I* think she's full of shit," Mal shouted over the engine. "Completely and totally full of shit."

I wanted badly to agree with her, but I simply couldn't.

I knew what I'd seen.

35

HOLMES

Friday, April 27, 1821

After a moment of sinking, something sharp struck the back of Holmes's head. He flipped over, his body instinctively ready to swim again, but his hands, and then his feet, touched ground.

Rock.

It seemed impossible he'd made it to the mainland shore already. He blinked the salt water from his eyes and stood tall, glancing around.

He was not on the mainland at all. The current had, instead, taken him to the central islet of Li Galli, known as La Castelluccia.

Holmes knew these islets well; they were visible from much of the Amalfi Coast. He wondered, now, if the hazy form he'd seen from the *Aquila*'s main deck was not the shoreline at all, but perhaps one of these islets. *We are not far from land*, Imelda had said. She hadn't specified what land, exactly, this meant.

He didn't care where it was: he was just glad to be on solid ground. He heaved himself up the rocky slope and lay on his back, breathing hard, a fine mist swirling above him, its dampness cooling his cheeks and the tip of his nose.

He inspected his wound beneath Imelda's scarf. The bleeding hadn't stopped, but it had slowed.

The morning sky was bright. The fishermen would already be out in their *gozzi*. Someone might see fragments of wreckage and send word to the village if they had not already. They would come looking for survivors.

But Holmes was a criminal, and with both Mazza brothers dead, their men in Naples would be out for revenge. Holmes would be hunted down and killed. Imelda's sacrifice would be for nothing.

He needed to flee.

Indeed, the only way to save himself now was to pretend he was already dead.

After catching his breath, he waded back into the water and reached for a piece of flotsam, something resembling the side of a cabinet. He threw himself over it and began to kick, best he could, making his way for the mainland. It was much easier this way, having something on which to rest. He felt he could swim this way for as long as needed.

As he kicked, he laid his head on his arms, breathing hard and praying he wouldn't be seen. He concentrated only on propelling himself forward by whatever means possible. He did not even look where he was headed, for he knew he would arrive at the shore eventually. He was too tired to care much about when.

Suddenly, the wooden flotsam on which he supported himself collided with something else.

He heard a scream. Then a cry of alarm. He looked up. And just as he'd asked himself long ago, so now did he ask at the sight of her again, *Who was this woman that had just emerged from the sea?*

It was Mari. His beloved. Like an apparition born of the mist.

"Mari," he said, looking up at her like a fool. This was proof of it: he'd gone completely, entirely mad.

"Holmes." She gazed back at him, dumbfounded. "Holmes."

"It cannot be you, Mari."

"But it is. How are you—" She studied his face, his hands. "How are you alive?"

He opened his mouth to reply, but he snapped it shut at the sight of what was tied around her: a length of rope, wrapped several times around her waist. It was knotted in the front, like she'd done it to herself.

As he heaved himself upward onto the flotsam to have a better look, he shuddered. At the end of the rope was an iron anchor, hand-forged, as wide across as Mari's shoulders. He hadn't any idea how she'd lifted the thing into the boat. But should she manage to drop it into the water, it would yank her under in an instant. She would not stand a chance.

"Help me up," Holmes said.

"No," she said, beginning to cry now. "No, I must do this."

"But my love, I am here now."

She shook her head. "Oh, Holmes. I did not think anything could make this moment worse. And yet, your being alive nearly does."

He frowned, not understanding what she meant.

"We sunk the *Aquila*," she explained. "There is so much I haven't told you. Matteo Mazza, he is still alive. There is something I must do now, to protect the village from him and his men."

"You're wrong, Mari. Matteo is dead. He was on the *Aquila*."

"No," Mari insisted. "I thought he was, too. But this morning, I learned he was not. Corso spoke with him just last night in Naples."

"That doesn't make any sense. Days ago, I heard the officers speaking very clearly about it. Matteo was on the brig."

"Then, he must have disembarked. Perhaps without your realizing it."

Holmes nodded. He'd been imprisoned, after all, so how could he know for sure? "Please, Mari, help me up so we can talk about this."

Together, in a terribly unwieldy way, they managed to get him into the *gozzo*. It nearly turned over at one point, which gave Holmes a great fright. He kept his eye on the anchor, ready to lunge for it should it go over with Mari still attached.

In the boat, he went to work at her very good knots. There were several of them, and he hardly took a breath until he had successfully released her from the rope.

"There is something you must know about me," Mari went on. "There is a group of us women, and we have special—"

"I know it all already," he interrupted. "I met someone on the brig. She told me of *stregheria* and your abilities."

"*She?*"

"Your mother," Holmes said. "Imelda. She set me free. I was imprisoned in the cargo hold, and she helped me get out. She was just above me, locked in the second mate's cabin."

Bewilderment crossed Mari's face. "My...mother?" She gazed up at the sky. "I must be dreaming," she said. "All of this, a dream."

He shook his head. "It is not a dream." He pointed to the scarf around his knee. "She was wearing this just this morning."

Mari bent forward, taking a long look at it. "I recognize it," she said. "She wore it often when I was younger."

Holmes reached into his pocket and withdrew the flask Imelda had given him, holding it out for Mari.

She eyed it warily. "What is that?"

"I haven't any idea. She asked me not to open it. To give it to you instead." He held it out for her.

"No. No." Mari averted her gaze. "She abandoned me and Sofia. I don't want anything of hers."

"Mari," Holmes said. "She did not abandon you. The Mazza brothers, they didn't know she had daughters. She turned herself over before they could learn you and Sofia even existed. She did it to protect you. That's who she rowed away with, the night she left. The two brothers. Did you recognize Massimo before you killed him?"

"Yes." Mari nodded, her tone softer now. "Yes, I did."

Holmes quickly relayed all he knew, including the fact that Imelda and Matteo Mazza had recently convened. They were, in this way, partners—though with very different values. Matteo was evil. But Imelda? She associated with the men so her daughters did not have to.

When he finished his story, Mari merely stared at him in disbelief. "This is why she called me her *cousin* on the night she left. It made no sense to me then. She was trying to throw them off."

"Exactly."

Mari reached for the flask in Holmes's hands. "I have spent a lifetime hating her," she said, carefully removing the cork stopper. She began to cry. "How unfortunate it is," she said through tears, "to have felt this way all my life. And then, in a single morning, she drowns—and I learn the truth."

Slowly, she turned the flask upside down, letting the contents spill into her hand. A small, folded note fell out first. Squinting, she read it once, quietly, then she read it aloud for Holmes.

My dearest Mari. I met your beloved only hours ago. The way his eyes light up when he speaks of you...it is something I have never seen in a man's eyes before. He cherishes you as much as I do. Perhaps even more.

He told me about Sofia. I have been dreaming about her nightly for almost two years. Somewhere, deep in the recesses of my spirit, I think I knew something had happened to her. Only, I had the gift of denial. You did not.

My girl, how much you have lost. I cannot fathom the pain you have endured.

I have been thinking about something for a very long while. I want to take them down, the Mazzas and all their men. I have been biding my time, waiting for the right opportunity.

That time, I know, is now. Holmes told me you killed Massimo. You began the work for me.

This leaves only Matteo. Holmes tells me he is after you.

I do not know whether Matteo is still on this vessel; moving around the brig is very dangerous for me, and I can only do so in the early hours of the morning. Matteo may be in the captain's quarters, or he could have called for a tender. He may be in Naples, or he may be on another vessel headed for Positano.

So long as Matteo is alive, you are not safe. Nor the village. I know the routes they run—I know they always skirt Li Galli.

There is a way to assure Matteo's demise. You will understand when you see what else I have put into the glass flask.

Do you remember the night I left, when I came to your bedroom and covered your and Sofia's foreheads in kisses? It is my sweetest, most treasured memory, and the one I will think of in my last moments.

Please forgive me for all those empty years, all the times you must have wondered why I left. I have always loved you. This, I hope, is proof of it.

Yours,
Mamma

Mari dumped the rest of the flask's contents out. All that remained was a strand of seashells, cool her in palm. "Her *cimaruta*," she breathed. Mari fingered the delicate charms, turning them over in her hand. "There is only one reason she would have removed it," she said, her eyes brimming with fresh tears. "A *strega* never removes her *cimaruta*. Never. Unless—"

She gazed out at the water, very near where the *Aquila* had gone down.

"Unless what?" Holmes asked.

"Unless she means to perform the *vortice centuriaria*."

Holmes frowned, confused.

"The spell endures for one hundred years. But to perform the curse, a *strega* must sacrifice her own life. And she cannot perform the spell while wearing her protective *cimaruta*." Mari leaned forward, clutching the necklace against her chest. "My mother sunk the brig, Holmes. This explains why the maelstrom was so strong—much stronger, even, than we on shore expected. The *vortice centuriaria* is very powerful."

But then Mari frowned. "Something still does not make sense. You said my mother was locked in the second mate's cabin? A *strega* needs to touch the water to perform an incantation. How would she have done so, from inside the brig?"

"She was able to get out a few times," Holmes replied, "as she mentioned in the letter. I wonder if..." Suddenly, he jerked his head upright. "A rope ladder. There was one in the cabin with her, just before I escaped. She must have slipped onto the main deck shortly after me and hooked the ladder from the railing. She could have crawled down it and—"

"Recited her incantation at the same time as those of us on shore," Mari said. "Though, of course, we didn't realize it at the time."

Together, they peered toward the eye of Li Galli, near where the *Aquila* had gone down. It was difficult to see sitting down, but as Holmes carefully stood in the boat, he could make out a cluster of wide, deep eddies. They spun viciously.

A trap, waiting for the next crew of unsuspecting mariners.

Holmes leaned forward, gently brushing aside the collar of Mari's shift. "You are not wearing your *cimaruta*," he breathed. He glanced at the rope he'd untied from her waist. "Did you intend to perform the *vortice centuriaria* yourself?"

Mari nodded. "Yes, after learning this morning that Matteo was not on the *Aquila*. He is on the next ship, *La Dea*, arriving soon. But it seems my mother—"

"Has already taken care of it," Holmes finished for her.

"Yes." She nodded.

Holmes lifted the rope and anchor and hovered them over the edge of the boat, ready to drop them.

"Wait," Mari said. She reached for something that remained tied up in one of the rope's knots. A bundle of paper.

"Your letters," she said, tucking them close to her chest. "Every one you have ever sent me."

"I—" he stammered, "I do not have yours. I kept them behind a plank in my berth." He gazed at the water. "They are now at the bottom of the sea, I'm afraid."

She gave him a small smile. "I am here. You are here. We don't need any more proof of it than that."

He threw the rope and anchor overboard.

"What can I possibly do now," Mari asked, "to honor my mother? To repay her?" She clutched the glass flask to her chest. "We have no spells for love or remembrance."

"I don't think she needed either of those from you." Holmes nodded to the letter in her lap. "She asked for one thing. Forgiveness."

"I wish—" Mari's voice was thick with tears "—I wish I could give her that so easily. I think it will take time."

Holmes nodded. "Of course it will. It is a deep wound." With his thumb, he swiped a fat tear from Mari's cheek, then dipped his hand into the sea. "But your desire to honor her death shows that, already, a tiny part of that wound has begun to close."

Suddenly, the boat gave a little shudder, startling both of them. Where Holmes's fingertips grazed the water, something dark and glassy spun beneath the surface of the water.

Mari leaned over the edge of the boat, softly exclaiming. "Dolphins," she said. "Three of them." She reached her hand into the water, letting one of them gently touch the tip of its snout to her fingers. The water around them began to shimmer, sparkling orange and pink. Sunrays, Holmes reasoned, though he couldn't remember ever seeing the ocean glimmer like this.

With the dolphins near, Holmes began to row to shore. The waves gently lapped the boat in; he hardly needed to pull at the oars.

As they went, Mari lay on the bottom of the small boat, her head resting against Holmes's leg and her hands wrapped around his calf. "I will never let you go," she whispered.

Holmes could not remember ever being so happy as he was at this exact moment. "Where shall we go," he asked, "when we are on land?"

"The little island of Ischia," Mari said immediately. "As soon as *La Dea* has sunk, we will go find Ami and Dante, and we will make for Ischia at once."

Nearly an hour passed while Holmes and Mari remained tucked away behind a boulder, anticipating the arrival of *La Dea*.

While they waited, Holmes withdrew his journal from its wax casing. It was damp in the corners but mercifully intact. He turned to the first blank page, noting the date. *Friday, April 27, 1821.*

He then recounted all that had happened that morning: Mari's mother, Imelda, helping him escape. Quinto's gunshots. Finding Mari wrapped in rope knots.

He mentioned nothing of *stregheria*, though. That was not his secret to share.

As he wrote, Mari withdrew a tiny plover feather from her gown. "I nearly forgot I had it," she said. "I found it a few days ago, and I've kept it with me since. It made me think of the story you once told me, saving the little bird from the boatswain."

Holmes smiled, tucking the feather tight between the pages. He considered his many great fortunes and lifted his pen one final time.

This voyage has come to an end, he wrote. *Both of us are presumed dead.*

And yet we are terribly, wholly alive.

36

HAVEN

Saturday

And yet we are terribly, wholly alive.
I read the last line of Holmes's journal again.
"Oh, my God," I said aloud. "Oh. My. God."
With the video paused, I zoomed farther in on the page, spotting a tiny gray-and-white feather stuck in the seam between pages. I wondered about the story behind it. Though, for the moment, I was more riveted by what I'd just learned.

It was Saturday morning, and Mal was still asleep in her bedroom. I stood to go wake her—I couldn't wait to tell her about this—but I felt so dizzy, I quickly sat back down.

I needed to tell Savina, too. This changed everything she thought she knew about Mari. *She shunned her powers over the sea*, Savina had said, *and look how it turned out for her.* Yet given what I'd just read, Mari's mother had not abandoned her. Her lover had not gone down with his ship. And she herself had not died by suicide.

The misfortunes Savina believed about Mari? Other than

losing her little sister, well, those things hadn't happened at all. If anything, Mari DeLuca suddenly seemed one of the luckiest women to ever have lived.

I jumped at the sound of a knock on the door. Was it Enzo?

I pushed myself off the couch, black spots flashing in my vision. I opened the door.

Conrad.

And by the look on his face, something was wrong.

"How did you find out where I was staying?" I asked, my fingers clutching the door frame.

"Gage told me." He peered around, taking in the double doors leading to the terrace. "Quite the rental for a project team on a limited budget."

I ignored him, not willing to waste my breath on an explanation.

"Can I come in?" he asked. "There's something I'd like to discuss."

Curiosity got the best of me. I opened the door wider, inviting him to have a seat on one of the bar stools.

"What's up?" I asked.

"Gage and I had a nice chat last night," he said, running his fingers slowly along the high-top counter. "You're aware, Haven, of the confidentiality clause surrounding the foundation's involvement in this project."

My underarms began to sweat. There was something about his manner that I didn't like. Something I didn't like at all.

"Yes, of course."

"I myself am intimately familiar with it," he went on, "as I signed the same contract a few days ago. It's one of their strictest tenets: HPI doesn't permit funding recipients to disclose their involvement. It's why Gage requires email encryption and the redaction of the foundation's name on documents shared with others. You remember signing the contract that agrees to this, right?"

"What are you getting at? I've never shared the foundation's name with anyone outside the project team."

Conrad pulled out his phone and flicked through a few photos, landing on a video. He pressed Play.

The first thing I recognized in the frame? Enzo's dive boat. It was footage from earlier that week when Enzo and I had the boatside encounter with Conrad and his crew. I thought he'd been taking pictures with his phone—but instead, he'd been taking a *video*.

I continued to watch as the camera panned over the waves, the water. Then the frame went still—this must have been when Conrad set his phone on the boat's center console.

He hadn't stopped the recording, though. He'd left it on as he began to fiddle with his equipment.

Proprietary. A prototype camera. It was his voice in the video. Clear and sharp.

But it was what I heard next that left a knot in the pit of my stomach. My own voice. *Did HPI loan it to you?* the video recording played aloud. *Or Gage Whitlock himself?*

This was followed by a pause I remembered well, even now. Conrad had glared at me after my question, then the video had picked up his under-the-breath comment. *Jesus, Haven.*

Now, he hit Stop on the recording and crossed his arms. "The foundation's involvement is to be kept confidential," Conrad said now. "Yet in this video, you state the name of the organization—and their CEO—in front of several people not involved with the project in any way."

"Enzo and your boat driver? That's a stretch. They wear swim trunks to work, Conrad. They're not interested in foundations and capital commitments."

He shook his head. "My dive crew isn't under contract, either. They had no idea this project was funded by HPI. Not until you said something. Now we're having to sort through NDAs."

I fumbled for an excuse, anything to exonerate myself. "Well, the contract I signed was null and void the moment Gage yanked me from the project," I said weakly.

"Wrong. It states that the confidentiality obligations survive even if the parties decide to end their agreement." He started tapping away at his phone again. "And they've got a hell of a team of lawyers back in New York who don't handle confidentiality breaches with a soft touch. Here," he said, showing me an obscure business journal article, probably something only a few had ever seen. The headline read *Well-Known Foundation Sues Funding Recipient for Breach of Confidentiality Clause*. Conrad scrolled down, pointing to the bottom. "Quarter-million bucks in restitution."

I threw my hands up, exasperated. "Okay, so I screwed up. What now?"

He shrugged. "I can delete the video."

"Cool. That's just great. Anything else I can do for you?" My hands shook as I gripped the edge of the counter.

"Yes," he said. "I want you to leave Positano."

I narrowed my eyes. "What? Is this a joke?"

"Not at all." He held up his phone. "You agree to head home, and I delete the video."

My mouth hung open in disbelief.

Then, finally, I braved the question I'd been scared to ask for days. "How do you know about it?"

He didn't flinch. "Know about what?"

"Jesus, Conrad. The *loot*. The gems my father saw on his last dive. I know that's why you're really here. Did he tell you about it himself? Or did you sneak around his office, his files, and—"

Suddenly, I stopped.

During our recent boatside encounter, Conrad had used my middle name, calling me *Haven Marie*. It might have seemed irrelevant, if not for the fact that the password to my father's cloud folder—the very one holding the images of the wreck—was my middle name.

Every so often, my father shared images of his dives with friends and family. Conrad must have snooped around on the cloud drive. "You figured out his password," I said now. It wouldn't have been very difficult to determine via my social media, or maybe my father had once mentioned it in passing. "You managed a way into the locked *Li Galli Potential* folder, didn't you?"

Conrad wouldn't meet my gaze. "Your dad shared plenty with me," he said. "He would have told me about it over beers, anyway."

I vehemently disagreed. "Let me guess," I said. "Your search is going well, but you need more time. You want me out of your way, don't you?" I didn't have the extravagant tech equipment Conrad boasted, but perhaps he feared I had other clues at my disposal—like information on the strange alphanumerical codes my dad had also left in the cloud folder.

Conrad didn't answer. Which told me all I needed to know.

Still—he wanted me to give up my father's discovery.

And he wanted me to *leave*.

Yet now more than ever, I needed to be here. There was something only I could take care of, something with huge implications.

I thought about what I'd read a few minutes ago in Holmes's log—*And yet we are terribly, wholly alive*—and Savina's erroneous beliefs. She thought Mari had drowned herself after a lifetime of personal loss. She also thought she and Renata were the last of the *streghe*. But if Mari and Holmes had lived, they could have gone on to have children. They could, for all I knew, have left a thriving line of descendants. If so, Savina needed to know this. She might not be the last of them.

Nothing was guaranteed, though. Staying in Positano to pursue this could be a dead end. And if that were the case, I'd have accomplished nothing in exchange for what could be a pretty little lawsuit.

"I need to talk to Mal," I said. "I'll be back in a minute."

I nudged Mal on the shoulder, waking her.

"Hey," I said. "I need help. It's about Conrad."

She blinked her eyes open, sat upright. "Are we burying a body?"

I didn't laugh. Instead, I summarized what I'd read in Holmes's journal, then my conversation with Conrad. "I don't know what to do. He wants me to leave Positano." I pinched the bridge of my nose. "How can I abandon this whole thing? Learning the truth about Mari, uncovering what my dad begged me to find…"

From Mal's stern expression, I could tell she was about to dive into one of her tough-love lectures. "Look, Haven," she said, her voice low. "This isn't about your dad anymore. I get that you're grieving him. I get that you're full of remorse. I get that you're trying to finish what he started." She stood and placed a hand on my shoulder. "But he's gone, Haven. And right now, everything that's at stake—not the least of which is the safety of the people on the water—means you need to let go of the search for your dad's gems—right now, anyway—and worry about the Something Bigger." She shook her head. "Think of it this way. If not for the journey to find his sunken treasure, you wouldn't have gone to the archive at all. You wouldn't have met Enzo, or his mother. You wouldn't know anything about the *streghe*."

She touched the worn, faded bracelet on my wrist. "Look at this thing. It's ratty and old and perfectly you. You, Haven, don't give a shit about money. Neither did your dad. He wanted to use the proceeds to start a scholarship fund, for God's sake. Conrad has always been about the yachts, the glitz. But you've told me yourself, your dad cared most for the joy of the discovery: the pursuit, the adventure, the deep dives with people you love. These are the things he wanted for you. And you've already made a hell of a discovery, haven't you?" She swiped away a tear that had slipped down my cheek. "You're a grown woman. You get to make your own decisions. You're allowed to do something different than what your dad asked of you."

She was so terribly, painfully right. For now, at least, I needed to stop worrying about the gems. I needed to get to the bottom of Mari and Holmes's story.

"Yeah," I finally said. "You're right."

"Well, obviously."

I shook my head at her—this blunt, wildly loyal best friend of mine—and left the room. I found Conrad still at the kitchen counter, eyes glued to the television. It was another news report about the nosedive in Amalfi tourism.

"All right, Conrad," I said. "I'll stay off the water, but I'm not leaving town." I nodded to his cell phone. "Do whatever the hell you want with that video."

He thrust his phone into his back pocket. "I don't get you, Haven. A lawsuit like this could ruin you."

I shrugged, making my way to the front door, then I opened it for him. "I've got bigger fish to fry."

At this, he frowned, and I basked for a moment in the satisfaction of it. Perhaps he thought I was on the trail of an even bigger pile of treasure. An even bigger, more valuable discovery.

Which in many ways, I was.

"Leave," I said, holding the door open.

With a slight nod, he slipped out of the house.

Given what I'd read in Holmes's log before Conrad's arrival, I was tempted to make my way to Savina's villa right then and there. But I still had questions, and I knew Savina would, too.

The log itself and the leather-bound case were both water-damaged. I'd assumed they were flotsam, since so much else in the archive room had been marked as such. But the journal couldn't be flotsam, not if Holmes had made an entry after the sinking, recording that he and Mari were both alive.

How, then, had this journal made it to the archive? And

might it shed light on Holmes's and Mari's eventual fates? This seemed crucial information before I went back to Savina with what would otherwise seem a preposterous tale.

I flipped through my phone's photos again, looking at an unusual stamp affixed to the bundle holding the log and its leather case: *FM-1842.1*. I hadn't any idea what this meant, and the only way to find out was to call Chloe—not exactly my favorite person. It was Saturday, but according to the archive's website, they were open this weekend for a special teaching event with university students.

Chloe answered on the third ring. After exchanging quick hellos, I asked her about the code on the journal.

"FM," she repeated. "Anything with that stamp means it came from the private collection that maintained the Fratelli Mazza company records until the early 1900s. Eventually, they donated those records to us. There were hundreds of boxes. The number 1842 indicates the year the private collection would have come into possession of the journal. And the *1* simply means they only had one record for that year. Which is logical, as the Fratelli Mazza business was all but defunct by late 1821."

This took me by surprise. "Why is that?" I asked.

Chloe let out a little laugh. "Well, the brothers were both dead. Massimo drowned in April of that year, and then two weeks later, Matteo was aboard a brig that sunk very near Positano. Their deaths, so close together, were all the city talked about for a year. We have dozens of old newspaper articles about the brothers if you're interested."

I paused. April of 1821 was the month of Holmes's final entry. "I wonder why the archive didn't get this journal for another twenty years, then."

"Could be any number of reasons," Chloe said. "The author of the journal might have sent it to the archive himself, believing its contents were historically significant. Or, after the author's death, his family might have mailed it to the archive, knowing there was mention of the Mazza brothers within."

I thought of my father, his home office still brimming with old dive logs, scattered Post-it Notes, and scribbled annotations on ship diagrams. I hadn't yet mustered the strength to review any of it in detail.

What would I do with it all someday? I wouldn't be able to throw his things away. Perhaps Holmes's family or children—if he had them—had felt the same, opting to send this personal document to an archival collection instead, where it would be forever preserved.

"Do you have any resources," I asked now, "that might shed light on the fate of the journal's author? Death records, for instance?"

"We subscribe to two genealogy databases, yes."

I thanked Chloe and hung up the phone.

A trip back to the archives was in order.

The next morning, Mal and I woke at the crack of dawn to take a taxi into Naples, a quicker trip than the bus. We arrived at the archive soon after it opened.

Before looking at the genealogy resources, I wanted to take a final look at Holmes's journal itself, to ensure I hadn't missed anything.

"I'd like to see the same document I viewed last time," I told Chloe. "No need to assist. I know where it is."

She pushed forward the clipboard with the visitors' log, and I scribbled my name. Mal did the same, then together, we went to the last archive room. I still had the shelf number written in my notebook, and I quickly located the bundle containing the water-damaged case and log. Together, Mal and I sat down at a small table.

For all the time I'd spent reviewing Holmes's log on my phone in recent days, it held significantly more meaning now, here in my hands. When I'd first held this journal, I'd chalked Holmes up to little more than another unfortunate drowned sailor. And perhaps even a criminal.

But now, I knew he was a man who'd fallen in love with a witch of the sea. A man who'd been determined to return to her.

A sailor who hadn't gone down at all.

I checked the journal for any overlooked clues that might shed light on how it had gotten into the archive's hands in 1842, nearly twenty years after the Mazza brothers were dead.

I could find nothing.

Frustrated, I gave the log and its water-damaged case a final look, then I patted it softly and placed it back in the paper bundle. I sensed, instinctively, that I would never see it again. It had given me everything it could.

"So we're done?" Mal asked. "I could go for a Bellini."

I shook my head. "No. This log isn't why we're here."

Mal raised her eyebrows. "Yay."

I chuckled as we made our way back to the entrance.

"Chloe," I said, "can you tell me about your genealogy databases?"

"Certainly," she said. "We subscribe to two. Il Portale Antenati and FamilySearch.org." She reached for a small card, handing it to me. "Feel free to use one of the computers in the back. Here is our log-in information."

A few minutes later, Mal and I scrolled through Il Portale Antenati, but it proved frustrating: the site was difficult to navigate and didn't return any records dated pre-1860.

We tried FamilySearch.org next.

"Let's try *Holmes Foster*," I said, typing his name into the search function. I left the dates wide-open.

"What about location?" Mal asked.

I tried Massachusetts first, remembering what I'd read in his log. Nothing matched the time frame. I trilled my fingers on the desk. He wouldn't have stayed in Positano, that much I knew. "Should I just put...*Italy?*" I gave a little laugh at the absurdity of it.

"Can't hurt to try."

I typed this in and hit Enter. Again, no results. "Okay. Let's try *Mari DeLuca*," I said. But again, nothing.

I leaned back in my chair, letting out a long exhale. Suddenly, Mal leaned across me, all but shoving me out of the way to access the keyboard. *Mari Foster*, she typed.

"That won't work," I disputed. "Italian women don't take their husband's surnames."

Mal glared at me. "They ran away after faking their deaths. Mari doesn't exactly sound like a rule-follower." Then, very dramatically, she hit Enter.

At once, a single result popped up on the screen. But it wasn't related to someone named Mari Foster; instead, it was a post made on a forum several years earlier. The user had posted the same message twice, once in English and once in Italian, stating that she was looking for an ancestor by the name of Mari who might have been involved with someone bearing the last name Foster. The time frame that this ancestor lived was early nineteenth century, with possible connections to Naples and the Amalfi Coast.

It seemed deliciously promising.

"You're welcome," Mal said, smirking.

My pulse quickened as I clicked on the profile of the woman who'd made the post. Her name was Lucille Detti, and she'd uploaded a photo, though she looked like countless other Italian women: olive skin, dark eyes. Interestingly, though, she had dark red hair, interspersed with gray. She was very beautiful, maybe midfifties. According to the profile, she lived in Venice.

Her profile listed an email address. I quickly sent her a message, asking her to call me regarding a *Mari/Foster* she'd posted about online two years ago.

It wasn't an answer to Holmes's fate, but perhaps it would shed light on Mari's.

"Now we wait," I told Mal. "Let's go find your Bellini."

Several hours later, as Mal and I were in a taxi returning to Positano, my phone rang with an unknown number and a +39 country code. I picked it up at once, sensing this might be Lucille.

I was right.

"You're the only person who has ever reached out about that post," she said, a delighted warmth in her voice. "I've been compiling my family's tree for many years, and Mari is one of the few places where I've found myself...*bloccata*."

She was at a dead end, then. I resisted the urge to start firing questions. What, if anything, did she know about Mari and Holmes? Was she familiar with *stregheria*? Was she, herself, a practicing *strega*?

Instead, I forced myself to start with pleasantries. I asked whether she still lived in Venice, which she did, and whether she had a family. She'd been married thirty-four years, she told me, and she and her husband had two grown daughters. Four grandchildren, as well: one boy, three girls.

"How interesting." I took a breath, steeling myself. "And what do you know about your ancestor, Mari?"

"Not much," Lucille said, voice resigned. "Have you ever tried researching your family tree? There are an infinite number of paths to take. If I can't make progress on one ancestor, I'll hop over a generation and work on someone else." In the background, I heard her sifting through papers. "Before I called you, I pulled a few files. Mari had four children. They took the surname *Foster*, which is interesting. Probably from their father, yet the surname is not Italian, of course. I never learned much about him. The parish registry records only referred to him as *Signor Foster*."

I stayed silent, feeling the need to keep Holmes's survival story to myself, at least for now.

"The cholera pandemic, which ravaged much of Europe in the 1840s, is what eventually killed Mari. Likely her husband, too. The parish registry shows that the family of six was living in Treviso in 1841, but there are no records for 1842. I would assume that if Mari's husband—this Foster man—had survived, he'd have remained at home with any surviving children."

Chloe's suggestion, then, had been correct: someone, whether Holmes or Mari or another person, must have sent Holmes's log—stamped *FM-1842.1*—to the archive shortly after the time of his death.

I looked out the window as the taxi sped down the freeway. In the distance, Mount Vesuvius rose high and clear into the sky.

Lucille went on, "Most likely a neighbor or friend of the family took the children in. Those children are my ancestors. I've traced a few of them, particularly one of Mari's daughters. Long family lines. I've got cousins all over the world. Thousands, I think." At this, Lucille laughed. "I've connected with a few of them. Made some good friends, really."

"Would you mind sending me pictures of the family tree?" I asked, remembering what Savina had told me. *A legacy stretching back thousands of years, and we are the last of it.*

"Of course," she said. "Once we hang up, I'll send the photos to you by email." I heard Lucille shuffling through papers. "I'm terribly curious myself. What is the reason for your interest in all of this?"

I explained to Lucille that I was an archaeologist researching a family whose lineage placed them in the Amalfi region. As I said this, Mal eyed me warily as though to say, *That is grossly short of detail, but okay.*

The answer seemed to satisfy Lucille, and I got the sense she was glad that someone, at last, had reached out. "Before we hang up..." I said, leaning forward in my seat. *Here we go.* "During my research, I stumbled on an old article mentioning *stregheria*. I'm curious if your family has passed down any stories or legends around it?"

"*Stregheria…*" Lucille repeated, her tone aghast.

"Right."

"I am n-not—" She fumbled over her words, then went silent. I wondered, briefly, if the line had gone dead. "I am not comfortable speaking about this over the phone," she finally said.

"I understand," I said quickly, wanting to put her at ease. Still, I'd caught the tremor in her voice. There'd been something there, something she hadn't wanted to share. Perhaps she would be more comfortable speaking with Savina if I could tactfully make the connection.

I thanked Lucille for her time and told her I'd be waiting for her email.

We hung up, and I checked my missed text messages—a few hellos from friends back home. Then I went to Instagram, curious if Conrad had posted any photos of today's dive.

I felt sick when I saw that he had. *Once-in-a-lifetime dive*, he'd captioned on a photo of himself pulling off his dive mask. With a pang of unease, I could only hope that my afternoon at the archive, and my conversation with Lucille, would make all of this worth it.

"Are you okay with a quick errand before we go back to the villa?" I asked Mal.

"Have I any choice in the matter?"

I laughed. "Touché."

I leaned forward and gave our taxi driver instructions.

37

HAVEN

Sunday

As the taxi pulled up to Savina's villa, I spotted Enzo's bright orange Vespa parked out front. He'd texted me a few times in the last day, but I'd been so preoccupied with everything else that I hadn't given him more than a few short replies.

The front door was slightly ajar, and Mal and I stepped sheepishly into the foyer. "Hello?" I called out.

"Haven."

I turned to see Enzo—shirtless—with a screwdriver in one hand and a bottle of water in the other.

"Hi," I said. "Enzo, meet my friend, Mal. Mal, meet Enzo."

The two nodded at each other, and Enzo leaned in to give me a gentle kiss on the cheek. "My mother mentioned that you two have chatted a few times," he said, "though, she wouldn't get into details. I didn't realize you had hit it off so well." He cocked his head to the side, an invitation for me to share more.

I glanced around the foyer. "It's for the project I'm working on. Turns out she knows quite a bit of local history." It was the best I could do.

"I'll go find her," Mal said. She rushed off, leaving the two of us alone.

I noticed a black hair band around Enzo's wrist. *My* black hair band. I gave it a playful snap.

"What's this?" I asked.

"Found it on the floor the other night. Next to the kitchen counter. Haven't taken it off since."

"I like it on you," I said, touched that he'd kept it.

Mal called me over from the other room. As I turned away, I felt Enzo's eyes on me. A rush of warmth spread through my chest: no matter what went down with Savina in the days to come, I knew Enzo and I weren't finished with whatever this was.

Savina rushed forward to give me a hug. "Come, come," she said, motioning for me to follow her to a small utility room off the kitchen.

Once we were alone, Savina leaned in close, her hands on my shoulders. "I can see it in his eyes," she whispered. "Enzo, he is falling in love with you—if he has not already. Oh, Haven, how—"

"Wait," I said, holding up my hand. Lucille's photos had come in soon after we'd hung up, and I'd already traced through them. Now, I zoomed in on one of the photos and showed Savina the handwritten name at the top of the genealogy chart. *Mari DeLuca.*

Beneath this, a spiderweb of descendants. Hundreds of them.

There were, in truth, *streghe* everywhere. All over Italy.

I took a deep breath. What I was about to share with Savina wasn't without risk. There was the possibility that, after telling her Mari had descendants all over, Savina might recruit them for her own wicked endeavors. But I had an incredible amount of leverage, including the discreetly recorded phone conversation with Savina from Friday evening. I'd gladly turn it over to officials if needed, along with every other bit of information I'd acquired.

"She didn't drown herself," I said. "Mari lived, and I have proof of it." I thought of Holmes's journal, tucked away at the archive. "I have proof her lover survived the *Aquila*'s sinking, too. And her mother? She didn't abandon Mari. Your mother's *legends and lore* might have had bits and pieces of the truth, but the real narrative looks much different than what you've been led to believe. Including," I added, holding up my phone again, "the fact that you and Renata aren't the end of anything. There are *streghe* everywhere."

Suddenly, it dawned on me that I served as the connection—the link—between these two separate lines of *streghe*. Savina believed she was the end of her lineage. Lucille was looking for the truth at the start of it. How could they have possibly known or discovered one another without my efforts?

Savina hadn't pulled her eyes from my phone screen. "I don't understand. Where did you get this?"

Briefly, I told her about Holmes's log and my online genealogy research. "I spoke with a woman, Lucille, earlier today. She's the one who sent me this. She's one of Mari's descendants and big into genealogy. She spent years compiling this information. Mari's data, for instance, comes from parish records in the nineteenth century." I navigated to my Gmail account. "Lucille sent me this, too."

Not sure what you've read, she'd written in the email, but *stregheria* isn't like other forms of witchcraft. Every *strega* I know uses her powers for good. For benevolence—change for the better. This lineage has been unspeakably rewarding, the greatest gift of my life.

Finally, Savina pulled her eyes from the phone. She gazed out the small window where, beyond, the small patch of olive trees had grown amid the thicket of evergreens. *"The greatest gift of my life,"* she repeated. "I think I would like to speak with her."

"Yes," I said. "Of course."

I thought I caught a glimmer of something like release, or deliverance, in Savina's eyes. "My, how I need to lie down…" she finally admitted.

I let out an exhale. I didn't consider Savina an evil woman but certainly a grieving, fearful one. She believed that catching up on a lifetime's worth of magic would keep her remaining child safe and well.

This didn't make her actions right. But I could, in a way, understand her motives.

I grabbed my phone, ready to put it in my back pocket. The screen lit up, revealing the image of my father on his boat: his hair dripping water, the indent of his dive mask on his skin. Everything that had unfolded in the last few days had been because of him—a result of my hunting down the treasure that had eluded him.

Of course, I hadn't found the jewels—not yet, anyway. In spite of my distaste for Conrad, I'd left them for him to find first.

But what I'd discovered was indescribably sweeter: Mari and Holmes's love story.

They couldn't have known it, but it was powerful enough—even now, more than two hundred years later—to save an entire region.

38

HAVEN

Three months later

Less than three months after leaving, I returned to Positano. I would stay longer this time, much longer—up to a year. Project Relic was back on, and this time, the project was entirely on my terms.

My team remained the same, with one bittersweet exception: Mal. She and Megan had decided they were ready, at last, to live in the same city, and Mal had proposed. Given their upcoming life changes, Mal wouldn't be able to resume work on Project Relic. Sad as I was to be without her, I was thrilled she'd found such happiness.

I hadn't thought I'd ever work on Project Relic again, not against the likes of Gage and Conrad. But a few days after my conversation with Lucille and my final trip to Savina's villa, Conrad had abruptly departed Positano.

Gage had been the one to tell me via a near-panicked phone call. "What happened with Conrad?" he shouted into the phone.

"I have no idea what you're talking about," I replied, staring at my dive gear, trying to strategize how to get back into the water as soon as possible.

"He ditched the project," Gage said. "Without explanation. Did something go down between you two?"

My shoulders slumped forward, and I took a seat on the edge of the bed, leaning forward to put my head in my hands. *He ditched.*

It could only mean one thing. He'd found my father's gems. And quickly, too: I wondered if his proprietary equipment had done the trick, or maybe he'd cracked the mystery behind the strange alphanumerical codes my father had left behind with the photos.

Either way, this was all the proof I needed: Conrad never cared a whit for the project's objectives. I could only hope that he was now too distracted by his newfound loot to forget about the video he intended to blackmail me with.

"Nothing went down between us," I muttered, thinking it was time to start packing and search flights home. "Maybe he got bored. Or maybe something better came along." I could hear the defeat, the frustration, in my own voice.

And…Enzo. I couldn't deny my still-smoldering feelings for him. We'd had lunch the day after my last visit to the villa, though it was somber at best, with everything so up in the air. Now I tried not to dwell on what our relationship might have become if Project Relic had gone forward.

There was a pause on the other end of the line, then, "You want back on the project?"

I froze. "You yanked me from the project, remember."

Gage exhaled on the other end of the line. "I acted rashly, Haven. I'm sorry."

"No, you're not, Gage. You're sorry that Conrad's team evaporated into thin air, but you're not sorry you pulled me from the project in the first place."

"What can the foundation do to get you back on?" In his voice, I heard eagerness—maybe, even, desperation.

I paused, sitting on the edge of the bed. Angry as I was with Gage, I could see an opportunity here. I could use this to my advantage. Renegotiate some of the terms I hadn't liked from the get-go. Demand more money for my team members. Draft a tighter contract between all parties involved, so the foundation couldn't renege on me. No matter what.

Still, renegotiating the contract would take time. Weeks, maybe months. And I wanted a different attorney overseeing the process—not someone on Gage's side but someone on *my* side, with my team's interests at heart.

"Let me think on it a few days," I said. "I'll get back to you next week."

"We don't have that kind of time, Haven."

"Gage. You don't have a team at all right now. If we do this, you're not strong-arming me again." I pulled my suitcase from the corner of the room and set it on my bed. Regardless what I decided, I needed to head home—for a short while, at least, to regroup and start calling attorneys. "I'll be in touch."

I hung up before he could reply.

Soon after my arrival in Positano—the second time—my phone rang.

I'd just finished unpacking my things. I was now in a single-occupant studio tucked on a side street toward the middle of town. Here, my window looked out onto an alleyway. It had no terrace, no view, no Mal. A decrepit stone oven doubled as a closet. The host told me it had once been a bakery, many lifetimes ago.

But it was cozy, inviting. It was more than enough.

I glanced at my caller ID. *Conrad*. I hadn't heard from him in weeks. In spite of everything, I answered, curious what he was after now.

"Back on the project, I hear," he said. His voice was raspy—like he was sick, maybe. It didn't sound like him. Gone was the usual tone of pretentiousness.

I raised my eyebrows. "News travels fast."

"I'm surprised you're still working with Gage, given all that went down last time."

"I got my own lawyer. Secured better terms. This project could make my career."

"Fair." He exhaled hard. "Proud of you, kid."

I rolled my eyes. Conrad might have saved my life, but he'd almost ruined my career. I would trust him with an underwater rescue any day, but not much more than that. "Is there something you need?"

"The gems," he said slowly. "Did you know?"

I frowned. In truth, I hadn't thought much about the gems in the last couple of months. I'd been busy gearing back up for the project, finding a replacement for Mal. I'd made peace with the fact that although I hadn't recovered the underwater treasure my father so badly wanted, I'd done something greater. Something undoubtedly more impactful.

Still, I imagined the gemstones would fetch a pretty penny. Hundreds of thousands, maybe. I wondered what sort of salvage reward Conrad had negotiated with the Italian government. If he'd told them at all, that was.

"Know what?" I asked now.

Conrad sucked in a breath. Then, very quietly, as if he hardly believed it himself, "They're fakes, Haven."

I sat down on the edge of the bed. "Fakes?"

I thought about the swindling Mazza brothers and Chloe's comment she'd made during my first visit to the archive: *They were swindlers...known for pulling tricks and planting decoys...*

"That's right," Conrad said. "Not a real gem in the lot. Just blue glass." He stopped, letting that hang in the air.

Blue glass? I frowned. The gems my father had spotted were pink, red.

Who's finding rubbish now? I wanted to ask him.

"Shame," I finally said, a smile creeping onto my face.

"Do you know about anything else, Haven? We can chase it down together if you do. I mean it this time."

Jesus, this man would not give up. "I don't know a thing," I said. It was an honest statement, though already, I was reaching for my bag. I wanted another look at the alphanumerical codes in the cloud folder. Maybe, having gotten some distance from the whole endeavor, I'd spot something new this time.

Besides, I'd never forget the phone call with my dad after he'd spotted the gems. He'd been convinced of their authenticity. And given Conrad's statement just now about the color of the gems, it was clear he'd excavated something different than my dad's discovery.

"I have to go," I told him.

We said goodbye, and I hung up, thinking of the different things that can bring a person joy. For people like Conrad, it was cash. For people like my dad, it was adventure.

Right now, for me, it was karma.

I fell backward on the too-firm bed and laughed until my stomach hurt.

I dumped the contents of my bag onto the bed, spreading everything out: my binder with the marked-up site plans and maps; my notebook, full of scribbles I'd made during my research and visits to the archive; the freshly drafted legal agreements; and my laptop, where I now reopened the Word document with the indecipherable list of letters and numbers.

I flipped through a few pages of my notebook, stopping on the page where I'd noted record indicators at the archive—the room number, cabinet code, and so on—for the original fourteen files I'd hunted down at the archive.

Then, I glanced at my dad's list.

His codes. I wondered for the first time if they could be some kind of archive-record indicator, too. But he'd parsed them into columns, instead of listing a string of digits like I had.

Further, even once merged, his records indicators didn't match mine.

I tapped a pen against my chin. Was it possible he'd been on a different trail of investigation altogether?

I gathered my things and called for a cab.

Chloe recognized me the moment I walked in. "Welcome back," she said brightly, pushing forward the clipboard with the visitors' log. "I wondered if I'd be seeing you again one of these days."

I signed my name, then paused, hovering the pen over the page. "Might I peek through this real quick?" I asked, holding up the clipboard. After all, the names in the log were visible for all to see.

She frowned, then said, "Sure. Not a problem."

I turned back page after page, searching many months ago, looking for one date in particular: the creation date as indicated in the Word document's metadata. If the list did indeed consist of archive-record locators, my dad probably would have visited the archive on or around that date.

Yes, just over nine months ago, there it was, unmistakably clear: my father's steady block handwriting, spelling out his full name, followed by his hurried, loopy signature.

Tears welled in my eyes as I brushed my thumb over his signature. I'd seen it a thousand times before but never had it wrenched at my heart like it did now. He'd been here, standing where I stood, touching these very pages.

"Thank you," I said, setting the log back on the desk.

"Is everything all right?" Chloe asked.

I nodded. "Perfectly all right, yes. May I?" I motioned to the door behind her, which led to the archival rooms I was now so intimately familiar with.

She gestured toward it. "Good luck."

I settled in at one of the large research tables, brushing it clean of dust and tiny flakes of aged paper. I reopened my dad's Word document, studying his codes.

From what I could glean, he'd listed three separate archive records.

I went in search of the first one, wondering if this record would have anything to do with the *Aquila*. It didn't, but I recognized something else almost immediately—the stamp on the brown paper bundle. *FM-1886.1.* This record, then, also came from the private archive housing the many Fratelli Mazza documents.

It was a newspaper article, published in Naples in August 1886, about a group of treasure-hunters who'd stumbled on a well-preserved wreck they traced back to the Fratelli Mazza. The men reported they'd found quite an assortment of goods still intact amid the wreckage, including—to their delight—hundreds of diamonds at the front of the vessel. They'd been hidden inside the copper-sheathed hollowed-out bowsprit at the front of the ship. The turquoise patina on the copper was what had originally caught their eye, leading them to the valuable discovery.

I made a few notes in my notebook, then returned the bundle to its shelf. I navigated to another room, another cabinet, another shelf, finding my dad's second record of interest. This, too, was a newspaper article, published in the 1970s after the advent of modern-day scuba diving. A pair of novice divers, exploring Roman ruins in the Bay of Naples, had stumbled on a gold-plated religious relic, estimated to be worth millions.

The location of the relic? The front of the ship, settled in the silt alongside several large fragments of copper casing.

My heart began to thump harder in my chest.

I quickly made my way to the third and final record, not at

all surprised when I withdrew yet another newspaper article, this one published in 1922. I read the headline quickly—*Free Diver Finds Stolen Pithos off Coast of Capri, Missing for a Century*—and skimmed the article, learning that this free diver had found the jar peeking out from beneath a sliver of bluish-turquoise copper sheathing near the vessel's bow.

Then, I gasped.

A Post-it Note was affixed to the bottom of the article, with a short note scribbled on it:

> This explains the copper-sheathed bowsprit on all Mazza ships. Inside is where they hid the good stuff! Those brilliant bastards.

The handwriting was my father's. Had he accidentally left the sticky note secured to the article? A moment of exhilarated oversight, perhaps?

With a lump in my throat, I carefully removed the note from the article and stuck it to my notebook, staring at it. Even the tone—the whimsical humor of it—was exactly like him.

It reminded me of what he'd told me so many times. *Sometimes the answers aren't in the water, but out of it.*

Here was proof of it.

I could only surmise what had led my dad down this path. Maybe he hadn't been searching for the *Aquila*, but instead he'd strategized more broadly, investigating the Fratelli Mazza as a whole. Then, making the connection across these articles—and possibly other resources he'd come across—he'd gone diving in the areas the Mazzas were known to sail, to sink.

Li Galli, for one.

Conrad, I knew, would never have thought to pursue this route of investigation. Conrad wasn't the archive type; he was the yacht type. He'd take one look at the database, written entirely in Italian, and call it a waste of his time.

Regardless, this discovery was meant for me. All along, I'd wanted to finish what my father had started. Little did I realize that even now, after his death, he still had a few things to say.

After dropping off my things at my new studio apartment, I made my way down staircase after staircase. I trailed along the beach sidewalk for a few minutes, doing my best to avoid the slew of fresh tourists, then I stopped in front of a shop window, quickly touching up my lip gloss.

A few steps later, I opened the door to Enzo's dive shop.

In the last few months, he and I had exchanged a few text messages but nothing of real consequence. I sensed the what-could-have-been was as painful for him to dwell on as it was for me.

I hadn't hinted at my return to Positano, either. I wanted to see the expression on his face when I showed up—in person—at his shop.

It was better than I'd even hoped. If I thought he'd be surprised, I was wrong. He looked *astonished*.

"*Buongiorno*," I said playfully. I stepped forward and leaned my hip against the desk. "It's great to see you again," I whispered.

I gave a quick glance around the interior. Enzo had made a great deal of improvements in the last few months. New merchandise, new signage. From what I could tell, the shop was doing well.

He bent forward, both arms braced on the top of the desk. My breath caught: my hair band was still on his wrist.

He caught me looking. "I haven't taken it off," he said. "Not once."

Had there not been a customer shopping for sunscreen a few feet away, I'd have thrown myself over the desk and pushed him against the wall. From his expression, I could tell he was fighting the same urge.

I took a steadying breath, willing myself to hold it together. For now. I told him about Project Relic, how I was back in charge.

The more I spoke, the brighter his eyes shined. "I can't believe it," he finally said. "That...you're here."

I glanced around. "I'm proud of you, Enzo. The place looks great."

"Thank you. Do you need a boat? Gear?"

I paused. I did need a few small items, but that could wait. Right now, I just wanted *him*.

"In due time," I said, locking my gaze on his. "Right now, I have other priorities."

He shook his head, ears turning bright red, and ran his hand over his jawline. I was certain, for a moment, my heart went still.

"How's business?" I managed.

"Never better," he replied. "I hired another employee. And things have been calm—perfect diving conditions. Along the entire Amalfi Coast, not so much as a distress call."

I knew this already. In the last three months, the Amalfi region had resumed its normal tourism levels. The hydrothermal readings had suddenly and inexplicably returned to normal. No more boats had sunk.

I couldn't say I was surprised. When I'd told Savina all I'd learned, I could see it in her eyes: she wanted free of this burden.

"If anything," Enzo went on, "conditions have improved. Visibility has been good all along the coast. Naples, too. Some of the clearest water anyone can remember. A lot of trash has been cleaned up. And all those oil slicks...gone." He lifted his hands and dropped them again as if to say *Who knows?*

I shrugged with him, playing along. Obviously, Savina and Lucille had wasted no time in getting to know one another. I'd never be privy to the conversations between the two women, but it was clear Lucille had picked up the baton I'd set down and had begun to undo the false narratives Savina had erroneously believed her whole life.

"How's your mother?" I finally asked.

He smiled. "Wonderful. Villa's mostly in order. She seems... happier. At peace, or something. I think the renovations had been stressing her out. She's made lots of new friends, too."

"Locals?"

"Some," he said. "Though, she's grown quite close with a woman named Lucille, who visits every so often from Venice."

"Interesting," I said, looking down so Enzo wouldn't see the edges of my lips turning upward.

"She'll be glad to know you're back in town," he said. "She adores you. Maybe you two can get coffee or lunch. Or she can join us on the boat one of these days."

I nodded, considering how very beneficial that could be for me. Savina, her strand of hagstones...

The thought was a fleeting one. It was the chase, the *hunt*, that invigorated me. Just like my dad. He'd given me a hell of a clue, after all, and I couldn't wait to get back to the *Aquila*'s wreckage and resume my search toward the front of the ship. I'd be looking, first, for fragments of copper.

The lone customer in the store walked out empty-handed. It was now Enzo and me, alone in his shop. Without a word, he walked over and flipped the sign to *Sorry, We're Closed*. Then he locked the door and pulled the blinds.

He stepped toward me and placed his hands on either side of my face. "Haven," he said, "how long will you be here this time?"

"A year, at least," I said.

He raised his eyebrows. "I cannot tell you how happy I am to hear that." Then he kissed me with such urgency, such need, I had to place my hands on the wall behind me, lest my knees give out.

I knew for sure, this time, that nothing about this moment was Savina's doing. She didn't even know I was back in Positano.

There was no magic here.

No witchcraft.

This was as real as it could get.

EPILOGUE

1841
Treviso

It was little Lia—who was not so little anymore but in her twenties, married and with three daughters—who, after the death of her beloved Mari and her husband, Holmes, mailed the log to the archive.

Their love story was too great to be locked away in an attic, forgotten and eventually lost. Mari had known this, and indeed, it was why she'd tasked Lia with caring for the log—and deciding its fate—once Mari and Holmes were long gone.

Despite the passage of two decades, Lia remembered her rescue from the tiny island of Ischia as though it were yesterday. It had been very late at night; she'd been sleeping fitfully on the stone floor of a damp, tucked-away cell in the bowels of Castello Aragonese. Only a barred window let in any fresh air.

Vivi and six-year-old Lia had been separated from one another upon their arrival at the castle, but their cells were next to one another, and they'd been able to talk through their open-air windows. Although, a few days into their imprisonment on Ischia, Vivi had stopped responding to Lia.

They must have taken her to another cell, young Lia reasoned.

Lia woke to the sound of whispers through the window. At first, she thought it a dream or the breeze or a bird flitting outside. Only at the sound of her mother's voice did she sit up, bleary-eyed, realizing this was no dream at all. She rushed to the window, overjoyed to see her parents, as well as Mari and a man she did not recognize.

Already, her father and the strange man were removing tools—chisels and saws—from a bag. Her father also withdrew her small wooden doll from the bag. He handed it to Lia through the window.

"I have carried it with me since the moment I learned you were gone," he said, his voice cracking. "I have not parted with it once."

Lia reached for her doll, hugging it close. It smelled like home. "How did you find me?" she asked. She remembered the maze of stone passageways she'd been led down days ago. It seemed a miracle they'd managed to locate her.

Her mother reached into her pocket, withdrawing something. She held it up for Lia to see. "It is Viviana's *cimaruta*," she said, eyes brimming with joy. "It was in the water, below where we stand now."

Lia frowned, not understanding.

Mari gave a sad smile. "Once we were near this island," she explained, "I performed the *incantesimo divinatorio*, begging the water to lead me to anything of the *streghe*. At once, the strand of hagstones began to tug us toward the north edge of the castle. It led us to the water below where we stand now. Among the rocks, just beneath the waterline, we found Vivi's *cimaruta*. She must have thrown it from her cell toward the water."

"From there," Lia's mother went on, "we climbed the rocks, and we found Vivi's cell. We…saw her."

"Is she all right?" Lia asked. "She has not said anything through the window in a few days."

Her mother looked down, and when she spoke again, her

voice was hoarse. "No, my love. We saw her body. She must have died in her cell. A few days ago, we think." Her eyes welled with tears. "Vivi might have kept her protective *cimaruta* on to keep herself strong. Instead, she threw it into the sea. It was a terribly brave decision, but it led us right to you."

Sacrifice, Lia was quickly learning, was the greatest form of love.

That night, her father and the other man—who called himself Holmes—chiseled their way around the metal bars, freeing Lia from the window. They freed the Fontana sisters, too, who were in another nearby cell. Together, the group escaped to a tiny villa on the western edge of Naples, where her father had family.

Lia had always been led to believe that no men knew of *stregheria*. She understood now that this was far from the truth. Some men, like her father and Holmes—who would not leave Mari's side, and Lia quite liked him for it—knew the women's secrets, knew everything they were capable of.

But, being the good men they were, they never breathed a word of it.

In the weeks to follow Lia's rescue, the Positano *streghe* left the village. Though the threat of the Mazza brothers had disappeared, it was too difficult to live among the memories of all that had transpired. Further, police officials and a few men within the Fratelli Mazza enterprise were performing an inquisition, wanting to dig more closely into the suspicious drowning of Massimo Mazza—whose body eventually washed up on shore, bearing no clues to his death—followed by the sinking of two Mazza-owned vessels, the latter of which sent Matteo Mazza to his early grave, as well.

In time, though Positano experienced no more seaborne attacks, it suffered some of the same misfortunes experienced by other nearby villages: bad fishing seasons, cliffside collapses.

Certainly not a place the *streghe* felt compelled to return to, anytime soon at least.

Most of the *streghe*—and their families—made their way to Treviso, west of Venice. It was close enough for the women who could not resist the call of the sea, yet far enough for those who preferred some distance from it, like Mari.

"Will you do me a very big favor?" Mari asked Lia, many years after the Ischia rescue, and long after the Fratelli Mazza had gone defunct.

"Of course," sixteen-year-old Lia said.

"A few *streghe* are returning to Positano," Mari explained, "to meet old friends and retrieve items from their abandoned villas. Holmes and I, we cannot go. We cannot be seen."

Lia nodded. She knew this well: the *streghe* understood that exposing the truth of Mari and Holmes's survival could put the pair at risk. Only the parish enumerator who recorded household births and deaths had any knowledge of them. But even then, Mari used Holmes's last name. Mari DeLuca did not exist any longer.

"I'd like you to go with them," Mari went on, "and see what there is to learn about my family. My father. Paola."

Lia had dutifully obeyed, spending several weeks in Positano with the others, gleaning what little information she could. Mari's father had passed away a year earlier. Paola had gone on to marry Corso, and the two were now living in Rome, though rumor had it his business interests had floundered and they were miserably unhappy.

Lia returned to Treviso to share the news with Mari, who was busy clearing out a small room off the back of the house.

When Lia walked in, Mari held up a tiny shirt, small enough for an infant. "I sewed it myself," Mari said proudly.

"Are you—" Lia gasped, eyeing Mari's belly, which revealed a subtle swell.

"Yes. I told Holmes only this morning. Already, he is making the baby a trekking pole." She pointed out the window. Holmes sat on the ground, whittling away at a stick. He and Mari loved trekking, especially in the great Pale Mountains north of Treviso, in Austria.

The two women hugged in celebration. "Have you thought of a name?" Lia asked.

Mari smiled. "Well, I feel sure it is a boy. And we have decided to name him Nico."

"Nico," Lia echoed, liking the name at once.

Mari approached a cupboard at one side of the room and removed a few items from a shelf in order to make room for the neatly folded shirts and tunics. Lia stepped forward to help her, spotting a water-stained oilskin pouch sitting on a shelf. She frowned, and Mari motioned for her to take it out.

"Holmes kept a journal during his sea voyages," Mari explained.

In years past, Lia had tried to ask Mari and Holmes about these voyages and why the two of them now preferred visiting the mountains over the sea. Mari explained that she'd always had a complicated relationship with the ocean. "It will take a lifetime to sort through my feelings about it," Mari once said, "but the sea was here long before us, and it will remain long after we are gone." She gave a little smile. "Something tells me it will be as patient as I need it to be."

Now Mari turned to Lia, a serious expression on her face. She placed her hand on the journal. "Will you promise me something, Lia?"

"Yes. Anything."

"I hope it is many, many years from now, but when Holmes and I are both gone, promise me you will not let this journal languish on a shelf to collect dust. There is so much within—not the least of which is the truth about our love story."

"You are not scared of it being exposed?"

Mari gave a little laugh. "After we are gone? Not a bit. Why, perhaps there is even something within that will help someone, someday."

Mari reached for another item on the shelf—a strand of hagstones. Lia recognized it as the same strand Mari had used to rescue her from Ischia.

"I want you to have this, too," Mari said. "Pass it down. Whether to your daughters, or my daughters, or nieces or cousins… No matter, just keep it among us women."

Lia took the stones in her hand, feeling the weight of them. It was a priceless gift, and unique, too: the second hagstone had a tiny starfish fossil embedded within.

"But remember," Mari said, closing Lia's fingers around the stones, "the treasure one seeks, whether by using the hagstones or by some other means, does not necessarily mean jewels or gems or expensive things. Your rescue from Ischia is proof of it."

Mari placed a tiny wooden baby rattle on the newly cleared shelf.

"Sometimes," she concluded, "the greatest treasure to be found is…love."

★ ★ ★ ★ ★

RECIPES

Please see sarahpenner.com/bookclubs for all recipes

Amalfi Coast–Themed Antipasti Menu:

Limoncello Spritz (recipe below)
Sliced Tomatoes with Fresh Burrata and Olive Oil Drizzle
Artichoke and Cannellini Bean Salad
Ricotta Dip with Crostini and Crudités
Sheet-Pan Lemon-Garlic Shrimp
Italian Ricotta Cookies (recipe below)

Limoncello Spritz

2 oz limoncello
3 oz prosecco
1 oz club soda
Fresh mint + lemon slices for garnish

In a glass filled with ice, add the limoncello, followed by the prosecco and club soda. Gently stir. Garnish and serve!

Italian Ricotta Cookies

15 oz whole-milk ricotta cheese
1 ¾ C white sugar
1 C butter, softened (not melted!)
2 large eggs
1 tsp vanilla extract
2 TBS fresh lemon zest
4 C all-purpose flour
1 tsp baking powder
1 tsp baking soda

For the glaze

1 ½ C confectioners' sugar
2 TBS milk
2 TBS fresh lemon juice
6 TBS fresh lemon zest

Note: Per below, dough must be chilled in advance. Plan accordingly!

1. Combine ricotta, sugar, butter, eggs, vanilla extract, and lemon zest in a large bowl. Beat with an electric mixer until blended. Mixture will be grainy.

2. In another bowl, combine flour, baking powder, and baking soda. Dump into ricotta mixture and stir until combined. Let dough chill at least two hours and up to two days.

3. Preheat the oven to 350°F (175°C). Grease or line cookie sheets. Working in batches, roll chilled dough into 1.5-inch balls and place 2 inches apart onto prepared cookie sheets. To prevent dough from sticking to your hands, dab a tiny

bit of olive oil onto your palms before rolling. This will result in a prettier cookie, too!

4. Bake in the preheated oven until edges are golden and cookies lift easily from the pan, about 13 to 15 minutes (do not overbake!).

To make the glaze: Mix confectioners' sugar, milk, and lemon juice together until smooth. Drizzle over cooled cookies, and sprinkle with fresh lemon zest.

Makes 55 cookies! Freeze if needed; delicious straight out of the freezer!

ACKNOWLEDGMENTS

I truly believe I hit the jackpot with my ride-or-die agent team at Janklow & Nesbit: Stefanie Lieberman, Molly Steinblatt, and Adam Hobbins. In the early days of *The Amalfi Curse*, when I was still fumbling through the outline even after months of work, they challenged me to sit with the struggle. We writers sometimes try to find the easy way out, but the best coaches simply won't let us. Thank you, Stefanie, Molly, and Adam, for everything.

To my ever-loyal team at Park Row Books and Harper-Collins, thank you. I'm not sure how I got so lucky to be surrounded by such a supportive and fun team. To my editor, Erika Imranyi, thank you for being such a fabulous cheerleader and sounding board. To my publicity team—Emer Flounders, Justine Sha, Kathleen Carter, and Heather Connor—I'm thrilled I get to do this again with you! To Margaret Marbury, Nicole Luongo, Randy Chan, Pam Osti, Rachel Haller, Lindsey Reeder, Amy Jones, Cory Beatty, Colleen Simpson, Ana Luxton, Loriana Sacilotto, Brianna Wodabek, Reka Rubin, Christine Tsai,

Nora Rawn, Emily Martin, Daphne Portelli, Katie-Lynn Golakovich, and the entire Sales team, especially Lillie Walsh and Andy LeCount…thank you for all you've done to support my books and writing career. Because of you, the publishing industry has not been an intimidating one. At the end of the day, we're all here because we love one thing—books!

A million thanks to author, teacher, and maritime historian Dr. Mary Malloy, who offered invaluable guidance on nautical terminology and maritime history as I revised *The Amalfi Curse*. I first met Dr. Malloy at the Historical Novel Society conference in San Antonio in 2023, and I knew immediately I needed to hire her. She coached me through hundreds(!) of tricky details as I revised Holmes's tumultuous journey aboard the *Aquila*. Thank you, Dr. Malloy, for your patience, enthusiasm, and candor.

Thank you to freelance editors Alyssa Matesic, Emily Ohanjanians, Heidi Pitlor, and Ronit Wagman for your insightful guidance on the early pages of this novel. And thank you to freelance editor Andrea Robinson, who tackled the whole of it: your feedback proved equally encouraging and constructive, and this book is a thousand times better for it.

Enormous thanks to the ilCartastorie Museo in Naples, Italy, especially Sergio Riolo and Andrea Zappulli, who were kind enough to grant me a private, behind-the-scenes tour of their archives. I've been to many an archive, but this felt like stepping into an old-world dream. Although ilCartastorie houses handwritten banking records—not seafaring logs!—the museum's myriad of documents, dating back hundreds of years, inspired Haven's archival research scenes in the story.

Thank you also to Mario Di Domenico, who led me on a private visit of the Museo del Mare in Naples, Italy. It's a can't-miss for maritime enthusiasts.

Thanks to the staff at the Florida Maritime Museum in Cortez, Florida, and the Cortez Village Historical Society, who answered my slew of questions about the customs and quirks of working fishing villages in the nineteenth century.

Thank you to copy editor Vanessa Wells, whom I've now worked with on two projects. I'm forever impressed by your suggestions and eagle-eyed fixes.

For those of you interested in learning more about shipwreck excavation and nautical archaeology, I highly recommend the e-learning modules provided by the Nautical Archaeology Society. And for those of you planning a visit to Positano, might I suggest the *zuppa di cozze* (mussels in tomato broth) and butterscotch *panna cotta* at Il Grottino Azzurro.

Special shout-out to Aimee Westerhaus and Mallory Hanson—namesakes for Ami and Mal in the story—as well as my sister Kellie and my dear friends Rachel LaFreniere, Lauren Zopatti, Taylor Ambrose, Kristin Wollett, Alex Vidal, and Steve Schaeffer, all of whom have influenced and inspired me in important—even life-changing—ways over the last two years. And to my mom, always one of my first readers: thank you for your unconditional love and encouragement.

Lastly, to my husband, Marc: it's a running joke that although he's the most important person in my life, neither of my first two books were dedicated to him. At last, here we are. Maybe third time's a charm? Thank you, my love, for your unwavering support over the last decade. You were there when the early rejections rolled in, and you were there when it all took off. Here's to all that's to come.